PAY for PLAY

Reed Bunzel

AVON BOOKS 🔷 NEW YORK

In memory of Deborah

PAY FOR PLAY is an original publication of Avon Books. This work has never before appeared in book form. This work is a novel. Any similarity to actual persons or events is purely coincidental.

AVON BOOKS
A division of
The Hearst Corporation
1350 Avenue of the Americas
New York, New York 10019

Copyright © 1992 by Reed E. Bunzel
Published by arrangement with the author
Library of Congress Catalog Card Number: 92–90556
ISBN: 0-380-76589-6

First Avon Books Printing: November 1992

AVON TRADEMARK REG. U.S. PAT. OFF. AND IN OTHER COUNTRIES, MARCA REGISTRADA, HECHO EN U.S.A.

Printed in the U.S.A.

RA   10   9   8   7   6   5   4   3   2   1

In his new life, Stuart Logan had but one rule. No requests.

Then again, in his new life he didn't have much to worry about. He didn't play the sort of music that inspired many people to want more. Nor did he play the sort of places where folks made a whole lot of requests—or demands of any sort, for that matter. Fact was, the people he entertained seemed fairly content just to sit and sip and listen while Logan's fingers plucked musical memories out of the thick, heavy summer night.

The chords drifting out of the Yamaha baby grand were scored by the hush of whispers and the clink of ice. The room was dark and smoke billowed near the ceiling in dark cumulous folds. A warm breeze eased through the open-ended lounge, carrying a thick mix of aromas: tobacco, salt, sea heather, sweat, rancid perfume. Supple waitresses in short red skirts and cotton halter tops cut above the navel weaved about the room, dispensing sex on the rocks and sloe comfortable screws, and other concoctions that somehow had survived this year's "out" lists. Flames flickered inside red glass lamps, each wrapped in white plastic netting and set in the center of tables placed in a lazy arc around the piano. The walls were hung with marine netting and glass floats and dead starfish. A 300-pound fiberglass-reinforced albacore tuna was mounted beside the door. After all, this was the Albacore Lounge, serving the thirsty patrons of the beachfront Albacore Club in Avalon By-the-Sea.

Logan had first noticed the man at the start of the third set. He was sitting at a corner table, hunkered down over his glass, flanked by two steamy L.A. dolls. Logan recognized the man's face but did not know his name, a sometime customer who drifted in several times a summer to escape the din and dirt of the city. The same as a lot of the faces staring up at him tonight, eyes lit by the glow of the candles and the booze and the warm tropical night. Eyes trapped in the romance of the island, the spirit of the evening, maybe even the magic of the music.

Logan always looked at their eyes; that was where most true secrets were stored away.

The man drained his glass and rose from his chair. He edged past several tables and lurched toward the piano, righting himself on tenuous legs as he approached. Yeah, Logan knew him; he'd seen him out here before. Always with a different chick, always dripping of casual L.A. haute couture. Tonight he was dressed in a light cotton shirt, unbuttoned halfway down his chest to reveal a mat of dark fur. He wore a simple gold chain around his neck. In the low light of the lounge his black hair seemed tangled with strands of silver, plastered back as if flattened by a ferocious Santa Ana gust. His skin was tan, crinkled, leathery, the result of too many years spent in the Southern California sun.

His eyes were unfocused, fixed on a point halfway between himself and the piano. Such secrets, Logan thought.

The man stumbled up in front of Logan and leaned against the piano with sweaty hands. " 'The Way We Were,' " he whispered, his voice oozing of too many Manhattans.

"I'm sorry." Logan shook his head sadly, as he did a dozen times a night. "No requests."

The man blinked, creased his brow as if his ears again had failed him. He drew his eyes to Logan's and thrust his jaw forward. "I want 'The Way We Were,' " the man insisted, the words coming out slow and measured.

Logan turned his palms up in apology, then shrugged. "Sorry."

"You play goddamned lounge piano in a goddamned piano lounge," the man growled. "So play me 'The Way We Goddamned Were.' "

"Why don't you do us both a favor." Logan smiled brightly as his fingers tripped lightly up the keys. "Why don't you go back to your table, shut the fuck up, and listen."

The man simply stood and stared, dumbstruck. No one talked to him this way, no one had the gall, his eyes said. "Jesus goddamned Christ on fucking rye," he grunted, scowling at the piano man's benevolent smile. His upper lip quivered as he wove his way back through the darkness to his table.

Logan watched as the man angrily sank down in his chair.

Then he returned his gaze to the crowd of drinkers and lovers, laced his fingers and cracked them with ease, and settled down to a standard rendition of a standard middle-of-the-road piano lounge tune. He smiled softly at a polyester woman sitting with her polyester husband at a corner table: *This guy's in love with you,* the music assured her as faint applause of distant memory momentarily filled the lounge.

A short three minutes later, as the song ended with a whimper, Mr. Request angrily rose to his feet. He slapped some money on the table, shot a last piercing look at Logan, and jutted out his elbows. His two babes dutifully slipped their arms through his crooked elbows and followed—assisted was more like it—their escort through the maze of tables.

Both women were real lookers, lookers being a dime a dozen in L.A. Hanging off the man's left arm was a blonde, and from the way the candlelight danced off her hair she looked like a peroxide junkie. She was stuffed into a skintight white sundress with no back; Logan couldn't see the front. She looked like she was trying to appear much younger than she was, and in the dim lounge she might well have succeeded. She whispered something into Mr. Request's ear, or nibbled on his neck. Whichever it was, Logan easily interpreted the message.

The other woman looked much younger. She had darker hair, brunette or red, Logan couldn't quite tell in the flickering darkness. She glided between the tables toward the door, her light cotton skirt moving like a breeze around her silky legs. As she accompanied her host, Logan's eyes were fixed on the tightly stretched cotton top hugging her bosom. The woman hesitated in the doorway, then slipped out into the night.

The last set of the evening ended two songs later, with a hammed-up version of the old Four Preps' ditty "Twenty-six Miles." The finale was met with a round of polite applause, followed by the tinkle of more ice on glasses as the tired drinkers turned bottoms up. Logan checked his watch: twelve thirty-six. He folded the cover down over the warm piano keys and rose from his bench. At this point most pianists also gathered up their sheet music and slipped it back inside the bench, but not Logan. Logan had no sheet music because he couldn't read it. Fact was, musically Stuart Logan was illiterate. Everything was by ear, by memory. That's the way he had put himself through college, a dubious talent he had misplaced until Molly's passing had reminded him that sometimes memory serves you best.

Which was another of the reasons he didn't do requests.

He pushed his way through a doorway carved in the whitewashed latticework wall that separated the lounge from the bar. The four tiny tables in here were occupied, as were all but two of the bar stools. Logan selected one that wasn't, down at the end of the counter near the waitresses' station, and scooted up on it. He flexed his fingers as if preparing for a Mozart concerto, drummed them rhythmically on the polished oak bar, reflexive fingers that moved of their own accord. Then he glanced up at the vast array of bottles that seemed doubled in size by the immense mirror behind them. His eyes thirstily roved to the top shelf.

The bartender was named George. He wandered down toward Logan's end of the bar, wiping the counter in front of him as he went. He swept a pile of gunk onto the floor, then leaned both palms on the slick wooden surface.

"Good show tonight, Stu," he said, raising a brow in a slim show of sincerity. "What's your poison of choice?"

Logan hesitated, sizing up the single malts. "Double dose of Glenmorangie, up," he said at length, his tongue already tasting the musty flavor. "And get one for yourself."

"Twin twelve-year-olds, coming up." George grinned, pivoting away, pulling down the bottle, and pouring out two double shots of Scotch, all in one practiced move. He slipped the bottle back into its assigned space and swept one of the glasses onto the counter in front of Logan. "Run you a tab?"

"Not tonight." Logan shook his head, raised his glass and clinked the edge of George's, then tipped it back for a long, glowing sip. The smooth liquid warmed his throat as it eased down; it felt good, so he did it again.

George smacked his lips at the malty sting. "What was that little fracas all about, a few minutes ago? You been leering at the guests' lady friends again?"

"Some L.A. lard-ass didn't know the rules," Logan grumbled. He tipped his glass and another wash of warmth oozed over his tongue.

"What was it this time?"

" 'The Way We Were.' "

"Christ, Stu. What's the big deal?" George raised a skeptical brow, then settled back against the stainless-steel shelf running along the rear of the bar. He eyed the Scotch in his glass as if he were examining a urine specimen, then indulged in a long, slow sip. " 'The Way We Were' is a nice song," he said. "What gives?"

"I don't do requests." Logan stared at the wavy amber reflection of himself in his glass. That's how he saw himself most nights; most days, too. George was right: "The Way We Were" *was* a nice song. And easy, too. And he'd played it last night, and both nights last weekend. And he would have closed with it tonight, if Mr. Gold Chain from the city hadn't reminded him so much of what he'd left behind.

One of the waitresses, a bleach-blonde UCLA coed named Lydia, trotted up next to him and took her place at the waitress station. It was shaped like a stall, separated from the rest of the bar by two curved brass rails that gave it the appearance of a starting gate at Hollywood Park. Lydia looked as if she had just stepped down from a *Sports Illustrated* calendar. Her hair was short, cropped just above her neck, and framed a pair of caramel-colored eyes. Her body was meant for spandex and tonight was pushing the limits of her halter blouse, knotted in such a way that it seemed as if one good tug would easily pull it open.

"Nice show." She smiled at him, running her tongue lightly over her soft lips. Then she glanced down the bar and smacked a bell with her palm. "Yo, George. Two white wines, a rum and Coke, Seven and Seven, and two Bud Lights." She smiled furtively, a smile that turned suggestive as she drew her gaze back to Logan. But she found his gaze already was drawn somewhere else.

He had turned away because he had felt *her,* felt a presence behind him, staring. Not necessarily staring at *him,* but staring just the same, looking, sizing the place up. His eyes roamed the bar, the diamond-shaped openings in the lattice walls, through the lounge, the door leading out to the street. And then he saw her, framed against the streetlight, a silhouette against the sparkling bay. The redhead, if indeed that was what she was. From where he sat he still couldn't be sure. But he knew it was her, the woman on Slick Prick's right arm, the one with the flowing skirt and skintight top. He caught her eye; she smiled. Then she glided into the lounge and slowly worked her way toward the bar. Logan glanced at the empty stool next to him, signaling her. Without a word she eased up beside him.

"This seat taken?" she asked, her hushed voice sexy and

light, almost sung with a thick accent. British, maybe Australian, but he didn't have an ear for those things.

Logan said nothing, just swept the stool with his hand as if sweeping off the dust. Not quite Sir Walter Raleigh, but what did she expect at these prices?

The redhead slipped up onto the stool and set a small white purse on the bar. She patted her thin skirt in place over her tan legs and crossed her ankles, resting her feet on the brass rung that was part of the stool. She licked her lips, her tongue working a slow figure eight over the upper one first, then the lower one. Then she looked over the bar at the selection of rail booze. It gave Logan plenty of time to soak her in, up close and personal.

Her hair flowed in waves way past her shoulders, the hue of a brilliant L.A. sun setting through the smog. Her dark-jade eyes were lined in black and shadowed with a violet haze, and her cheeks were doused with a faint rouge. He now noticed that her top was a light-pink, and he could make out the distinct impression of her nipples pressing against the supple ribbed cotton. Her skirt was of a faint pastel floral design, and rode up a bit on legs that could only be described as shapely and svelte. She glanced impatiently down the bar at George, then flashed Logan a pretty smile. Just a split second, but he quickly availed himself of the opportunity.

"Stuart Logan," he introduced himself, offering her a firm but friendly hand. She grasped it politely, held the touch for a moment, then glanced back at the bartender. A pert smile brought him right over.

"Gin and tonic," she requested. "Lemon, not lime."

George nodded but said nothing, just flashed a lascivious wink in Logan's direction.

"And you're—?" Logan asked, drawing her eyes back to his.

"Excuse me?"

"I'm Logan," he repeated. "And you're—"

"Thirsty." She sighed, her voice like a breeze easing through the palm fronds down on the beach. He noticed that her eyes held a pink, watery tint, and her eyeliner had widened to puffy smudges. Either she was coked-up or cried-out, he couldn't tell which. Maybe both. "Very thirsty."

"Came to the best place in town, then, Miss. . . ." He looked at her hopefully, waiting for her to finish the sentence.

"Hope so," she cooed as George flipped a cocktail napkin

onto the bar and set her gin and tonic on it. She picked up her glass and smiled at Logan, then looked back at George. "Run him a tab," she said, cocking her head toward the piano man.

George glanced at Logan, who raised his brow and nodded.

The lady sipped her drink in silence, her busy eyes reflecting a busy mind. She seemed to have traveled somewhere else, another time. She held her glass with both hands, as if it were her only possession left on earth. Then she turned to Logan and studied him over the rim of her glass.

"Why wouldn't you play it?" she asked at great length as she ran her tongue over her perfect white teeth.

"Play what?"

"My song. 'The Way We Were.' "

"I didn't know it was your song."

"You would have played it if you had?"

"I usually do."

She regarded him suspiciously, confused, as if some element of humor were eluding her. Then a smile creased her lips, forming lines that made her look older than she probably would have liked.

"You musicians are all the same," she announced, drowning her scorn in gin and quinine. "So temper-fucking-mental."

Logan grinned. "Thank you."

"It was only 'The Way We Goddamned Were,' " she said, dwelling on it, taking another long sip. "You got something against passion and romance?"

"Two of my favorite pastimes," he assured her.

He gazed deeply into her eyes, momentarily unnerving her. She pried her eyes from his and quickly looked away. He left her alone with her thoughts for a moment, watching as the droplet turned into a tear and spilled down her cheek. She quickly wiped it away.

"What about your friends?" Logan asked softly, edging just a bit closer on his stool.

"Friends." She nodded, reflecting on something, maybe the evening, where it had been and where it was going. Then she turned her head toward him and rolled her eyes upward.

"Three's a crowd?" he prompted her.

"I'm just an old-fashioned, duet sort of girl."

"Do you prefer the melody or the harmony?"

"The melody. That's the one that's on top, isn't it?"

Logan grinned and rested his hand on her soft thigh. To his

surprise she didn't knock it away; instead, she returned the gesture. She moved closer on her stool and rested her head on his willing shoulder.

"I'll play harmony under your melody any time," he purred.

"I thought you didn't do requests," she reminded him, gently plying his leg with kneading fingers.

"There's an exception to every rule," Logan said softly. He leaned forward and planted a gentle kiss on her forehead. Jesus, he thought, it doesn't get any easier than this.

She smiled up at him. Her lips were moist, tempting, and they met his halfway. A spark exploded as they touched. She giggled, he grinned, and they tried it again. No spark this time, just a fathomless kiss. Eventually she pulled away and gazed up into his waiting eyes.

"Your keyboard or mine?" she whispered as she reached for her white purse.

He felt her hand rub firmly between his legs, and whatever physical lust that might have been secret was quickly revealed. "I just tuned mine this morning."

"Then what are we doing here?" She smiled at him and rose on wobbly legs, like a newborn fawn just exploring the fresh mysteries of life. "Let's go tickle your ivories."

Daggers of sunlight sliced through the venetian blinds, hacking bright diagonal wounds on the dusty floor. Logan rubbed his parched eyes, trying to dispel the disorientation that always followed a night away from home—not that his life was filled with many such encounters. He despised waking up somewhere else, with someone else, briefly wondering who he was, who she was, and trying to recall last night's escapades that led him to where he was.

Not that he did this a lot, but the few times he had at least he'd tried to keep his wits about him.

This was not his bed, of that much he was sure. Nor was this his bedroom—but it *was* his apartment. He squinted through the darkness and made out his TV, his ragged overstuffed chair, his stereo cabinet with the JVC music system and the CD player and his collection of records. His IBM Selectric, covered with dust and untouched since he moved out here. His potted palm, yearning for sunlight toward the shaded window. And his piano.

His piano. The keys. Ivories. He remembered something about duets and crowds, and tickling. He breathed a relaxed sigh, then sat up with a start. He swung his legs over the edge of the seedy couch. Of course: that's what it was. The couch, *his* couch, and he had slept on it. Which meant that she must have slept in the bed. But he and she, they had come home together, arm in arm, strolling in the moonlight. Of that he was sure. And then . . .what then. . .?

He ran his tongue over his teeth, rubbing off the dry morning fuzz. He cleared his throat, sniffed, took a deep breath, scratched himself. He expected his head to throb, but it didn't. He really hadn't had that much to drink. He reached for the ceiling in a slow stretch and found he was in his undershorts, overdressed for this part of the summer. Usually he slept naked, with or without female company. So what was it with the Fruit of the Looms this morning?

Coffee, that's what he wanted, what he needed. A big mug of harsh, thick coffee, like the tar over on La Brea. He snapped the waistband of his briefs and padded across the rug.

Halfway to the kitchen he stopped. He hesitated, then turned and padded back out into the living room. There: the bedroom door was closed, latched tight. Was she still in there? Had she slept in there, with him out here? Instinctively he glanced at his wrist, but his watch was not there. Of course not; he always took it off before going to bed, for whatever purpose. He shifted his legs into reverse and backed further into the living room. The blue LED readout on the VCR told him it was twelve thirty-four.

His brain took two seconds for the numbers to sink in. Twelve thirty-four, on a Sunday afternoon? Had he really slept—or whatever—that long? His mind seemed to click into rewind, gears spinning as his memory sped backwards over the last twelve hours.

Forgetting about the coffee, Logan returned to the bedroom

door and regarded it curiously. He hesitated, then wrapped his fingers around the ancient glass knob. Quietly he turned it until he felt the bolt retract and door give way. He pushed it inward on silent hinges, and poked his head in. Light spiked the darkness through a torn shade. He focused his eyes on the old bed backed up against the musty wall, the yellow flowered wallpaper hanging in dusty curls from an ancient stain at the ceiling. The sheets and spread were neatly tucked in under the mattress, army corners as tight as any he'd ever seen. The pillows were neatly fluffed and placed at the head of the bed, and Molly's heart-shaped lace pillow was arranged carefully between them.

She was gone. He crossed the room and raised the blinds. The room seemed to swell from the sharp infusion of bright sunlight. He blinked back the glare and stared out at the street below, then turned and surveyed the room. Draped neatly, over a chair he found his white trousers and his blue-and-white-striped shirt; his brown leather boat shoes were placed neatly under the chair. On the dresser he found his Seiko watch and eelskin wallet, the latter still clogged with his driver's license, AT&T calling card, thirty-six bucks in cash, and his American Express green card. In the top drawer of his dresser he found the .35 snub-nose Smith & Wesson he'd bought after the burglary. At least the woman hadn't drugged and rolled him.

He grasped for whatever pieces of last night he could find, trying to assemble them in whatever order he could manage. Sort of like assembling a jigsaw puzzle picture-side down. A distant scrap of memory seemed to slip back into place. He tried not to reach for it, then let it go, afraid that any effort would push the memory, however slight and brief it might be, beyond his grasp.

They had been giggling, holding onto each other, she on his left, leaning on his shoulder, something in his hand. What? A glass. She had asked for a drink.

"You got anything to slick my tongue?" He remembered her words now, the slow way with which she seemed to hypnotize him.

Of course. A glass of Scotch; two glasses. He had poured them both a drink when they came in. He had unlocked his front door and flipped on the light; she had followed him inside and flipped it off again. Then she had come toward him, draping her arms over his shoulders, gently folding her hands behind his head, firmly pressing her body against his. Their lips had touched, lingered long and full, and she had drawn her nimble fingers down his sides, slowly, suggestively hooking them in his belt loops.

He had lit a candle, two of them. He remembered the amber glow dancing on her face, the flame smoldering in her bottomless eyes. So he had poured them both a Scotch, no ice, and they silently moved into the dark bedroom. He carried the two glasses, she held one of the candles. She set it down on the night table, and he handed her a glass. They had toasted something, perhaps the night, perhaps the moment, and then they had drunk.

The candle was where she had placed it, on top of last year's copy of *Life: The Year in Pictures*. Red wax had dripped onto the magazine like the flow from a volcano. He wondered how long it had burned: the candle, not their passion. At least an hour, from the looks of the spill. Long enough for them to strip out of their clothes, climb into bed, and pay homage to Shakespeare's notion of the beast with two backs.

And then, in that instant, he knew.

Amidst their giggling and fondling the mystery woman had every chance to slip something into his Scotch, most likely a Quaalude or three. Whatever it was had knocked him out like a horse, kicked into a deep slumber void of a single dream, a solitary memory, even a simple goddamned headache. He took a deep, resolute breath, pulled on yesterday's clothes, jammed his bare feet into his shoes, and marched out into the kitchen.

It's your own fault, a voice told him. That voice, that same voice he had heard too often lately, that voice that had no timbre or accent or tone, but a voice all the same. It was *her* voice, he knew, Molly's voice, as he imagined it in his sleep, as he thought of it while showering in the morning, while walking the beach at noon, while playing the piano in the evening. It was her voice, the last shred that gave his life a hint of continuity.

Yeah, it was Logan's fault, all right. What was kindergarten rule number one? "Don't talk to strange redheaded women who approach you in a bar and put their drink on your tab and don't tell you their name and then come home with you at the drop of a hat." Only problem was, barfly rule number one said, "Opportunity missed is opportunity lost."

* * *

The rock was his place, a boulder the size of a Volkswagen half-submerged at the edge of Avalon Bay. It was part of the fill upon which Crescent Street long ago had been built, and from this particular vista he could see all the way from the breakwater beyond the red-roofed casino on Sugar Loaf Point, across the turquoise depths of the protected anchorage, to the massive loading dock that protruded from the southern reach of the bay. At that point the rocky coastline angled south, defined by a small road—carved from the granite and scrub—that wound its way to Pebbly Beach and the island heliport. The harbor itself was clogged with boats: sailboats and ketches and power yachts, mostly large, mostly from Marina del Rey. Out at the far fringe of the bay Logan noticed the flashing blue light of the Harbor Patrol, probably chasing down a drunk speeding in excess of the posted 5 MPH limit.

Past the breakwater, punctuated by points of sail cutting through the pale horizon, lay the deep blue waters of the San Pedro Channel. Beyond that—some twenty-six miles distant—sprouted the parched coastline of the California mainland: Newport, Long Beach, the Palos Verdes Peninsula, Los Angeles. On this particular Sunday that mass of land was shrouded in a thick yellow pall, concocted from the stale air and the clog of hydrocarbons steaming up from the miles of asphalt tentacles that constricted the terrain. To Logan the dense blob resembled a giant fungus conjured up in a special-effects lab for some low-budget horror flick.

It was a world that didn't exist, not in Logan's mind, out here on Catalina. The island of romance as the song said; an island of escape more distant from the city than the twenty-six miles the lyrics would lead one to believe. Actually, it was more like twenty-two miles from the dock at Cabrillo Mole to the ferry terminal in Long Beach, but P.R. has a strong way of blending fact and hyperbole.

A stiff wind blew down from the stark ridge above him and whipped through his hair. With a shudder of reality he looked up from the green water rhythmically lapping the base of his rock. The sun kissed his skin with its warmth and he stretched his arms like a cat waking up from a midday nap. He slowly gathered his legs under him and stood up, glancing once again at the boats bobbing in the harbor. As he started to pick his way down the rock to the street, his eyes were drawn to the commotion out at the end of the town pier. The

Harbor Patrol boat, its light still churning in great blue circles, had docked alongside a growing crowd of curious onlookers. One of the Sheriff's Department's two Ford Broncos on the island was parked at the beach end of the pier, its glaring blue strobe similarly flashing.

No man, especially the war-torn writer still lurking deep within Logan's self-ascribed exile status, could resist the scene. Flashing lights had a mystic power, like the sirens' song luring sailors ever nearer the rocks, or a fresh accident inviting rubberneckers to check for roadside carnage as they pass by. Whatever the force, whatever the lure, Logan was drawn by an inner sense he thought he'd long ago exorcised from his brain. But as he scrambled from the rock and pedaled his Fuji twelve-speed back toward the beach, he felt what he inwardly had feared. The exorcism had been a sham, he could never be free of what tugged at his insides.

He arrived at the pier at the same time as the bodies. Logan knew they were bodies before he saw them: It was his reporter's sixth sense at work. The somber crowd, the unnerving quiet, the ghostly faces of the men carrying the collapsible stretchers, the cold chill on a warm afternoon—all defined the absolute value of death. It was a chill with which Logan was very familiar; it seemed a mere fact of his life. During his six years at the *L.A. Times,* four on the city desk and two as special investigative editor, he had acquired the displacement and remoteness that a daily association with death requires. Still, it had never prepared him for the sight of his Molly lying in the cold hospital basement. The perfect horror of the empty hole where her eye had been still swarmed over him in his dreams.

The circle of onlookers parted like the Red Sea as Deputy Sheriff Jack Woods, one of two sheriff's deputies posted on the island, followed the stretchers off the pier. Woods hovered over them, studying the white sheets that covered the bodies, almost scratching his head as if he didn't quite know what to think or do.

Woods was a large man, six-two at least, and looked as if half a keg of old beer hung over his belt. His dark hair fell in loose strands around his head, uncombed and windblown, and the skin on his face hung in folds that seemed ready to slide off at the slightest touch. His eyes were dark and drawn, and quizzical, the eyes of a no-nonsense cop. He had come to the island some five years ago, made it his business to know every resident and regular tourist, and in so doing had established casual communication with Logan. In the last twelve months they had grown accustomed to saying hello on the street, but their passing acquaintance hardly ever left time for a good-bye.

The deputy glanced up and saw Logan standing about four feet away. "What is it 'bout dead bodies that attracts people like flies to shit?" he asked, his words drawn out in a laid-back island drawl developed over the years. "You stringin' this for the *Times*?"

"Nope. I just love a good party," Logan said.

Woods shook his head grimly. "You see any cake and ice cream?"

"Seems I was misinformed," Logan quipped, shamelessly stealing from his favorite late-night classic. "What've you got?"

Deputy Woods shrugged. "Man and a woman, shot clean through the head. A real pisser."

Yeah, a pisser, Logan thought. He nodded but said nothing.

"Dead man's Neil Novak," Woods mumbled, raising his brow. "Some record biz hotshot." He glanced at the paper license in his hand. "This here says he's forty-six, lives at 3569 Stradella Road in Bel Air."

"Pretty ritzy." Logan noted. "What about the girl?"

"We think she's Lynn Sutton, age forty-three. Lives ... lived ... in West Hollywood—2522 Spaulding Avenue." Woods flexed his shoulders in a slight shrug. He glanced over his shoulder at the milling crowd. "The license photo sorta looks like her, but shows her with short black hair, weighing one-ten. This chick's a blonde, probably from a bottle. But the eyes and mouth match up, and I figure she's had a love-fest with the groceries since then."

"Mind if I take a look?"

"It's your party."

Logan moved toward the two bodies, neatly laid out in the hot afternoon sun. Woods bent down beside him and hurriedly raised one sheet and lowered it, then did the same with the other. As usual, the smears of dried blood and the ooze of tissue and other viscera churned the beer in Logan's stomach. Gastric acid roiled like waves in a storm fighting to rise up into his throat. He forced it down and gulped another lungful of salt air.

Logan felt the harsh afternoon sun digging into the back of

his neck, and several dozen pair of eyes watching his every move as the crowd continued to hover. Slowly he rose to his feet, his arms hanging limply at his sides. He'd come out here a year ago to get away from all this, but death seemed to follow him. He found his breathing was forced in short, rapid gasps; his skin had erupted in a clammy sweat. He'd seen worse, of course, scenes that made this look like a Sunday cruise in a glass-bottom boat. But it wasn't the murder itself, or the gore, or the clean holes that so neatly pierced the foreheads of their victims, that made the blood rocket into Logan's brain.

No, it was not the blood and ooze itself—just whose blood and ooze this was. Because the man and woman lying under the sheets were the lifeless forms of Mr. "The Way We Were" and his peroxide-blonde companion, last seen leaving the Albacore Lounge arm in arm.

With a lovely redhead hanging on the other arm.

3

The Neil Novak murder story was journalistic fast food.

Logan fixed himself a stiff gin and tonic and carried it out on the small deck that overlooked the street below and enjoyed a distant water view if he leaned way out. He set the glass on the wooden rail, then wheeled the portable TV to the doorway. He settled into his favorite webbed chair and watched the reporters and anchors stumble over each other in their wild scramble to scoop the competition.

According to evidence so far pieced together by the Sheriff's Department and the Coast Guard, L.A. record magnate Neil Novak and his companion—now positively identified as Lynn Sutton—were murdered in their sleep aboard Novak's yacht, the *Rhapsody on Blue*, early Sunday morning. Both victims had been shot once in the head; the bodies were found later that afternoon by a neighbor from a nearby yacht.

That same neighbor also reported seeing a beautiful redhead leaving the boat just after dawn.

Redhead? *His* redhead? The word shot a bolt to Logan's brain. He awoke from whatever stupor into which the tube had lured him; he leaned forward and shut out the passing street noise drifting up from below. Redhead? Leaving the boat just after dawn? He absently fished the wedge of lime from his glass and sucked it between his teeth, then plopped the shredded rind back into his drink. A gentle breeze stirred the fronds of the khaki-colored palm tree that poked out of the rock-hard backyard and bowed over the deck. He aimed the remote control at the TV and adjusted the volume up a bit.

The news report switched to a brief profile of Neil Novak, show-biz baron and entrepreneur extraordinaire. Novak was president of Rhapsody Records, a small, publicly traded record label that over the past five years had discovered a number of chart-topping acts with such names as Metal Sponge, Pyret Chip, the Chrome Kittens, the Metric Geese. The Metric Geese, the bubbling reporter was quick to point out, was led by an arrogant young genius named Billy Keenan, who had produced five straight chart-topping hits for his record label.

Next, a brief cutaway focused on Rhapsody's corporate lawyer, a Mr. Joseph Minetti. Minetti provided a short profile of the record company, from its founding fifteen years before to a catalog of artists that now totaled more than thirty. When asked, Mr. Minetti refused to speculate on what would happen to Rhapsody Records, and its publishing subsidiary, Rhapsody Blue Music, now that Novak was dead. Further, he declined to offer any conjecture of who might have wanted Novak and his lady friend out of the picture.

Logan eased the volume down on the TV and kicked his feet up, resting them on the edge of the peeling railing. He cradled his drink in both hands in his lap and closed his eyes. The breeze was building now, as it did most summer nights when it eased in from the west, shifting down from Avalon Canyon into the streets of the town.

He took a long sip of gin, swallowed slowly, took a full, even breath, and tilted his head back. He felt an old comfort sweep through him, for a moment forgot where he was, who he was, what he was doing out here. For just an instant he was back on his small backyard patio in Sherman Oaks, stretched out under the dying elm tree that once had shaded the yard. The aroma of lighter fluid and smoldering charcoal and teriyaki marinade and night-flowering jasmine and the dry Valley evening invaded his memory. Funny how, of all the senses, the sense of smell triggered the most basic shot to the past. He sensed the ache of despair trying to take root again, the past grappling with the present. He shook it down, drowned it in another gulp. The feeling was familiar now, even comforting, symptoms of a desperate wish to return to a former life, a wish countered by the knowledge that the clock always moves forward, never in reverse. Dismal as it was, he had found his comfort zone.

Screams and shouts echoed up from the beach, a few summer visitors lingering another night out on the island before going home. The bars along Crescent Street would be hopping, their doors open to the soft August wind and the foot traffic and the music drifting down from upstairs windows. The last swatches of orange and scarlet were disappearing over the inland mountains, and a bright neon moon had risen in the purple umbra to the east. Logan tipped his head back and stared up at the thickening sky, the first stars winking open in the new night.

He sat that way for a long time, motionless, absorbing each new flicker as it appeared in the heavens. He watched as the blinking lights of a jet climbed skyward over the Pacific for parts unknown. Time was when Sunday night was his one moment to relax, to stretch out under the canopy of stars and listen to the distant whine of cars and trucks on the freeway. They had shared a joke, he and Molly: if you closed your eyes and lost yourself in the evening noises and pushed away the smog and soot, the freeway sounded like the gentle crash of surf on the beach somewhere up the coast. And then one weekend they had driven up to Carmel and found themselves walking the clean, cold hard sand at dusk, a thorough blackness seeping into the deep orange where the ocean met the sky. And as the surf hit the shore, they had laughed at how it sounded just like the muffled freeway back home.

That was his Molly. Pretty but not beautiful, tall but not statuesque, thin but not like a model, well-formed but with parts that he knew eventually would break down. She was real, with a laugh on her lips and a glow in her eyes that radiated a special love for him and everything about him. And because of all this love he gave it back, pound for pound. It was not his way, had never been his way until she came into his life and swallowed him up. The distance, the reserve, that had gripped him from early childhood had dissipated like grains of pollen on a spring breeze. Maybe their love was no more special or real or wonderful than what a million other young lovers feel, but those other millions didn't matter as long as he had Molly in his life.

A life suddenly taken one early August afternoon. He knew the story only by the facts, what he'd seen in the police report. Molly had come home early from work to shed her corporate skirt and blouse and nylons and shoes, to soak up whatever warm rays she could wring from the waning summer sun. According to evidence found at the scene, Molly had pulled her Honda into the driveway, bundled her briefcase and computer printouts under her arm, trudged up the walk to the front door. She had paused on the front step, inserted her key in the lock, pushed the door open, and promptly caught a bullet square in the left eye. The surprised intruder apparently slipped out the sliding door he'd broken to get in, spilling what little jewelry and money he'd managed to find on the floor and back lawn. Shredded ivy on the back fence indicated he'd climbed over the chain link and disappeared into the dry wash of the L.A. River.

When Logan came home from the hospital that night, his body drained from the horror and anger and emptiness, he vowed to Molly that he'd find the bastard who did this, if it was the last thing he'd do.

He never did, of course. A career of investigative reporting betrayed him, and so did the cops. L.A.'s finest turned every stone, checked out every slim lead, ran every print through the computer, checked every ballistics report in the state for a match. But the motherfucker was still out there, and until the bastard slipped up no one—not even Logan—could do a thing about it.

He wondered what the estimated half-life of self-pity was.

The harsh rap of fist on wood snagged him from his bout with melancholy. Someone was at the door, a quick knock-knock-knock, followed by an obligatory moment of silence, then repeated. Logan was opting for ignoring whoever dared to interrupt his gin-inspired meanderings, but on the fourth series of knocks he finally gave in. His feet felt heavy as the blood rushed back into his toes. He shuffled across the deck and walked inside, taking his sweet time, not giving a damn who had chosen this particular moment to pry into his life. Still, he was inexorably drawn by the hypnotic hold that curiosity enjoys over free will.

He opened the door and found Deputy Woods standing squarely at the top of the landing, his feet poised for yet another series of staccato taps. He unclenched his knuckles and let his hand fall to his side.

"Evening, Stu," he greeted Logan, bureaucratic tedium evident in his lack of enthusiasm. "You got a second?"

"Just doing slow-mo arm curls," Logan said lightly, indicating the glass of gin in his hand. "Come on in."

Woods wasted no time, pushing past him and stomping heavily into the living room. His dirty brown county-issue boots deposited clumps of dirt on the threadbare Oriental carpet. He stopped in the middle of the floor, shoved his hands in his trouser pockets, and made a quick visual survey of the place.

"Home sweet home," Logan mumbled, waiting for Woods to get to whatever point he'd come for, then get the hell out.

"Nice digs," Woods grunted when he'd finally brought his gaze back to Logan. He headed toward the glass slider that led to the wooden deck, a hasty non-code add-on that perched over the side driveway of the two-story frame house that had been carved into three apartments. He leaned his head out and smelled the ocean, looked down the street at the beach a block away. When he pulled back in he grinned mischievously. "Bet the ladies go nuts up here, what with this view and all, huh?"

Logan eyed the deputy tentatively. He did not consider the two of them close friends, just enigmas passing on the boulevard. Woods did his thing, whatever it was, and Logan did his. They were fellow travelers in an island refuge, and they shared an unspoken understanding that personal inquiries were strictly taboo. Even in the line of duty.

"It's not the view that drives women nuts up here." Logan grinned, but a sharp edge in his voice conveyed his annoyance with Woods' predictable line of thought.

"Not last night, at least," Woods pressed, stumbling his way into a clumsy line of questioning. Obviously out of practice with his interrogation skills. "Can't see much of the harbor after hours."

"Who's looking at the water when there's better things to do on a Saturday night?" Logan answered rhetorically.

"Such as?"

Logan exhaled a deep gush of air that he'd been holding in. He took a sip of his gin, then rolled his eyes wearily. "Please, Jack. Get to the point. I said I wasn't busy, but beating around the bush isn't my idea of a quiet Sunday night at home."

Woods shot him a look that said *Screw you,* then straddled the back of a kitchen chair. Logan sighed to himself; just about every cop he'd ever met felt inclined to sit like that, rather than use furniture in the manner for which it was designed. An exhibition of repressed machismo, he figured. Logan leaned against the deck doorjamb, cradling his drink in both hands as he waited for the routine to begin.

"Last night," Woods began slowly. "After you finished your last set, you were seen talking to a woman, red hair, medium height, average weight—"

"Green eyes, perfect teeth, great legs, nice tits," Logan finished for him.

"So you admit you were with her?"

"I *admit* nothing, Woods," Logan corrected him. "But I *agree* I was with her."

"And you brought her back here."

"I left with her."

"But you didn't come back to your place?"

"No."

"No, you didn't?"

"No, we did."

"So you did bring her here."

Logan shook his head and stifled a yawn. "For chrissakes, Woods. If this is about the beautiful redhead seen slipping off Novak's boat in the wee hours of the morning and disappearing into dawn's early light, get on with it."

"What do you know about that?" Woods demanded accusingly.

"Just what ten million TV viewers in the L.A. basin already know."

Woods rose from his perch on the chair and took a step toward Logan, like a barrister approaching the jury. "Come on, Stuart. You're telling me you came back here, had a drink, gave her a little pop, and she went on her merry way?"

Logan cocked his head and shrugged. "Nope." He took another sip of gin and tonic. "I'm not telling you anything. You know about as much of this as I do."

Woods eyed Logan suspiciously, shifted his weight to his left leg, then jammed his hands back in his pockets. "You got into a fight with Novak last night, am I right?"

"We had words," Logan allowed.

"Words." Woods hesitated, as if turning the concept over in his mind to see how it fit. "Words about what?"

"He wanted me to play a song."

"What song?"

"Jesus friggin' Christ," Logan growled with mounting contempt. "He asked me to play 'The Way We Were,' and I told him no."

"Why?" Woods pressed.

"Because I don't do requests."

"I mean, why 'The Way We Were'?"

"Why?" Logan lanced the sheriff's deputy with a dark glare and held him with it. "It's just a goddamned song."

"And she was just a goddamned redhead," Woods added. He worked something over in his head for a moment, stroking the dark stubble on his chin. "What was her name?"

"The redhead? I don't know."

"You don't know? You bring a girl home and jump on her bones and you don't even know her name?"

"It spoils the mood," Logan offered, playing off Woods' patent incredulity and mounting envy.

"Love and sex in the time of viruses," Woods mumbled, shaking his head. "So you don't know who she is, and you don't know where she went after you left here—"

"I take it she went out to Neil Novak's boat," Logan observed capriciously as he polished off his drink.

"Why?"

"I don't know." He moved forward and set the glass down on a teak coaster on the coffee table, then resumed his position against the doorjamb.

"You don't know much, do you?"

"Too much knowledge spoils a good thing," Logan said, as if reciting some eloquent axiom. "Now, if you don't mind, I'd like to get back to being not busy."

Woods said nothing. He studied Logan with measured scorn, then moved toward the door. He pulled it open, then turned around to level the classic parting shot. "Thanks for the few moments of your precious time, Stuart," he said with a sneer. "And I'm sure you know the routine in all this. You get any urge to leave the island, you let me know. Got it?"

"You'll be the first to know," Logan agreed dryly. He turned to retreat back out to the deck, not even waiting for the door to close. On his way he made a pit stop in the kitchen for a refill of Beefeater and Schweppes. Then he settled into his webbed deck chair and contemplated the heavens.

He should have been pissed, would have been pissed a year ago. Maybe even a week ago. This was his goddamned life, and he had every right to live it any way he damned well pleased. To hell with Woods, to hell with Neil Novak and Lynn Sutton, and to hell with old Red, whoever she was.

One thing was certain: he'd come out here to Catalina to escape death, but it had followed him. Of course, deep down he knew someday it would find him; it always did. Death framed his life; he got paid writing about it. Over the years he'd come to know it the way a sportswriter knows all the nuances of a hometown team. He had been trained to reduce death to a passionless science, to detach himself from its taunts and jeers. His years on the city desk had served him well, bringing him close to every kind of death imaginable: domestic stabbings, street corner shootings, back-alley brawls, carved-up whores, emasculated pushers, burned dopeheads, drive-by massacres, mangled hit-and-runs, even the occasional death by natural causes. And each time he had to look the other way and force his stomach closed, Logan could say two things about death: it had a great imagination, and it had a great sense of humor.

Molly's death had changed all that. No longer could he look at death—much less write about it—impassively. The startled look in her right eye, the red hole where her left eye should have been, created an identity to death that until then he had been able to keep separate. But from that moment to this he saw Molly in every corpse: the pain, the anguish, the surprise, the loss. Now, whenever he saw the intimate mask of death he no longer felt disconnected; in the words of John Donne, he felt diminished.

Until today. Until he sauntered across the beach and found himself standing over two lifeless mounds, two puffy bodies stretched out under the hot sun, waiting to be carted off to the lab so some detached medical examiner could pry them open and have a look. Logan had seen the wounds, recognized the faces, known them as two people who had lived and laughed and argued just the night before. And their deaths had done nothing to him. In their faces he saw vacant effigies of death where life had surged just hours ago. He had stared, but he had felt nothing.

Of course, the redhead only fueled the fire.

Impulsively he made a decision, one that instantly felt good.

He picked up the phone and dialed. As the anonymous ringing echoed back over the wires, he sensed a sudden chill merging with a nagging dread. Did he know what he was doing, did he realize what might happen, what he might feel, when he set foot on the other side? Twenty-six miles was a long way coming over; could it be such a short step going back?

The flood of fools rushed in where the city's few wise men dared not tread. Normally Logan would have traveled the surface streets, but today he was forced to tackle the L.A. freeway system.

This was the 405, the San Diego Freeway. Eight lanes of dry, stale pavement bisecting the Southland, slicing from the upper reaches of the San Fernando Valley sixty miles through the basin into Orange County. Then, just north of Laguna Hills, the smog-choked interstate intersected with Route 5 and continued southward to the Mexican border.

Behind him lay the snarled tentacles of overpasses and underpasses and exits and entrances of Long Beach. Ahead loomed the gray outline of the Santa Monica Mountains that formed the north edge of the L.A. basin. It was a view that by two o'clock would be blanketed with a billowy consommé of steaming brown haze. The mercury had already begun to soar, no end in sight to the heat wave that had oozed into the city over the weekend. Valley temperatures had slipped past the hundred mark on Sunday, and every TV weather clown was preparing another space in the record books for today. The heat gagged the earth with a certain stillness.

A blast of warm air caught Logan in the face, forcing him to squint through the slope of glass before him. He adjusted the dark shades that hardly protected his eyes from the raging sun, then flipped the visor down to shield his eyes from the blowing dust and grit and airborne filth. He watched as a top-down Mercedes surged up behind him, then swerved into the fast lane and sped past. Next came an early-model Chevy Camaro, black on black, Hollywood pipes jutting out the side. It edged past Logan on the right, a heavy bass beat thundering from its radio, pounding out the latest processed music. Logan eyed the scooped hood and the black tint and the bronze arm hanging from the window, a lone, fleshy palm beating rhythmically and mindlessly against the door. The arm belonged to a kid who probably wasn't even born when that classic rolled off the Motown assembly line.

The warm air felt refreshing on Logan's dry face, blowing through his tangled blond hair. First thing he had done when he pulled the car out of storage was put the top down, just as he used to do every morning during the ceaseless dry spell that lasted from late April to early October.

He'd bought the 1967 Plymouth Fury for such days, which in Los Angeles were just counted among so many other givens. It was a heavy, gas-guzzling silver-over-black convertible tank with wire wheels and a 389 V-8 that smacked of impulse and freedom. The engine purred at ninety, and it handled with an ease that showed an understanding of center of gravity. It was an impractical car that somehow had survived into an era of conservation and retooled logic. When it came time for Logan to part with his worldly goods and become an island hermit, he found he couldn't do it. He also knew he couldn't take it with him. So he'd stored it in a rental storage garage a half mile from the ferry terminal in Long Beach. He received a ten percent discount by paying for a full year up front, which he applied to an extra month's rent. Then, ferry ticket to Catalina in hand, he locked the Fury in its space and walked on down to the docks.

This morning when he had unlocked the metal door and exposed the car to the sun for the first time in twelve months, it had started right up. A thin film of dust had settled over the lacquered body and the upholstery smelled musty, but in all other regards the car looked and felt like it had only spent the night.

Logan tuned the AM-only radio to KFWB, the all-news station that promised to give you the world in twenty-two minutes. At the mention of the name Novak, Logan instinctively reached over and turned up the volume. He listened intently as the droning announcer added a few details to the sketchy facts Logan had reviewed in the *L.A. Times* during the two-hour channel crossing: Neil Novak and his female companion reportedly were on a weekend outing in Catalina; they arrived Saturday morning and had moored in Avalon Harbor for the night. The couple had motored ashore for a romantic evening of dinner and entertainment, then returned to the *Rhapsody on Blue* for a nightcap. The following morning they were found murdered in their sleep in the aft stateroom of the forty-two-foot yacht. Novak's wife of twelve years had *not* accompanied her husband on the weekend jaunt. Authorities were looking into rumors of illicit sex or drugs, rumors which the media, intimately and vicariously familiar with the entertainment clique, accepted as a matter of course.

L.A. was a town that thrived on sex and drugs. More than once Logan had been called up from Hollywood to the industry netherworld that seemed to exist only in the show-biz gossip rags. There he found a bizarre array of rapes, drug ODs, sex for pay, and shootings and stabbings and drownings, all part of a parallel world that seemed to exist in an orbit all its own. He'd seen enough to last a lifetime, and he was only a newspaperman. How the hell the cops survived with their minds somewhat intact was the true mystery.

L.A. traffic always had a marked cathartic effect on Logan. The mesmerizing pace at which it barely crawled, the thick stench of exhaust, the practiced ritual of the freeway waltz. Cars changed lanes like swingers changed partners, as if life was all just a frantic binge. Maybe that's all it was. Logan shrugged as a black Mazda Miata cut in front of him to make a right turn onto Venice. He leaned on the horn and the phantom driver gave him the finger. Logan thoughtfully returned the gesture.

He checked his watch: just before noon. Getting his car out of storage had taken a good hour, and the freeway traffic had slowed his northbound progress. No matter; he didn't have anywhere to go for another two hours. He pulled to the right and took the Santa Monica Boulevard exit, keeping to the left

as he neared the end of the exit ramp. He waited for the light
to change to green, then made a wide turn and pulled into the
westbound lane.

He lumbered along the broad boulevard, through the lower
reaches of Brentwood, past car dealerships and franchise
pizza parlors and Chinese restaurants and flower shops. By
the time he felt the cool sea breeze drifting in from the ocean
he didn't give a damn.

At Ocean Avenue he hung a left and slowly glided down
the curb lane beside the seafront promenade. Pensioners in
dirty trousers, widows with little silver-colored dogs, winos
with paper bags, transients carrying matted sleeping bundles
all shuffled along the concrete walkway, slowly, as if defying
time to pass any quicker than they did. He weaved in and
around the bicyclists and joggers and skateboarders, past the
entrance ramp to the Santa Monica Pier, past the opulent
Santa Monica galleria on the left and seafood and hot-dog
stands on the right.

He continued southward for a half mile, parallel to the
beach, several blocks back from the sand. When he spotted
several ancient neon signs announcing motel rooms by the
night or week, he slowed to a crawl. Three two-story motor
courts were set side by side, postwar L.A. stucco, faded paint
chipping from years of neglect. The Bay View Inn, the Santa
Monica Beach Motel, and the Breakers. Logan pulled up in
front of the Bay View Inn first and read the accompanying
marquee: ALL ROOMS SEA VU, HTD POOL. LO WKLY RATES. Palm
fronds rustled high above him, and a distant roar of surf induced him to pull into the inner courtyard.

For twenty-six bucks a night, seven-night minimum, Logan
got a queen-sized bed in a sparse but clean room on the second floor with a deck overlooking the beach. It was furnished
with a low dresser, a wooden chair with a ruptured seat cushion, a junkyard coffee table, and a small boxlike fridge that
amazingly started humming when he plugged it in. The bathroom was small, equipped with two towels barely large
enough to dry a small child, and a small stack of individually
wrapped soap samples. A two-cup electric coffeemaker sat on
the back of the toilet, along with two plastic cups, a packet
of coffee, and a lone paper filter.

Logan tested the bed for tired springs, then threw open the
sliding-glass door and stepped outside onto the small concrete
deck. Below him was a kidney-shaped pool with clean water

and an ample supply of lounge chairs neatly lined up against a chain-link fence. The pool and patio were empty; so was the rest of the motel, as far as Logan could see. He gulped a deep breath of clean ocean air, then retreated back inside. Then he locked the door, grabbed his keys and headed out the way he came in.

Logan turned the car away from the ocean and caught the Santa Monica east. He got off at the Overland exit and cruised a few blocks up to Olympic. There he turned right and hugged the center line until he hit La Cienega; from there he angled his way up to Hollywood, turning right on Santa Monica, left on Highland, right again on Sunset. Traveling the surface streets was much quicker than crawling along on the freeway, where early rush hour now was pushing toward twenty-four-hour-a-day tie-ups. He slowed a bit as he passed the Shell station at the corner of Wilcox. A landmark, still there in a vast, ever-changing landscape of car washes, mini-malls, diners, and adult bookstores. He pulled the Plymouth up in front of a row of parking meters, then glanced up and down the street to reassure himself that he wasn't tempting fate by leaving an open ragtop on the streets of Hollywood. He hiked up his white denims, ran a rough hand through his tangled hair, and darted across the street toward a row of dilapidated storefronts with the windows painted out.

Marty's was wedged between a movie-poster shop and a boutique that sold cheap lingerie. It was marked to the world only by a white neon martini glass tipped at an angle, with a green neon olive hovering near the bottom. It was dark and quiet, more a joint than a bar. A home for some and an alibi for others. A musty odor saturated the place, especially at this lazy time of day when business was slow and the air was still. Four maroon Naugahyde booths stretched along one wall of the narrow lounge, while a dark oak bar and eight stools lined the other. The tin ceiling was dark and grimy, laced with sagging cobwebs. The front window had been slathered with countless coats of black paint; faint scratches allowed in slivers of light, which cast jagged patterns on the chipped linoleum. The overhead lights and jukebox were kept low. Perry Como was playing, well-suited to the half dozen drooping pensioners slouched over their drinks. It was as good a place as any for an *L.A. Times* reporter to share a beer with a fair-minded deputy medical examiner. No one but they and the neighborhood regulars even knew the place existed.

If Langston Post was anything, he was large. Not fat, no-where near it. His bulk was muscle, and all of it wore very comfortably on his massive frame. His rugged face sported a pair of intelligent, inquisitive eyes that likely had witnessed more in just one day than most folks saw in a lifetime. He'd grown up on the streets of this city, raised by his mother and six older sisters in a roach-infested hovel in Watts. Somehow he'd managed to escape the riots and fires, in body if not completely in spirit.

He sat at the bar twisting a cocktail straw in a fashion that would have made Alexander Calder nervous. A Budweiser long-neck sat on the polished wood counter in front of him.

"Dr. Post, world's finest corpse-cutter, I presume?" Logan greeted the tired M.E. with a hearty slap on the back.

"Stuart Logan—and I thought I'd already seen enough dead meat for one day." Dr. Post grinned, raising his brow. He rose from his stool and they stood motionless for a sec-ond, sizing each other up like long-parted father and son. Then Langston Post gripped Logan's hand and shook it vig-orously. "Good to see you, my friend. Thought maybe you'd plum dropped off the face of the earth."

"That was the intent." Logan shrugged and drew a foot up onto the tarnished brass rail. "The best-laid plans, et cetera."

Langston Post slowly sipped his beer, slid back onto his stool, and motioned for Logan to sit next to him. Logan hes-itated, then took a seat and glanced down the counter at the bartender. He was a short, wrinkled man who looked like life had thrust too many disappointments his way. He regarded the two men at the bar warily, as if they looked familiar but not familiar enough.

"Hey, pal ... what'll it be?" the bartender finally said, wiping down the polished wood with a cloth.

Logan gestured at Langston's Budweiser. "One of those, coldest you got," he said.

The bartender nodded, fetched a bottle from the cooler, and popped the top. He set it down on the bar, then grunted, "Glass?" in such a way that Logan knew only fags and girls dared drink from anything but a bottle in this place.

Logan shook his head. "Bottle's fine."

The bartender nodded, then returned to his bored place in front of a Dodgers game slowly unwinding on a TV sus-pended from the ceiling.

Logan and Dr. Post each sipped their beers and fell into a

quick silence, as if the lack of conversation helped them re-cap the last twelve months. Finally, enough ground silently covered, Langston swiveled on his stool and faced Logan.

"What d'you say we go into my office," he suggested, cocking his head toward the most distant empty booth.

Logan shrugged. "Whatever you say, boss." He left a five on the counter and followed Dr. Post across the room. He eased into the booth across from Langston, leaned against the dark wall, and stretched his legs out on the slashed-and-taped seat.

Post took a long drink, wiped the foam from his lips, then rested his bottle on a cocktail napkin. He pulled his knee up to his chest and regarded Logan curiously. "So, my friend . . . what's this all about?"

"Just like that? No small talk, no chitchat, no 'How do you think the Rams are going to do this year'?" He studied Dr. Post over the neck of his bottle but did not drink. The man had changed in twelve months, gotten older and harder. Logan wondered if he'd fared similarly.

"I know how the Rams're gonna do," Langston said. "They're gonna choke. Now . . . what's up?"

Logan paused just a second more, then leaned forward and gave the good doctor his most sincere hushed tone. "Neil Novak and the girl," he said. "Lynn Sutton."

"What about 'em?"

"Anything you got."

"That's what I was afraid of," Dr. Post said, nodding slowly. He fidgeted, twisting the beer bottle in his hands as he thought. "Look, Stuart . . . it's not like the old days, when you could just ask me for shit and I'd be happy to help you out. You were legit press then, and I could justify a legit leak."

"But now I'm just persona non grata," Logan mumbled, acting properly miffed.

Langston said nothing, just sipped his beer and looked down at the grimy table. He wasn't going to buy into Logan's act, and Logan didn't expect him to.

"Okay, Langston. I'll deal right off the top. All I'm looking for is what I might have read in the paper if my replacement down at the *Times* ever got his act together. Just the who, what, where, when, why, and how."

"Official press briefing's tomorrow morning," Post stalled.

Logan flashed him an offended look. "Shit, Doc.

Briefings're just Q-and-A kibble to keep the press satisfied."
Logan folded his hands in front of him and looked plaintively
across the table.

"Just tell me why this is all so goddamned important." Post
nervously bit a sliver of ragged nail. Then he looked back at
Logan, doubt still creasing his weathered forehead.

"Okay." Logan sighed, peering into his bottle. Christ, it really was too early for this. "There's a girl—"

"Ain't there always."

"Saturday night—"

"I'm so happy for you," Dr. Post said, heavy sarcasm in
his voice. He sipped his beer, then listened attentively while
Logan recounted his tale. The story and the beer ran out at
the same time, and Logan sat back for the reviews ...

The twenty-year veteran of the L.A. County Coroner's office scratched at the day-old bristle on his chin, rubbed his
nose, cleaned his ears, all the while studying the ex-writer sitting across the table from him. All this studying took a long
time, tested Logan's patience. But Dr. Post knew that only
eternity could outwait Logan, and the six bodies waiting for
him back at the lab were only getting riper. He took another
sip of Budweiser.

"Okay, pal," he said finally. "This is just between you and
me. Just a source, unidentified. You got it?"

Logan gave him an offended, intelligence-insulted look and
nodded. "As always."

"This one's real tight, don't ask me why. In my book, this
Neil Novak is just another scrap of human flotsam that
washed ashore. Some guys are just autopsies waiting to happen, and this fella was one of 'em. Sooner or later, he was
gonna come to Papa." Post grinned, drained his beer, set the
bottle softly on the table.

"Kinda odd, don't you think?"

"How so?"

Logan cradled the empty bottle in both hands, picking at
the foil Budweiser label. "Sounds like a hit."

Langston laced his thick fingers on the table in front of
him. Hard to believe that fingers the size of small trees could
wield a scalpel. Maybe that's why he felt more comfortable
with patients that were already dead.

"You breathe a word of this, my ass is fried. And yours."

"Stack of Bibles," Logan assured him.

Langston regarded him skeptically, then shrugged it off. "I

told you this is a tight one, right?" His voice had lowered to a light whisper, almost lighter than the dust that caked the walls. "Well, for some reason the feds had been keeping an eye on Mr. Novak for quite some time now. Organized Crime Task Force."

Logan nodded. He'd heard vague grumblings from the District Attorney's Office when he was still at the *Times*, rumors about the feds' probe into alleged connections between certain Sicilian families and the entertainment biz.

"Anyway, Novak and the girl never knew what hit 'em. Both of 'em were gone to the world."

"Drunk?"

"Point one-eight for him, two for her. Plus other assorted substances that the lab's still trying to get a fix on."

"So how do the feds fit in?"

"Well, what I hear is that they were keeping a pretty close eye on Novak, his comings and goings."

"And you think one of these comings or goings was carrying a loaded gun?"

"I cut up bodies, Logan. I'm not a dick."

"That's not what I hear."

"You keep my old lady outta this." Langston grinned, running a tooth-sharpened fingernail over his balding head.

Which one, Logan could have asked, but decided to remain prudent and fair. Instead he asked, "This girl, Lynn Sutton. She was just out for an overnight trip?"

"From what I hear, Lynn was good at overnight trips."

"A pro?"

"An aging pro. She worked in spurts, so to speak. Here and in Frisco. Her sheet shows she was employed by a couple of escort services over the last few years, the latest being a place called the Sachet Social Club. S'posed to be upscale."

"So what're the cops saying?"

"Not much," Langston said, checking his watch, rolling his eyes at the time. "Word has it, the feds're figurin' hit, Italian-style. That's what Sheriff Criley'll say tomorrow, and the government lads'll probably back him up." He regarded Logan for a second, then began to push his way out of the booth.

"Going so soon?" Logan asked rhetorically. Over the last five years he'd grown accustomed to the doctor's abrupt trademark. Here one second, gone the next.

"Gotta get back to the old body shop," he lamented. "Been

a real killer of a day," he added, pleased with his own sense of gallows humor.

They shook hands, then Langston turned and quickly marched toward the door. He pulled it open, hesitated for a moment in the blast of sun that invaded the peace and quiet of Marty's, then disappeared into the anonymity of the city.

5

When Logan had first met Jeffrey Rhodes, he found the cop's boundless energy amazing. Now it was simply depressing.

When Rhodes wasn't pulling a stakeout or bracing witnesses or writing reports he usually could be found in some gym, lifting free weights, entwined in some Nautilus machine, or otherwise engaged in a game of racquetball or a game of pickup basketball. Even when Rhodes was off the court, his frenetic energy was still unbearable: the man simply couldn't remain in the same place doing the same thing with the same person. His eyes were always darting, calculating, absorbing vague nuances. Signals of being, he called them. Of being what, he never said, bouncing from place to place and woman to woman. Always searching, prowling—almost desperate for the brass ring to reward his unlimited libido. Twice married and forever divorced, the sight of blonde on flesh gliding down Sunset was his ticket to adventure.

Twice a week in the afternoon Rhodes descended on the L.A. Sports Club for an hour of some never-ending elimination tournament for the terminally active. Today was no different—except that he had agreed to knock off twenty minutes early to meet Logan for a quick post-workout break before heading back to Hollywood Division. Flexing biceps on department time was a definite violation of department policy, which to Rhodes made it all the more attractive.

The homicide detective was already seated at a small Formica table in the elevated restaurant, bent slightly over a colorful fruit salad as Logan approached. Rhodes glanced up, grinned widely, but didn't stand.

"Shtuart," he announced as he slurped, wiping a smear of melon from his lips with a napkin. "Pull up a chair, ol' buddy."

Fact was, they *were* buddies, although they hadn't started out that way. They'd started out adversaries—Rhodes the cop, Logan the probing reporter sticking his nose where authority didn't want it. For five years theirs had been a working relationship founded on professional courtesy born out of a respect for the system and all its foibles. And when Molly died, when the cops came up empty-handed, when Logan lost hope in the system, Jeffrey Rhodes was there to cushion the impact that he knew would come.

"Same old J.R. . . . all work and no play," Logan quipped as they shook hands and awkwardly embraced each other. He gave the place a visual once-over. "Nice gig."

"Fitness-a-go-go," Rhodes agreed. "You oughta give it a try."

"I bend my elbow every night."

"Poison," Rhodes condemned scornfully. "You gotta get on a program, get that old heart pumping. And this is the place to do it. First-class all the way, and top-grade ass. State of the art. Eighteen racquet courts, basketball, coed gyms, cardiovascular conditioning center, junior Olympic pool, spa, indoor track, paddle tennis, three restaurants. I tell you, it's a palace."

Logan grinned. "You sound like a vampire trying to convince your victim that being dead isn't going to be all that bad."

"You'd be surprised, *mi amigo*." Rhodes waved Logan into a chair. "Anybody who's anybody comes here. It's a walking *Who's Who in L.A.*, in the flesh."

Logan glanced around, noticed two women sharing secrets under a ficus tree several tables over. One had short, bobbed blonde hair; the other had a mound of auburn tossed on the top of her head. The requisite painted-on Danskins encased their ample bodies; the brunette flashed Logan and/or Rhodes a demure smile, then returned her attention to private matters.

"In the flesh is right," Logan said, raising his brow.

"That's just one of the fringe benefits. Fact is, you're right: this is work."

Rhodes subtly signaled to a waitress across the room. She

hurried over, and Logan thought she fit in nicely. She was clad in pink spandex leggings and a black-and-green striped cotton top. Her hair was pulled back in a ponytail, revealing pale skin blanched by all the right amounts of fiber and vitamins and fruit and no red meat. She took Logan's order for a tonic and bitters, smiled politely if not completely vacuously, and jazzercized over to the bar. She was back in two shakes, her pretty smile intact.

"Anyway, enough about this place," Rhodes continued, when she once more had danced off. He swallowed the last of his grapefruit and wiped his chin. "What brings you back to civilization, if that's what you call all this?"

Logan took a long, healthy breath, gulped his tonic and bitters, cast a sideways glance at the two ladies, noticed they were getting up to go. His eyes trailed them as they eased down the steps, then he drew his eyes back to Rhodes, who was waiting patiently for Logan to get on with it.

"A triangle," he finally said. "Of a sort."

"Good man, Stuart. I believe congratulations are in order."

"A love triangle involving a mysterious red-haired nymph," Logan added. "And a dead man and a dead woman."

"Jesus," Rhodes breathed, his voice a whisper. He glanced around, an automatic reflex to see if anyone was listening in. Job hazard. "Looks like I've been hanging out in the wrong place. These stiffs . . . who are they?"

"Neil Novak and Lynn Sutton."

This time Rhodes whistled, low. He stared at Logan, waiting for more, wondering what sort of shit Logan had gotten himself into. Logan fed off the curiosity building in Rhodes' face, played the suspense to the hilt as he took a casual sip of tonic. Then he set the glass on the table and slowly briefed Rhodes on everything he knew—and everything he didn't.

"So all you're aiming to do is find this girl?" Rhodes said at the end of Logan's tale.

"Call it a quirk."

"I'm sure Criley's boys'll do a bang-up job."

"I'm not interested in Criley's boys," Logan said, shaking his head. "Whoever this girl is, she used me."

"Hey, pal. Friend. *Amigo*. That's the name of the game, the call of the wild: use or be used."

"In this case it was kill or be killed."

Rhodes nodded; Logan had a point. He rubbed his chin, glanced at his watch. "So what do you want from me?"

"Whatever you can tell me. This Novak guy, the Sutton girl, whatever might be lurking around the gutter. Friends, enemies, husbands and wives, that sort of thing."

"And when you find your mysterious redhead? What then? You going to ask her if it was as good for her as it was for you?"

"Maybe." Logan shrugged. "Maybe I'll just ask her how good it was for me."

Rhodes cracked a grin. "Stuart ... what's mine is yours, you know that. If this girl's so straight-up important, I'll see what I can find. But this one's real sticky, way I hear it. Novak was a longtime fixture in the record biz—not exactly your greatest-American-hero sort."

"So I've heard. How 'bout this Lynn Sutton?"

"The girl who bit the bullet with Novak? Lynn's business was pleasure. She also worked days, at a trendy boutique on Rodeo. Frangi Pangi, I think. To each his or her own, I guess." The waitress walked up, asked if everything was all right, was there anything else the two men wanted. Rhodes shook his head and sent her on her way. "If Neil Novak wanted to spend the weekend with some aging hooker, that was his business."

"Pleasure," Logan corrected him. "There's a wife—"

"Yeah. Name's Leslie. A few years younger than Neil, onetime studio singer. Don't know much on the personal side, but I hear she's a bit of a nympho, so watch out. I get the feeling they had some sort of arrangement."

"Arrangement?"

"Sort of an open marriage, I guess."

Logan wrapped his fingers around his highball glass and studied Rhodes suspiciously. The Novak murder was under the sheriff's jurisdiction, not L.A.P.D., but Rhodes seemed to know more than what usually fueled rumors at division briefings. On the way over here from Marty's he'd had plenty of time to digest what Langston Post had told him, and one thing kept coming back at him.

"What about this business with the feds?" he asked, a measure of suspicion cloaking his voice. "What's that all about?"

Rhodes sat still, said nothing, just regarded Logan with great interest, maybe even a little awe. He drummed his fingers on the table, then inched forward in his seat.

"I'm not going to ask you how you know that," he began.

"I don't want to know. All I can tell you is that some pretty heavy shit is going down."

"It's hardly been twenty-four hours—"

"Since Novak bought the farm, yeah. But something else has been cooking for a lot longer than that."

Rhodes leaned forward and cocked his head toward a dapper man sitting alone at the bar. "Recognize that man down over at the bar, Jack Armstrong, Jr.?"

"Looks like David Carbone, with his seersucker."

"You know him?" Rhodes' eyes opened wide in genuine wonder.

"Tracked him for two years, back when Justice tried to nab him but let him slip. I noticed him when I came in, wondered when you'd bring him up."

"Yeah, well, his old man's in deep doo-doo right now. Gouging a couple dudes named Eduardo DeSola and Chico Escabar."

"Colombian slime," Logan said. DeSola and Escabar were reputed to be direct links with the cartels in Medellin, and at one time the feds had an airtight case against them, adding up to twenty-five-to-life at San Quentin. Then a protected witness was found dismembered in his new home up in Lompoc, and the case fell apart. The federal judge assigned to hear the case was not pleased.

"Anyway, we got little Davey covered twenty-five hours a day," Rhodes continued. "What we hear, they're trying to get a bigger slice of the pie: drugs, sex, gambling, a little laundry on the side. And the Colombians ain't too pleased."

Logan didn't say anything immediately. Instead he let it sink in slowly as he raised his glass, looked at Rhodes over the rim. Then he asked, "So how does Novak fit in?"

"Strictly business. Primarily with Papa Luigi and Uncle Niki. Remember them?"

Hard not to. While the entire undercover effort had ended in embarrassment for the feds, it had earned a promotion for Logan and a circulation boost for the *Times*. And all the months spent trailing DeSola and Escabar brothers and uncles and cousins all kept turning up the same players, like a bad recurrent dream: Luigi Carbone in New York, Niki Carbone in Chicago, David Carbone in L.A.

"What are they looking for, besides drugs?"

"Whatever there is." Rhodes shrugged. "But the Task

Force on Organized Crime is operating in full cooperation with the L.A.P.D."

"And that's where you fit in?" Logan asked.

Rhodes nodded. "Temporary assignment. Maybe permanent after this is all over."

Logan glanced up at David Carbone, who had straightened in his chair and was digging his wallet from his back pocket. If the man was getting ready to leave it didn't seem to bother Jeffrey Rhodes.

"And Novak?"

"His ties are strictly through a middleman, slimeball named Frank Kennedy." Rhodes noted the surprise on Logan's face and grinned. "I know, doesn't sound very Ey-tie, does it? Kennedy's related by marriage, his mother's a cousin or something. Still, they're related, in a way only those people can understand."

"Blood is thicker with water."

"And you don't fuck with blood."

Logan started to say something but held back, taking his cue from Rhodes, who hushed up as the waitress glided over with the check. Rhodes signed on the dotted line, flashed his membership card at her, and she dutifully trotted off. He glanced over at the bar and watched as the young Carbone stood, collected his sunglasses from the bar, slipped them in his shirt pocket, and strode purposefully through the lounge.

"There goes your boy."

"Don't worry. Little Davey goes nowhere we don't see him."

Of course. Logan watched as Carbone crossed the massive sports complex lobby, heading for a door. Immediately a short man with thin red hair rose from a plush green chair and followed him out into the sunlight.

"So what's the record connection?" Logan said, hopeful that maybe this time the Justice suits were doing things right.

"Between Novak and Carbone? Strictly coke. Amazing what just a little blow'll do for you, 'specially if you want some deejay out in Podunk to play some lousy record."

"Payola?"

"For starters. Trouble is, it's tough ass shit to prove. The crime that doesn't exist. You need sources, witnesses who'll cross the mob and cooperate with the Justice Department. And we both know what happens to snitches."

Logan gazed in awe as a tall black-haired beauty, her aer-

obics outfit slicked down with sweat, entered the lounge and
stretched out in a chair two tables away. She shook her hair
back from her tan face; the arch of her back made her nipples
press stiffly against the thin pink fabric.

"I presume we're talking big money?" Logan pressed,
drawing his eyes back to reality.

"Absolutely. It's a billion-dollar business, Stuart. Over
seven billion last year alone; biggest year ever. Just one percent of that means tens of millions. If one CD sells five million units, that translates to twenty million bucks. A lot's
riding on every record a label produces, considering that over
ninety percent of all records are bought and sold because of
radio airplay. And a twenty-million-dollar profit packs a lot
of incentive to get radio stations to play a record."

"Anyone I should talk to?"

"Well, I hardly see how all this's gonna help you catch
your redhead, but if you've really got a hankerin', talk to Leo
Gold." Rhodes glanced at his watch, then fished in his pocket
for his parking stub.

Logan could sense that Rhodes was getting impatient. David Carbone had flown, so now any time spent with Logan
now was on his own time.

"Gold? Who's he?"

"He's a record producer, has a state-of-the-art studio just
off Fairfax. Sonnet Sound, it's called. Novak was real tight
with Gold, used him almost exclusively. Feds are taking a
real close look at him. Big counterfeit scam."

Logan scribbled the name in his notebook. He sat for a
moment, his hands wrapped around his glass, eyes absently
roving from the withered ficus trees to the low-key pastel
walls and Black Beauty.

"What about this Kennedy?"

"Hard to track down. Works out of his home out in Playa
del Rey." Rhodes pushed back his chair and slowly rose to
his feet. Logan drained his tonic and bitters, sucking an ice
cube into his mouth. He set the glass on the table and stood
on tired legs.

"What's his angle?"

"Commodities."

"Such as—?"

"Cocaine, prostitution, racketeering, smuggling—all that
good stuff."

"American capitalism at its best," Logan said dryly. He

followed Rhodes through the lounge and down the tile steps into the main atrium. He felt self-conscious among so many trim, tan bodies.

They walked each other out into the torrid afternoon sun. The day had settled in heavily into the L.A. basin, turning the vast summer sky a pale gray. The sting of soot bit at Logan's eyes; not like the soft salt spray in the face he was used to, sitting on his rock along Crescent Street. The buzz of traffic rushing past on the San Diego Freeway announced an early start to Monday rush hour. Logan tried but was unable to force his mind to conjure up the distant crash of surf from the roar of tires on the dry asphalt.

Rhodes handed the parking attendant the green claim check. He was a young kid, probably UCLA, and he nodded politely as he took the card, turned, and fished for the proper set of keys on a plywood board. Then he hurried off around the corner of the building, leaving Rhodes standing at the curb.

"Listen, Stu. Why don't we get together over the weekend? Just the two of us. We'll catch a game on TV, find us a couple chicks."

Logan hesitated. "We'll see."

"You fall off a bike, you gotta get back on," Rhodes reminded him. Then something struck him: he thought for a moment, frowned, then brightened, all within the space of a second. "Scratch that—I got Brian this weekend. Hell ... come out anyway, we'll burn some burgers on the grill. Brian'll love to see you."

Brian was Rhodes' son, from his first marriage, his only progeny and his only claim to a life of sanity.

Logan nodded. "I'll give you a call." Better not to make plans that far in advance; no telling where he might be by the weekend.

Logan crossed the street to where he'd left the Plymouth under the watchful eye of a parking meter, turned to watch as the valet attendant delivered Rhodes' black Toyota Celica. He shook his head as he yanked open his own door and slid onto the hot seats: where else but L.A. would you find a subculture that thrived on exercise and fresh air, where folks spent upwards of a hundred bucks a month to stay in shape, just so someone else could fetch their car?

6

Logan's memory was hardly photographic, but at times it bore a close resemblance to a bad Xerox. That's how he recalled Neil Novak's address on Stradella.

He fished in the glove compartment and drew out a worn map: Molly's tourist map, her guide to stars' homes. It was worthless the day she'd bought it and he knew it would be just as worthless out on Catalina. He could have thrown it out, just as he could have sold the Fury—but deep down he knew he could never part with the past. He unfolded the ragged sheet of paper in his lap, then folded it back until just one accordioned section of Bel Air rested against the wheel in front of him.

From Sunset he hooked a fast right at Bel-Air Road, took the second left, and wound his way up through the opulent neighborhood of exotic French chateaus and Italian villas and Arabian mosques. He hung another right at a fork and climbed a half a mile more. He worked his way into the hills with ease, each passing house more expensive and extensive than the last. Pink haciendas decked out with bougainvillea and oleander and palm trees were crudely plopped down amidst English Tudors and Frank Lloyd Wright replicas.

The Novak house was hidden from the street by a ten-foot whitewashed adobe wall. A pair of gates was carved out of the thick masonry wall, and each was adorned with ornate Spanish grillwork. A brick courtyard led up to a Mediterranean portico and sculpted rose gardens. A canopy of trees—willows and magnolias and oaks—shaded the red tile roof from the malicious sun.

Logan continued up the street a hundred yards. He made a U-turn at the next intersection, then slowly coasted back down the street. He pulled to a stop just past the lower gate and cut the engine. A warning sign from Bel Air Security Patrol threatened armed reprisal if he touched anything. The last thing he wanted was to attract attention from whatever gun-toting guards might be cruising the hills. He carefully approached the gate and peered up the short driveway into the circular courtyard.

A red convertible Mercedes 450 SL was parked at the far end of the cobbled drive. Its top was down, and a man Logan could only assume was its driver was standing in the shade of the front portico. The oak double front door stood ajar, and the man was standing in the doorway talking to someone in the inner shadows. Conversation was hushed; even in the stillness of the hot afternoon Logan couldn't make out a word. But the manner in which they were saying whatever they were saying told him more than could any words could. Close, delicate, intimate, light hands holding each others' sides as the figure of a woman finally inched into the sunlight. The man stepped back a bit, drawing her further out onto the front step, and Logan noticed her gentle fingers running up and down his open neckline. She glanced around nervously, reluctantly, pulling back. But the man wouldn't let her go.

Leslie Novak, no question. She was tall and thin, and from where Logan stood she seemed to epitomize the perfect L.A. poster child. Only this was no poster, and she was no child. Sun, surf, sprouts—all had provided her skin a healthy glow. Her auburn hair clung closely to her sculpted cheeks, framing her eyes and lips. A tuck here and there, and a hint of liposuction and four days a week at Matrix One tied the bow on an already tight little package. She looked a little more war-torn than she probably wished, no doubt attributable to the sudden, tragic loss of her husband. But the way she was touching this man, the way he was touching her, suggested that grief was not presently a strong part of her emotional repertoire.

The man stepped closer and touched his hands to her hips, then slowly moved them around back until they found comfort on the curve of her ass. Again Mrs. Novak glanced around nervously—but only for a second. The man drew her into his arms. Their lips met, tentative at first, then more violent, a full, passionate lock. At great length she pulled back, shared a few more loving words with him, and retreated inside alone.

The oak double doors shuddered closed and the man turned toward his Mercedes. Logan ducked back around the edge of the gate, ran for his car, and unfolded the celebrity map across his lap just as the Mercedes emerged from the drive and pulled alongside.

"You lost?" the man asked, leaning across the passenger seat. His voice was tempered with all the suspicion that comes with discovering a strange face in such a neighborhood.

"Yeah," Logan grunted. "I was looking for Nick Nolte's place." He handed over the ragged map. The man regarded it with contempt but consented to have a look, giving Logan time to assess his rugged looks. His skin was pure Hollywood, eternal tan, not too leathery but definitely on its way. His face was angular, his chin squared with a slight cleft. A full head of black hair swept over the ears, and his steel-gray eyes seemed tired but aware, the type that often knew more than they were showing.

The man gave Logan directions back to Sunset and made a comment about how that map had to be five years old if it was a day. Logan thanked him, refolded the map, and chucked it on the seat beside him, then followed the red Mercedes down the winding grade.

As they descended the hill he pulled out his notebook and copied down the license plate bolted to the red 450 SL: PLAYTYM. *Tres. L.A.*

Back at Sunset he hung a quick left, then another at Beverly Glen. He followed the road as it snaked its way up through a narrow canyon, one of the few cuts through the Santa Monica Mountains into the Valley beyond. A canopy of trees protected the street from the harsh August sun, and Logan inched the Fury in among the homeward-bound stream of traffic. As the road began to climb into the golden hills the houses began to shrink in size. Gone were the whitewashed mansions of Beverly Hills with the Rolls-Royces parked in the driveways; up here the houses were stucco and redwood and were perched on small, funky lots that backed directly against the sun-parched hillside. At Mulholland the stream of traffic crested the mountains, and Logan began the steep descent into the bowl of thick, putrid smog that was the Valley.

The freeways and cross streets and buildings and palm trees of the towns that anonymously blended into each other were obscured by the noxious haze. Logan's eyes stung and he felt like holding his breath as he guided the car down the ribbon of roadway, past the houses cantilevered out from the hillsides on stilts, past the gray scrub that clung for dear life to the barren, dry cliffs.

Selling the house was the wisest thing Logan had done in the last two years. It had been *their* house, his and Molly's, their first. A charming little fixer-upper, under-appraised for a neighborhood so close to Ventura Boulevard. It had not been expensive; in fact, it was cheap by Sherman Oaks standards. Still, with ten percent down, plus taxes and insurance, two salaries had barely covered the mortgage. A handyman's dream: nothing a little work couldn't fix. New paint, inside and out. New carpeting in the bedrooms, refinished hardwood floors throughout the rest of the house. New cabinets in the kitchen, new tile in the bathroom, custom draperies and new light fixtures. Fresh lawn in front and back, full landscaping, refurbished plumbing, and extensive repairs on the roof. He and Molly shared in the sweat and agony, and eventually pride of ownership replaced buyers' remorse.

He'd signed the purchase agreement at the start of last summer and moved out in late July, the hottest weekend of the year. It was a choice dictated mostly by financial necessity; any reduction in emotional baggage was a fringe benefit.

When it had happened, when Molly had died, he refused to accept that his world was shattered. He went into the office the following Monday—a hot August morning, as he remembered—and tried to block the pain. He almost made it to the lunch hour before his spirit crashed. At home he couldn't sleep facing the emptiness where Molly used to sleep. He couldn't eat where he and Molly used to eat. On their anniversary two months later he set two places for dinner, and he'd celebrated her birthday in November. The Christmas tree that year still held her handmade ornaments, and he still hung her stocking by the chimney with care. He had consulted his "Molly conscience" on a daily basis, seeking benign approval from her memory, pursuing dreams they once shared but which he refused to accept were now as dead as she. His life came from hers; they had formed each others' worlds. But as hers had come to a skidding halt, so had his.

Of course, his friends and family commended him for handling it all so well. People don't know what they can't see, and Logan did what he could to make it easy on them. All the books and articles sent by friends and family said it was best to let go, to identify the stages of grief. The pain, the anger, the resentment, the fear, and emptiness. Logan knew all about the stages, he'd reviewed them with Dr. Gillette, and as much as all the psychiatric terms and axioms serviced to structure and identify, they did little to lessen the loss. Molly was gone and there was nothing he could do about it, except to work through the hurt during the day and bear the boiling nightmares of the night.

He sat for a long time, across the street, motor idling low. He sat and stared at the house, a part of his former life, a part of his history with Molly. He had carried her across that front doorstep the day they moved in, and she had died on that same step, shock on her face, a bullet through her brain.

Whoever bought it had painted it gray. Logan frowned; he'd spent eight agonizing days in the hot sun painting it white. The driveway had been repaved; it looked good, but the lawn had gone to weeds and the walk had been heaved upwards by the pesty mulberry tree roots. The bougainvillea had flourished, now covering the side fence, but the roof shingles still hung like a coal miner's teeth. The rosebushes Molly had planted along the front of the house were in full bloom, but the ivy Logan had pulled down from the garage had taken hold again. And a pane of glass in the garage door had been broken, not repaired.

He waited for the tears, even if there was to be just one. He wished it to come, as if he were wishing to drain one last drop from the bottom of a Johnnie Walker bottle. He felt it in there, but there it stayed. One could not indulge emptiness, wallow in depression, at whim.

Logan threw the shift into drive and stepped on the gas. As he pulled out from the curb and turned the corner he gave one last backward glance at the little house that no longer was a part of him, and headed off toward the freeway.

Logan edged the Plymouth into a small space to the side of the L-shaped motel structure, a tight fit in the days of Japanese compacts. He pressed the power top button and waited as the giant canvas roof crept out of its recessed slot. It flopped down, the front edge aligning with the top of the windshield. Logan snapped the two locks, rolled up the windows, and locked the doors.

The motel consisted of twenty-six units, thirteen up and thirteen down, each one with a glass door opening out on the pool yard. The place was landscaped with fresh flower beds and rock gardens. Bright arrays of alyssum, roses, wisteria, and begonias cast a rainbow of colors across an otherwise drab complex. The paint was peeling, the drainpipes hung at odd angles, and rust stains had formed under the aluminum windowsills. The place looked like a ma-and-pa operation, with Ma getting the upper hand.

He grabbed the two bottles he'd picked up at Ralphs—a liter of Beefeater and a liter of Johnnie Walker Red—and started toward his room. On his way to the concrete aggregate stairway he glanced at the pool, found himself drawn toward it. He fumbled with the latch at the chain-link gate, finally working the rusted U-shaped catch away from the galvanized stanchion. He pushed the gate inward and walked into the pool area. The air was heavy with salt and street smells; from the crystal water came a stiff odor of chlorine and other chemicals. Logan set the two bottles on the concrete apron surrounding the pool, slipped off his shoe, and dipped a toe in. The water was warmer than he expected, almost like a tub. Solar-heated, probably piped up through a system of tubes on the roof, then pumped back into the pool.

Logan slipped his shoe back on, picked up his two bottles, and went upstairs.

Two minutes later he was sitting on his balcony, his feet up on the rail, a plastic cup with a healthy measure of gin balanced on his knee. The scent of backyard barbecues sifted through the air from the next block over, screening out the pervasive aroma of exhaust fumes that filtered in from Ocean Avenue. A gentle breeze rustled the brown palm fronds towering high overhead, striking a soft melody on a set of copper wind chimes probably set in someone's backyard down near the beach.

Logan lifted his exceptionally dry martini as the wind tousled his stringy blond hair. He realized now he hadn't had a good cut in over a year, just the quick hack jobs that comprised the $5.95 men's special offered every Wednesday at Narscissors in Avalon. Maybe this week he'd go back and see Liz, the Rubenesque Beverly Hills blonde who used to work wonders with his mangy mess.

Then he realized something that hit him harder than it should have: a week ago he wouldn't have given a damn about his hair. And now he was considering paying someone thirty bucks to snip it.

What exactly was he searching for? What the hell was he doing over here on the mainland, having sworn to himself that he'd never lay foot on L.A. soil again? Was he really here because of the redhead, in hot pursuit of the truth of last Saturday night? Did he really care that much to violate a promise, albeit an impossible one, that he had vowed on Molly's memory to honor? Or was it deeper than that? Was he scratching an itch, a nagging, pestering rash from which he had fled, but not escaped? Maybe he had needed something like this, someone like Neil Novak, to excite the hornets that once had buzzed in his gut.

Then again, did he really give a shit about Neil Novak? Did he care, did anyone care, that the man was dead? Did anyone care how it had happened, or why? Who, but just a small handful of family and friends, would suffer more than a few months? Who would really give a damn four weeks from now? He'd seen it before: studio head suffers nocturnal coronary, industry mourns. Industry takes stock, then goes on despite the tragic loss. That's the way it was, life in general. Someone dies, those around him form personal holes. Holes which eventually fill in to the satisfaction of all. Life goes on. Ob-la-di, ob-la-da.

One thing was certain: Logan's life had been all too quixotic since he'd lost Molly. And now, somewhere deep within, he sensed a stiff wind building.

7

Logan awoke to strange surroundings for the second time in three days. A thin swath of light cut through the gap in the ragged curtains that barely touched over the glass sliders, and as he tried to identify objects in the room he remembered where he was. He groped for his watch on the nightstand: just after seven. Not bad, still early. Too early to do much except to roll over and try to stave off the headache he knew would hit him if he sat up.

Or he could attempt to make an early start of the day. Without allowing too much time for mental dissent, he swung his legs over the side of the bed and tentatively stood. No headache yet. He padded across the crusty carpet and stepped into the bathroom, his bare feet feeling the grit on the floor. He ran a razor over his stubble, brushed the fuzz from his teeth, studied his eyes in the mirror. No more tired or red than usual, he thought as he splashed cold water on his face and watched the remnant blobs of shaving cream slide down the drain.

In the other room he dug through his duffel and found a pair of balled-up swim trunks. He wrapped a dry towel around his waist, grabbed the room keys, and trudged out to the pool. The motel was dark and quiet, windows closed off to the new day. He tossed the towel and keys on the nearest lounge chair, walked around the edge of the pool to the deep end. He stood over the marking that read 7 FT., contemplating the flat surface of the water. Not a ripple, not a breath of wind: just a few hapless moths that had been trapped overnight and finally had given up the struggle. Logan took a full breath, exhaled, stretched, dove in.

The water was cooler than last night, but still comfortable. He swam the length of the pool underwater, pulling himself along through the crystal depths, then surfacing near the far end. He pushed out of the water, gasped, shook the water from his nose and ears, scooped ropes of wet hair back up on his head. Then he turned around and pushed off again, this time skimming the surface in a splashless crawl. The pool was too short to make much of a lap, but the surge of water refreshed his body and mind.

He swam for close to an hour, then retreated inside to shower off the heavy dose of chlorine. Then, after a quick do-nut and a cup of bad motel-room coffee, he was set for the day.

He checked his watch again: ten-fifteen.

Thirty-six minutes since the receptionist told him to please have a seat. He'd obeyed, and had waited patiently. Twenty minutes had passed since he'd exhausted every magazine on the wicker table in front of him, ten minutes since he'd identified every celebrity in every framed black-and-white glossy gratuitously hung on the white lobby walls. Five minutes since he'd drained his Styrofoam cup of decaf. And in the last five minutes, the white couch in Rhapsody Record's lobby began to really piss him off.

Then came the voice. A voice like a song, a voice that instantly quelled the anger swelling inside him. The voice dazzled him before he ever looked up.

"Stuart Logan? I'm sorry. I hope I didn't keep you waiting."

He stood, his annoyance suddenly fading in the fluorescent glare, his eyes gazing at what, to an island-happy recluse, could only be considered a living vision.

"Thank you for seeing me on such short notice."

"My pleasure. I'm Corie Chapin," she introduced herself, offering him her hand. "Goddamned newspapers and networks calling me right and left, can't even think straight."

Corie Chapin defined everything that was Southern California. Eyes that were wondrous and blue, intense and intelligent. Lips meant for forms of magic only fantasy could fulfill. Skin smooth and soft and creamy, a hint of rouge blended into the scant tan on her cheeks. Blonde hair, darkish but natural, pulled back from her high cheekbones, cascading at will around her soft shoulders. To her body clung a tight gray knit dress which dared every confident curve to tempt and tease. She wore no jewelry except for two gold studs in her ears.

"Please . . . let's go up to my office," she invited him with a practiced smile.

He nodded, following her down a short hallway which opened onto an expansive open work space set off by nose-high partitions. Soothing green carpet, exposed brick walls, and recessed lighting transformed this once-barren warehouse into a comfortable, all-purpose office area.

"Innovative setup," he commented as Corie led him past a grouping of desks furnished with IBM clones. No one seemed to be working very hard, nor did they seem to care. Understandable. The Protestant work ethic symbolically was flying at half staff.

"It was all Neil's idea," she replied, still sniffling, like a cokehead on a bad night. "He hated leases. This building was an abandoned furniture warehouse when he bought it. He converted it to office space, burned the mortgage three years ago. Now, while all the major record labels are frantically renegotiating their leases and paying their landlords' kids' tuition, he just watches his own property value go up. Watched."

Logan studied her. She was putting up a strong front, almost succeeding. He sensed the shock in her patriotic eyes—red, white, and blue—and in the frailty of her slightest moves.

"And you. How are you holding up?" he asked her, a genuine question that he hoped didn't come off as too condescending.

She glanced around quickly, her movement tempered by nerves. The question was unexpected. "I'm okay, Mr. Logan. It's just . . . a strain, that's all. Total chaos. Please excuse . . . everything."

She led him up a wide staircase that opened off from the rear of the massive first-floor work space. Her office was at the top of the stairs, actually an anteroom to what Logan assumed was Novak's executive suite. The half dozen chairs and end tables suggested it served primarily as a holding pen for visitors waiting for an audience with the president of Rhapsody Records. Clean and corporate, comfortably appointed, highlighted by ferns and tropical vegetation placed at strategic visual points around the room. The lighting was indirect, recessed, the furniture carefully selected for warm familiarity. The walls were hung with gold records, posters of Rhapsody's hottest acts, a bulletin board covered with memos and Post-its. Logan checked for names of people he might want to meet, found a few he recognized and committed them to memory. He noted that the office had very little other personal character except for a small bud vase with a single yellow rose in it, its wilting petals sobbing onto the desk.

Corie invited him to take a seat in one of two overstuffed chairs; she sat in the other, facing him. She handed him a blue folder with Rhapsody's corporate label on it: a big "R" formed by a looping piano keyboard.

"You'll find a lot of background material in here. When the company was founded, a complete catalog of artists and records, that sort of thing." She hesitated, sighed tiredly. It had been a hard couple of days. "I still don't understand what all this has to do with Neil's insurance coverage."

"Standard procedure," Logan lied, feeling a twinge of guilt. He thanked her for the file and quickly browsed through the contents: clippings from *Forbes, Barron's,* the *Wall Street Journal,* virtually every trade paper covering the entertainment industry. Standard P.R. hype, touting Neil Novak as industry genius and entrepreneur. He set the folder on the floor and fixed on Corie's sapphire eyes. He felt as if he might drown in them.

"What can you tell me about Mr. Novak?" he ventured.

"What do you want to know?" she asked, a bit defensive.

Logan studied her, pondering the proper approach. The proper lies. He hadn't had to work up a cover in over a year, and he shifted uneasily in his chair. Did she detect the hesitation? He doubted it; she seemed too distracted by other things.

"Ms. Chapin, Mr. Novak died . . . was killed . . . on board his private yacht, the *Rhapsody on Blue*, presumably while he was entertaining friends. A friend. That much we know for certain, and we have no problem with that. As you may know, his policy with Pacific Mutual Insurance was a personal umbrella policy, strictly supplementary to any other policies that might cover his business operations. Do you follow what I'm saying?"

"Not particularly," she said bluntly.

"Ms. Chapin, Pacific Mutual is interested in determining whether Mr. Novak was indeed out on Santa Catalina for personal reasons, or if business also was being conducted. If so, we'll need to contact the corporate underwriter." Logan had no real concept of what the hell he was talking about, but figured—hoped—Ms. Chapin was similarly confused.

"I'm not sure I can help you."

Logan raised his brow and continued. "I understand if you weren't aware of every detail of your boss' personal life, Ms. Chapin. Most executives refrain from sharing personal matters with their secretaries—"

Corie Chapin suddenly leaned forward, her blue eyes roiling. Evidently he had hit a nerve. "First off, Mr. Logan, I am not . . . I was not . . . Neil Novak's secretary, business or personal. I'm his executive assistant. Don't worry, I know how it sounds, especially to members of the sexist male establishment. But Mr. Novak was extremely conscious of chauvinistic labels, and he ran Rhapsody Records in a very progressive manner. Second, Mr. Novak never mentioned any umbrella policy, business or personal. That's not unusual; he wouldn't mention such matters to me anyway, which suits me just fine. All I can tell you is, if you want to talk insurance, talk to his wife. Third, the man's body is barely cold, and here you are, snooping around, as if the only thing that matters is how much you're going to have to shell out to cover your financial ass and satisfy your shareholders. That may be the way you people operate, but it's pretty low on my list of priorities."

She glowered at him, then settled back in her chair. She kept her eyes on him, waiting patiently, the ball now in his court.

"Please excuse my abrupt manner," Logan apologized softly, genuinely. "I certainly didn't mean to be abrasive or obtuse. I'm afraid sometimes we fail to give proper consideration to the strain that death can inflict on close acquaintances. Blame it on the insensitivity of business. All I need is a few names, and I'll be out of your hair."

"Names? What kind of names?"

"Friends, business colleagues, people he may have entertained on his boat in recent weeks. We know about Ms. Sutton, of course, and our lawyers are examining that accordingly." He paused a moment, suddenly deciding to go for the gold. "What we're looking for is anyone who might have accompanied Mr. Novak out to Catalina this past weekend, if only for the day." Someone like a striking redhead with a seductive smile and a pocket full of knockout pills, he declined to add.

"I'm sure I can't help you, Mr. Logan," Corie Chapin said stiffly. She twisted a paper clip uneasily in her hand. "Mr. Novak was a very private person. At the office he was an open book, very outgoing, flamboyant even. But when he went home the book closed tight. Except for occasional parties, which he considered business, not pleasure."

Logan sensed in Corie a need to remember, to eulogize the man in her thoughts. Secretaries—executive assistants, *por favor*—often grow quite close to their employers. Logan sensed that sort of bond here, a bond of friendship if not surrogate paternity. Or maybe something more, something sexual.

"Tell me about him," he urged her, his voice softened to take the edge off her sadness. "What sort of man was Neil Novak?"

She sniffed, studied Logan for a moment, her need for grief battling her sensibilities. Logan felt like a vulture, hovering over a fading soul in the parched desert.

"Neil was a perfectionist, and he sought the same in everyone he knew." She reached behind her and extracted a tissue from a box, dabbed her eyes with it. "He felt there wasn't enough excellence in the industry, believed it gave him an edge. He had a dream, and he turned it into reality from the ground up. Look at Billy Keenan and the Metric Geese."

"Billy Keenan?"

Corie again reached behind her and picked up a stack of plastic CD cases. "Billy Keenan's released three albums in the last three years, sold twenty million copies. Neil discovered him. He discovered the Chrome Kittens, Rienna King, Metal Sponge, Green Virus. Hell, he goes all the way back to psychedelic rock. Remember Lilac Tradewind? Johnny Rand, teen idol and rock legend? In a business full of geniuses, Neil was a genius' genius."

Logan didn't subscribe to most genius theories, but Novak did seem to exhibit a knack for being just ahead of the current trends. And over the years he had turned that knack into the driving force behind Rhapsody Records. In the last year alone Rhapsody had released thirteen gold or platinum records and won six Grammys.

"And now that he's gone—?" he ventured.

"Hard to tell." Corie plucked another tissue from the box and blotted her eyes and nose. "It's only been forty-eight hours."

"What about you?" Logan pressed.

She looked at him, bitterness in her eyes. But the bitterness wasn't directed at him, it was for sudden twists of fate.

"Who knows." She shrugged. "He always said he structured the company so it could run without him, but no one will ever be able to replace his ear."

"And his wife?" Logan asked, wondering if other parts were equally irreplaceable.

"Leslie? What about her?"

"You said Neil was a . . . private person . . ."

"I did." She looked at him warily, a mechanism of defense.

"Meaning he was . . . entertaining someone other than his dear, loyal wife over the weekend."

Corie didn't even bother to translate fact to rumor. "Every marriage has its ups and downs."

Logan nodded. "Of course." He sensed a growing impatience, pending termination of their impromptu meeting.

"So, tell me . . ." he said at great length, his eyes fixed on hers, as if maybe that could keep her in her seat.

"Tell you what?"

"Did Neil ... did he have any enemies, anyone who might want to see him ... gone from the picture?"

"What's it to you?"

"There's a double-indemnity felonious death clause in his policy," Logan lied simply.

"I see." She nodded. He noticed she'd stopped sniffling. "Neil Novak had a number of acquaintances who wouldn't mind if he never stepped on them again."

"When you last saw him, did he seem ... worried, upset?"

She focused her darkening eyes between his. "Neil always seemed worried. Not that it has anything to do with you or your insurance policies, as far as I can see."

"Try me."

"Sorry." She rose to her feet, reaching out to her desk to steady herself. "And now, if you don't mind, I have a meeting. I'm sure you'll understand"

Logan took his cue, pushed back his chair and stood. "I can show myself out." He extended his hand, but she wasn't ready to shake it.

"Sorry. Door-to-door escort. Company policy."

Logan consented with a shrug. Corie led him down the stairs, out into the hallway, back through the maze of office cubicles. She walked briskly, and he had to move fast to keep abreast of her.

"If it's possible, I'd like a quick word with Mr. Minetti."

She slowed her pace and eyed him with suspicion. "He's in meetings with the accountants and lawyers. Won't have time for anything until he's gone over all the company records, sometime next week."

"How 'bout Frank Kennedy?"

Her suspicion narrowed but she tried not to show it. "Sorry."

"What about Mrs. Novak? Do you have her number?"

She turned and shot him a dark glare. "That should be in the policy, Mr. Logan. If not, that's your problem. I know you think you're just doing your job, but so am I. And I've given you all I can."

They reached the lobby and the end of the conversation at the same time. He apologized for putting her through such mind-bending hardship and thanked her for her help. She smiled sweetly, looking like she couldn't wait for the day to end—and for him to leave.

As he trudged back out into the baking sun, he felt an old

feeling, comfortable yet unnerving. A need to labor unto the truth and report it, to cast aside everything except his work. Molly had been understanding about it, deriving perhaps a heightened eroticism from her driven husband, absorbed in his work like a mad obsession.

8

From Culver City Logan cut over to the Marina Freeway. As he headed west the scent of salt air poured over the broad windshield. A gentle breeze had kicked up, still warm but a welcome respite from the torrid fever hanging over the basin just a half mile inland.

An uneasiness had started to seep through him, a sense of wonder. What the hell was he doing back here in L.A.? Why *had* he returned? Was it really to find some anonymous red-haired knockout artist, or was there something more?

Logan turned right onto Admiralty Way and wound around the marina to Palawan. He cruised past the endless landscape of masts and flying bridges gently rocking in the calm water and pulled up alongside the ramp that marked the 2400 pier; an accompanying sign read NO PARKING. He circled around the waterfront condo complex and parked in the open lot across from the swimming lagoon. The sea breeze chilled his shirt and pasted a loop of damp hair across his bronzed scalp.

A chain-link fence separated the boat slips from the public, and a locked gate prevented Logan from walking down the gangway to the vacant slip at the far end of the dock. He checked his watch: eleven-forty, still a few minutes early. He studied the boats tied to the dock: a Uniflite and a Bayliner cruiser, several day sailers, two Pearsons of differing lengths, a Swan 42, and one double-masted ketch with a teak deck and blue sail covers. As he surveyed the scene two pairs of soft footsteps approached behind him.

"Mr. Logan?"

Logan turned to greet a middle-aged couple crossing the

one-way drive from the underground parking garage beneath the condo structure. The man, tallish and stringy and sporting a captain's hat, was dressed in a tattersall shirt, chinos, and boat shoes with no socks. He carried a small Igloo cooler in one hand and was fidgeting with his keys in the other. His wife wore a pastel scarf over her tightly coiffed silver hair. A pilled pink sweater hung loosely over her bare shoulders and lime-green blouse, and she wore a pleated navy-blue skirt. In her arms she hugged a bag of groceries, from which was sprouting an enormous celery stalk.

"You must be the Kirbys," Logan said, extending his hand. "Let me help you there."

"Thank you. And it's Ross and Sylvia," Mr. Kirby insisted.

Logan helped Mrs. Kirby with her grocery bag as her husband unlocked the gate, then held it open for both of them. The Kirbys reminded him of the type of couple he'd expect to find at a plumbers' convention in Las Vegas: wonderfully middle-American, had saved all their lives for retirement, and nurtured through the years by conservative wisdom and conventional morality. The Channel 4 newscaster who identified them as the witnesses who discovered the two bodies Sunday morning in Avalon Bay had described them as "average middle-American," and he had been right on target.

A quick call to a network contact out in Burbank had procured Logan their address and phone number, and a two-minute conversation had earned him an eager invite out to the marina.

Mr. Kirby glanced up at the sky, pale-blue with just a distant upper-layer haze blotting out the incessant glare. "Perfect morning for a sea cruise," he said, getting a start on idle chatter.

"Absolutely," Logan agreed as he followed them out to the end of the dock.

The Kirbys owned the Bayliner he had noticed from the curb, and as Ross helped his wife aboard Logan read its name on the stern: *Sea Spirit*, out of Marina del Rey. He climbed over the rail and followed them into the compact galley. Mrs. Kirby invited him to set the bag down on a table and make himself comfortable.

"So you're an investigator," Kirby observed, a hint of suspicion breaking through his casual captain's banter.

"Pacific Mutual Insurance." Logan nodded as he handed over one of many cards left over from his newspaper days.

"Used to be with the L.A.P.D.," he added, embellishing the lie.

"Well, my heavens." Mrs. Kirby plucked a church key from a drawer and punched a hole in the top of a can of V-8 juice. "Just like on TV."

"This is real life, dear," her husband reminded her with a touch of chauvinistic embarrassment.

She shot a sharp glare at her husband, then smiled at Logan. "He thinks all I ever do is watch old reruns and read cheap paperbacks. He should only know the things I do."

"Yes, ma'am," Logan said, winking conspiratorially.

"So you're looking into the death of Mr. Novak?" Ross probed.

"Just routine stuff," Logan said, nodding vaguely, the untruth coming as easily as it always had.

Ross shuddered. "Such a tragic way to die."

"Ghastly," Sylvia agreed. "You *will* join us for a Bloody Mary?" It was more a command than a question, and Logan watched as she dumped ice into three highball glasses.

Logan consulted his watch. "It's a bit early."

"Nonsense," her husband insisted. 'The sun is over the yardarm somewhere, and Sylvia makes the best damned Bloodies in the whole U.S. of A."

Logan didn't need his arm twisted. He glanced approvingly around the galley. "I'd have no trouble getting used to this."

"Bayliner forty-foot convertible," Kirby acknowledged with pride. "Dual V-eight, twenty-two knots, flying bridge, sleeps six."

"Why don't you give Mr. Logan the full tour," Sylvia prompted her husband as she plucked a bottle of Absolut from a cupboard. She slopped three generous measures into the waiting glasses.

Ross obliged his wife. He led Logan into the forward cabin, custom-fitted with full teak paneling, queen-sized bed, plush carpeting, full head with shower. "It's not quite like Novak's boat, the *Rhapsody on Blue,* but it serves us just fine."

"You've been on his boat?" Logan pried cautiously.

"Once. He invited us to a party, and we went. What a mistake." He grimaced as if even the memory stung. "The party wasn't quite our style, but the boat was . . . grand. Same size as this, more or less. But his master cabin was more of a suite, set below deck in the stern. Ours is forward. Sleeps the same number of people, but the *Rhapsody* was ... more intimate. Cozy for couples."

"And parties," Logan ventured, trying to elicit the details.

"Sure as shit," Ross agreed. "Danced and played way into the night. I'm telling you, the characters he hung around with ..."

"What about his wife, Leslie? You ever see her down here?"

Ross Kirby thought on that, then shook his head. "Maybe once, I don't know. Trouble in River City, you know what I mean?"

Logan did, and showed it. "He ever say much to you?"

"About his marriage? Hell, no ... didn't have to, the way he had all those ladies around." He rolled his eyes disapprovingly.

Logan laughed. 'Not quite your style?"

"Our style went out with Benny Goodman," Ross lamented. "Anyway, he never brought his wife out to Catalina. Always someone younger, and always very private."

"You ever see him with more than one other ... date?"

"Not out on Catalina. Always one-on-one."

"You ever see him with this redhead before?"

Ross shook his head as if he'd been asked this same question before, probably a dozen times. "Never seen her. Coming off that boat she looked just like an orange ghost at sunrise." He raised his brow, surprised by the color of his own description. He thought for a minute as if about to say something, then turned and led Logan back to the galley, then out onto the rear deck where Sylvia was laying out the Bloody Marys.

"You've really got yourself a nice slice of paradise here," Logan complimented them as he accepted his glass. He sank into a folding deck chair and stretched out in the sun, thinking about the traffic that awaited him just a mile east of here. He shaded his eyes as husband and wife toasted the open sea.

"So, Mr. Logan," Mrs. Kirby began. "Tell us ... what is it you want to know that the cops won't tell you?"

Logan grinned and sipped his Bloody Mary. "Actually, the company is interested in who he was ... entertaining ... this past weekend. So far all we've got is this blonde woman, Lynn Sutton. And maybe the redhead—"

"That redhead again—" Sylvia said, taking a long gulp.

Mr. Kirby nodded, then took a long sip himself. He glanced at Logan suspiciously, as if wondering why an insurance investigator would be so interested in a striking red-haired beauty.

Logan sensed this and backed up a bit. "What I want to know, in your own words, is what you saw last Saturday, from the time Mr. Novak first tied up his boat."

"Sure." Kirby sounded a little bored. He propped his feet up on the teak railing and stared pensively out at the marina. "We went out there Friday, musta been about eight o'clock. We tied up, had dinner, and spent a quiet night. Next day, Saturday, we went into town for brunch, took a walk, then came back out to the boat around two. By that time the *Rhapsody* had already tied up and Mr. Novak was on deck, drinking champagne. So was his . . . lady friend."

"One lady?"

"That's right. The redhead."

"The redhead? Where was the blonde?"

"Never saw her." Ross Kirby deferred to his wife, who looked thoughtful for a moment.

"We've gone over this with the cops, so I don't know what else I can tell you." Mrs. Kirby sighed. "She was tan, wore a bright floral bikini. Barely covered her."

"*Just* barely," Ross agreed, drawing a stern look from his wife. "You know, if we knew we were gonna have to go through all this later, we woulda paid closer attention. Must've seen hundreds of girls out there, but to describe 'em all would be impossible."

The redhead, and not the blonde? He'd seen none of this on TV, read none of it in the papers. "What about later that night?"

Ross sat back and took a long, ponderous sip of his Bloody Mary. "Well, as we told the cops, they hung around the boat all afternoon. Around five o'clock they went below. Didn't see 'em again for another hour, hour and a half. Then they came back up and got into the dinghy. They were dressed for a casual dinner, which is pretty much all you can get in Avalon."

"When did they return?"

"Just after one. We were in bed."

Just after one—only minutes after Novak and Lynn Sutton and the redhead had stormed out of the Albacore Lounge, and the redhead subsequently had stormed back in.

"How do you know what time it was if you were in bed asleep?"

The Kirbys looked at each other with wicked grins. Finally Sylvia answered. "We were in bed. We weren't asleep."

Logan grinned, sharing in their obvious delight. "What about the blonde woman?"

"Never saw her." Ross shrugged. "Not until . . . the next day."

"After the redhead left?"

"That's right. It was a little before seven. I was making coffee, and I saw her get into a little dinghy and paddle off. Didn't look like Novak's, but I couldn't be sure."

Understandable. Logan nodded. A stolen dinghy, a fast approach at the bar, promises whispered in his ear, dancing candles in the dark, something slipped in his drink. A lovely lady disappearing in the dead of night, leaving only a trail of fingerprints and blood in her wake. He let the parts sink in, then glanced up at the sky and imagined he was out on his deck, feet up on the rail, drink in hand, breeze in the palms.

From the marina he took the surface streets to cross-stitch his way over to Hollywood. He slowly cruised past several blocks of clothing boutiques and secondhand shops and trendy eateries as he scanned for the street number: 6457 Franklin. He found it wedged between a crumbling stucco warehouse and a crumbling stucco antique shop. Sonnet Sound, the studio of the stars.

In a prior life it had been an equity-waiver theater set just on the fringe of Hollywood. Now the barren lobby had been split in two; one half served as a reception area and ancillary office space, the other was transformed into a small studio for solo recordings and mastering work. The theater itself, minus its ninety-nine seats and sloping floor, was refurbished in a complex array of soundproof baffles. The floor was covered with cork, foam, and a low-friction carpet which eliminated virtually all excess noise. Dual control rooms each were fitted with 48-track master recorders and digital mixers, and the result was a product unrivaled on either coast.

Logan had just barely sat down in a deep leather sofa in the lobby when a six-foot-wide barn-board door swung open on electric hinges, announcing the arrival of Leo Gold.

"Mr. Logan?" Gold greeted him as the door silently halted its gentle pivot.

"*L.A. Times,*" Logan said, shaking hands vigorously, be-

ginning to draw on the truth, however slim. "I know you've
got a busy—"

Gold raised an interrupting hand, waved off the obligatory
ass-kissing. "You're in luck. Rienna King canceled her after-
noon session. Probably the shock of Neil's death and all.
She's going on the road in two weeks, three-month tour.
Starts in Providence and ends here in L.A. on New Year's
Eve. We're having Scotch."

He touched a button on the floor and a large wood panel
slid aside, exposing a mirrored bar stocked with top-shelf
booze. Gold hesitated, then broke the seal on a bottle of
Pinch.

Logan looked around while Gold poured. The office reflected Gold's priorities and his name. The carpeting was a
rich gold color, and stepping on it was like stepping onto a
fleece Jason or Midas might have conjured from legend. One
of the walls was taken up by a massive sheet of glass that allowed him to look out over his studio. The other three walls
advertised his passions: wine, women, and song, one passion
per wall. Labels, head shots, gold records were crammed onto
every available inch of space. Two gold chairs faced a long
gold couch, all key-lit by overhead track lighting probably
designed by some unemployed studio decorator. They were
situated at right angles on an undersized shag run and set
apart by a massive black marble coffee table. On top of this
squatted an equally massive ashtray molded in the shape of a
cupped hand.

Gold himself was short and squat. He resembled a sloth,
with pasty skin and beady eyes. His entire body seemed to
sag slightly on invisible marionette strings. His polyester
slacks bulged at the thighs, seams straining from containment.
An open neckline completed the stereotypical bear-rug-chest-
with-gold-chain image. His hair was neat and plentiful, not
styled or moussed, cropped to the top of his ears. His lips belonged on someone with a bigger face. So did his nose. His
nostrils seemed to burn a bright crimson, and he sniffled constantly as he poured the drinks.

He hiked up his mailbag trousers, then plopped two perfect
ice cubes in Logan's glass. "Rocks okay?" he asked, handing
it to him.

They retreated to the sitting area, where Gold waved Logan
into one of the chairs. Logan sank down into what felt like a
twenty-four carat cloud, almost spilling his Scotch. He re-

garded Gold over the rim of his glass; there was something about the man's demeanor that made Logan immediately feel uneasy. Gut feeling or instinct, he felt himself slip-sliding back to the old ways. Back to the days of unyielding suspicion.

They squeezed off about five minutes of idle conversation. Logan gently built up Gold's ego with prattle about the glitter and glamour of Hollywood, and all the excitement of working with the stars. Molly would have been proud of him.

"So this is where you recorded Barbra Streisand?" he asked, drawing on the Rhapsody press kit stored in short-term memory.

"The same."

"She really as difficult to work with as they say?"

"A perfectionist." Gold shrugged. "She knows only two ways to do something: her way, and not at all."

"Sounds like Neil Novak," Logan observed, deftly steering the conversation back on course.

"Right. Novak. The reason you're here." Gold lifted his glass, examining the amber liquid inside. "To Neil, may he rest in peace."

Logan raised his glass, allowing a reverent moment to pass before sipping his Scotch. "You and he must go way back."

Jack Gold sat on the arm of the sofa, holding his glass in the palm of his hand. "Hard to believe he's gone. He was sitting right in that chair last Friday. He came by with Billy Keenan and his agent. They went over a couple arrangements for Billy's new album."

"And his band . . . what's the name? The Metric Geese?"

Gold nodded, gulped his Scotch. "Just Billy Keenan this time. The Metric Geese are just studio musicians . . . lay down tracks, maybe go out on the road for a couple gigs. Keenan . . . now there's a kid who's got something. Twenty-one years old, already he's topped the chart five times. Kid's right on top of things, genius songwriter. Tuned in to the times. Only Clapton was better with the ol' slow hand, and only Johnny Rand had a better pen. The Keenan kids' a whiz with a guitar, but he hardly knew how to brush his teeth before Neil found him. Took a real chance on him, Neil did. But that's how he worked. Real genius."

There was that word again. Logan frowned. "What about Novak . . . how'd he get his start?"

Gold fumbled in his shirt pocket for a pack of Camels and

poked a cigarette between his lips. He offered one to Logan, who shook his head.

"Novak moved out here from New York when the biz really started cooking out here, 'round '68, I guess. The golden years of rock and roll. I know, sounds like old-fogey shit. But it's true. Cream, the Dead, Jefferson Airplane, Iron Butterfly, Lilac Tradewind. Real music, not that computer shit we pump out these days. Anyway, he got a good gig in management over at Airtight Records, lasted there a couple years before he was cut."

"And that's when he started Rhapsody Records?"

Gold nodded, somehow scratching his head with the hand that held his glass of Scotch. "It was 1978. Named the company after his only idol. A Gershwin nut through and through. Good publicity, too; *Time* and *Newsweek* picked up on it. Meantime, Novak steamrolled over a lot of people, burned a lot of bridges in the process."

"These bridges he burned, any of 'em still around?" Logan asked as a waft of pungent smoke hit him in the face.

"Maybe a few," Gold allowed, drawing a gush of smoke through his nose.

"You figure maybe he burned one of 'em so bad the fire's still smoldered all these years?"

"Nothing surprises me."

"I guess in your business you see just about everything, huh?" Logan asked innocently.

"Which means just what?" Gold asked, a distinct note of caution creeping into his eyes and voice.

"Oh, I dunno. Whatever record people do. In my business we're always hearing something. Drugs, payola, prostitution, laundering, counterfeiting." Logan took a long, slow sip and let the mellow taste flow over his tongue. Playing the long pause for effect. "Maybe you could explain to me how it all works."

"If that's what you're looking for, Mr. Logan, you've come to the wrong place." A spark snapped in Gold's eyes.

"Whatever you say." Logan shrugged. "I just figured since you and he . . . well, with the exclusive arrangement you had with Rhapsody Records, I thought maybe you could shed a little light on some of Mr. Novak's business philosophies."

"I'm afraid you thought wrong." Leo Gold rose from his tentative perch on the couch. The first flicker of fury started

to ignite in his eyes; Logan could sense the anger by how
Gold's brow ruffled like the fur on a cat's arched back.

"You must have traveled in the same circles." Logan ran
his eyes around the room, over the framed black-and-white
glossies and the gold labels and the rest of the typical Hollywood pretentiousness hanging on the walls. "From what I
hear, the two of you were bosom buddies. Helped you carve
your niche, made you what you are today."

"Get to the point," Gold growled.

"So what I wonder is, what happens when things go bad?
Growing debts, bad loans, wrong connections. You get stuck
between a rock and a hard place, maybe, only the rock
doesn't budge. Or, more like it, you get stuck under a pretty
heavy thumb."

"Listen, Mr. Logan . . ." Gold glared. His nostrils flared
and his eyes burned red. "I don't know what sort of bug the
Times has got up its ass, or what you think you picked up off
the street. But I think it's time I told you to get the hell out
of here."

Logan's instinct for self-preservation told him it was time
to make a proper exit. He stood; their eyes met in a duel of
rage versus repose. Some of what he was throwing at Gold
was speculation, the rest of it pure guesswork. Neither element had failed him in the past—well, rarely—and a short
twenty-four hours in L.A. was rekindling the old instinct, the
old gut feel.

"Counterfeiting's a nasty rap," Logan observed as he
started past Gold toward the door. "But I guess it's easy
enough to pull off. Just slip out of the studio with the master
tape, make a copy, slip back in with it."

"Get your ass out of here," Gold snarled.

"Just press a few hundred thousand copies, get 'em into
the stores, no one'll ever know the difference. That how it
worked?"

Gold didn't bother with another warning. With his right
foot planted, he aimed a right hook at Logan's protruding
chin. Slothlike as Gold was, the fist moved like a locomotive.
Logan saw it coming, but not in time. He pulled back, and
Gold's heavy fist glanced off the side of his jaw. Logan shot
up a hand, grabbed Gold's arm, and in one deft move twisted
it up behind Gold's neck.

He studied Gold through glassy eyes. Then he said, "I'm

on my way," sarcasm easily injected into his voice. "Just one question before I go."

"The little shit just doesn't know how to make an exit—"

Logan rolled his eyes, yanked Gold's arm back a bit tighter until the man winced, either with pain or humiliation or both. "One question. Nod if that's okay with you."

Gold nodded.

"I'm looking for a woman—"

The look in Gold's eyes seemed to say, *Aren't we all, pal.*

"A redhead." Logan released the pressure on Gold's twisted arm. "Blue eyes. Medium height. You know her?"

"Maybe I do, maybe I don't."

"I want a name," Logan pressed. He let go of Gold's arm, offering a ray of hope.

"Go fuck yourself." Gold shrank back, placing a couple of quick yards between them. He quickly moved around his marble desk and flashed a crazed grin at Logan, like a little kid just waiting for the fireworks to begin. Then he pressed a button on the intercom box. "Shirlene, get Bruno in here. Now!"

"Forget the question." Logan shrugged smugly. "I just hope you have better luck with your family friends than Neil Novak did."

Leo Gold lunged again, but Logan slipped through the oak door into the hallway, well out of harm's way. He grinned tauntingly, turned on his heel, dodged the hulking bouncer marching down the dark hallway toward him, and disappeared outside into the L.A. heat.

9

Frangi Pangi was wedged in between two chic clothing boutiques on the mezzanine level of the Rodeo Connection in Beverly Hills. It was a small jewelry shop, elite yet funky, gaudy and overblown in the best definition of L.A. style. The shop was bright and perfumed, fashioned out of pink marble

and frosted glass. Windham Hill music wafted pleasantly
from speakers placed as indirectly as the custom lighting.

Logan instinctively shrank inside his customary island attire, no match for the leather-and-lace fashion sense of B.H.
He lingered outside for a moment, then pushed his way in-
doors and edged toward a glass case containing a collection
of gaudy silk scarves. Within two seconds he was approached
by a sensuous statue of a girl whose ivory face was framed
by straight black shoulder-length hair.

"Is there something I might help you with, sir?" she asked,
her voice an expert mix of seduction and salesmanship. "A
gift for a lady-friend, perhaps?"

Logan lost his train of thought. The girl was a whisper,
black on black. Her body was almost boyish, innocence offset
by a wayward sexuality. Eyes deep, dark, hypnotic, anything
but innocent. Her lips, painted a blackish purple, seemed to
drip blood.

"Yes," he said at length. "And no."

She smiled. "We'll start with the yes first." Her voice
echoed her deceiving chastity. "Perhaps you're looking for a
gift—"

"No gift," Logan said quickly.

"Something for yourself, then?"

Logan swept the shop with a quick once-over glance and
smiled, then shook his head. "Not my style, I'm afraid."

She gave his clothing a desultory glance and shrank back
half a step, as if his style might be contagious. "In that case,
what might we be able to do for you?"

Many things—and all of them for a price, Logan considered. "Maybe we can go someplace and talk?"

The girl looked at him warily, shook her head. "Sorry."

"Just a few questions. Two minutes . . ."

"I don't like questions," she said, her face drawn in doubt.
"And I've got a store to watch."

Logan extracted a business card from his wallet and
handed it to her. "H. L. Price, Pacific Mutual," he said.

She read the inscription, then palmed the card. "I'm not interested in insurance," she told him skeptically.

"I'm not here in a sales capacity," he assured her. "Actually, I'm an investigator. I'm handling certain matters having
to do with the estate of a Miss Sutton. I believe she worked
here."

"Lynn?" Her forehead creased in a frown.

"That's right," Logan said. "You look surprised."

The girl nodded, remained skeptical. "Doesn't sound like her, not Lynn."

"How do you mean?"

"Insurance. She wasn't the type to think ahead, worry about death and all that. Not like she had anything to leave behind, either. Whatever she had, which wasn't much, she didn't have very long. And she never mentioned insurance."

"Most people don't. Now ... about Lynn Sutton—"

"What kind of insurance?" the girl interrupted. Her voice was tainted with skepticism, derived either from knowledge of Lynn or suspicion of Logan.

"Whole-life. She'd fallen behind on the premiums, and the billing has to be brought up to date before we can pay out."

"Not to her scumbag brother, I hope." She raised a single brow in a sign of contempt.

"Sorry. Privileged information." He shifted his weight and watched as a Mr. and Mrs. Trend entered the store and headed for a rack of clip-on rhinestone bow ties. "Maybe you could fill me in ..."

The girl hesitated, trying to figure out what was best. Logan had learned long ago that the more people think, the less they intend to say. "Were you two close?" he prodded. "You and Lynn?"

The woman thought for a second, shook her head. "We worked together. But Lynn wasn't the sort you got chummy with."

"She kept to herself? No close friends?" Or family, Logan almost made the mistake of adding.

"Not really. She was closest to her niece, I suppose."

"And *her* name?"

"Kynnie. Kyndall Wyatt. She worked here, too. Fell off the turnip truck a few months ago. She's taking a few days off." The girl glanced around, then lowered her voice to a whisper. "Lynn's death kinda hit her hard. You know how it is."

Logan knew, and didn't push. "What about Neil?"

"Neil?"

"Novak. She see much of him?"

"Look, Mr.—" She looked at the business card again. "—Mr. Price, if that's really your name. I don't know what sort of game you're playing, but it sure don't sound like insurance. And whatever it is, you can keep that slimeball Neil out of it."

Logan gazed intently into the girl's piercing eyes. First a scumbag, then a slimeball. "Okay. You tell me your name, I'll tell you what the score is."

She bit her lip for a moment, and folded her arms across her slight chest. "Randi. With an 'I.' "

"Pretty name," Logan allowed.

"The truth?" she asked, not impressed with niceties.

"Right. The truth." He pursed his lips as if puffing on a cigarette. "My name really *is* Price," he lied. "Howard Lee Price. And I *am* in insurance . . . in a roundabout way."

"Roundabout?"

"Independent appraisals. Personal probes, corporate checks, credit references—"

"You're a private detective."

"I prefer to think of it in terms of free-lance surveillance," he suggested. "Keeping an eye on things."

"You're a little late with Lynn," she said testily, as if closer scrutiny on his part somehow might have prevented her death. "Who hired you?"

"Wouldn't be very private if I told you that, would I?"

She thought this over for a moment, seemed to accept it. "So . . . what's Mr. Novak got to do with it?"

Logan shoved his hands in his wide pockets and rolled on the balls of his feet. He was tired, he didn't want to be here, and the smog was digging at the corners of his eyes. "You tell me," he suggested. "I heard he was a ladies' man."

"Look, Mr. Price. I wasn't the man's social secretary—"

"You ever see him with a redhead?"

She huffed, glanced around the shop, then regarded him conspiratorily. "Maybe, maybe not. You want all the juicy details, go talk to Mrs. Novak."

"She's not exactly going to roll out the red carpet," Logan lamented. He'd gone after her confidence, and it seemed he might be winning it.

She hesitated, puzzling over how much she should reveal. Then she sighed and ran a nervous hand through her hair. "Novak came in here once in a while. His wife would get her hair done upstairs, and he'd sort of drift in and browse. You ask me, I think Leslie Novak saw Neil's wayward libido as her meal ticket to divorce."

"Adultery isn't grounds for divorce," Logan pointed out.

Randi reacted to this as if it was news to her, which it probably was. "Still, I wouldn't trust that . . ." Her voice

trailed off as she searched her brain for a suitable word.
"... witch. And come to think of it, if you're looking for a
word with her, you're in luck. Today's her hair day."

"Say what?"

"Two o'clock appointment, every Tuesday." Randi checked
one of three plastic watches strapped to her wrist, a definite
fashion statement. "She should be up there right as we
speak."

"You think even today? After all that's happened?"

"Especially today. The bitch ... excuse me ... Leslie,
she's gotta look tops, right? I mean, tomorrow's the funeral."

"And she's upstairs?" Logan asked.

"Jean Michel's. Up the stairs, to your left."

Logan thanked her for her valuable help, and she told him
that if he ever needed something in the way of a gift, to come
back and let him know. He assured her he would and backed
out of the store.

Jean Michel's was located directly above Frangi Pangi. It
was a small, elite shop, catering to a small, elite clientele. A
large mirror ran the length of one wall of this sterile, swanky
joint. The walls were salmon, almost smoked; the floor was
Italian tile. A floral pattern of what appeared to be calla lilies
was etched in the plate-glass window overlooking the sunny
courtyard. A small wine bar featuring four reserve Napa char-
donnays was set off in one corner. The wines were selected
by Jean Michel himself. All complimentary, of course.

A nubile Oriental girl with saffron skin greeted him. He regarded her dubiously, wondering if her pumpkin-orange hair
was one of Jean's personal creations. She was stuffed into a
pair of skintight white leggings and wore a white blouse decorated with hand-painted pink and purple flowers. She looked
up from her perch behind the marble counter and smiled at
Logan.

"Jean—" She pronounced it *Zhawn*. "—is very busy at the
moment, as you can see," she explained in an accent that
teased of Japanese and French. "May I help you?"

Logan glanced over at Jean and the woman he was working on. Leslie Novak in the flesh, reclining in one of the
plush chairs, Monsieur Michel's nimble fingers deftly snip-
ping her wet hair. Logan checked his watch: Two-twenty.

"I'm here for an appointment," he said.

"Mr. Michel does not do men."

Logan studied old Jean and suspected the slight hairdresser

was the type who most certainly *did* do men, in one fashion or another. "I'm not here to see Jean," he said casually. "I'm meeting someone. Mrs. Novak."

"Mrs. Novak is also busy at the moment, as you can see," the girl told him. "You can come back—"

"I'll wait."

The orange-haired girl kept a wary eye on him as she stepped over and whispered something to Jean. Mr. Michel cast a cursory glance in Logan's direction, then whispered something in his customer's ear. It was now Leslie's turn to glance over; she pondered him for a second, raised her brow, then gave a careless shrug and went back to being bored. The Oriental girl sauntered back and informed Logan that the wait would be about thirty minutes. He thanked her for this piece of good news and relaxed in a chair.

"How the hell did you find me?" Mrs. Novak demanded. "I've already told you people all I'm going to."

"Ingenuity and instinct," he answered evasively.

She'd left the shop with him, angered at his persistence but intrigued enough to tolerate his presence as she examined what she could see of her reflection in the plate-glass window. She kept one eye on him while she studied her fresh cut with the other. It was a refined, simple look, almost matronly, reserved and solemn. She obviously didn't feel the slightest bit comfortable looking so tight-assed, but she seemed resigned to it under the circumstances.

"Jean should use a lighter tint on your highlights," Logan observed, banking on her vanity to distract her from his impertinent invasion of her personal space.

"And the *L.A. Times* should use more inspired tactics on its intended victims," she countered.

"Touché." Logan grinned. He'd decided to cut the crap with the insurance; Leslie Novak seemed too classy and sharp to bite on anything so clichéd. The *Times* seemed most appropriate on the spur of the moment, and it was the closest lie to the truth that he could muster on such short notice. She seemed to accept it, and when he also had extended his deepest sympathies and said he understood what she was going through, she granted him two minutes to make his case.

"It's too dark," she agreed as she brushed a few strands over her eyes, then blew upwards to make the arrangement seem more windswept. "So you're after an interview?"

Logan affected a shudder. "That sounds too ... formal. And stiff. No, I really just want a chance to talk. One-on-one, off the record. Just a chance to get to know you, maybe get to know Neil a little better. It'll only take ten minutes—"

"Ten minutes won't do it."

"I'm in no rush."

"But I am."

"Tomorrow?"

"Tomorrow's the service." She said it with little emotion, just a matter-of-fact appointment, almost a nuisance.

"I'm sorry." He recalled how he'd felt when some prying reporter from the competing daily showed up at his door the morning after Molly had died, trying to snoop into the personal side of the tragedy. Logan had felt no remorse when he slammed the door in the sucker's bewildered face, and he knew Leslie Novak had every right to do the same thing to him now.

"And Thursday and Friday are no good." She thought for a moment, then drew a deep breath. "I've had cops and reporters and lawyers practically trying to blast my door down for two days now. They hang out at the end of the driveway, they call all hours of the night, even follow me into town. Hell, one of 'em even tried to pretend he was looking for stars' homes the other day. Vultures, the whole lot of 'em."

Logan choked down a flush of guilt. "What about the weekend?"

She thought for a moment, then shrugged lightly. "I don't know why I'm doing this, I ought to have my head examined. But I honestly think you're the real thing. At least I hope so. Give me a call Sunday morning, maybe we can set up a time."

"You'll be there?"

Leslie Novak smiled. "I'll instruct Maria to let you in."

He thanked her for her confidence as they arrived in the underground parking garage. When the valet attendant brought her yellow BMW M5 around, Logan held the door while Leslie gracefully made herself comfortable behind the wheel.

"You think I should have Jean lighten the streaks?" she asked as she set her white leather handbag on the seat next to her.

"Maybe just on the sides and in front," Logan suggested. "I think it would catch the sun a little more."

She smiled up at him, touched him lightly on the arm. He

thanked her once again and gently closed the door. As she shifted the car into drive she flashed him a sensuous smile. Then the car leaped forward, tires squealed on the red brick, and the car shot up the driveway into the L.A. sunshine.

Logan covered the distance from Rodeo Drive to Spaulding Avenue in less than ten minutes, lacing his way through West Hollywood over side streets and boulevards, the shortcuts coming back to him as if they were etched in his brain. He just hoped to Christ Lynn Sutton hadn't been like half of all Californians, who moved a half dozen times since they last had visited the DMV.

She wasn't. Her name was still listed below the mailbox set back under an overhang near a flight of stairs. Logan scanned the four rows of red embossed plastic tags, most of them peeling at the edges, until he found one that read SUTTON, L. He noted the number—206—and mounted the stairs that led off to his right.

The apartment complex was typical L.A. postwar nondescript. Constructed in the fifties, solid stucco, painted a dirty cream color that had not aged well, palm trees that had long ago outgrown their usefulness as shade trees. The building itself was an open-ended rectangle, with three sides framing an inner courtyard that housed a kidney-shaped pool and a stone aggregate patio. The first-floor apartments each had a glass slider that opened directly onto the patio, aesthetically divided by concrete planters into quiet little sitting areas in front of each unit. The upstairs units lacked such individuality; instead, each opened directly out onto a communal balcony that ringed the inside of the complex. Several tenants had placed cheap patio chairs and tables in front of their units in proclamation of squatters' rights; the rest evidently feared neighborhood theft. Makeshift locks, crossbars, braces, and curtains drawn over the glass sliders echoed that concern.

Lynn Sutton's apartment was at the far end of the complex, set in a corner where the balcony cut across the back. Like the others her shades were drawn, and a folded webbed chair leaned against the stucco wall. No one had yet thought to either move or steal it. Next to her apartment was a short corridor that housed a Coke machine, which long ago had succumbed to the ravages of time. A sign next to the machine proclaimed LAUNDRY, and an arrow pointed down the hallway around the corner to the rear.

No question the cops had already gone through the place, but Logan wasn't searching for trace evidence. No, his instincts instead were directed toward the *feel* of the place, the sense of living that occurred behind closed doors, one which only personal belongings could reveal. Vibes. He grinned to himself at the ambiguous nature of left coast terminology. He studied the glass door, then glanced over the balcony at the pool below. A young kid, high school age, probably delinquent, lay sprawled on a lounge chair, soaking up the rays and probably humming the unemployment blues. An elderly woman, stuffed into a swimsuit that had been in style about the same time as tail fins, sat at the edge of the pool. She splashed her legs to and fro, kicking up slight ripples in the clear blue water. Other than that, no company.

He knocked twice on the door, waiting an appropriate measure between knocks. He didn't expect an answer, but decided he'd better err on the side of prudence. He leaned an ear to the glass and heard nothing other than the rustle of palm fronds overhead. Then he checked over his shoulder again, looking for any telltale movement behind a curtain, a set of prying eyes peering out from the darkness. Nothing.

From his pocket Logan extracted his wallet, and from that he pulled a nail file that had been cut down into the shape of a master key. The pick was designed for simple locks like the one on this sliding-glass door, part of a set of B & E tools he'd scored from a snitch just before the young dope head was found dead in a trash dumpster down on Alvarado. The entire set could have provided easy access to almost half of all locked doors in the city of Los Angeles, but he'd found little use for them on Catalina.

He slipped the nail file into the lock, and went to work. The whole process took about a minute, not the simple twist and jerk like on TV. But sixty seconds later he felt the click . . .

Once inside, Logan quietly slid the door closed, locked it, and waited a few seconds for his eyes to adjust to the low light. The apartment was dark, with just the curtained glass sliders providing a touch of illumination. He wanted to turn on a light, but feared that any illumination might stir the interest of some resident busybody.

One brief look around told Logan that Lynn Sutton was a collector, a friend of flea markets and yard sales and dumpsters. Small china and plastic figurines in strawberry and mushroom and flower motifs cluttered her shelves, and her walls were hung with framed stills of old movies. A good half dozen tables set around the living room held a wide array of cheap memorabilia that looked like it had been won at the state fair. An odd collection of witches fashioned out of gourds sat on an end table next to the couch, and an arrangement of crystal dogs and cats and goats and pigs seemed to graze on the coffee table. A table set in a corner held a porcelain carousel, complete with handed-painted horses, music box, and a wind-up mechanism that provided movement. A glass case on one wall displayed a dozen Hummel figurines, while another housed a collection of Royal Doulton porcelain dolls. English Christmas plates were displayed in an oak sideboard set in the corner of the dining nook. A trio of framed Ansel Adams prints was hung in a stepped design along the opposite wall.

The room itself was plain, drab white walls with dirty beige carpeting. An old yellow couch and an overstuffed chair faced a portable color TV, and a pole lamp next to it was squeezed between the rug and ceiling. The place was barren of books, except for a beat-up old leather photo album that sat under a small stack of magazines on a shelf under the TV. The apartment was that of a single career woman on the climb, which in a way described Lynn Sutton to a T. But by the looks of things, Miss Sutton had either retired altogether or at least worked far from the madding crowd of Hollywood and Vine.

The leather-bound volume caught his attention. It was an old scrapbook, two brown leather covers encasing some fifty pages of ancient family memorabilia, bound together with a brown lace tied in an ornate bow. Logan lifted it gingerly from its shelf beneath the TV and spread it open on the carpet. He turned to the first page, brittle paper that imparted an ageless quality. Six black-and-white prints were neatly set on each page, two rows of three each, held in place with archaic paper photo corners.

The prints mostly consisted of baby shots, with inscriptions that proclaimed such things as "A King Is Born" and "J.J. Turns Two." The respective dates were scrawled under the photos, with the first-photo identified as "4 Ap, 49." Subsequent shots were dated similarly, and went on to depict "the newborn King" in a series of infantile shots: baby taking his first step, baby using his first fork, baby building his first sand castle, baby painting first picture, baby glaring at newborn sister brought home by mother from the hospital.

On 12 Mar, 51, baby "Princess Lynette" was born, and promptly was rewarded with her own set of priceless posed candid shots. Lynette in her high chair, Lynette snoozing in her crib, Lynette taking a bath, Lynette standing naked in front of the Christmas tree in all her toddler glory. Meanwhile, little J.J. was growing up, sporting his first tooth, sitting on the potty, catching his first frog. And thus the competition began: two shots of Lynette, three of J.J., four of Lynn, two of Jay. All the baseball, hot dogs, and apple pie of childhood bound within two leather covers.

The volume ended when Jay reached twelve and Lynn was ten. Was Jay the scumbag brother Randi had referred to, and if so, where was he now? Were there other volumes, or was this the only one? What happened to Mr. Sutton, whose face was so prevalent in the first few pages of photos, but whose absence Logan had duly noted. Death, divorce, dishonor? He gently closed the scrapbook and replaced it under the TV, allowing a vague but unclear notion of discovery to lodge somewhere in his brain.

Lynn's bedroom was a stark contrast to her living room. Piles of laundry lay scattered in every corner, in the closet, on the bed, presumably poked and prodded by some grinning sheriff's voyeur. Logan checked his watch, then quickly probed the billowy piles of lace panties, low-cut bras, garter belts, slinky wash-and-wear dresses, cotton halter tops, silk stockings, fuck-me jeans. Her closet contained a rainbow of leather miniskirts, studded leather vests, leather pants, sheer see-through blouses, and an array of belts to match any occasion and taste. Tucked in her dresser he found a few tricks of Lynn's ageless trade: handcuffs, body paint, ticklers and feathers and massage oils, and an ample assortment of lubricated condoms. In a career of many hazards, she at least showed a touch of concern about minimizing the hazards of the workplace.

A brief check of the kitchen turned up little else than a storehouse of ice cream, Sara Lee pound cakes, donuts, and Snickers bars. A cupboard next to the stove was stuffed with several brands of Scotch, vodka, bourbon, and gin, and a case of cheap French bordeaux. Jack Woods had wryly observed that Miss Sutton had added a few pounds since her last license photo was shot, and Logan could see why.

Logan drew his glance to the pile of L.A. telephone books stacked on the pass-through counter that connected to the dining alcove. The sheriff's deputies already would have lifted whatever address books, bills, opened mail, and notepads might have been scattered about; an empty wicker basket beside the phone further convinced him. Whatever once was in that basket now was probably scattered all over a cluttered desk in the county building downtown. Logan was too late to find anything that might be of interest to him, which was just as well. Better not interrupt the wheels of justice while they're turning, no matter how slowly. As long as they were turning. After all, he was only looking for a lovely lady with auburn hair and Carribean-blue eyes, not some hideous multiple killer who'd plugged his—her?—two victims through the head while they slept.

Or was he?

He visually worked the kitchen one more time when his studying eyes fell on the telephone. A cord ran from where a standard wall-mounted phone would plug in, but it was connected to a counter-top unit customized with state-of-the-art time-saving features. Auto redial, mute, volume control, and an electronic memory to store and dial up to twenty different phone numbers at the touch of a button. Logan regarded the phone almost reverently; eleven of the twenty possible memories were identified with names hastily scrawled in light pencil. He scanned the list, trying to place the names or initials. Only a few even remotely rang a bell: Sachet (he'd heard the name somewhere), N.N. (Neil Novak?), F.P. (Frangi Pangi?), Mane Stay (a beauty parlor?), Kyndall (her niece?). A few of the other names meant nothing to him—Roger, Allysa, Jones—and four (Tony Roma's, The Palm, Spago, Michaels) belonged to what must have been her favorite upscale restaurants.

Using a paper towel torn from the roll beside the sink, he

carefully lifted the receiver and pressed the first button. After two rings a quiet, polite voice answered: "Sachet Social Club. How may we serve you?"

"Oh . . . excuse me, I must've dialed the wrong number," Logan quickly apologized, and hung up.

He pressed down the next button and waited. Again two rings before someone picked up the other end. "Rhapsody Records," came the pretty, light reply.

This time Logan recognized the voice: Corie Chapin in Neil Novak's office. He considered saying something cute, decided against it.

He started to press the next button in line when the sound of voices stopped him. Two voices outside the apartment, coming closer, hesitating outside the door. One voice saying, "This was Lynn's, Officer," the other answering in an off-hand, almost embarrassed tone.

Officer? Shit. Logan hurriedly surveyed the room. Not many places to hide: a hall closet, a closet in the bedroom, the shower-tub in the bathroom.

"Thanks. This'll only take a few minutes." The second voice was muffled, but obviously male.

The first voice, evidently belonging to the resident manager, said something again, something causal like "Here it is," probably referring to his master key.

Logan padded across the living room toward the drawn floor-to-ceiling drapes. Thank God he'd been swift enough to lock the glass slider behind him when he sneaked in; now if only he could sneak out equally undetected. He checked behind the curtain, which was wider than the double glass door it covered and thus was hung so it covered about eighteen inches of wall as well. Logan slipped behind this part of the curtain just as the manager heaved the door open and stepped into the room.

"You don't mind, I'll just wait out here," the manager said from the doorway as a set of footsteps came into the room.

From where he stood Logan heard only the one set of steps move around the room, padding knowingly down the short hallway into the bedroom. On cue, Logan slipped out from behind the curtain and tiptoed across the threadbare carpet toward the door. Not only did he not want a run-in with the cops, the set of picks in his wallet would do little to curry favor with any judge.

Logan pulled back the edge of the curtain covering the

door, which had been left open a few inches. The manager was just standing at the balcony railing, leaning slightly over the patio below, his back turned to the apartment. As silently as possible Logan gripped the edge of the glass and pushed the door open a few inches wider. He studied the manager's repose, his casual demeanor as he soaked in all the glory of his domain, like a king standing at the tower window gazing out upon his serfs. Trying not to think about the cop ransacking the apartment inside, probably armed, he edged through the door and tried to slip around the corner to the corridor that led to the laundry room.

He actually might have made it undetected had it not been for the folded webbed chair leaning against the wall of Lynn's apartment. As he tried to slide out of the line of the manager's peripheral vision, his foot caught on the arm of the chair and sent it tumbling to the concrete. Instantly the manager wheeled around, but Logan already was halfway down the short hallway, and in a flash had disappeared around the rear of the apartment complex.

"Hey! What the hell—?" the startled manager called out.

The walkway around the back of the building dead-ended just past the laundry room, which Logan would have realized had he staked out an escape route before his attempt at B & E. As it was, Logan found himself up against a wrought-iron rail that, along with a good ten feet to the ground, separated him from a clean getaway. No matter. Without thinking, he swung himself over the rail and held on with both hands as he calculated possible bodily damage. He maintained that stance until he heard the scamper of feet rushing down the hallway toward him.

"Stop! Police—"

Logan didn't look back; instead he recoiled his knees and jumped. The fall wasn't all that far and the pavement not that hard, although harder than he remembered and much harder than it appeared on TV. His feet took all his weight upon impact, and his ankles shuddered as they absorbed the shock. He rolled to the left, then scrambled to his feet and disappeared down the alley toward the street.

He circled the block on foot, taking great pains to avoid the front of the apartment complex and to keep an eye out for any stray squad cars that might have been alerted for a man in tan slacks and a light-blue shirt. Logan estimated a minimum four minutes ETA for any cop cruiser to answer the dispatch and get down to Spaulding Avenue. Keeping this in mind, he made it back to the Plymouth in just over three. Not bad time, considering he'd parked around the corner in the next block, just in case.

Ten minutes latter he was stalled in traffic on Santa Monica, part of the never-ending snake dance that for Los Angeles was just another part of the daily ritual of life.

11

Over forty-eight hours had passed since the Novak–Sutton murders had hit the airwaves, and it summarily had been relegated to the number-four position on the nightly newscast. The anchor introducing the story revealed that the ubiquitous "authorities" were leaning toward mob hit, which to the news media suggested organized crime.

An "in-depth" exclusive report began with a recap of the Novak incident, as it was now being called, followed by an investigative report on the link between organized crime and the record business. The four-minute story, obviously rushed through the editing room to complement the impact of the headline story, opened with a wide-angle shot of two dressed-to-kill record execs scrambling into the back of a black stretch Mercedes limo. Narration was provided by Ted Smart, the network's L.A.-based pretty-boy whiz kid whose reports on mob activities and connections had incurred dozens of real or imagined death threats, as well as several libel cases. But Smart was still alive and the suits had all been dismissed, a dubious badge of distinction, if not courage.

Logan sipped his Scotch and watched the drama unfold.

". . . was seen leaving the Century Plaza Hotel last month with late Rhapsody Records president Neil Novak," Smart was saying as the two dark-suited men, unaware of the grainy network nightscope, assisted a leggy brunette into the back of the limo. "The two-high-powered label presidents were taken here—" Cut to a shot of an oceanfront Malibu retreat. "—for a meeting with reputed crime family head Nicholas Carbone."

Guilt by association, Logan mumbled to himself, knocking back his Scotch, shaking off the taste slashing the back of his throat.

"Niki Carbone and his brother Luigi are under investigation by a federal grand jury for racketeering, conspiracy, and tax evasion. In addition, this man—" Cut to another long shot, this of a man leaving a stark, monastic low-rise office complex. "—independent record promoter Frank Kennedy, has been linked by federal investigators to an alleged scheme to obtain airplay for records in return for the payment of cash, sex, and drugs—"

Kennedy. At the mention of the name Logan leaned forward and studied the grainy footage.

"Kennedy, under contract with a half dozen record labels, including Rhapsody and Pacific, denies the charges, calling them malicious innuendos and falsehoods."

Next came a shot of a darkened room, focus on a silhouette of a mysterious witness, backlit, melodrama for effect. Ted Smart introduced the mystery man as Mr. X.

". . . This man has worked in the radio and record business for twelve years, and claims he has been on Kennedy's dole for the last four," Smart droned on.

Then the Shadow spoke, his voice distorted by a sound baffle, electronic and hollow: "It started slow, no strings attached, you know what I mean? Just business as usual. Then a record would come along and he'd lean a bit, use a little pressure, ask if I was makin' the payments on the 280Z. Hell, an extra hundred a week can make all the difference. At the end I was gettin' five hundred a week, and all the blow I could want, just to play some stiff record."

Cut back to Smart: "Such allegations have sparked an interest on Capitol Hill, where a bipartisan panel of senators, including California's own Al Livingston, are looking into the possibility of establishing an investigation of their own."

"*Is,*" Logan corrected him. He savored another swallow. "A panel *is* looking into the possibility."

The story finished with Ted Smart's network I.D., and the TV cut back to the studio in Burbank. The superficial information gleaned from the short report contained little substance other than circumstantial innuendo. Smart was schooled in an era of theatrical journalism, and he pushed the scope of the fifth estate ever closer to the precipice of satire, probing no deeper than four minutes of network time allowed, caring no more than his most recent Nielsen numbers dared him to care. Cotton-candy journalism: flavor but no substance, an eyeful of angel hair wrapped around a paper cone.

Professional jealousy? Logan wondered as he dribbled another dose of Scotch over what ice remained in his glass. He took another slow sip, then extracted another slice of cold pizza from the box on the bed and bit off a blob of congealed mozarrella. Then he dropped another ice cube in his glass and wandered out onto the balcony.

Logan drew his feet up on the railing and stretched his body out in an attempt to close off his mind to everything but the pulsing surf on the distant sand. He listened for a long while, lost in the tangerine sky and the pink sea and the mellow taste of malt. At great length he reached over for the yellow legal pad he'd picked up at a stationery store on the way home. Pensively he chewed on a number-two Berol, while he played imaginary, but elaborate, chords on the pad of paper. Homesick?

He started by jotting down a few names, scribbling "Neil Novak" in the center of the page and printing "Lynn Sutton" just below him. To the right of her he added "Red," followed by a question mark. Under these names he penciled in "Frank Kennedy," and in parentheses added the notation "promotion and whatever."

Beneath the heading "Rhapsody Records" he listed Joseph Minetti and Corie Chapin, leaving enough spaces to add whatever other names might later turn up. Off to one side he noted "Leo Gold," a name that might—or might not—be of future value. Then he connected all these names by solid lines to Novak. On the left-hand side of the page Logan listed Leslie Novak, whom he connected to her husband by a solid line, and to Mr. PLAYTYM by a dotted line. Under this last entry he noted "drugs, sex,?" and extended dotted lines to Lynn Sutton and Novak. At the bottom of the page in dark lettering he carefully printed the Carbone connections—Niki, Luigi, and David—beneath which he added another question mark and again left room for any late additions. He then filled in the names Chico Escabar and Eduardo DeSola, and drew dotted lines from all of them back to Kennedy, Gold, PLAYTYM, and Neil Novak.

He balanced the pad in his lap and evacuated his mind of all excess shit. He thought for a moment, then reached over and grabbed the telephone he'd dragged outdoors. He thought for a moment, then dialed a number from distant memory. Jane Belisle answered, interrupted in the middle of dinner, but happy to hear from her long-lost confidant. Ms. Belisle was an *L.A. Times* legend, one of that rare breed of career women content with assisting a long succession of reporters and editors without ever expecting—or desiring—additional responsibilities. She had a husband and a passel of kids, and her life was perfect just as it was. No need to screw it up just for the sake of ambition.

Logan spent the next five minutes fielding the dreaded questions of what he was up to and where he'd been hiding the past year and whether he was seeing anyone new and why didn't he stop by the office, everyone would love to see him.

Finally he was able to get around to why he called, omitting all but the barest essentials. "So, Jane . . . think you can get someone to run it?"

"Stuart," she said, pretending to sound hurt, "you think I've maybe lost my touch? Couple of calls, I'll get right back to you. What was the plate again?"

"P-L-A-Y-T-Y-M," Logan read to her slowly.

"Got it," Jane purred over the phone. "Give you a call when it comes through."

He gave her his phone number and hung up. He hefted the legal pad in his hand, as if divining its substance by its weight. He was beginning to get a fairly clear impression of Neil Novak and his world, which included many of the players and motivations Logan had encountered in previous investigations into crime or passion. The entertainment business—records, TV, radio, and film—was rife with an element of sleaze. Like politics, it was an industry that banked on greed, power, and opportunity, and thrived on all the ancillary aspects of corruption. A few honest souls notwithstanding, the nebulous entity that was Hollywood was everything it was cracked up to be, and more. The business was one pervasive perversion, an immeasurable melting pot of deviates who used, and were used by, virtually every brand of vice Logan ever encountered on the streets. Designer drugs of every style and color and effect, men and women with on-demand sexual practices and persuasions, and boys and girls far too young to understand either.

Logan's eyes roamed over his penciled scribbles, his brain absorbing the names and analyzing the connections, how they all might trace back to Novak. And, ultimately, how the missing redhead fit in to all this. She was his first link, but the chain went deeper than that, all the way to a double murder. He closed his eyes to the sunset, allowing a few questions to form behind that dark curtain.

Number one: was she involved in Neil Novak's and Lynn Sutton's deaths? He suspected she was, but more as an impassive observer than as an active participant. Number two: had she staked out Logan as a possible alibi, just so he would take her back to his apartment and provide her with cover? Possibly, but then why draw attention to herself by knocking him cold with a 'lude or two? And why risk detection by slipping off Novak's boat by dawn's early light, to boot? And what had happened in the slim twenty minutes between her departure from the Albacore Lounge with Neil and Lynn and her return to the bar? Had the friendly little trio had an argument, convenient or otherwise? Or had Red been told to scram by a jealous Miss Sutton? And, speaking of Lynn Sutton, just what was she doing out on Santa Catalina? Conducting business or pleasure?

He sucked on his Scotch, then his pencil. First things first: motive. The old standbys were greed, jealousy, revenge, and any and all combinations thereof. The mere fact that the feds had been keeping an eye on Novak told Logan that the label president probably was up to his ass in the mob. But to what end? Again, the old standbys were bad debt, money-laundering, drugs, maybe even a little payola.

Playing all sides of the picture, Logan suspected that Novak probably was into the Carbone brothers for big bucks. Seed money, operating finances, maybe even gambling debts; in any event, maybe he'd finally balked and the debtors had collected. maybe the organization wanted a bigger slice of whatever pie was baking, and had tried to force him into a deal of which he wanted no part.

Then again, maybe the Carbones, or Escabar, or DeSola, or all three, were using Rhapsody as a Laundromat. No secret among L.A.'s finest—or those that reported about them—that Niki Carbone routinely washed millions of dollars in Colombian drug money through legitimate institutions. Four banks in L.A. alone, several real-estate conglomerates, and a New York brokerage house—all were reputed to be wringing the dirt out of Carbone drug-money reserves, despite a lack of concrete evidence. With a two-percent service charge, cleaning $100 million a year provided a nifty profit, untaxable. If the Carbones were even remotely involved with Novak, his label was a perfect front. Rhapsody was a legitimate, highly visible corporation, perfect for passing unwashed drug money.

But was it worth killing for? Possible, but unlikely: if Novak was funneling cash offshore, why kill the goose that was laying the golden egg? Of course, if Novak had been called to testify before the grand jury, who could guess what he'd spilled. Such proceedings were tightly held, and any suspicions easily could have triggered the fireworks.

Then, of course, there was Mrs. Novak. Maybe Leslie hired the job out, or did it herself—with or without an accomplice. Maybe she'd grown tired of her husband's philandering and decided his fortune was better off in her name than his. She could have enticed her friend in the red 450 SL, whose blatant intentions Logan had seen displayed outside the Novak house just yesterday afternoon. If theirs was an affair of the heart Leslie could come forward—after a proper period of mourning, of course—and confess her love for Mr. PLAYTYM and retire in the newfound splendor of her inherited millions.

The revenge angle also was easy. Novak's business practices left him open for eventual retribution. No question: the man's career must have left a trail of crushed toes along the way, some of which might not be so willing or able to simply walk away. Neil undoubtedly had royally screwed a friend or associate in the past; maybe that someone finally decided to exact payment. Someone with enough pent-up venom to carry out a .38-caliber fantasy.

Logan was still nibbling on his pencil, still pondering the puzzle, when the phone rang. His hand swung over and picked up the receiver after the first ring.

"You got a pen, Stuart?" Jane Belisle asked.

"In my teeth," Logan said. "What do you have?"

"Plates P-L-A-Y-T-Y-M belong to a Mr. Roger McNulty, address 3812 Oakfield Drive, Los Angeles. Driver's license number C134566-dash-B. Born 4/26/48."

"You're a sweetheart, Jane."

"I know," she acknowledged sweetly, then hung up.

Logan replaced the handset on the table and picked up the

pad of paper. A name for the face. He used the eraser to rub out the "PLAYTYM" entry, then scribbled in "Roger McNulty" instead. He set the pad back on the table and stared at it from a distance, as if the whole picture was worth more than the sum of its parts. Then he rose from his chair on legs that were a bit too affected by the Scotch. His muscles seized up: his neck was stiff, and his back felt as if nails had been driven between each of the vertebrae. He ran his fingers up along the base of his skull and rubbed hard. What he needed was a good full-body massage, front and back. But, since that wasn't in the cards at the moment, he opted for a long swim in the pool.

The cold water rejuvenated his skin. It sent his body into momentary shock as he dived in and angled toward the bottom. A wave of relief washed through him. His nerves adjusted to the sudden drop in temperature as he glided along the pool bottom, eyes open in the dark, the tall palm trees overhead casting wavy shadows on the dark gunnite. At the other end he surfaced and shook the water and chlorine from his eyes and nose. A crystal moon punctured the black sky, painting a deep silhouette against the motel roofline.

For the next half-hour he swam slowly, pushing off and gliding through the silent water, feeling almost reborn as the cool wet rippled past him.

Finally the night got the better of him. He pulled himself from the pool and wrapped a towel around his body, then trudged back to his room. He fumbled for his keys, then remembered his suit didn't have any pockets. That's why he'd left the door unlocked, so he wouldn't have to take the awkward plastic key out to the poolside and leave it bundled up in his towel while he swam.

But he hadn't left the door ajar, he suddenly remembered as he pushed his way inside. Water dripped from him while he toweled off, forming little puddles on the carpet. No, he'd distinctly felt the door click shut as he pulled it closed.

What—who—had pushed it open?

But it was a thought that came too late, as the hard shadow smashed into the back of his head and he slowly, painfully, crumpled to the floor.

12

Logan woke up in a confused fugue, the third time in four days. His mind had slipped into a time lapse. No way could it be nine twenty-two—he'd gone out for his swim much later than that. Then he realized that the light biting into his eyes was streaming in through the open glass slider, the hot sun rising into a new day.

He'd been asleep—out cold?—for twelve hours. Whoever had conked him—he remembered that much—had done an expert job. The base of his skull throbbed, and a tender welt the size of a golf ball pressed against his bruised skin. A similar area of tenderness—no lump, just a deep purple tattoo in the shape of Africa—colored his left temple, where his head had hit the floor when he collapsed from the single blow. A distant ringing clogged his ears, and he tried to shake it loose. But the noise was built in, powered by pain.

So was the rest of his body. Twelve hours in the same tangled position, arms splayed out over his head, legs tucked under him almost fetally, his spine twisted. As he gingerly sat up he felt the torment in every cramped muscle, every stretched ligament.

A quick shave and shower provided temporary relief. He studied himself in the steamed bathroom mirror, gently prodding the dark continent that loomed on the side of his head. His eyes felt tired but seemed clear, no glossy hint of concussion. His skin seemed pale and pasty and his head felt like a ball of wet Styrofoam. He twisted his neck from right to left, tolerating the spasm that stabbed into his brain. Then he held his arms outstretched, touched his fingers together. Contact.

Eventually deciding he was fit to travel, he pulled on his trousers and the most somber-looking short-sleeved shirt he could find. He unhooked his dark-blue sport coat from where he'd hung it in the alcove that served as a closet. He started toward the door, then hesitated; something was out of place, missing. The room was pretty sparse when he'd moved in, and he hadn't added much. His wallet was still in yesterday's back pocket, money and plastic still intact. The keys to the Fury and the room were where he'd left them on the TV, and his waterproof Seiko was still strapped to his wrist. Maybe Logan had interrupted the thief at the start of his heist.

Logan pushed the recurrent image of Molly out of his head.

He picked up his keys, jiggling them in his hand. Something was out of place, something minuscule, probably nothing. Still, nothing could be something, he thought as he faltered, running his eyes one more time around the room. And that's when he saw it.

The top page of the legal pad was missing, hastily ripped off so a jagged edge of yellow remained. Whoever had slipped in last night wasn't a burglar after a quick fix; he was after Logan, most likely had trailed him here. Or had him followed. In any event, he'd broken in and found what he was looking for. And then lingered around for something more.

He felt a fresh chill race up his tired spine. He absorbed a lungful of sea air, then wrenched the door open and stepped out into the hot August morning. Whatever the hell was going on—redheads and murder aside—whatever gentle breeze for which he'd been searching was beginning to stir.

The receptionist in Rhapsody's front lobby smiled benignly at the bunch of roses cradled in Logan's arm.

He complimented her on her tight-fitting black dress, which was cinched at the waist with a studded black belt. Her seven earrings, two dangling from one lobe and five from the other, constituted some sort of fashion statement. Her hair was the color of Concord grape, short and stiff and straight.

"I'm here to see Corie Chapin," Logan explained after a brief exchange about the individuality of fashion. He winked, giving a sideways nod to the roses. "It's a surprise."

"You a courier?" she inquired.

"Nope." He shook his head. "Personal."

The receptionist regarded him sympathetically, then smiled. "All the way to the back, up in the loft," she told him, then wished him luck.

Logan grinned a thank-you, winked again, and disappeared through the maze of work stations. What did she mean by luck?

Corie Chapin was not at her desk, but was definitely nearby. Sixty megabytes of hard drive memory were humming in the corner, and the Diet Coke on her desk was still ice-cold. Probably went to the ladies' room or the supply room. Logan lingered at the top of the stairs for a moment, then quietly padded across the thick carpeting and peered into Novak's office. Still no sign of her. He paused for a moment in the doorway, surveying the setting, curiosity beckoning him. He listened for approaching footsteps, then set the flowers on Corie's desk and wandered into the dead record mogul's expansive office.

Neil Novak's private sanctum was eerily empty. His personal effects lay scattered everywhere but his presence seemed faded, after only four days. A lifetime of spirit snuffed out like a candle in a storm. The office was designed around the same free-flowing plan as the rest of Rhapsody Records, except for one major difference: it had windows. Not windows opening to the world outside; no, these overlooked the ground floor of the Rhapsody Records work area. Sort of like looking down on the New York Stock Exchange, keeping tabs on the ups and downs of the day. From up here Novak had a clear view of his entire empire, except for the private offices and conference rooms set off along the two sides. Who said Big Brother wasn't watching?

The wood-paneled walls contained a random patchwork of Novak's successes. They were cluttered with framed posters, autographed publicity shots, various trade press articles, concert memorabilia, gold records. Virtually every square inch of usable wall space was covered, floor to ceiling. A genuine antique Wurlitzer bubbler jukebox sat dormant in one corner, and a full-sized model of RCA's Nipper the dog—"His Master's Voice"—stood guard next to it. A long walnut credenza housed a state-of-the-art Harmon Kardon stereo system, complete with multi-play CD turntable unit and a set of Bose speakers. VHS, Beta, and three-quarter-inch video recorders and an NEC forty-inch color monitor rounded out the equipment. An immense glass table, set with only a telephone and pen set, served as his desk, while a grouping of leather chairs and matching sofa was clustered on a Swedish wool rug. A system of Scandinavian wall units and a globe fish tank flanked the doorway. Levolor blinds set against the mezzanine windows were angled slightly, permitting a one-way view of the work space below.

Logan moved quickly around the room, picking up odd items of memorabilia and weighing them in his hands, like a psychic divining their significance in Neil Novak's life. His eyes roamed from coffee cups to wooden African statuettes to a model airplane on a stand, to a small collection of wooden duck decoys that filled an otherwise unused shelf unit. Everywhere was a Novak memory: photographs taken with the stars, a collection of porcelain dogs, autographed album covers and concert posters. And a hand-carved ebony address case crammed with numbers and addresses.

Logan kept one ear tuned in lest anyone surprise him. How could the cops have missed this? He assumed they'd already searched the place, but maybe he assumed wrong. Or maybe they hadn't seen it, wedged in among the odd assortment of other collectibles scattered around the room. He quickly sorted through the pages; most of them contained home numbers and addresses of fellow label presidents, managers, agents, producers, artists. A treasure trove of Novak lore. He flipped through the alphabetized listings, picking out random names: Lynn Sutton, Roger McNulty, Leo Gold, Frank Kennedy, Joseph Minetti.

At the first sound of footfalls coming up the steps Logan slipped the address case into his coat pocket. He tiptoed out of the office and picked up the arrangement of roses just as Corie ascended the stairs.

"For you." Logan smiled sweetly. "I just thought you could use these, after everything you've been through."

"Just what the hell do you think—?" She eyed the flowers suspiciously, then relaxed her guard. "Thank you," she finally said, as if it was a real chore.

"I figured . . . since everybody is probably sending flowers to Mrs. Novak, while here you sit, in this—"

"Drab, colorless, lifeless office? It's quite easy, when I'm left in peace," she told him, her voice still a caustic barb. "How did you get past the front desk?"

"We persistent types have our ways."

Corie cocked her head warily, as if expecting more of an attempt at an explanation. Or at least an excuse.

"I lied," Logan obliged her.

"Of course."

"I wanted to talk to you. We didn't get much of a chance the first time."

"You think you're doing better now?"

"I hoped you'd give me another chance."

"And you thought the flowers would help."

"So I was dumb."

She frowned. "You just lost your second chance."

"But—"

She moved around her desk, keeping her eye on him the entire time. "I'm sorry, but I really don't have time—"

"Just five minutes. Everybody's got five minutes."

"You're right. I've got five minutes, and if I have to spend it telling you to get out of here, I will."

"Please. Think of it as a favor to a friend."

"Since when are you and I friends?"

"I meant you and Novak."

"Neil Novak is dead, Mr. Logan. And right now I've got—" She checked her watch. "—about three hours to get things in order for his memorial service. Now, I'm going to ask you one more time. Nicely and succinctly. Please get the fuck out of here."

He sighed and looked forlorn. "The chance of a lifetime—"

"In a lifetime of chance. And you just lost your last one."

Another set of footsteps started climbing the stairs, this time heavier, more forceful. A dark, scowling man with wavy black hair peppered with strands of silver strode into the office. He stopped short, looking first at Logan, then at Corie.

"Do I have an appointment with this gentleman?" he asked her.

"I'm sorry, Mr. Minetti. He got past the front desk. I've been trying to get rid of him."

"Not with any success, I see." He glowered at Corie, then turned back to Logan. "The stairs are that way."

"Mr. Minetti? Joseph Minetti? Stuart Logan—"

"He *says* he's an insurance investigator," Corie explained to Minetti, rolling her eyes in doubt or disgust. "But that was yesterday. I don't know who he thinks he is today."

Minetti waved a hand at Logan, almost an effeminate brush-off. "I'm busy." Then, to Corie: "Get him out of here."

"Just two minutes," Logan begged.

"Sorry." Minetti turned and headed for his—Novak's—office. "Now get out."

Corie smiled victoriously, but Logan didn't flinch.

"It'll be worth your time," Logan assured him.

"I think not."

"Trust me," Logan pressed.

Minetti stopped, turned in the doorway. "Concerning—?"

"Concerning your pal Novak, and his pals. Frank Kennedy, Roger McNulty, Leo Gold, the Carbones ... you know who I'm talking about." Logan had only a slight idea himself what he was talking about, but the scowl on Minetti's suddenly scarlet face told him he'd hit a raw nerve.

"Fuck." Minetti checked his watch. "All right. Five minutes."

He led Logan into the office that Logan had just skimmed. Minetti offered him a seat on the voluminous sofa, while he perched on the back of one of the padded chairs. His eyes had acquired the slate hue of a Pacific storm. "Your five minutes begin now."

Logan wasted no time. "Mr. Minetti, I've been hired to look into the death of your late colleague, Neil Novak. I didn't really feel at liberty to explain that to Miss Chapin—" He nodded toward the door that led out to Corie's anteroom. "—and I really can't go into detail right now."

"What the hell—?"

Logan dug into his pocket and produced another business card with his own name on it, followed by the description PRIVATE SECURITY OPERATIONS. The address on the card listed a nonexistent address and phone number in Studio City.

Minetti studied the card dubiously and slipped it on the end table next to his chair. He said nothing.

"I'm not sure exactly what I'm looking for, but I think you can help me piece a few things together."

"Such as?"

"I'm not going to waste your time, Mr. Minetti. I'm looking for a redhead—" And if one more idiot says *Aren't we all,* I'm going to bash him, Logan thought.

"Aren't we all," Minetti said.

Logan stifled an inner groan and continued. "This redhead, she was last seen leaving Novak's boat the morning of the murders. You know her?" Hope surged in his blood.

"Look, Mr. Logan. I've already told the cops all I know, and that's the end of it. Period."

"All I need is a name—"

Minetti shook his head, rose from his seat. "Your five minutes are up. Now, get your ass off my couch and move it out of here."

"I thought it was Mr. Novak's couch," Logan said as he pushed his way out of the depths of the sofa.

"Mr. Novak is dead," Minetti reminded him irritably. "And despite what they tell you in business school, it doesn't matter how many toys you have, you still die."

"Exactly," Logan agreed. "Which gets me to thinking, how do you fit in? Was it Novak's arrangement that you move into his office, or just part of the posthumous corporate power grab?"

"I'm executive vice president of this company," Minetti explained with more patience than even Logan expected.

"And now you're acting president, at least until Rhapsody's legal situation is completely determined. I'd say there's a lot of incentive here for you."

"I don't think I like what you're implying."

"I'm implying nothing." Logan shrugged. "You're inferring."

"Whatever." Minetti frowned, displaying a row of gleaming dentures. "Look, whoever the hell you are, I'm an attorney. I've been an attorney for upwards of twenty years, as a partner in one of the largest firms in the city and then here at Rhapsody. My reputation in the legal community—and in this business—is impeccable. So for you to suggest that I have committed any impropriety—"

"No impropriety. I simply stated that you may have had a lot to gain from Neil Novak's death—"

"And I think I've allowed your rantings to continue far too long." Minetti crossed the room and opened the door. "Now get your butt out of here, you little fuck. And if you're as smart as you think you are, you won't show it around here again."

Logan decided prudence followed the open-door policy. As he stepped past Minetti and into Corie's custody, the new label chief glared at his harried lame-duck executive assistant.

"Make sure no one slips by again," he admonished her, then slammed the door.

Corie winced at the noise. "Please, get out of here," she fumed, sotto voice. "My job's on the line as it is."

"I should hope so, for your sake," Logan whispered, cocking his head toward the closed door. He dug in his pocket and pulled out his parking stub. "I almost forgot. Do you validate?"

"Front desk," she snarled. "You know the way."

13

The Los Angeles District Attorney's Office was a study in tradition. Rich wood paneling, thick wool carpeting, table lamps instead of the high-tech track lighting that pervaded the California life-style. The suite of offices suggested a somber reality about the law: the front reception lobby was decorated with overstuffed leather couches, separated by a massive oak coffee table and matching end tables. These sported a vast collection of magazines, newsletters, newspapers, and copies of bills of interest to California voters. Just in case visitors forgot that the D.A.'s job was highly political, with more than a handful of them going on to much higher state and national positions.

Cal Mitchell was one of those aspirants, one of a dozen assistant D.A.'s who'd come to work for the county fresh from the bar exam. Now in his mid-thirties, he was a spry man with a penchant for truth, justice, and the American way. He'd joined the D.A.'s team after finishing third in his class and serving as editor of the Law Review at Bolt, and approached his work like a hungry justice machine. His experience with criminal law earned him a reputation around the office of a determined, exhaustive (and exhausting) prosecutor, with an excruciating eye for detail and due process.

This morning the man was as consumed with work as ever, almost brushing past Logan before he recognized the long-lost face. Then he stopped, performed a nifty double-take, then nearly pumped Logan's arm right out of its socket.

"Stuart Logan, as I live and breathe—"

"Cal," Logan said simply, perplexed by Mitchell's animation. The two of them had met a total of five times over the last three years, including Logan's twelve-month hermitage out on Catalina. In their roles of hard-nosed prosecutor versus probing reporter their contact had not always been one of great camaraderie, and they were not what either would de-

92

scribe as bosom buddies. Still, it was hard not to be over-whelmed by Cal Mitchell's practiced enthusiasm.

Logan eyed Mitchell's customary attire. He wore a dark suit, too hot for L.A. in August, but a guarantee of professional ascendancy. Button-down shirt, cuff links, yellow tie, suspenders, black Italian shoes. The power struggle was alive and well. He grinned to himself. "Good to see you," Logan returned.

"I thought you'd moved up north, Monterey or San Jose or something. What gives?"

"It's a long story, worthy of a beer or two," Logan said, knowing Mitchell didn't drink. In fact, Mitchell never had time or inclination, for anything other than an office brown-bag lunch.

"Rain check, pal," Mitchell sighed. "You said you wanted to pick my brain about something—?"

Logan dipped his head in a slight nod. "Neil Novak."

Mitchell eyed Logan as if he'd just painted a swastika on the wall, then glanced briefly at the receptionist to see if she was listening. The woman appeared to be deeply engrossed in the latest issue of *Elle,* and Mitchell seemed to heave a sigh of relief.

"I think maybe we'd better step inside," he suggested, his voice suddenly taking on an overcast tone. He opened a door that led to the inner sanctums of justice and motioned for Logan to precede him down the hallway, first to the left, then to the right. Logan remembered the way to Mitchell's private office, but allowed himself to be waved properly in the right direction.

Once seated behind closed doors, Mitchell leaned forward on the hard surface of his walnut desk. His eyes fixed on Logan's, and for a disturbingly long moment he said nothing. Then: "This is classified shit, Stuart."

Logan smiled and slowly shook his head. He made a stee-ple with his fingers, then turned his hands back inside out to look at all the people. "Save your breath, Cal. I know what you're going to say, and I'm not going to push. All I want is a little fringe info, completely off the record."

"That's all you've ever wanted—"

"This time it's a matter of personal business."

"Yeah?" Mitchell raised a skeptical brow. "What's the payoff?"

"Payoff!"

"Your motive. You working a book deal, maybe a free-lance piece for one of the national news rags?"

"I told you, Cal. Personal. No ink."

They studied each other closely, as if trying to stare the other down. Then Mitchell rose from his chair and walked over to the window. He stopped beside the floor-mounted American flag and California bear flag and peered through the dusty venetian blinds. Then he abruptly turned and faced Logan squarely. "No attribution, right? We never talked."

"I don't even know who I never had this conversation with," Logan agreed. He shifted in his chair; Mitchell was playing power games with him. Prosecutor standing, witness seated. He'd seen it before, countless times while covering countless hearings and trials. This was Cal Mitchell's office, his chairs and flags and his view. But Logan wasn't here to be stepped on like some annoying bug. He stretched his legs, then slowly rose to his feet.

"Hope you don't mind if I stand up," he said. "Been sitting all morning."

Mitchell shrugged, waited while Logan wandered over to share the vista. The power struggle thus equalized, Mitchell began: "Neil Novak ran with some fascinating folks, Stuart. As I'm sure you already know."

"The record industry makes for a lot of strange bedfellows," Logan nodded, reflecting back on his evening with Big Red.

"Anyone in particular?"

"The Carbones—Niki, Luigi, David. Frank Kennedy. Roger McNulty. Maybe Leo Gold. Did I leave anybody out?"

Mitchell turned away from his own reflection in the glass. He wandered back to his desk, found an empty corner, sat down. Logan remained where he was, but turned to face the assistant D.A.

"No one of any consequence." He wandered back to his desk and plucked a cigarette from a carved teak box. He stuffed it between his lips, but didn't light it. "There's not much I can tell you; just about everything I know is classified, and I don't know shit."

"Look, Cal. I don't want to kick up any dust, and I sure don't want to jeopardize an ongoing investigation. Not after last time. I'm just interested in Novak and his friends, and how they were using Rhapsody Records to do their dirty work."

"Assuming there is some dirty work."

"You don't usually see feds trailing after Mr. Clean." He flexed his shoulders; his neck still ached and his muscles were growing more tired by the minute. "What I want to know is how the circle operated, the extent of Novak's personal network. Who did what for whom, what the connections were, how far the network extended, who got what. Stuff above and below the table."

"You want to know a lot."

"I'm a naturally nosy guy."

"And you say this is all personal?"

"Call it a new image."

Mitchell regarded him carefully, closely, weighing the pros and cons of the request.

"Stuart, the record industry is just about the last frontier for the feds. Our prelims suggest this whole thing goes deep, really deep. Everyone in the business has a first- or second-hand story. Rumors. We've heard more rumors of mob connections and bribes and threats and payoffs than you can count. Nothing I'm sure you don't already know. And as you also know, we've been looking for years to pin something on these guys, and this time we're getting real close. But until we connect, the well is dry."

Logan sighed and shoved his hands into his jacket pockets. "Cal, I appreciate all this hooey about sensitive issues and confidentiality and closed hearings and allegations. Believe me, I don't want to interfere with that. But if you can feed me anything—a name or two, a little info, I'll be out of here in under sixty seconds."

Mitchell nibbled on the cigarette, finally fueling it with a carved lighter that matched the teak box. He inhaled deeply, then blew a halo of smoke over his head.

"Try me," he sighed. "Give me a name."

"The mob. Niki and Luigi and David."

"What about 'em?"

"What's their interest?"

"In the industry?"

"In Rhapsody Records."

"Confidential."

"What about Escabar and DeSola?"

"*Nada.*"

Logan shrugged, then slowly walked around the front of Mitchell's desk and rested his hands on the back of the chair he'd been sitting in just moments before.

"Okay," Logan began again. "Payola."

"What of it?"

"Widespread?"

"In theory."

"In practice?"

"It's your guess." Mitchell shrugged a genuine apology and drew another big breath of smoke.

"How 'bout Rhapsody Records?"

"Confidential."

"But it does exist?"

"Payola or Rhapsody Records?"

"Come on. Just give me a crumb."

Mitchell plucked the cigarette from his mouth and knocked an ash into the waste basket. He examined the tip, then stuck it back in his mouth.

"You see the piece Ted Smart did last night, that guy they had backlit? He talked to us. Gave us a lot of good stuff, but they ironed out the wrinkles in his face. Literally. Hell, anyone finds out who that dude is, he's dead meat. These guys mean business. A year ago one of the networks did a report, got a radio guy down in Florida to talk. A week later the poor schmuck was in the hospital with shattered legs and a fractured skull. Now he says he made his story up and won't talk. Down in Nashville some deejay refused to comply with a certain promoter's demands; two hours later someone pumped a load of bird shot into him."

Logan winced from the pain, imagined as well as from the steady throbbing coming from the base of his skull. "This payola: it's mostly money, drugs, sex?"

"Cash, cars, coke, cunt. The four C's of record promotion. It's a wonder what a little blow of any type can do to get a record played on the radio."

Logan felt a sneeze building in his nose and stifled it. Secondhand smoke did it every time; the curse of the ex-smoker. "How 'bout counterfeiting, bootlegging?"

"Highly profitable. And highly sensitive." Mitchell exhaled a blue cloud of noxious smoke and moved off his desk. This line of questioning was quickly coming to a close.

"Leo Gold?"

"I wish I could be of more help." Cal Mitchell turned up his palms in apology. "Maybe at a later date—"

"A later date may be too late."

"For your personal purposes, maybe." Mitchell smiled. "But not necessarily for ours."

Logan felt like inviting Cal Mitchell to go jump off the Santa Monica Pier, but burning a bridge would gain him very little.

"Well, I appreciate the time you've given me," he said instead as Mitchell led him toward the door. He thanked California's future hopeful attorney general, then stepped out into the vast corridor and merged into the hallway with the madding crowd of the L.A. legal system.

Lynn Sutton's memorial service was a short and simple affair. No chapel, no casket, no three-piece suits or Rodeo Drive fashions draping the shoulders of the throng of mourners. Instead, it was held on a bluff overlooking the ocean ten miles north of Malibu.

It was a placid setting, a tranquil meadow of wildflowers and scrub bordering an aromatic grove of towering eucalyptus trees. Golden sun danced off a glimmering sea of undulating Mylar, and a gentle breeze cut through the heat. A faint scent of dry heather enfolded the field.

The air was quiet. Quiet except for the gloomy presence of a dozen people paying their last respects to a woman whose short but hard life had ended on the same sea that would soon carry her ashes into eternity.

Logan pulled the Plymouth to the side of Pacific Coast Highway, waiting for a stream of traffic to pass, then made a wide U-turn and headed back toward the wide shoulder where the small group had parked their cars. He inched onto the gravel shoulder and surveyed the scene for a moment, then cut the engine. He inhaled a deep breath of clean air, holding it in his lungs before letting it out again. He remained behind the wheel, watching the informal service through the barbed-wire fence partitioning the field from the public. A menagerie of cars was scattered along the road, the newest being a new black two-door Ford Bronco with black-tinted windows; the oldest was an early sixties Ford Fairlane wagon with fake fiberglass wood paneling sagging from its rusted frame. Parked a short distance behind these was a black stretch Cadillac limousine with license plates that read STRWD 23. Leased from

the Starwood Livery Company of Hollywood and Long
Beach.

Logan left them alone, the twelve, their private words fading in the wind. He counted nine women and three men, each
of them alone in their thoughts. Logan suspected that the
women, mostly well-dressed but not overdone, were Lynn's
colleagues from some point in her varied history. So were the
men, for all he knew. From this distance he recognized no
one. The men comprised an odd lot: one was tall and large,
muscle turning to fat. Another was young and stubby and
topped by a mop of dark hair, dressed in white jeans and a
black shirt; the third was the minister, casually adorned without regard to denomination, sporting William Hurt blond hair
and a John Ritter face. He held a small book in his hand and
seemed to be reciting some sort of prayer or other eulogistic
utterance.

Eventually the remembrances trailed off and the minister
picked up a brass urn. The rest of the crowd formed a semi-
circle a few yards distant, heads bowed in silent remem-
brance. The minister stepped forward and handed the urn to
one of the women. From Logan's angle she seemed no more
than a teenager, maybe eighteen or twenty. She accepted the
heavy cannister, with solemn determination. She held it quietly for a few moments, gazing down at the rocks below. At
great length she slowly unscrewed the cap, then let the contents drift over the edge of the precipice, into the hungry sea.

That was it. The service was over. Solemn hugs and kisses
were shared all around, except for the other two men, who
both remained somewhat distant. The minister slipped his
arm over the girl's shoulder and slowly meandered back
across the field with her, their heads bowed in low conversation, comforting her as they approached the highway. She still
carried the brass urn, holding it clearly at arm's length. Several other women approached her, but she didn't want to talk
and they understood.

Logan wondered who this girl was, what her relationship
to Lynn had been. Sister, daughter, friend? Maybe even
lover? Maybe she was the girl that Randi had mentioned:
Kyndall, her name was. Lynn's niece, she had said. He continued to watch from afar as the girl reached the fence and
bent down to squeeze under the barbed wire that seques-
tered the meadow from PCH. She snagged herself on one of
the spikes and dropped the urn, and the minister recovered

it for her. They talked for a moment, she hugged him, then she briskly turned and walked toward her car.

The girl gingerly laid her memorabilia on the passenger seat of her old Volkswagen and climbed behind the wheel. She glanced around nervously, closed the door, and for a long moment sat behind the wheel. She started the engine, which throbbed to life with a characteristic high-pitched whine. Then she threw the car into gear and swerved out onto the four-lane highway.

Logan started his own car and watched the VW merge into the thin southbound traffic. That's when he noticed the red Mercedes and its obvious licence: PLAYTYM. He hadn't seen it before, parked a hundred yards down PCH, pulled over into the shade of a thick eucalyptus grove.

As the girl's car crested a distant rise in the road, the Mercedes edged out onto the highway and fell into the stream of traffic behind it. And just two cars back, the black STRWD 23 Cadillac limousine pulled out behind them both.

Neil Novak's service was scheduled three hours after Lynn Sutton's. Logan felt morbidly promiscuous as he pulled through the gates of Forest Lawn: two memorial services in one day, and it was only two in the afternoon.

It originally was intended to be quiet and private, a somber affair in a pastoral setting. Just a few dozen of Neil's business colleagues and a smattering of friends, plus his loving wife. That was the agenda, but the press, oblivious to decorum, managed to turn it into a media event. Cameramen, photographers, sound crews, and a gaggle of reporters jostled for position outside the chapel perched high on its solemn knoll above the city of Glendale. Logan swept a few errant locks of damp hair across his sticky forehead, slipped on his dark shades, and joined the quiet procession to the top of the oak-shaded knoll.

A string of limousines lined the curving drive, which meandered up from the smog-shrouded depths of Grand Avenue to the chapel. Strains of Bach swept eerily through the parched trees, over the rolling lawn kept green by the *pftht-pftht* of a crescent sprinkler. Family members, friends, and colleagues milled about outside the chapel door, conversing in hushed tones while fanning themselves. The growing covey of press reverently kept their chaos to one side of the expansive front patio. Reporters whispered as if they were calling the play-by-play of a golf match, while cameras panned the crowd for familiar faces and the distant Valley vista for cutaway shots.

Logan surveyed the throng of mourners, most of whom he decided were present more to be seen than to pay their last respects. He recognized some of the faces but few of the names. That was Molly's forte, not his. If she were here now, standing beside him, her arm in his, she'd be reeling off names faster than he could keep track. Then again, if she were here he'd be here in an official capacity with the *Times* rather than as part of the curious milieu.

Logan's gaze fell on Joseph Minetti, who was speaking softy with Leslie Novak in a quiet corner of the expansive stone patio. He was dressed in obligatory black pinstripes, she in black silk. A pair of black glasses probably masked tears and reddened eyes. She tried to smile as he spoke, her face bleached of all emotion and her eyes strained with distress.

The doleful carillon music broke, and as if at some unspoken cue the crowd flowed inside. Logan hovered near the back, not wishing to disrupt the sanctity of the moment. He studied the mourners with detached interest. Heads were bowed during the minister's invocation, couples held hands, many wiped tears from their eyes. The thought struck him that he had no reason to be here, that he should have left these people to their private peace. And to their respect for the dear departed Neil Novak. But the growing voyeurism that now reached far beyond the identity of a red-haired woman kept him here. Fact was, a double-murderer might be sitting in this chapel at this very moment, paying his or her last respects and having a few chuckles at the same time.

Five minutes of this was all Logan could endure. Two minutes later he was outside in the putrid heat. He removed his jacket and tie, rolled up his cuffs, and untucked his shirttails.

His collar and armpits were already dripping and his hair was plastered in wet, slick streaks across his scalp. He sauntered over to the side of the courtyard and took in the sweeping view of the Valley, spread out below in a mass of freeway cloverleafs, boulevards, car dealerships, shopping malls, discount spa warehouses. All crowding the base of this lush hill: Forest Lawn–Glendale, one of several convenient Southern California locales serving your burial needs.

He drifted over to the line of limos, each with a driver comfortably ensconced behind the wheel, passing the afternoon in air-conditioned luxury. As he meandered down the winding drive, a familiar license plate caught his eye: STRWD 23. The black-tinted windows were rolled up against the stifling heat, and the driver thoughtfully had parked the car in the shade of a flowing willow.

Logan sauntered up to the car and peered through the passenger window, cupping his hands against the glare.

"May I help you?" called out a sweet, sunny voice from behind him.

Logan turned and found himself facing the car's chauffeur, a young woman with porcelain skin and blonde hair that spilled over her shoulders. She was dressed in a black tux and stiff wing-collared shirt; her black jacket was neatly folded on the grass beside her. She held a dog-eared Danielle Steel novel in her hand.

"I was . . . just curious who—"

"Who belonged to the car, right?" She smiled, folded over the corner of the page, and closed the book. "Sorry."

"You work for Starwood?" Logan inquired as he stepped up on the grass and moved closer.

"I do. And it's our policy never to divulge the identity of our clients." The words sounded as if they came from a sheet of official rules. "Not for love or money."

Logan raised his brow in accompaniment of a slight shrug. Maybe this girl was too naive or moral to have a price, but someone down at Starwood maybe could use a couple extra twenties.

"Nice day for a funeral, anyway," he said, smiling. Her eyes lingered on his for just a moment; then she cracked the book and immersed herself back in its sorrowful love triangle and grand passions.

Logan drew his gaze down the winding drive to the vast array of other cars. Rolls, Ferraris, BMWs, Jags, two Aston

Martins, a DeLorean—and a red Mercedes parked against a distant curve. He didn't even need to check the plates. The top was down, and the car's driver was leaning against the left front fender, hands in his pockets, shirt halfway unbuttoned. Roger McNulty.

Logan strolled down the hill toward him. "Hotter 'n hell," he called out, breathing heavily in exaggerated emphasis.

"Fuckin' A." McNulty regarded Logan curiously, a flash of recognition in his face.

"You could fry an egg on this thing," Logan said, nodding at the car's hood. Without thinking he ran a hand over the tender lump on his forehead.

"Looks like you already got one," the man said, glancing at the bruise on Logan's temple.

"Cliff-diving," he explained succinctly, extending his hand. "Stuart Logan."

"Roger McNulty," the man responded in kind. "Have we met?"

Logan thought quickly. Tell the truth, or play ignorant? What was this man doing at Lynn's service just three hours ago, and why was he waiting outside while Neil Novak was being eulogized in air-conditioned comfort? Was it because of his relationship with Mrs. Novak, in whose arms Logan had seen him just Monday afternoon? Or maybe it was his connection with Novak himself, and with Rhapsody Records. Logan wondered just what that connection was: dealer, pusher, pimp? In just three short days back in L.A., Logan had crossed the man's path twice now, not including whoever paid him a nocturnal visit at the motel last night. Could that have been McNulty as well? A shard of pain stabbed up his neck.

"Two days ago," Logan replied. "Bel Air."

"You were looking for some fucking house. You had a map—"

"Nick Nolte."

McNulty's look of curiosity faded into a decidedly noxious scowl. He pushed himself up from his relaxed lounging and took a step forward. "Listen, pal. I don't know who you are—"

"I told you . . . I'm Stuart Logan."

"Okay, Mr. Logan. Smart-ass. Whatever you're up to, I'm tellin' you right now, right here. Fuck off!"

"Sure thing, Mr. McNulty. Give my regards to Mrs. Novak."

McNulty's face paled and his eyes grew dark and narrowed. "You little shit . . . you got just about ten seconds to beat it," he warned, taking a step forward.

"That what you do when your little girlfriend's not around?"

McNulty grunted and grabbed for Logan's collar, which ripped at the seam as Logan sidestepped the frontal attack.

"Nasty, nasty. This here's a thirty-dollar shirt."

"Just stay the fuck out of my business," McNulty growled, his glare more piercing than the hot sun.

Their eyes fixed on each other's long enough for Logan's mouth to turn up in a mocking grin. "See you around, maybe up in Bel Air—"

McNulty looked ready to lunge, but he showed respectable reserve. "Motherfucker," he cursed under his breath.

Logan idly climbed back up the long drive, not bothering to turn around, still curious as hell to see what McNulty was up to. Twenty seconds passed before the answer came. The powerful Mercedes engine roared to life and Roger gunned it in anger for a few seconds. Then came the squeal of raging rubber and a high-pitched whine as the car fishtailed and sped down the hill. Roger McNulty would have to postpone till later whatever visual rendezvous he had planned with the grieving widow Novak.

By the time Logan reached the crest of the hill the carillon again was playing soulfully. Mourners were filing out of the chapel, quiet and somber. He took up position at the far end of the courtyard, at the top of the short flight of steps which led down to the line of parked cars.

Corie Chapin wandered out into the sun, the first person whom he recognized to emerge from the chapel. Her eyes were streaked with red, and her skin seemed flushed. She was dressed in the same black dress she had worn in the office that morning, obviously no time to change. In natural light her skin reflected the sun in even tones, her lips radiant yet somehow subdued. Her deep-set eyes reflected the afternoon sky, clear up here above the smog. A flood of golden hair washed over her shoulders.

Logan approached her slowly; she didn't see him until he was barely ten feet away.

"That was touching," he observed cynically.

"Please . . . just leave me alone," she said flatly.

"I will. I promise. Just let me explain—"

"Not now, Mr. Logan. Not ever." She tried to move away, but Logan blocked her path.

"I know this is neither the time nor place—"

"And it never will be. Now, please—!" She stepped around him and headed across the expansive slate patio. Logan instinctively trailed after her.

"Corie, just listen. Ten seconds."

She slowed, turned to face him as if she were going to launch into a tirade, but he caught her by the arm. Lightly. She shook loose, but looked into his eyes. Her body seemed to ease up, the tension evaporating in the dry heat. She sighed, took a halting breath, looked around at the sweaty mourners filing past her. Then she dug into her purse, pawing around for something elusive. Finally she extracted a small green package. "Gum?"

Logan shook his head. "What do you say we start over."

"Not here, Mr. Logan. If that's really your name."

"It is." He sensed her doubt and smiled. "Trust me. And you can call me Stuart."

"I'll call you Logan."

Logan shrugged; that was fine with him. "So. What do you say?"

She answered by saying nothing; instead she slowly made her way toward the mass of parked cars. Logan accompanied her, this time walking at her side rather than running after her like some smitten twelve-year-old.

"Let me think on it," she said finally as they neared what Logan assumed was her car. A metallic-blue Honda Accord with a trunk rack, very practical. She unlocked the driver's door and pulled it open, then noticed the puffy, swollen bruise on Logan's face. "Don't tell me . . . someone throw you out on your ear?"

"I walked into a door."

Corie almost grinned, a near-victory for Logan. Her eyes settled on his for a second or two, then gazed up past Logan.

Logan turned and followed her glance. Sweeping down the stairs was a woman dressed in a sleek gray dress, her dark hair protected from the sun by a somber gray scarf. She vaguely looked familiar, but he couldn't place her. Maybe from TV or films. She raised a hand toward Corie as she crossed the driveway.

"Sorry, Corie," she apologized as she glided up, seeming to ignore Logan's presence. "I got caught by Johnny Rand and couldn't get away."

"Johnny Rand?" Corrie sputtered. "You're kidding."

"Old teen idols never die."

That voice. Logan recognized it, placed it immediately. What was it, English? Australian? He stared at the woman, her beautiful green eyes those lips, that soft skin, hair the color of burgundy, wisps brushed back and bundled under that scarf.

Corie glanced at Logan, returned her attention to her friend. "Anyway, I didn't mean to abandon you back there. Just had to get out."

"I understand." The woman nodded. She turned toward Logan. "Aren't you going to introduce me . . ."

Her lilting voice trailed off as a spark flashed between them.

"Jenny, this is Stuart Logan." Corie smiled politely, still not sure what to make of him. "Stuart, Jenny Baxter. There. How'd I do?" She looked from Logan to Jenny, back to Logan, but neither of them seemed to have heard her.

"You—" Jenny Baxter flinched, involuntarily shrinking back.

"No shit," Logan countered, his voice a mixture of anger and awe. "Jenny, huh? Jenny Baxter?"

"Please . . . not here . . ." Jenny Baxter, redhead extraordinaire, pleaded, her voice faltering.

"A lot of folks're are looking for you," Logan pressed. "But then, I guess you know all about that, now don't you?"

"You know each other?" Corie interrupted, her eyes narrowed in a look of confusion and puzzlement.

Jenny nudged her and glanced at the car. "I think it's time we split this scene. I still have work to do."

"What? So soon?" Logan asked sarcastically as he followed Jenny around to the passenger door and opened it for her. "I think it's time you started hanging around instead of ducking out."

"Please," Jenny begged, turning her eyes from Logan to Corie. "Can we go?"

"So . . ." He looked closer, eyeing her roots. "Is it really red, or is that just for appearances? Don't tell me . . . only your hairdresser knows for sure."

The blood had drained from Jenny's face, and her upper lip quivered nervously. "It's not what you think."

"So . . . now you know what I think, is that it?" he sneered. A man has his own brand of venom.

Corie was thoroughly confused, and looked it. "Could someone here please tell me what the hell is going on?" She glanced from her friend to Logan, waiting for an answer.

"I'm sure Jenny will fill you in, if and when she wants to." Logan shrugged tiredly. "Of course, I wouldn't mind hearing the story myself."

Jenny slid inside, gathering her gray dress underneath her. She started to pull her door closed, but Logan caught it.

"We need to talk."

"Do we, now?" Jenny smiled sweetly, pried his fingers from the door, and pulled the door tight.

Corie tumbled into the car and started the engine before she even closed her door. Logan stepped back as she swerved away from the curb, roared up the hill to the end of the cul-de-sac, and stopped. The two women conversed for a few moments at the top of the knoll, Corie talking first, demanding, then throwing up her hands. Jenny answered back with great animation, her hands flailing with whatever she was saying. Then Corie shifted the Honda into gear and the car sped back down the crowded drive. As it careened back down the road it veered toward him; for a second Logan thought Corie was trying to run him down. Then she stopped next to him, the engine idling, Jenny Baxter's side nearest him.

The window rolled down and Jenny crooked a finger at him. *Bend down,* it beckoned.

Logan walked over and did as he was told. Jenny motioned for him to lower his ear closer. He did, not knowing whether she was going to kiss it or spit in it. In fact, she did neither.

"Rive Gauche, Sherman Oaks, seven-thirty," she said, her Kiwi accent betraying her loose nerves, but coming out gentle as a breeze nonetheless. "Tonight."

She smiled warily, then rolled up the window as Corie plunged her foot on the gas. Gravel popped under the tires as the car shot down the hill into the steaming Valley soup. Logan waited and watched as the car disappeared around the corner; then he wiped a clump of soaked hair from his eyes and retreated up the hill to fetch his own set of wheels.

15

Logan took Los Feliz Boulevard back toward Hollywood. He passed the entrance to Griffith Park and was momentarily tempted to detour up the winding drive to the observatory.

He'd only been up there once, seven years ago, right after he and Molly had bought their house in Sherman Oaks. Christmas Eve afternoon: a filmy fog had rolled in from the coast, reaching its wispy fingers through the canyons, tickling the Hollywood sign perched precipitously on a scrubby cliff. A distinct December chill hugged the air, the closest the Southland ever got to winter.

They had driven up to the observatory, closed for the holiday, and sat on the granite ledge overlooking the damp L.A. basin. Up here they could find a little peace, feel a little solace. It was their first year in L.A., and the holidays were a shock: pink- and blue-flocked trees in the lots on Hollywood and Ventura Boulevards, plastic Santas and reindeer and snowmen and angels on every other lawn in the Valley. And as the sun began to slip into the gray veil to the west, Christmas winked on in the distant streets below. Twinkling lights and palm trees and warm Santa Anas bathed the city with an unreal quality, and for a brief fantastical moment Logan and Molly fell in love all over again. They said they should come back up here every Christmas Eve, to make it a tradition born from their first Christmas together.

He hung a left at Western, then turned onto Franklin and continued west until he passed under the Hollywood Freeway. He worked his way through the disintegrating Hollywood neighborhoods until he came to Hawthorne, then hung a right onto Gardner. Which building was it? he wondered, as his mind raced back to the last time he'd been down here. When was it—two, maybe three years ago? Closer to four, back when he was still working the crime desk. He'd been called out of bed at three in the morning because onetime two-bit drummer Chick Tedesco was found lying on the small lawn outside his West Hollywood apartment with a bullet through his gut. Fortunately the slug had just missed his heart and Chick survived to tell about it. Two weeks later a vigman named Raul Rodriguez was behind bars, and yet another hole in L.A.'s drug sieve was plugged.

Tedesco quickly dried out and eventually started bartending for a catering service, mixing Manhattans and sloe gin fizzes and Harvey Wallbangers for the Beverly Hills set. As such he was vital to the interests of both the L.A.P.D. and the *L.A. Times,* and more than once had tipped Logan off about a drug deal or a sex ring.

Logan wasn't sure he'd find Chick home, because business tended to start at the cocktail hour, but he was in luck. After the obligatory it's-been-so-long greetings, Chick invited him inside the small first-floor apartment. Logan followed him into the living room and assessed the ex–studio musician. His dark hair had gotten longer, his skin tanner, his muscles tighter, his face healthier. A few years in the sun had worked wonders for the former cokehead.

"Got a gig up in Benedict tonight, but it don't start till six," he explained, waving Logan toward an arthritic Naugahyde sofa, tufts of fluff spilling out of a jagged wound. "So till then it's 'General Hospital' and 'Days of Our Lives.' "

Logan glanced around the gritty apartment as Chick sauntered into the kitchen alcove and grabbed two beers from the fridge. Unlike Chick himself, the place was the same wreck it was four years ago, the mess simply rearranged. The floor was littered with newspapers and empty Fritos bags and a Domino's pizza box with cheese and tomato sauce dried in a pattern of telltale wedges. A ghetto blaster sat on an upturned apple crate in the corner, flanked by a stack of cassettes and old clothes. A rusted ten-speed sat upturned in the middle of the room, its chain draped over the coffee table and grease caked on the natty yellow wall-to-wall. The only new addition to the Tedesco household that Logan could see was the twenty-five inch Sony in the corner.

"Hot?" Logan asked, cocking his head toward the TV.

"Yup." Chick shrugged. "Least it works." He handed Logan a Budweiser, then pulled out a kitchen chair and straddled it.

Logan popped the can and enjoyed a long slug of ice-cold

foam. He ran his sleeve across his mouth, then gulped again. "That truly hits the spot," he sighed.

"Right on," Chick answered, draining half his can in one swallow. He leaned forward on the back of his chair, cradling the beer in both hands. "So, Mr. Reporter, if that's still who you are . . . to what do I owe this distinct pleasure?"

Logan said nothing for a moment, only gazed at Chick Tedesco intensely. Finally, hunching over his beer, he asked, "You still run with the same weasels? Rodriguez, Del Gado, Garret, Cujo?"

"Hey, pal. No way. I been clean, close to four years now. After Rodriguez went to Napa, that was it. Finished."

Logan creased his brow, fixed Chick with a penetrating eye. "But you still hear things."

"Like what?"

"More like *whom.*"

"All right . . . I give. *Whom?*"

"Roger McNulty." From the instant look of pain on Chick's face, Logan knew he'd hit a mine.

"Two-faced sombitch. Kill his own kid if there was a profit in it." Chick Tedesco set down his beer and clumsily rose from his chair. He crossed to the television, which was sitting on a large wooden steamer trunk. With a low grunt he lifted the Sony and set it aside, then raised the trunk lid. He pawed through some boxes and papers, digging deep for whatever treasure he was seeking. Finally he mumbled, "Ah!" and rose to his feet. When he turned around Logan saw that he was holding a .32-caliber nickel-plated Smith & Wesson in his hand. He hefted the gun, spun the chamber, then sauntered back over to his chair. As he sat down he tossed the pistol on the couch next to Logan.

Logan picked the gun up and examined it with a perfunctory grunt, then glanced up at Chick for an explanation.

"I got that piece because of old Roger," he began, holding the cold beer can to his forehead. A slight grin found its way into his eyes. "We crossed paths when I shoulda turned tail. No sense going into it, it's all old vomit." He sipped his beer, wiped his lips. "So what's the little bastard up to now?"

"Circumstantial shit, far as I know," Logan said. He sighted down the barrel of the gun, tested the tension of the trigger, then set it on the coffee table next to the bike chain. "That's where I thought you might be able to help me."

"I'm sorta out of the info biz, case you ain't heard."

"Same here."

"Wondered why you ain't been bugging me. What gives?"

"As you said, old vomit," Logan explained. His eyes roamed the room; the walls were bare except for a few old posters hyping Chick's few concert and recording gigs.

Tedesco stroked his chin nervously, shifted his weight in his chair. "So . . . what do you want to know?" he finally said.

"McNulty, his friends . . ."

"People old Rog called friends most people don't call, period. The man worked the edges, all of them. Middleman extraordinaire. Bought drugs from guys like DeSola and Escabar on one end, sold pussy to Carbone and Casselli and Sanchez on the other."

Casselli and Sanchez: Logan hadn't heard those names in years. Casselli was the prime connection for the West Side, Sanchez the runner down in East L.A. And, of course, the Carbones ran most of what was in between. And Escabar and DeSola had slipped through everyone's fingers, thanks to the stuffed suits from Washington.

"You ever heard of a guy named Frank Kennedy?"

"Francis Fitzgerald Kennedy has got his finger in every pile of slime from here to Vegas. If it's crooked and goes into the human body, Kennedy's right there behind." He picked up the Smith & Wesson from the coffee table and turned it over in his hand, as if by touching it he somehow was protected. "What's this all about, anyway?"

Logan finished his beer and crumpled the can. He eyed one of the posters tacked to the wall: "Skeezoid Blues," an all-night rock party at the Aquarius featuring Chick Tedesco and Lisa Asil and the Palindromes. It was Chick's last stage gig, gonzo box office, but no one remembered who the hell any of them were.

"It's about how two people got bullet holes in their heads while spending a quiet little weekend out on Catalina," Logan finally said, resting the can on the table.

"Neil Novak." Chick nodded slowly. He hefted the gun in his hand, then set it down again. "Don't look at *me.*"

"Don't worry. It's the wrong size. Besides—" Logan gingerly touched the lump on the base of his skull. "—you've been clean for four years. What would you have to gain?"

"Right on." Chick Tedesco inhaled deeply and cleanly

through his nose, then exhaled proudly. "See ... works again."

"Tell me about the Kennedy connection."

Chick seemed to think this over, as if he were editing his thoughts. "You know, Logan, you hang around long enough, keep your ear in the right place, you hear things."

"That's why I'm here," Logan reminded him.

"Fuckin' A," he agreed, impressed by his role in the general scheme of things. "And when you hear things, you start hearing more things."

"And what sort of things did *you* hear, Chick?"

"I heard a lot. Things about records, things about radio, things about a little crack here and there, grease the old nose. And things about records and radio and crack and those who knows."

"You talkin' payola or poetry?"

"I'm talking incentives. You play, you pay. Everyone's got a price, no one ever gets caught. Hell, what's it matter some record gets played just 'cause some radio jock's all strung out and lookin' for a fix? That's just the way it goes, right? Someone hears a rumor about someone who heard a rumor, and before you know it the fed pinstripe geeks start pokin' their noses in, shake everybody down, and in the end can't find any evidence to support a damn thing. The IRS dances a little jig, then everybody goes away for another five years."

Tedesco leaned forward, squinted at the clock on the VCR. He picked up a remote control from the coffee table and zapped the TV. Instantly one of his afternoon soaps flickered on the screen, and Logan knew it was time to go. He slowly rose from the couch and stretched his muscles. His neck still ached and his head had been throbbing intermittently all day.

"Look, Chick. Suppose you keep an ear open for me, huh? You hear something, you give me a call?"

Chick looked at him expectantly, his hand eager for a little green padding before committing.

Logan read the look and scowled. "Hey, pal, this one's private. No cops, no slush. Let's just say I owe you one."

The disappointment was scored deep in the wrinkles on Chick's face, but he shrugged it off. "Sure, man," he agreed, but the sport clearly was taken out of the game. "I'll call you."

Logan wrote his number on a slip of paper and handed it over. "Any time, night or day. Ask for my room."

"Bay View Inn," Chick read from the scrap, then tossed it on the coffee table. He watched it flutter onto the surface, then smiled at Logan. "Movin' up in the world, huh?"

A long, cool swim in the pool. A quick stop at Carl's Jr. to stave off the hunger. A top-down, moonlit drive through the canyon to the Valley.

The house at 3812 Oakfield Drive was literally life on the edge, that special kind of L.A. house that was cantilevered out over a steep precipice in a direct taunt to the San Andreas fault. McNulty's abode was connected to solid ground only where a strip of concrete had been poured along a fragile lip of fragile canyon shale, and supported in the rear only by three long stilts supposedly anchored firmly in bedrock. Oakfield was a graded dirt track that seemed carved out of the uphill side of a tree-filled ravine.

McNulty's residence must have had a splendid view of Sherman Oaks and the rest of the San Fernando Valley. As Logan pulled up into the scant dooryard he spotted the red Mercedes wedged into the undersized garage. Parked directly behind it was Leslie Novak's yellow BMW. A light was on in what must have been the kitchen. Inside he noticed a shadow moving past the frosted window, pouring something from a bottle. Another shadow moved into view, became one with the other, then disappeared from view.

Logan sat there for a moment, engine idling, imagination racing. Then he stepped on the gas and spun gravel as he hooked around a sharp S-turn.

He glanced at his watch for the tenth time in as many minutes. Quarter after nine. Jenny Baxter had said to meet her at Rive Gauche in Sherman Oaks at seven-thirty, and it was coming up on two hours past that now. No way he could have missed her—he'd kept one eye on the door all night and the other on the procession of glasses that quickly came and went. Even after his six Dewar's, his vision was pretty clear. Or so he thought. He even tried calling Corie Chapin at Rhapsody Records, but she'd cut out early and gone home. Understandable, with the memorial service and all.

He sucked another melting ice cube into his mouth and started to crunch it, debating whether he should start in on another Scotch or forget Jenny and bag it for the night. The happy-hour crowd had thinned out long ago, and only a few diehards remained at the bar. The bartender, a classic olive-skinned beauty very much in love with her own striking presence, shared girl talk with the lone remaining waitress. Both of them actresses, probably, each trying to convince themselves they were practicing their craft every night as they worked the crowd and played with men's hearts. The town was full of such desperate hopefuls, actors every one of them whose dreams faded quicker than their summer tans.

His glass was empty, which to Logan created a mental tug-of-war. Go or stay? Drink, drank, drunk. Pour or poor? Eventually the waitress glanced up from her engrossing conversation to see how he was doing, the poor guy sitting alone in his corner, stood up by his date, drowning his sorrows and killing the pain. She and Logan had shared a little chatter five times during the evening, each time as she brought him a refill. But they had nothing real to talk about, no connection beyond simple barroom prattle.

He signaled for the check. Time to go. He'd catch up with Jenny tomorrow, find out where the hell she was and what the hell was so important that he had to wait two hours just to face rejection, for the second time now. Now that he knew her name she'd have to face facts. Or, in this case, fantasy.

Logan rose on wobbly legs and grabbed his coat from the back of the empty chair across from him. Right now all he wanted was a designated driver and a handful of aspirin and his bed. And Molly's gentle nuzzling beside him as he tried to ward off the nightmares that roiled so clearly in the darkness.

16

Logan's brain felt as if someone had driven a sharp spike into it. His skull felt like cork, and his scalp seemed ready to peel from his forehead in shreds. His stomach was empty and queasy, like a lump of Styrofoam soaked with Sterno. His eyes stung, and his tongue tasted as if a dog had urinated on it.

Steam rose from his first cup of black coffee as he scanned the front section of the *Times* he'd picked up down on the corner. He skimmed the headlines, his sodden brain soaking up the latest skirmishes in the Middle East, fanatical bombing in London, the latest aborted skyjacking.

Time was, he couldn't even bring himself to buy a paper, much less read one. He couldn't watch the news on TV, couldn't listen to it on the radio. That had been right after Molly's death; he'd made the mistake of browsing through the newspaper the morning after her murder, finding the picture right there in black-and-white on page three. Two uniformed cops hovering over a body covered by a blanket, her lifeless form twisted across the front steps where she had fallen. Logan had felt like his insides had just been kicked. And he'd felt embarrassed for her; death was the most naked part of life, and there she was for everyone to gape at. A 130-dot screen of her passing.

But this morning there was no photograph, only the headline on the third page of the Metro section. As Logan turned the page the familiar wave of nausea rushed through him again, brought on by that instant of horror and denial and sickness and disbelief that somehow connects, even before the hard facts had time to travel the circuit to his brain.

And then he read the story:

WOMAN KILLED IN MULHOLLAND PLUNGE

A Studio City woman was killed shortly after nine P.M. last night when the car she was driving went out of control and plunged down an embankment in the hills above Sherman Oaks.

The California Highway Patrol says the driver of the car, Jennifer Baxter, was apparently traveling up Nicada at a high rate of speed when she failed to stop at Mulholland Drive. Her car rolled 200 feet down an embankment, coming to rest just ten yards from the rear of a hillside residence.

Paramedics pronounced her dead on the scene.

A shiver rattled up his spine. He saw Molly's death all over again. He heard Molly's voice on the phone the afternoon she died, telling him she'd be home early and would take something out of the freezer for dinner, so don't pick anything up. See you when you get home. Love you. Bye.

And he saw Jenny Baxter as he last saw her, just yesterday afternoon. He saw the worry on her face, remembered the nervous tremble in her voice as she suggested they meet for a drink. And he saw her as she was four nights ago, sitting on a bar stool next to him, her hand on his thigh, the candle-light playing off the walls and her perfect body. And he saw her as they walked in silence back to his place, the moonlight glistening in her auburn hair. Wondering what could have been, what actually might have been.

And suddenly he felt very guilty. His mind was wandering the path of sexual fantasy about a woman who now was dead. After Molly had died he couldn't allow himself to fantasize about her; he'd pushed that part of her from his mind. There was something grossly wrong about that, even sick. And now the same was true of Jenny Baxter.

He forced himself to read through the rest of the story. Authorities believed Jenny had been drinking, which unnamed sources said "may have contributed to the accident." Evidence found at the scene suggested she came speeding up the hill toward Mulholland, trying to turn either right or left. Instead she lost control and sailed over the ridge. Her skull was fractured and her spine had snapped in two places. Her body was badly bruised.

And she was survived by her husband, James.

Husband? Jesus Christ, the lady was married? He felt his stomach churn, bile rise up in his throat. What the hell was going on here? Who the hell was this Jenny Baxter, and what game had she been playing? She'd played with Logan's heart, she played with Neil Novak's and Lynn Sutton's lives, and now she'd played with her own.

Logan didn't even hear the phone until the sixth or seventh burp. Then, as if on time delay, he absently reached over and picked it up.

"Yeah," he said with detached simplicity.

"Stuart." It was Jeffrey Rhodes, his voice drawn and weary. "You seen this morning's paper? Page three of Metro—?"

"Looking at it right now."

Rhodes hesitated, maybe trying to get a fix on Logan's

mental state. "You think that's your girl? . . . Your red-head?"

"Who?" Logan said as he sipped his coffee.

"C'mon, Stu. This is getting mean. Buy you a hot dog? Winkie's, twelve o'clock?"

Logan agreed and hung up.

Married.

He concentrated his energy on a little core in the center of his throbbing brain and hauled himself out of the sinkhole of despair. Jenny Baxter. He felt a heavy rush in his veins. He felt his bones growing heavy and unable to move, as if he were burdened by a lead vest. His eyes roamed the ceiling, his brain blank but racing, mental shots ricocheting off each other, synapses clogged with pent-up charges of grief and sorrow and guilt.

He dialed Corie Chapin and, after being transferred around the building a half dozen times, she finally came on the line. Her voice was leaden and thin and tired, as if she'd been up a good part of the night.

"Corie . . . this is Stuart Logan."

"You . . . bastard—!" Her voice broke off with a sudden sniff.

Logan paused a beat, softened his tone. "Please . . . don't hang up. If there's anything I can do . . ."

"You've already done enough."

"I know how you feel. Believe me. Jenny and I—"

"She told me."

Logan hesitated. What did she tell Corie? How much do women speak of such things? "Did she tell you that half the cops in L.A. county were looking for her?"

"Jenny had her problems."

"Damned straight."

Corie said nothing. He heard her inhale, maybe dab a tissue to her eyes. She was trying to come across stoic and hard, typical of the denial stage of sudden violent death. The shock of unexplained loss was an acid eating away at her. Jenny Baxter was dead and a pit was forming, but the full reality probably wouldn't hit for hours, days. Maybe even weeks. "Now, if you don't mind—"

"Just one thing."

"No. Not now."

"Corie, listen." He took a deep breath, glanced again at the picture of the crumpled car. "She was on her way to see me when she was killed."

Another beat. Then: "And the guilt . . . is killing *you.*"

She was right; the guilt was having its run. But that was something he could deal with later, something he was used to dealing with. Guilt was a solitary board game to keep the mind occupied when too much infected it. He started to say something, maybe to plead once more, but that's when the phone slammed down hard, and all he could hear was a dull buzz in his ear.

Winkie's was an L.A. landmark on Olympic Boulevard between La Cienega and La Brea, a legendary eatery serving 242 varieties of hot dogs and grease to a loyal and varied clientele. Three-piece suits could be found next to ragged denim, silk jumpsuits next to spandex leggings. Among this varietal crowd of tube-steak worshippers Logan spotted Jeffrey Rhodes. The detective was sitting on a low cinder-block retaining wall cautiously devouring a concoction of chili, cheese, sauerkraut, and jalapeños. Logan paid for his own blend of sauerkraut and horseradish and somberly joined his once and former informer.

"Sloppy little devils," he noted as he leaned up against the wall and watched a blob of mustard splat on the pavement.

"Looks like the sorry son of a bitch we pulled out of the gutter last night," Rhodes commented wryly. "Chicken hawk sat on a bottle."

"Please." Logan choked. "Not today."

"Sorry. Hazard of the trade. You know how it is." Rhodes shoveled a mammoth bite into his mouth and wiped his lips. They chewed a few bites in silence before Logan broke the solemn spell.

"So . . . accident, you think?"

"You know me, Logan. I don't see anything as an accident, not unless everything points that way. But this one's not up to me."

"Meaning?"

"Who knows what it means." Rhodes flexed his shoulders in an official shrug. "Jenny Baxter's only been dead a few hours, and no one's saying boo. Official word is they're checking it out."

"Bullshit." Logan started to take another bite but suddenly

felt his appetite drain away. "Three people buy the farm within five days, and the cops're 'checking it out'?"

"A lot of people are dead, Logan," Rhodes reminded him. Just a like a cop: always jumping to the defense of his brethren, county or not. "Listen, pal. All interdepartment bullshit aside, the Sheriff's Office has the best solution rate in the county. One of the best in the state. Fact is, there's no evidence to indicate that Jenny Baxter's crash was anything other than an accident."

"Was it an accident?"

"Maybe, maybe not." Rhodes leaned forward, allowing a blob of ketchup to drip on the sidewalk instead of his white trousers. "On the surface it looks like an accident, but Hollyweird's the special-effects capital of the world. She got pretty banged up in the car, and that's pretty convenient. And I don't like convenient, and I don't like neat."

"Neat?"

Rhodes pried the plastic lid from a cup of coffee that by now had grown lukewarm. He swallowed a hearty gulp, then popped the last bite of grease into his mouth.

"The chronology. Girl leaves the office at five, spends four hours getting bombed, alone. No one sees her. She drives home through Beverly Glen, then sails off a cliff."

"I know the place," Logan said with sad distraction. He'd traveled it twice a day when he and Molly moved to Sherman Oaks.

"Then you know there's twists and turns everywhere, you can't do more than forty, forty-five max. She comes up to the top of the hill, turns off on Nicada. Now, you and I know that street's a rush-hour shortcut to Mulholland, heading west. But she wouldn't head west, because she lives in Studio City. She'd head east, then turn left back down Beverly Glen. Okay, maybe a few drivers take Nicada as a shortcut to bypass the rush-hour congestion backed up at the Mulholland light, but that time of night there wouldn't have been any traffic. Fact is, after nine it's pretty quiet. Plenty of opportunity to put her behind the wheel of her car, give it a little push . . ."

Logan nodded slowly, working on the mental image. "Any witnesses? People who saw the car? Maybe heard something?"

"Give 'em time. It's only been—" He looked at his watch. "—fourteen hours."

"What about skid marks?"

"Nothing."

"Even drunks know how to use the brakes."

"Exactly."

"So you think there's a connection? To Novak, I mean?"

Rhodes dabbed his chin with his napkin. "Jenny's death may not have been an accident, but that doesn't mean it was murder. 'If not P' does not necessarily mean 'Q.' That's what the cops'll tell you. And the lawyers. Right now they're going along as if it was just another fatal O.U.I. Pretty girl gets tanked, flies off a hill."

Logan gulped down the rest of his chili dog. He watched as a low-rider Buick Riviera bounced at a red light, then soared through the intersection at the first glimpse of green. Then he said, "She was on her way to see me."

Rhodes' eyes bugged out. "Excuse me?"

"We were supposed to meet last night. Seven-thirty."

"So you finally located her."

Logan nodded. He stared dumbly at his paper plate, then folded it in two. "She was at Novak's service yesterday."

"She was going to talk to you?" Rhodes said with controlled, but still obvious, irritation. "Why not the cops?"

"I found her first."

"And if you'd bothered to tell someone—me, even—she might be alive as we speak."

Logan considered this as his gaze focused somewhere between Winkie's plaster-and-neon sign and a Winchell's donut shop. Then he shook his head. "If someone wanted her dead, they'd get her that way sooner or later."

Rhodes raised his brow and shrugged. They both knew there was no point in talking about what-ifs. He slowly sipped his now-cold coffee, stared off at the waltz of cars and trucks and buses grinding by on the street, plumes of blue smoke rising up into the gray ozone. Finally he turned to Logan, leaned forward, lowered his voice.

"There *is* something—"

Logan cocked his head in interest.

"And I'm laying my ass on the line with this," Rhodes added quickly, shaking his head briskly.

"Spill."

Rhodes filled his lungs with smog, then exhaled. "They found a piece of iron in her car."

"A gun?"

"Thirty-eight-caliber," Rhodes whispered. He took another sip, grimaced at the mouthful of grounds he swallowed, and emptied the cup over the cinder-block wall. "Ballistics is checking it out, but it looks like it might be the piece that killed Neil Novak and the Sutton woman."

"Any evidence linking it to Jenny?"

Rhodes rose from his perch on the wall. He wadded his napkin into a tight ball and chucked it at the trash can: two points. Then he turned toward Logan as a flicker of doubt creased his face. "You mean aside from it being found in her car? Yeah, there's evidence. Her prints are all over the damn thing."

"You think she did it?"

"Look, Logan. I think your redhead either plugged Novak and the Sutton woman, or she knows . . . knew . . . who did." Rhodes ran a hand through his hair and adjusted the collar of his light-blue jacket. "They're running a check on the gun as we speak. If it turns up registered to Jenny Baxter, or her husband—"

"James?"

"James." Rhodes nodded tiredly. "If it belongs to either one of 'em, this case is sealed tight."

"And if it doesn't?"

"Sorry . . . gotta fly," Rhodes shrugged. He slapped Logan on the back, as if trying to dislodge a glob of frankfurter. Then he shoved his hands in his pockets and jaywalked across Olympic to his easily recognized unmarked sedan. A set of bubble lights on top couldn't have made it any more conspicuous. Logan watched the car pull away from the curb into the continuous flow of traffic, hanging a left at the next light.

17

An angry sun beat down on the L.A. basin, and seemed to suck out whatever life had somehow evaded the stifling heat. The lack of an offshore wind held the hydrocarbons within the rim formed by the mountains and cooked the Southland like a pot of polluted stew.

Logan pulled into a self-serve Arco station on La Cienega and parked the Plymouth alongside a cinder-block wall around back, next to a pay phone. Lacking a phone book, he first tracked down Jenny Baxter's number in Studio City, a number she shared with her husband James. The operator patched him through to an electronic voice that read off the correct sequence, which he scribbled on the back of a year-old Visa invoice. Then he called back to verify the Baxters' address, giving the operator an incorrect street number on Laurel Canyon Boulevard. She corrected him, and he scribbled "12340 Valleyheart Drive" below the phone number.

Next he tried the same thing for Kyndall Wyatt, but with no luck. After badgering an increasingly annoyed operator for close to two minutes, checking every Pac Bell sector and neighborhood, he concluded the girl just didn't have a phone. Either that, or she shared some flop pad ... maybe splitting the tab with a bunch of girls who conducted business from a pay box down on the corner.

His third call was long-distance, twenty-six miles out to Catalina. He checked his watch while he counted the rings: five, six, seven ...

The ringing stopped after the twelfth ring, and a gruff, flustered voice answered. "Teskey here ..."

"George ... Logan here."

"Logan. Where the fuck are you? Jack Woods was in here the other day, Monday I think it was, looking for you. I don't have time to be no answering service for my piano players."

"George ... hold onto your pants." Logan wiped the grit from his eyes and shifted the phone to his other ear. "I'm in L.A. And I'm gonna be here for a few more days. That's why I'm calling."

"L.A.? For chrissakes, Logan, you're playing tonight."

"You're gonna have to find a stand-in."

"What the hell you tellin' me, you bailin' out on me?"

"Just for the weekend, pal," Logan said apologetically. He spent the next five minutes explaining his way out of his weekend obligation, until George finally caved in and wished the curse of Coronado on him, or something like that. When Logan finally hung up he felt wrung dry, except his forehead and shirt were soaked from the sun and nerves. He pocketed the Visa bill and the rest of the change, and returned to his car.

The 12300 block of Valleyheart Drive was a neighborhood in transition, houses on one street facing new condo complexes on the other, backing up against the L.A. River. To call it a river was to crack a joke; long ago it had been paved on the sides and bottom to direct the winter floods where the army engineers wanted it to flow, diverting it from the streets and backyards and an occasional orange grove that so far had eluded the developers. During the building spurt of the mid-eighties much of the R-1 real estate between Fulton and Laurel Canyon had been rezoned to R-4, and suddenly a flock of multiunit dwellings had popped up where traditional L.A. tract houses had stood.

The mailboxes at the front of 12340 Valleyheart said that the Baxters lived in unit 12, which was located around back overlooking the dry wash. The builders had omitted any locked gate or fence as a safety feature for the complex, probably because they considered the area safe from murderers and burglars. Ignorance is bliss, Logan thought grimly as he entered the inner courtyard. He wandered along the bricked path to the back of the development, counting numbers as he went.

He stopped for a moment outside number 12, finding himself on the uncivil side of curiosity. Just as reporters had tried to grab a minute with him right after Molly had died, and he'd felt repulsed by the circling vultures of the media, now here he was in virtually the same role. He swallowed his pride, stepped up to the door, and knocked.

On the other side of the door he heard a sound, like something being dropped heavily on the floor. Then he heard a loud curse, followed by a few more loud thuds: footsteps approaching the door. Then the door swung inward, and Logan found himself staring into the dark, suspicious eyes of the grieving, of not somewhat cuckolded, husband of the late Jenny Baxter. He was tall and thin, with a wispy black mustache seemingly pasted to his upper lip. He was dressed in an Izod shirt with a blue crocodile on the left breast, and a pair of tight Levi's 501s. A gold hoop pinched a hole in his left ear. His face was red, his eyes redder. Logan recognized the signs of grief and sympathized with him.

"Yeah?" he growled.

"Mr. Baxter," Logan said, feeling almost parasitic in a situation that he once would have considered standard reportorial procedure. "I'm Stuart Logan. I knew your wife."

"I'm sure you did, Mr. ... Mr. Logan. Now get the hell out."

"I know how this must seem, sir—"

"You deaf or something? I said get the *hell* out!"

"If I could just have a word—"

But evidently words were not what Mr. Baxter had in mind. The swinging door sharply interrupted Logan's pleas as it crashed against the jamb three inches from Logan's face. The sudden force of the blast sent a shock wave of wind into his face.

On the way back to Santa Monica Logan considered what Jeff Rhodes had told him, that the cops were leaning toward the execution theory. Logical and convenient, typical of the modern course of law-enforcement cleanliness. It explained a lot of things: the bullet through the brain, the stealth in the middle of the night, Novak's connections to the underworld, and a great opportunity to pin two 187s—three, counting Jenny—on the Carbone crime family. If motive and opportunity could be found to fit the crime, maybe the whole thing could be tied up in a nice, neat bundle.

Maybe. The Carbones were the prime target of whatever fed investigation was going on, and Logan wasn't ready to cross the family off his shortlist. He also didn't rule out the connection with Frank Kennedy or Roger McNulty, with or without the Eastern syndicate's blessings. Maybe Novak had indirect knowledge of Frank Kennedy's promotion tactics—drugs and sex in exchange for radio airplay—but had looked the other way until the feds moved in. Maybe Leo Gold was feeding the Carbones a continuous supply of counterfeit records and CDs, and Novak stumbled upon the deal. Then again, maybe one of the Carbones had approached Novak with a laundering scheme that Novak found unacceptable or excessive. Whatever the case, if Novak had known enough to throw the whole organized crowd behind a lifetime of bars, his reward may have been his own death.

Logan couldn't rule out Leslie Novak, either. The poor, grieving widow stood to inherit a major portion of her late husband's holdings. In addition to Jenny's death, the morning paper had noted the just-released dispensation of Neil Novak's estate, and most of it went to Mrs. Novak. The trimmings of Leslie's life were lavish and plentiful, but she had to share them with a boor of a husband, a philanderer who had drifted off course since their marriage fifteen years ago. A divorce would have been messy and drawn-out, and only half as profitable as a quick tragedy in a common-property state like California.

Enter Roger McNulty. Logan's brief run-in with this snap-shot of L.A. slime left no doubt that he could have mastermined the whole sordid mess. No telling what sort of motivation would have induced the glorified pimp and pusher to rub out a trusted and respected customer.

When Logan arrived back at the room he set up a make-shift office out on the balcony, facing the sun and the waves and the sand. He grabbed a Bud from the fridge, then reclined in his chair and propped his feet up on the deck rail. He popped the beer, took a long swig, then balanced the yellow legal pad in his lap. From memory he redrew the diagram that had been pilfered two nights ago, mentally drawing lines from Lynn Sutton to the other names on the page. Too bad he couldn't have a word or two with old Lynn. The woman had been around the block a few times but, like a kid running away from home, hadn't traveled far. The last person she had talked with was Novak, and *that* hadn't gotten either of them anywhere. If only he could find her niece, Kyndall. Undoubt-edly the girl's name was listed in her aunt's address book, which Lynn undoubtedly kept. Working girls like Lynn always kept phone books; it was their link to business. And somewhere in that book, which now was somewhere deep within the halls of the L.A. legal juggernaut, was Kyndall's phone number and address.

And then Logan remembered: in all the chaos following Jenny's death, he had forgotten about the ebony address case he'd lifted from Neil Novak's office. He'd slipped it into his pocket when he heard Corie Chapin returning to her desk, and eventually dumped it in his glove box when he got back to his car.

He grabbed his keys from the dresser inside and dashed downstairs to the car. The baked aggregate patio scorched his feet as he danced from one cool spot to the next, both coming and going. On the way back he dipped them quickly in the pool to ease the potential blisters, then returned to his perch on the balcony.

He flipped through the address case, turning first to the "W" heading, looking for Kyndall Wyatt. Aside from a few business associates he found nothing. Next he perused the "S" entries: Sachet, Sardi's, Sawyer, Sidon, Schaumberg, Siestas, Sonnet . . . but not Sutton. Strange: Neil and Lynn were . . . what were they? Close friends, at least close acquaintances. They'd even died together. But she was not listed in the file. Maybe Novak's book was strictly business; if so, Logan still suspected he'd find Lynn Sutton entered somewhere. He rifled through the "S" entry again, and was ready to give up when this time the listing jumped out at him.

Sachet Social Club.

Sachet: Langston Post had described it as an upscale outcall escort service.

The phone number was a windfall, but even more vital were the names hastily scrawled below it. Names of Neil's four favorite girls, each accompanied by a star rating system. The name "Lynn" was penciled off to one side, with a separate phone number.

The first of the four entries was Penny Macklin, who earned a dubious three-star distinction. Heather Geer also earned three stars, with the notation "straight, Norma Jean, no act." Diedre Buck was four-star material, tagged with "accurate last name." He wondered about that one for a moment, then drew his eyes down to the last entry.

Kyndall Wyatt, five stars. "Lay of the land." Lynn Sutton's sweet little niece.

He looked at the top of the card for the number, then picked up the phone.

Six rings later he was greeted by a young voice, sweet and sexy. "Sachet Social Club," she said.

Logan hesitated a second as instinct took over. Then he began: "Yes, I'm calling ... on a recommendation. I'm from
... out of town ..."

"Of course," the sweet thing purred. "And your referral?"

"My ... what?"

"Your referral. We only take new clients who are referred
by established customers."

Logan paused for a moment, for effect. "Neil Novak."

A gasp, then a short silence followed. Then the voice
spoke hesitantly. "Mr. Novak is ... well ... he's ... no
longer with us."

Logan wondered if the Sachet Social Club missed the man
more as a fine customer than as a human being.

"I know. I'm in town from New York for his service. I
thought it would be fitting ..."

"I understand," the sweet voice cooed. "*Your* name,
please?"

"Ted Duncan," he said, quickly recalling Molly's brother's
name. What the insurance agent didn't know couldn't hurt
him.

She accepted this, then asked if he was aware of the policies of the Sachet Social Club. Two hundred dollars an hour,
one hour minimum. Tipping was permitted and encouraged.
The club employed high-class escorts, and that's just what
they were: escorts. If something else developed, something
extracurricular and personal, that was strictly between the cli-
ent and the employee. Did he have a preference? Tall, short,
thin, full-figured? Brunette, blonde, Afro, strawberry? Bald?

"Kyndall Wyatt," he said flatly. "Neil's recommendation."

"Of course." There was a long pause, which Logan
guessed was spent checking on the availability of Novak's
five-star favorite. Then the girl was back on the line, with a
question he hadn't been expecting: "Where are you staying,
Mr. Duncan?"

An unexpected twist. He hesitated briefly. A close associate of Neil Novak would hardly have a room at the Bay View
Inn in Santa Monica, but one night at a respectable hotel
would run him about the same as he was paying for a week
in this dive.

"Century Plaza," he said simply, still not sure he wasn't
throwing good money after bad.

"Very well, Mr. Duncan. We'll contact you there for final
arrangements. Thank you for calling Sachet. And just in case

Mr. Novak didn't tell you—rest his soul—we accept all plastic."

She hung up, leaving Logan to wonder what the hell he was getting himself into. No less than two hundred bucks an hour for a call girl, one-fifty for a room.

He called the Century Plaza and booked himself an executive queen for the night.

Two minutes later the phone rang. He looked at the receiver suspiciously; who the hell knew he was here? Jeff Rhodes, Langston Post, Chick Tedesco. He waited four rings before he decided to answer it.

"Hello."

"Yeah, Logan. What the hell's your butt doing over there?"

Logan recognized the voice: Deputy Woods. "What of it?"

"Seems you left town pretty quick. Didn't even drop in to say a proper good-bye."

"Sorry. I didn't know you were running Catalina as a penal colony," Logan quipped. He cocked his head toward the sun, lest this phone call be a total waste of the afternoon.

"Yeah, well," Woods grumbled. "Still shoulda let me know."

"So I'm telling you now." Logan wiped his forehead with his arm, then shifted the phone to the other ear. "Look, Woods. I'm not as sharp as you are. I need things spelled out in plain English, okay? What gives?"

"What gives is this," Woods started, hesitating as he collected his thoughts. "Last Saturday night, early Sunday morning, a man and a woman are killed on their boat. Around the same time a mysterious redhead is seen leaving the scene of the crime, and she disappears. Then witnesses say the same redhead was seen earlier in the evening with the piano player at the Albacore Lounge—"

"We've been through all this," Logan interrupted.

"And now a redhead is found dead at the bottom of a cliff, right after that very same piano player sails over to L.A."

Logan sighed deeply and rolled his eyes at the beige sky. The palm trees seemed to droop like dead umbrellas. "Okay, Woods. You found me out," he said with obvious sarcasm in his voice.

"This is not a joke, Logan."

"Look . . . anyone wants me, they know right where I am," Logan growled. "They know where I am because you'll tell 'em, I'm sure. But if you're not gonna shit, then why don't you get off the pot and leave me alone?"

He slammed the phone down, briefly wondering how the hell Woods had trailed him to the Bay View Inn. His wonderings were cut short by the sharp shrill of the phone. Logan snapped it off the hook and barked into the receiver.

"Listen, Woods. Fuck off. I got better things to do."

He started to hang up when he heard a voice, deep and resonant, yet softer and more hesitant than Woods.

"Uh ... is this ... Stuart Logan?"

Logan looked at the receiver, then pressed it back to his ear. "Yeah. Who's this?"

"Good," the man said, ignoring Logan's question. He hesitated, anxiety written into the beat. "I've been trying to reach you all day. I wanna talk to you."

"I'm listening," Logan said, his boredom quickly fading. He sat up, propped his shades on the top of his head.

"Not on the phone. In person."

"What's this about?" Logan inquired.

"No tape recorders, no pix, no notes," the man said, again ignoring Logan's question.

Too many people watched too much cloak-and-dagger television. "You got it. When and where?"

"Carousel, the pier. In an hour."

Logan started to object, but the voice was gone. The pier, in an hour. No more than a good ten-minute walk from where he now sat. He glanced up at the sun; at least he could get a few good moments of peak time before he trudged up the boulevard for whatever clandestine rendezvous this nameless voice had in mind.

He retreated inside, grabbed a towel, and trekked down the back stairs for a quick dip in the pool.

18

The throng of Santa Monica perpetuals shuffled along the dusty, hot drive leading out to the pier. Joggers, skateboarders, tourists, lovers, an occasional car looking for a nonexistent parking spot—all crowded the roadway. Sea gulls wheeled overhead, eyeing the die-hard fishermen with their buckets of fresh bait. Drifters in torn denim and worn leather eyed the girls in ass-hugging bikinis and filmy skirts wriggling along the beach.

The pier had been rebuilt completely since the great storm of '82, when it had been decimated by the pounding sea. Timbers, planks, stone seawalls gave way to the tremendous force of nature, and in the course of this anger much of the old landmark pier disappeared. Now the structure was back, with the same old gift shops and seafood stands and other honky-tonk delights cluttering the pier while fishermen and ocean gazers straddled the railing and peered out at the phantom sea.

Logan approached the reconstructed carousel and stood in the doorway, gazing inside. The horses were painted in muted hues, bittersweet-coral and grayish-blue and forest-green. They pumped up and down with an almost sexual rhythm, prancing in a circle to the accompaniment of the haunting strains of the calliope. Logan stared through the blurring action at a tall, muscular man standing opposite him along the far wall. The man was dressed in black jeans and an orange T-shirt, and was staring out at the beach. But as Logan approached he sensed the man was watching him in the glass.

Logan slowly wandered around he cacophonous merry-go-round and slowly drifted up behind the man, who turned at the last minute and faced him.

"Logan?" The voice was low and drawn, and sounded ravaged by various substances, alcoholic and otherwise.

Logan nodded, offering a hand that went ignored.

"We'll walk," the man said.

He led Logan outside and began strolling, casually, out toward the end of the pier. He was a big man, over six feet, with broad shoulders and thick arms straining his sleeves. The front of his T-shirt read IN CASE OF RAPE, I'VE GOT AIDS. His face was masked by a wild beard, his forehead scarred by a large, triangular continent that hinted of some childhood catastrophe. Car accident or burn, maybe. His skin was coarse and rugged, making him look older than he probably was, with telltale signs of excess abuse. His eyes had the same telltale red rivulets.

Their casual steps took them past a man studying a paper on a bench. Scarface checked over his shoulder for any undesired company. Logan wondered if all this secrecy was really necessary.

"You're poking into this Neil Novak thing?" the man finally said, more a statement than a question. A kid on a skateboard weaved past them, tauntingly close.

"I'm interested in his friends," Logan acknowledged with a nod. "Kennedy and McNulty and the Carbones."

"Interesting bunch. Never know when one's gonna turn up."

"That why you keep one eye in the back of your head?"

The man shrugged, not without a sign of fear. "Some folks don't like other folks talking to nosy reporters."

"I'm an ex-reporter," Logan explained matter-of-factly. "How'd you get my name and number, anyway?"

"Wild horses couldn't drag it out of me," the man said with a slight grin. "But I do have a low threshold for pain."

"I don't suppose you're going to tell me your name, either?"

"Not important." The man looked toward the sea as they walked, then leaned on the rusted railing and took a deep breath of salt air. "I know these guys. Know 'em real well, Kennedy especially. We worked together, ten, twelve years back. I was in radio at the time, back East. Trying to work my way out here."

"Looks like you made it."

"I paid the price," the man said, a resigned note in his voice. A voice that at one time probably sounded good on the air.

"Everyone's got his price," Logan observed wryly.

"So they say."

"And you?"

Scarface stopped to gaze down at a covey of near-naked nymphets naughtily splayed out on blankets. He undressed what little there was to undress with his eyes, then looked back at Logan. "Yeah, I had my price," he finally admitted.

"Which was?" Logan pressed.

"At the end? Five hundred, cash. Once a week."

They started walking again, casually strolling through the nauseating blend of asphalt and fish and chips drifting out from the Surf and Sand pub.

"Nice arrangement," Logan said, his mind working on the calculation. "Comes to—"

"Twenty-six grand a year, more or less. Plus perks." He shoved his hands in his pockets, but his shoulders remained tense. "I was living in Baltimore, playing music director at some shitbag station, picking the records we were going to add and drop each week. Every Monday the promoters would start calling, pushing this record or that record. Sometimes two or three. Most of these records were real turkeys, but out of twenty, twenty-five, one or two might be hot."

"And Kennedy fits in how?"

"He was the worst of the bunch. He knew he was sitting on stiffs, but didn't give a shit as long as they got played. They made their nut on quantity, not quality. The more records they got on the charts, the more they'd get paid. It was worth it, whatever the price."

"And everyone has their price."

The man nodded. "Exactly." They walked the pier in silence for a moment. The dull roar of surf slurped past the pilings while the persistent sea gulls screeched overhead.

"And when you moved out here?"

"I got in over my head. I bought a Porsche 911, bought a condo down in the marina, took off for Vegas every other weekend. So I get this offer, ten crisp Franklins a week, enough fresh powder to keep the lift lines operating all year."

Their pace slowed, and Logan turned to face him as they passed a couple of fisherman futilely casting their lines out to sea and reeling them in.

"I'd gotten into Kennedy so deep I thought I'd never get out. Drugs, gambling, broads. I owed the fuckers over a hundred grand. And they started to make noises about collectin'. I tell you, I was up to my ass in slime. Worked my way in real deep, felt like a fag who suddenly wakes up, realizes what he's doing. So I kicked it. And I talked. To the grand jury."

"Took a lot of balls." Logan recalled his conversation with Cal Mitchell.

Scarface shook his head, as if he was still trying to figure it out. "Lack of brains. Christ, I was so burned out I couldn't even get my pecker up. Days were nights and nights were days. These guys said jump, I was already high."

"So what happened?"

He thought this one over long and hard before answering. "My old lady left me. Then I lost the house and the car, and somewhere in there I lost my self-respect. And now I'm beginning to sound like some self-pitying public-service TV commercial. So I chucked it all and checked myself into the hospital."

Logan knew all about self-pitying and chucking it all and making a mad dash for the fringes. "What did Kennedy do when he found out?" he asked.

"You mean when I squealed?" The man pulled back his hair to expose the red smear on his forehead, a rounded triangle. "They ironed my face."

"Jesus!"

"Actually, I was lucky. They gave me a choice: the Gorbachev make-over or the old eunuch surprise."

Logan winced; these fuckers played hardball, all right. "And Neil Novak fits into all this?"

"Novak and Kennedy were like flies on shit. Neil paid big bucks, Kennedy got the records played. And Neil didn't care what Kennedy did as long as the records climbed up the charts."

They had arrived at the end of the pier, among the fly-casters who stood out here all day, vainly trying to reel anything but sludge up from the depths of Santa Monica Bay. If there were any fish in these waters, and Logan saw no such evidence, no one would dare fry one up for dinner.

"And the Carbones?"

"They set Kennedy up in business, still get a percentage. Plus they got a great avenue for coke and pussy."

"I thought that was McNulty's bag."

"It is. But they get their cut."

"So many sticky fingers—"

"There's more where that comes from. Way I hear it, Novak discovered they were ripping him off. Kennedy and

Carbone. Neil wasn't exactly the king of scruples himself, and he'd fucked over enough guys in his day. But when someone did it to old Neil, the man didn't turn the other cheek. Story is, he caught 'em red-handed in some sort of bootleg deal."

Scarface turned his face into the wind, breathed deep, then elaborated. He recounted how he'd heard that someone working for the Carbone organization sneaked out the master tape and artwork for the last Billy Keenan album. Rhapsody Records was slated to ship three million CDs and two million cassette tapes, and a few hundred thousand extra units on the market would hardly be noticed.

"Had to be someone on the inside." He shrugged. "Word is, Novak got wind of it and set up a trap."

A gentle wind wheezed in from the west. Points of sail cut across the horizon, headed back for the marina before the sun settled in for the evening and the lingering breeze faded. They stood at the end rail for a moment, then turned and began working their way back. Again, Scarface scanned the pier for familiar faces as they walked.

"This counterfeiting deal," Logan said. "How'd it work?"

"All I know is what I hear," the man breathed. His gaze fell on an old man sitting on the wooden curb spending an inordinate amount of time perusing the *Daily Racing Form.*

"And what do you hear?" Logan pressed.

"Nickel-and-dime stuff, mostly. Cutouts: you know, the remainders sent back from record stores. The corners are drilled or sliced to identify them as returns, and they're sold in the cut-rate bins. But if someone takes these records, presses a few thousand extras, packages 'em in identical album covers, and ships 'em out, who's to know? No accounting, no inventory, no taxes."

"Perfect setup."

"Almost. But the greed factor always takes over."

Logan nodded slowly; the man was right. Greed multiplied geometrically, if not logarithmically. He'd seen it so many times before, a two-bit delinquent lifting car radios for a lark, then graduating to grand theft auto and armed robbery. Just a case of believing your own P.R., becoming a legend in your own mind.

"These guys figured they could make more from new product than from cutouts," Logan's snitch continued. "All they needed was a copy of the master tape, a few hours to re-pro the artwork, then maybe press a couple hundred thousand discs. With Rhapsody's own distribution network already intact, the whole scam was tit. The only true way to account for sales was by counting returns. Bogeys are impossible to track 'cause they're pressed from the same master and have the same artwork. Only way to know for sure is when the record's a bomb. If a label gets back more units than it pressed, they know something's up. Even a moron knows two plus two doesn't equal five."

"Got any ideas who the insider was?" Logan wanted to know.

"What I hear it was Leo Gold. He's a producer."

"I know the man. Sonnet Sound." Logan ran a hand through his windblown hair. The salt air made his scalp itch. "Gold had access to the master tapes?"

"Access? Hell, they're practically his. He produced most of Rhapsody's top acts—Billy Keenan, Pyret Chip, Rienna King. Had access to everything, completely above suspicion."

Suddenly a quartet of kids on skateboards was headed directly toward them, full speed ahead. Scarface stopped in his tracks, holding firm ground. Logan did the same. As the skateboarders came closer they split down the middle, two heading off around to the left, two to the right. Now Logan knew how Moses felt at the Red Sea. As the skateboarders fell back into formation, they cackled maniacally in unison.

"And Novak caught him red-handed?"

"So it goes. Gold was sneaking out of the studio one night with the master tape. Neil ran into him."

A sea gull squawked overhead, dived toward a bucket of bait sitting next to a fisherman who so far was having little luck.

"What'd he do?"

"Kept it quiet. You want my opinion, I think he had Leo by the balls." The man winced, as if remembering the choice that had resulted in the painful red smudge on his forehead. "Leo agreed to play along, set up the next Billy Keenan job—so Carbone and friends would be nailed for good."

"I thought they were all buddies."

"It's not public knowledge, but the Carbones own a big chunk of Rhapsody—and Novak didn't like it one bit. They'd already set the place up as a shipping joint for laundered cash; now Novak found 'em ripping him off on the back end. I think he went to Niki and Luigi and laid it on the line."

"And their reaction?"

"Neil is dead."

The two men ambled along in silence for a few moments. They were nearing the shore end of the pier, and the carousel music blended into the wind.

"So . . . what happens now?" Logan asked at great length.

"For me?" Scarface shrugged. "Seems no one 'round here'll touch spoiled goods. Been offered a gig up in Reno. It's kinda pretty up there, the air is clean. If I can only stay away from the tables." He looked pensive, and Logan wondered if he doubted his own resolve.

"Think they'll leave you alone?"

"Kennedy?" He nodded but seemed unconvinced. "They made their point. But if some real heavy shit starts coming down, it's best I'm not around."

"I wouldn't mind if a lot of shit comes down."

"So I hear."

"From whom?"

"Not important." The man cocked his head, raised his brow. "Just keep your brain up and your pecker down, you'll do okay."

They shook hands in farewell, Logan regarding the man curiously. He still had a lot of questions, but knew he wasn't going to get any more answers. And he wasn't sure what he was going to do with those he already had. As they parted the man made another cautious check of the pier, then disappeared into the shadows of the carousel pavilion. Logan watched as he faded into the shadows: the man living on the edge, gripped by constant paranoia and fear. The long-term dividend of vice and fraud.

19

He put the room on plastic. If Kyndall Wyatt was everything she was cracked up to be, the price was worth it. If not, he could amortize the cost over twelve months through Citibank in New York.

The desk clerk gave him a room on the twelfth floor, facing west. The hour was too late and the night too dark to see the ocean, but the lights of Santa Monica winked at him through the glass sliders leading out to the lofty balcony. A breeze gusted in from the sea, pushing the rancid stagnation further inland.

Logan quickly surveyed the room: king-sized bed, floral spread, matching drapes. Cream-colored carpet, a few stains from high-spirited revelry or wild passionate sex, and a cigarette burn on the French provincial desk. He flipped the TV on, clicked through the channels, watched a couple minutes of CNN, then shut it off again. He checked his watch. Nine-fifty. Kyndall was due at ten. He paced the room, feeling like a young kid preparing for the senior prom.

Kyndall Wyatt appeared promptly at the top of the hour. She tapped softly on the door and waited politely for her paying host to answer. Logan felt a wave of nerves surge through his system as he quickly surveyed the room one last time. Everything looked neat and tidy, as if a ranking Fortune 500 was in residence. He opened the door.

One look at Kyndall was all it took to understand the rationale for her five stars. She was young, no more than twenty, but she exuded a confidence that made her seem much older, more mature. Relaxed and comfortable, yet innocent, still touched by a flagrant naiveté. He sensed this was not a streetwise middle-American-farm-girl act, acquired from years of pain and calluses. This came from within, a cross of genuine self-reliance and natural dependence. A sense of being, one that years of cold professional street wisdom might not crack.

"Miss Wyatt?" he inquired, his voice edged in bedroom lust.

"Call me Kyndall." She smiled as she stepped inside.

She floated into the room and instantly blended into it. Her blonde hair whispered over her shoulders like glowing strands of Rumpelstiltskin's straw. Blue eyes, deep-set and electric, studied her surroundings with practiced grace, as if she were checking for any infinitesimal difference between this and other Century Plaza rooms she may have worked. She wore a black silk skirt embossed with a cobalt-blue paisley pattern, and a thigh-high slit flashed great glimpses of leg and more. The whole ensemble loyally clung to every ample

curve. Her sheer black blouse revealed vast visages of her
soft, full breasts. She looked alluringly, alarmingly at ease as
she turned her beautiful face toward him. Her eyes penetrated
his with genuine warmth; the seduction would come at its
own pace.

"Please ... make yourself completely comfortable while I
call the office and let them know I'm here." She spoke with
authority, as if this were her room and he was the guest. He
felt like he knew her, but couldn't sense just why.

Did 'completely comfortable' mean undressed, he wondered, or just completely comfortable? Fact was, he had no
intention of getting undressed, because the moment she
walked in he knew he wanted to take her in his arms, to have
her be all his, to make long, slow, silky love with her. And
that was out of the question. This was business, his and hers,
and his would be lost as soon as he succumbed to whatever
delicate touches were the tools of hers.

He picked up the bottle of Mumm's he'd bought at
Gelson's and carefully worked the cork from the bottle. Then
he poured two ample glasses and handed one to Kyndall, who
was just finishing her check-up with the home office.

She quietly replaced the phone and faced him, deviously
surprised to find him still clothed.

"To encounters," he toasted, suddenly feeling pretty stupid,
at a complete loss for anything better to say.

"Encounters," Kyndall agreed, and swallowed heavily, with
great need. She seemed to enjoy the champagne's sharp bite,
but her nose seemed set for much more than a little bubbly.
She placed the glass on the night table, breezed closer to the
bed, and kicked off her near-stiletto heels.

"Here ... let me make you feel at home." She stepped
close, her hand lightly brushing across his shoulder. He shuddered.

"Mmmm," he breathed as she ran one hand through his
hair and lightly kissed the top of his head. Her other hand
took his and gently guided it to her breast.

She deftly removed his tie and started to unbutton his shirt.
She ran her hand across his chest, lightly massaging his
shoulders and neck. "You're so tense," she sighed. "Relax."
Her fingers expertly plied his stiff muscles.

"Neil said you were ... attentive," Logan purred, trying to
assemble what was left of his wits.

"Neil?"

"Neil Novak."

She pulled back, hesitated for just the briefest of moments, then slid his shirt off and draped it over the foot of the bed.

"Shhh," she whispered.

"He told me he ... knew you ..." Logan said as she kneaded his knotted shoulders. Had his self-control taken complete flight?

"Who?"

"Neil."

"Oh, I see," she sighed in his ear. "You like hearing that sort of thing. My ... other men." She nibbled his earlobe, then turned his face and touched her lips to his. He tasted her tongue as it darted toward his. She drew her hands down his chest, running her fingers through the wiry hair and then pulling him close. She tried to nudge him backwards on the bed, but he wasn't ready to succumb to her gentle urgings. He could easily see how Novak, how any man, might have fallen, time after time.

"Was it like this?" Logan persisted, fighting nature.

"You're really into that sort of thing, aren't you? Okay then, just lie back and I'll tell you." She gently edged him onto his back and knelt over him. "Better yet, I'll show you."

Her hands traveled to his fly, which she had down in two seconds. She groped inside, deftly started to take him out, but he instinctively jerked back. She sat back on her heels, confused and wary for the first time.

"You have to tell me what you want."

"Neil Novak."

She stiffened and sat back on her knees. Then she looked at him sharply and got off the bed. "Look, Mr. Duncan ... are you a cop? 'Cause if you're a cop, I ain't done nothing. Law says you have to tell me you're a cop if I ask you if you're a cop. So are you?"

"I'm not a cop." He sat up, wearily. "And I'm not going to arrest you." He took a deep breath and collected whatever sane thoughts remained following her amazing, gentle touch. "But my name's not Duncan."

She stared at him dumbly.

"I'm sorry," he apologized. "I ... I had to meet you. You came highly recommended."

"From your friend Neil."

"In a roundabout way."

She stared down at him, then in one abrupt move icily

pushed away from the bed and edged toward the open balcony slider. She collected her purse and shoes. "I think I'd better get outta here, in a 'roundabout way.' "

"No. Please. I'm not a mugger, and I'm not a pervert." He wasn't so sure about the latter, not at the moment, but knocked the thought from his head. "I had to . . . lie." He felt a river of sweat ready to break through his forehead. "I needed to meet you."

Kyndall stood with her shoes in her hands, no doubt questioning why she was even giving this guy the time of day. But her curiosity was aroused: Neil Novak had no friends.

"How do you know him?" she demanded.

Logan assessed her face. Skeptical. He stared at her blankly, half-expecting her to split but desperately wanting her to stay. "My name is Stuart Logan," he finally told her. "I was a friend of Jenny Baxter." Not exactly the truth, but not a lie, either.

"Who?" Kyndall studied Logan intently, as if she wanted to believe, needed someone to trust. Finally she sat on the arm of the chair set to the side of the sliding door.

"Jenny Baxter. She was with Neil . . . and your Aunt Lynn . . . last weekend when they were killed. And she was killed last night."

Kyndall fell silent, swallowed up in thought. Did she want to go or stay? Was she interested or unimpressed? She stared at him, then set her shoes on the table beside the iced Mumm's.

"Please," Logan said, seeing his opportunity. *Everyone wants to be sold, they're just looking for a good enough reason.* That's what his car-salesman father always said, and it worked on women as well as potential Buick customers. "You and Lynn were close."

"Look . . . I'd like to help you . . ."

"I need all the help I can get."

She considered this, crossed back to the bed, and sat next to him, close. She picked up her glass from the night table. "I met her once," she said softly. "Jenny, I mean. She was nice."

Nice. That wasn't the first adjective that came to mind.

"We met at a party," Kyndall continued. "She was Billy Keenan's manager. You do know who Billy Keenan is?"

Logan nodded. He took a long, steady sip from his glass, then poured some more champagne for Kyndall. Did he look so old that he appeared beyond rock and roll? Probably the hair, or lack thereof. Unconsciously he swept a few errant strands back onto his head and tried to fix his eyes on something in the room that didn't provoke or excite him.

She smiled as if she understood his plight. She couldn't get much closer on the bed, so she crossed her legs and hiked up her skirt, just to make things more difficult. Did she know what she was doing to him? Of course she did—that was her job. She glanced at the wall, focusing on a distant spot hidden in the floral wallpaper. When she turned back, her eyes were wet with tears.

"Why?" She snuffled. "Why would anyone do something like that? Why Lynn?"

"I don't know," Logan said softly. He took her hand, drew her close. A fine line, he thought. Tread carefully. She smiled at him, then rested her head on his shoulder, squeezed his hand. "That's why I need your help. You might know something, someone. Someone you don't even realize you know."

She shook her head and took another sip, then sniffed again. "I just spent an hour at a time with them. Come and go, that's the biz. Except maybe Neil." She thought on that for a moment, then added with a touch of guilt, "I feel like I'm betraying some kind of doctor-patient thing."

"As you said, the man is dead," Logan reminded her. He was beginning to wish he didn't have money resting on this hour, and that she was motivated by reasons other than profit. Under other circumstances, less professional on both counts, he could really ravage this living vision. He shook back these thoughts and looked her in the eye. "So. How did you meet him? Neil."

"You never give up," she groaned. She let the champagne trickle over her tongue, savoring every bubble. "It was about ten months ago. I'd just gotten into town and I met Roger—"

"McNulty."

"So the pleasure is yours, too." She raised a brow, accepting this small bit of common ground. "He said he had some connections in the industry."

"I'll bet."

Kyndall shrugged. "I know. I was naive, and full of dreams. I thought he meant movies. Not that I had any grand delusions about acting, but ... well, people said I had the looks and I thought ... well, anyway, *this* wasn't exactly the kind of business I had in mind. But Sachet's not a bad outfit.

Fourteen girls on staff, quite an elite little organization, really. Not like those dirty services you see in those sex rags. It's a classy setup, and Roger gives us half." She took another sip of champagne.

"And what about you?"

"You mean, what's a nice girl like me doing in a place like this?" She gave the room a once-over and grinned. "I came down here from north of San Francisco. Place called Occidental."

"Redwood country."

"That's right. I was born in the City, Haight-Ashbury. Mom was tripping out, Pop was a musician. He played clubs all over town, ended up doing all right for himself. Kicked Mom and me out just before he hit it big. So she packed up the Bug, put me in a cardboard box in the backseat, put some guy in the front seat to keep her company, and headed north over the bridge."

She flashed him a matter-of-fact look; all this was ancient history. Little emotion left, just the scars. Mother and child got as far as Occidental before the car broke down, ended up spending the last eighteen years freezing their respective butts off in an old Airstream trailer. Haight-Ashbury dropouts growing beans and tomatoes and selling tie-dyed shirts over in Santa Rosa and an occasional crop of weed to the other dropouts in the area.

"This is for real?"

"Cross my Living Heart bra." She drew an X in the air over her chest and he had to look away again. Did this girl know just what a talent she had for driving men nuts? "Speaking of which, then I got these." She pulled out her already-low neckline to expose nature's generosity. "Nice set, don't you think?"

"Eighth wonder of the world." Logan grinned, feeling his face grow warm.

"That's what Momma's old man thought, too. Him and his friends, and they all took a shot." She flexed her shoulders as if it didn't matter, but the mere gesture told him it did. More than she ever admitted, or probably wanted to remember. "Then last year, after high school, I took off, came down here to visit my aunt."

Her grip on Logan's hand had tightened as she recounted her tale. She sat stiffly on the bed, staring out the door at the lights winking in the distance, and the black horizon beyond.

Somewhere out there were the ends of the earth. Logan turned toward her, studied the lines of her face strong and sensitive and beautiful lines that had no business being in this business. He couldn't picture this five-star woman growing up in an abandoned Airstream trailer in a redwood grove, or opening herself up to every rich bastard with a little money to blow.

"And your aunt?" he pressed softly. "She took you in?"

"Lynn." A name, a memory, a frown. "My father's sister. She lived in the house up in the Haight when I was born, or so I hear. The scene was pretty much winding down, but they had this good thing going. Played clubs all over town, always had steady work—and all the dope they could handle. Then they split up, sort of a falling out, and he cut out."

"What happened to him?" He ran a finger along her hand, soft but reassuring. "Your father, I mean."

"Didn't even know the S.O.B. was alive until last year." She tipped her glass and let the rest of the champagne trickle down her throat. "Screw him."

She tried to sound in control, tried to convince him she was inured to the past and optimistic about the future. It didn't work for him, and he knew it didn't work for her. Suddenly she pulled her hand away and stood up. She glanced down at Logan, then strolled the few steps to the open balcony door. She took a deep breath, savoring the fresh coastal scent as if it might have been her last, maybe her first. Then she turned and leaned against the side of the door. She sniffed, looked almost hungry. "You carryin'?"

"Huh?"

"Carryin'. Stuff. Blow. Cocaine."

"Sorry." Logan shook his head.

She frowned, fidgeting with her glass, holding it in both hands as she crossed her legs, still leaning. She rolled her eyes up, as if drawing out a memory.

"Lynn knew I was coming." She sniffed.

"And Roger greeted you with open arms?"

She nodded. "I'd written to Lynn; took me a long time to find her but I finally did. Roger picked me up at the bus station, said he'd give me a job. I had a pretty good idea what he was into, but I didn't care. Figured I might as well make some money for what Mom's boyfriends took for free."

As if to punctuate her break from the past she ceremoniously tossed her glass over the balcony rail. They both waited for the splinter of glass as it struck whatever was below, but the room was too high up to hear anything.

She checked her watch, offered him a sad smile.

"Only ten more minutes of agony," he informed her.

The smile widened and she picked up the bottle. Her glass gone, she drank straight from the mouth. Then she returned to the bed and started kneading his tight shoulder muscles again.

"You sure I can't do something for you?" she inquired softly. "You can't be all talk and no action."

"Talk tonight, give me a rain check on the action?"

She shrugged. "It's your money."

"That's right," he said. "So what's the connection to Novak?"

"You're relentless." She sighed.

"It strengthens the character."

"Of course." She chugged a bit more bubbly, then touched her gaze to his. "If anyone hears about this—"

He glanced at the bottle and grinned. "Mumm's the word."

She thought this over, then got the joke. She giggled. "You're all right, you know?" she said giddily.

"Novak and McNulty?" he pressed, playfully.

"Okay already. Jesus." She considered the two men, a dire scowl etched on her face. "They deal in goods. Roger sells and Novak buys . . . bought."

"One call gets all."

"Something like that." She took another slug from the bottle, wiped her lips with her arm. "There's two ways to do it. One is the way you did it, just call up and make a date. Most of it's done that way. But for preferred customers, those who buy bulk, Roger offers a package deal. Same minimum wage to the girls, but a discount to the customer."

"Say Novak had a party down on his boat—?"

"He'd hire three or four girls for him and his friends."

"Such as?"

"You name 'em." She shrugged, glancing at the floor as if looking for her pride. "They pay for it, we'd do the dirty work."

Logan said nothing for a moment. He held out his glass for a refill; Kyndall simply handed him the bottle instead. He accepted it and gulped heartily. She smiled.

"You ever go out on his yacht?" he finally asked, handing the bottle back to her.

"Purely professionally," she explained as she took another

swig. "Amazing what a man will agree to when he's been laid."

"Power to the pussy," he suggested.

She laughed, leaned over, and kissed Logan on the cheek, checked her watch again. Then she smiled sadly.

"Well, I hate to be businesslike, but your hour's up." She ran a hand up his leg, resting it where the one met the other. "Always feel like a shrink when I say that."

"In a manner of speaking, that's just what you do."

She laughed. Kyndall Wyatt was no dumb hooker trapped in the body of an angel. Whatever downward spiral had brought her to this point was a twist of fate that had no right to be dumped on her.

Kyndall checked her blonde hair in the mirror, then turned toward him. "I hate to charge you for this, but—"

"You do take Mastercard, I hope." Logan said as he opened his wallet.

"But of course." She smiled lusciously as she took his card. She pulled a black card roller from her purse, ran off a credit slip, and handed it to Logan. "Gratuities go there." She pointed to the proper space on the receipt slip.

Logan added $50 to the $200 charge, wondered how the hell he was going to write this one off, and handed it back.

"I hope you got your money's worth."

"I hope *you* did." He grinned as she slipped his receipt in his pocket and walked with her to the door.

"Won't matter anyway. Coupla weeks I'm blowin' this job, so to speak."

"Retiring?" Hundreds of rich hearts were going to be broken.

"Tired of spending my life in bed. Gotta be more to see in the world than the cracks in the ceiling of L.A.'s finest hotels. Now maybe I can put my friggin' life in order, thanks to Lynn."

"Lynn?"

"She managed to save a little money, planned to open her own jewelry store. She left it to me. And as soon as the lawyers get through screwing around with it, I'm kissing ol' Roger on the cheek and saying fuck this job."

She lightly touched Logan's lips with her own, drawing out a bit more than the moment. Then she opened the door and glided out, as if on a cloud of eternal hope. And at that instant Logan realized his instincts again were on track.

When she'd first come through the door, he knew she arced a gap in his brain. Kyndall Wyatt was the girl at Lynn Sutton's funeral. The girl who sifted Lynn Sutton's ashes into the raging surf, the girl who gingerly carried the brass urn across the meadow after the service.

The girl who had driven off toward the city, McNulty's Mercedes and the black stretch limo close behind.

Logan settled into his chair on the balcony and slowly gulped a hearty swallow of V-8 juice. He drew a discerning hand over his unshaved chin, then swept back a tangle of hair from his forehead. He needed a shower, but didn't have the legs. He needed coffee, but didn't have the energy. He rubbed both eyes, still burning from the impurities of champagne and no food since the hot dog yesterday at Winkie's.

So. Just what had his four-hundred-plus bucks bought him, besides an hour of temptation with a quick-witted woman-child? Few answers, more questions—but he'd expected nothing less. He'd been able to crawl inside Neil Novak for a few minutes, except he hadn't gone where Novak had gone, or felt what Novak had felt. A woman Logan had wanted to love but wouldn't. Or couldn't.

And that's where the difference lay, pun intended. Novak was a different customer and got what he wanted, all five stars' worth. But what had Logan received? A vague insight into the world of a call girl? A growing connection between Roger McNulty and Rhapsody Records, maybe Frank Kennedy, maybe Niki and Luigi Carbone? Maybe even a little insight into the woman herself. All that, but nothing tangible, no hard facts, no motive, no desire for any of Novak's few close friends or enemies to desire the man dead.

One look inside at the clock on the night table told him it was ten-fourteen. Time to get a move on. All he wanted was to crawl back into bed inside or, better yet, grab a towel and a pitcher of something cool and spend the day out by the pool. He faced a momentary battle of wits, and as usual no practical side won out.

He thumbed through Neil Novak's address case, picked up the phone, and dialed.

Frank Kennedy's secretary said Mr. Kennedy had a breakfast meeting and wouldn't be in until later in the morning. Logan told her he had an urgent message, prompting the efficient woman to demand details. When Logan refused to comply she harrumphed and explained that her boss might be calling in for messages and she'd be glad to leave word with him if Logan wanted her to.

Logan thanked the sweet, soft voice, and told the woman he would be out of the office himself and would have to call back later in the day.

Next he made his daily attempt at contact with Corie Chapin at Rhapsody Records, but she allegedly was away from the office. He considered leaving a message with her, too, but figured he'd have no better luck than with Frank Kennedy's nose guard. He politely thanked the receptionist, wondering what color she had chosen for her hair today, and hung up.

Logan remained motionless in his chair, the sun already baking his dry skin, the languid post-slumber drowsiness seeping back into him. He started to close his eyes, then violently shook off the waves of sleep. With equal parts reluctance and obligation, Logan swung his feet to the floor and slowly rose on wobbly legs. Tentatively at first, he pressed them into service and managed to stumble into the bathroom, where a hot shower awaited him.

Playa del Rey was a funky neighborhood tucked into a strip of coast just south of Venice beach and north of LAX. Most of the houses were postwar patchwork, single-story dwellings set up on a ridge overlooking the Pacific. Some of these were owned by retirees who hadn't moved in forty years; most were rented out to groups of four or six Angelenos all scrambling for a speck of the beach and willing to sacrifice a great deal of cash to achieve it.

Kennedy's office was located in this dubious little pocket, two blocks up Redlands Street in a lime-green house badly in need of repair. Paint was shredding from the weathered stucco walls. The lawn was begging for a close clip, and crabgrass sprouted from the cracked sidewalk. Every window was covered with folding interior shutters, and wayward roses climbed up to the rotting roof gutters. Logan double-checked the address in Novak's address case and pulled his car up behind a red Ferrari parked at the curb.

He didn't figure this at all. Except for the Ferrari, this hardly fit the style or form of a two-bit, grade-A L.A. slimeball.

Logan was greeted at the door by the sweet face behind the sweet voice. Another California blonde, sun-drenched hair, short black leather skirt that tempted even the weakest imagination, eyes that wouldn't quit.

"You the messenger?" Her voice even softer than it had been on the phone. "I got a package to go óver to Capitol—"

"I called earlier," Logan explained, consciously averting his eyes from her tight skirt. He seemed to be doing a lot of that lately. "I said I'd call back, but I just happened to be—"

"Casing the neighborhood. Of course." She studied his eyes for a moment, then forced an apologetic shrug. "Frank's still out of the office. I told you—"

"That's his car parked outside, isn't it?" Logan interrupted.

"One of them. He took the Jeep today. Sorry." The waiflike look on her face seemed so genuine, so honest, that Logan almost bought it. Almost.

"I'll wait," he announced.

"I don't know when he'll be back," she fussed.

"I'm in no hurry." Logan smiled. He stepped through the doorway and made himself comfortable on the overstuffed leather couch.

"What did you say your name was?" Her ire was quickly and understandably mounting.

"Stuart Logan." He introduced himself, extending a hand that went ignored.

She glowered at him, his dubious welcome wearing even thinner. She sat for a moment, then stood and disappeared through a doorway. When she was gone Logan surveyed the place. No doubt an office, but try telling that to the IRS. He was sitting in what was, and someday again would be, a living room. At the moment the brick fireplace was closed off by a low Art Deco sideboard, and a matching desk occupied the dark corner under one of the shuttered windows. Swivel chair, IBM Selectric, digital phone system, computer terminal, and file cabinets completed the picture. The rest of the room was similarly decorated in haphazard American workplace, except for an extensive collection of Art Deco trinkets that illustrated a style frozen in time, if not in taste. His critical appraisal was interrupted by a sudden shadow lurking in the hallway.

"Yes?" a heavy voice grumbled from the doorway.

Logan stood up. If this was Kennedy, he was shorter, stumpier, more disheveled than Logan expected. Probably in his forties, Kennedy looked almost anemic, except for his eyes and nose, which were a faded pink. He had a scrubby beard, frosted with telltale signs of white powder. His chin sagged, and a small gold earring pierced his left lobe. He wore white denims and a pale-blue aloha shirt; his feet were bare and dirty. He was eating a banana.

They sized each other up for a moment. Logan spoke first. "Frank Kennedy?"

"Sandi here says you've been bustin' your balls to see me."

"Figure of speech." He extended his hand, which he knew Kennedy had no intention of shaking. "Stuart Logan."

"Logan, huh?" Kennedy hesitated for a moment, then peeled the banana a little lower. "I'm supposed to know you?"

"No." Logan shook his head, taking his time picking out the appropriate lie. "I'm writing a book."

Kennedy sneezed. He wolfed down the rest of the banana and tossed the peel into a nearby cardboard box. He swallowed almost without chewing, and didn't take his eyes off Logan the whole time. "What kind of book?"

"Is there someplace we can talk?"

Kennedy studied Logan longer than felt comfortable, then shot Sandi an exasperated glance. "Hold my calls," he told her as he motioned for Logan to follow him down the hallway.

"I appreciate—"

"Right," Kennedy interrupted as he ushered Logan into his office and briskly closed the door behind them.

The room was more a storeroom than an office, a study of clutter. A blond oak file cabinet in one corner was stacked with papers, and every wall was lined with old records, all stacked vertically as if never played. Piles of promo 45s and compact discs and videos lined the floor; a revolving magazine rack was stocked with the current issue of every radio and record trade journal published. A dead pinball machine jutted from one corner, while a Bally's quarter slot machine invited suckers in another.

"So, to what do I owe this pleasure?" Kennedy said, waving Logan into a folding chair.

"Neil Novak," Logan said at length.

Kennedy took a seat behind his desk and tapped a cigarette from a crushed pack. He offered one to Logan, who refused. "Seems he's all anyone's interested in these days."

"The man is dead."

"If that's what it takes ..."

"That's what sells."

"And you're here to get the skinny, am I right?"

"Right."

Kennedy nodded as he lit his cigarette. Everyone knew he was always right, and everyone knew he was a goddamned genius.

"So ... you want me to tell you all there is to know about your man Novak? You mind I ask who you're working for?"

"Confidential."

"Right." Kennedy shrugged as if he didn't care, but Logan could tell the question was nagging at him. Novak was dead five days and already the vultures were hovering. Vulgar business, all this. But then again, Frank Kennedy's whole business was vulgar. He sat on the edge of his desk and picked up an autographed baseball. He turned it over in his palm, then tossed it in the air and caught it. Vultures.

"You're a goddamned piranha, you know that?" Kennedy said matter-of-factly.

"And you're a goddamned pimp and pusher," Logan countered with a polite smile.

Kennedy thought this one over, impressed with Logan's brashness. Didn't see a whole hell of a lot of that in this business, where everyone's on their knees puckering up. A smile crept into his eyes.

"Let me guess ..." he began. "You're workin' against the clock here, cranking out some mass-market paperback to get to the checkout stands before Novak's ashes cool. Am I right? Damned right I'm right. An' you know what else, I think you're tryin' to beat the cops. And the papers. You aim to scoop the shit right out of those creeps, am I right. Fuckin' A I'm right. You're lookin' to make your nut here, and what you need is someone to pin this on, but before that you've gotta have a motive, a purpose. Desire, lust, greed, revenge, something that would get someone to plug the man through the noggin. But as it looks right now, you ain't got diddly. Don't say it . . . I know I'm right."

Logan sat patiently, hands in his lap. Let the man ramble, let the white powder work its paranoid course. "You're right," Logan said anyway. "Except you left out one thing."

"Which is?"

"That you were one of those someones."

Kennedy's face turned sour, his eyes dark. "You read too many newspapers," he growled.

"Better to read them than to be in them." Logan studied Kennedy's eyes intently, brown meeting brown. Curiosity facing intrigue. "What can you tell me about Neil Novak?"

"We've met, on occasion."

"Please. Don't insult your own intelligence. You and Novak, you were like this." He crossed his fingers. "Same with Roger McNulty, and Niki Carbone and Jack Gold. And every major record label in town. You make the hits."

"Strictly business," Kennedy said, his glare tempered by his grandiose ego. "Speaking of which, I have work—"

"You and the Carbones go way back, don't you? Family ties."

Kennedy jolted to his feet, hands pressed to the desktop. "This has gone far enough."

Logan made as if he didn't hear or care. He rose from his chair, giving the impression he might be getting ready to leave, but instead walked over to one of the shuttered windows that kept out the hot August sun—as well as any stray eyes or cameras.

"You'd be surprised what I know about the family," Logan continued, turning and facing Kennedy, who stood squarely at the door. "Way I hear it, Niki and Luigi made a healthy loan to a cousin, by marriage, to set up a record-promotion business a few years ago. A business that, by all accounts, has turned into a thriving little entrepreneurial venture."

"I don't have to listen to this." Kennedy's hands tightened into little fists that began to match his eyes and nose in color.

"Seems they also had an arrangement with Leo Gold, a cozy little partnership that Novak found out about."

"You're fuggin' ranting—"

"Now, Novak really didn't give a shit about the payoffs, the payola, am I right? Damned right I'm right. Didn't give a rat's ass what you had to do to get his songs up the charts.

But the counterfeits, and the Billy Keenan album—that's what really set the guy off."

Kennedy lost it. Fury streamed into his face, and he lunged at Logan. "You goddamned son of a bitch!"

Logan was losing his touch. For the second time in a week he had misjudged the rage factor of a cornered man, a miscalculation that cost him another shirt. He wriggled free from Kennedy's grasp and slipped past him toward the door.

"It's been a real pleasure, Mr. Kennedy." He considered offering his hand, but decided on a vexing smirk instead.

Logan toyed with the idea of making a run out to Malibu to pay a surprise visit on David Carbone, but he knew it would be useless. He had tried that stunt twice before, when he was with the *Times,* ending with the same result: a bruised head and dents the size of baseball bats in the side of his car. He already felt bruised enough as it was, and he had no desire to start poking through auto graveyards for replacement quarter panels for a 1967 Plymouth Fury.

As he pushed northward, toward the Sepulveda Pass, his brain worked on the Carbone connection. Any of the clan could have had any number of reasons to want Neil Novak dead, but for each reason there was probably an equal and opposite reason to want the man alive. Logan doubted that Carbone would have signed a death warrant over something so trivial as exposure of a counterfeit record plot. Who gave a shit if Leo Gold was caught with his pants down, and probably had squealed to Neil and begged forgiveness? Even if Gold had vowed to expose Carbone, and assuming Uncle Niki was actually the force behind the scheme, what could Novak do? Call the cops? Five grand juries, the IRS, dozens of Justice Department attorneys, and two assistant D.A.'s were keeping close tabs on every member of the Carbone organization. Even if Novak and Gold wore wires twenty-four hours a day, Carbone wouldn't be stupid enough to kill one but let the other go free.

Yet Leo Gold was alive, and Novak was dead. And one does not kill one's golden goose.

It didn't make sense. It wasn't logical mob behavior, an oxymoron if he ever heard one. So was organized crime. But the fact was, these guys had their own sense of logic, their own way of operating. And so far it didn't add up to squat. Let the cops think what they wanted, to dig up enough dirt on the Carbones to declare victory on organized crime. Logan didn't have the same priorities, or the same slate to wipe clean. He wasn't running for attorney general; he wasn't running for anything. If he was running at all, he was running *from*, not *to*.

Logan's thoughts meandered through the meager facts dangling before his brain, and before he realized where he was going he found himself at the Mulholland cutoff. He veered up the exit ramp, then started the long, winding trek east toward Nicada, the dead end where just the night before last Jenny Baxter had plunged to her death.

He slowed down as he approached the intersection and pulled off on the rough shoulder. A steep driveway climbed up the hillside to the top of the mount, leading to the house that Logan assumed had the rare view of the San Fernando Valley to the north and the L.A. basin to the south, a view that—on a clear day—probably extended all the way out to Catalina. He sat at the wheel for a moment, staring across the road at the gaping hole carved in the thick scrub, a half dozen mailboxes plowed over in the wake of Jenny's wayward car. His hands still gripped the wheel as he gaped, then slowly loosened as he mustered the courage to get out and take a look. Traffic was light this time of day; he waited for a Corvette and a Luv pickup to pass. Then he opened his door and climbed out, hesitantly making his way across the highway toward the roped-off scene.

An orange Highway Patrol ribbon lay limply over the parched, mowed-down brush; Logan moved to the edge of the precipice and peered down. Deep gashes were carved in the dry earth, indications of Jenny's roller-coaster ride over the edge. A massive oak tree some fifty yards down the hillside had suffered a deep wound in its ancient trunk, and sparkles of crushed safety glass winked in the hot, hazy afternoon sun. Twenty yards beyond was the fenced backyard of a hillside home, perched treacherously on the rim of disaster.

Down there, somewhere, Jenny Baxter's life met a quick and tragic end. Logan felt a shiver run down his spine, the same shiver he felt during those first empty days without Molly. Could there actually have been a time when his life had included her, when they had laughed and hugged and loved and battled, when his life hadn't felt so . . . empty, so lost? How long had it been, if not a lifetime? So little time since the Carbones, and so much to remember.

He stepped back from the edge and gazed down at the Valley. A thick, brown soup filled the bowl that stretched interminably to the north, ending against a ridge of mountains reaching out of the veiled horizon. Only the tops of the tallest buildings lining the boulevard in Encino jutted out of the goop; everything else was wrapped in a cloak of pungent exhaust, just waiting for the afternoon drive time rush to descend into its stifling depths.

And somewhere out there, maybe cruising down Ventura Boulevard, maybe breaking into another of so many Valley houses, was the bastard who two years ago so quickly and completely had brought down the curtain on the first act of Logan's life.

The sun was tumbling toward the horizon in a broad palette of orange and red and lavender. Logan pulled to a stop at the light at Sunset, and waited for the traffic to stream by. The road was thick with southbound sun-worshippers heading home, passed by the northbound rush of beachniks ready to crack the night wide open. It was summer, it was Saturday, and it was sunset.

When the light changed he eased through the intersection and jostled over a speed bump into the valet parking lot. Gladstones 4 Fish, dinner at the beach. Corie had suggested this place; seven-thirty. Noisy and boisterous: better than some quiet, intimate place where too much emotion might be on tap. He glanced at his watch and groaned: fifteen minutes late. He hoped she would understand. He exchanged his Fury for a parking stub and averted his eyes from whatever horrors the parking attendant might inflict upon it.

The surf was light. Waves gently washed up on the beach as couples strolled arm in arm along the sand, shoes in hand, absorbed in each other. Logan gazed upon them with sad envy, then forced himself out of the automatic melancholy that arose every time he saw other people in love. He pushed his way inside.

The bar hadn't changed since he'd last been here. How long had it been: two years? Three? Sawdust and peanut casings dusted the floor, men and women competed for position at the bar and crowded the lounge to claim their dinner reservations. Logan edged past a party of four pushing their way out and squeezed through the crowd of thirsty drinkers watching Phil Collins on MTV. The tide of bodies shifted as another "Jones party of four" was announced.

He surveyed the lounge area, then edged over to the hostess to see if Corie had already checked in. A light tap on the shoulder stopped him mid-stride.

"Glad you could make it," she greeted him politely as she was wedged against him by a party of eight crowding into the paddock. She gave him a friendly peck on the cheek, close enough for him to smell the Black Russians on her breath.

"I'm glad you caught me." He smiled, still amazed that she had called him. "I was on my way out to Burger King."

"Lucky you." She gripped his arm, probably to steady her footing. "And yes, I'd love another." She smiled as she lamented her empty glass. "You?"

He nodded and strolled up to the bar. Two minutes later he was back, with a refill for Corie and a Dewar's and rocks for himself. They clinked glasses and as the cold Scotch flowed down his throat Logan felt a wave of anxiety subside.

A few minutes of idle chatter filled the awkwardness that existed before the hostess seated them at a table near, but not next to, a window overlooking the white-water surf. She inquired whether they wanted anything further to drink, noted what they were already having, and disappeared toward the bar.

"You sure do get around," Corie observed as she made herself comfortable at the table.

Logan grinned. "You keeping an eye on me?"

"News travels fast. Folks are wondering what you're up to."

"What sort of folks?"

"Folks who are naturally curious."

"And what do you tell them?"

"That they should talk to you."

"Is that why you're here? To talk to me?"

"I have my reasons." She winked at him, then sipped her

vodka and Kahlúa. Her eyes tonight were the color of a deep blue coral lagoon, and he felt perilously close to drowning.

"Why the change of heart?"

She pursed her lips, smearing lipstick on her teeth. She dug into her pocketbook and pulled out a folded white form. She handed it to him. "I thought these were supposed to be pink."

Logan read the bold print, skimmed the short note, then stared at her with shock. "You ... they ..."

"Fired me," Corie finished for him. "This afternoon. Standard procedure, really. New boss comes in, brings his own way of doing things. Including his own secretary."

"But you're not a secretary."

"Semantics," Corie sighed as she swirled the brown liquid in her glass. "Mr. Minetti prefers the standard job descriptions."

"Minetti?"

"Who died and made him king, right? Minetti was Neil's hand-picked prince-in-waiting. Attorney and one grand S.O.B."

"You left out 'prick.' "

"And manic-depressive," she added with a shudder. "You'd think he was heavily into coke except he's too fat."

A busboy brought a loaf of bread on a cutting board, then darted back into the kitchen. When he was gone Corie glanced down at the menu.

"Entertainment law?" Logan wanted to know.

"Corporate. Neil found him in some downtown firm about four years ago. He was on retainer with a lot of respectable concerns."

"Respectable concerns like the Carbones?"

"Please ... keep it down," she whispered, shooting him a stinging glance of reproach over the top of her menu. "In this town you never know who's listening."

"Or who's paranoid," Logan countered brightly.

"Look," Corie said, missing the levity. "I'm going to level with you. I'm here for Jenny, not for my health. She was into something deep, something that got her killed. And I'm with you in whatever you're doing to find out what that was. But right now you're dangerous to be around. I've spent nine years in this business, and at the moment I'm out on the street. I don't have time to end up on somebody's blacklist."

"You'll do just fine."

"Not if it gets around I'm spilling every Rhapsody secret to some half-assed ex-reporter from the *L.A. Times.*"

Logan grinned sheepishly and set his menu on the table. "I didn't tell you I was with the *Times.*"

"You're not. But you were." When he looked at her curiously, she added, "I have my sources, too."

He blinked, decided not to pursue it. There was a time for all things, and right now it was time to finish his Scotch. He emptied the glass down his throat, set it on the table. Then, for the first time that evening, he studied Corie. She was dressed in a coral dress that hugged every tight curve like a steel-belted radial. Her hair was pulled back and shimmered at the tips, her cheeks were flushed and delicious. A silver moon dangled from one ear, a constellation of stars from the other.

"Half-assed?" he finally asked, breaking the spell, bringing the moment back to earth.

"I told you, I have my sources," she assured him. "And why don't you take off your crusader hat for the evening, okay? If you want to talk, we'll talk. Feed me, ply me with spirits. But don't push. Let me go gentle into this good night."

"So let us melt and make no noise, no tear-floods, nor sight-tempests more?"

She smiled softly, her tongue darting around the rim of her glass. "That's more like it," she purred. "Donne, right?"

"Donne and finished." He grinned. "So . . . how and when did you meet him?"

"Meet who?"

"Novak."

"I knew it was too good to last," she sighed, rolling her eyes in exaggerated exasperation. "All right . . . here goes. Four years ago I was a secretary at Melrose Management. We handled a couple of Rhapsody artists—Metal Sponge, Feeled in Scream, Pyret Chip. Neil had a party up at his house, a lavish catered affair with endless food and drink and the absolute worst heavy-metal band he ever tried to break. I went with the man who was to become my husband—"

"Husband?"

"More of a brain tumor, really. A massive cerebral hemorrhage. He was in radio, gonzo Hollywood. That's the type I attract."

"Maybe your luck is changing." Logan winked.

"We'll talk about luck later." She winked back. "But that was then, and this is now. Anyway, later in the evening Neil was doing a few lines in the game room, had them spread out on the Ping-Pong table. Everyone was getting into it. Never saw so much blow."

"And you joined the fun?"

"Yes, Mr. Morality. I admit, I cut loose every now and then. Who doesn't? Well, I mean except for *you.*"

Logan shrugged off the droll, yet deserved, dig. This was L.A., after all; half the town was putting Colombian gold up its nose, and the other half was chasing down those who did. If not, Logan would have been out of a job long before he ever screwed himself out of the one he had.

"But that was then, and this is now," he suggested.

"Exactly." She grinned. "Anyway, Neil and I got to talking, and a few months later when he fired the bitch who was working for him he called me."

"How closely did you work with him?" Logan glanced about for their waitress, who obviously was teaching them discipline by avoiding their table.

"You mean, did I know the intricacies of his business deals, and will I tell them to you? Yes and no."

"Don't get ahead of me. I just want to know if he ever took you into his confidence."

"I'll just bet you do." Corie was becoming a touch defensive, but managed to maintain a friendly edge.

The waitress finally decided to return. She took up an officious stance, whipped out her order pad, and looked at them expectantly. Logan ordered dinner for both: endless steamers for her and broiled swordfish for himself. Salads and potatoes and wine taken care of, the waitress waddled off.

"What was their marriage like?" he asked when they were alone again. His attention focused more on her lips than her answer.

"It had its ups and downs."

"What about other women?"

"They were his hobby."

"And Jenny?"

Corie looked down at her place mat, then let her eyes roam over the crowded restaurant, looking anywhere but at Logan. This was not a subject she felt comfortable discussing, and a few awkward moments passed. Finally she allowed her glance to return to him, cautiously. "Neil was a very private man, and Jenny was my friend. They were both lonely."

Logan regarded her curiously, but decided to let it go for now. "And his wife?"

"They had what you'd call an understanding."

"An open marriage?"

"Approved indiscretions," she corrected him.

"And these indiscretions. Did they ever include you?" There. Go for broke. He half-expected her to take a swipe at him, or at least pierce him with that cobalt glare of hers. Wonder of wonders, she did neither. Maybe she realized that his curiosity was becoming personal as well as professional, something she didn't mind.

"Never." She smiled boldly. "Why do you ask?"

"Inquiring minds want to know." He shrugged modestly, soaking up her smile. A smile he longed to taste.

Corie stared at the bucket of clams sitting in front of her. She picked one up and pried it open, scooping out the meat with a fork. "What do the cops think?" she said, drowning the morsel in drawn butter.

"Hard to tell what they ever think," Logan hedged as he sliced off a bite of swordfish. He speared it with his fork, then held it in front of him as he continued. "Looks to me like someone's trying to use her as a scapegoat."

"The cops think she killed Neil and Lynn?"

"That's what someone wants them to think."

"But . . . why?"

"Jenny was out on Catalina with the two of them. She was seen leaving the *Rhapsody on Blue* just after they were killed. And the murder weapon was found in her car."

Corie had lowered her eyes, looking out the plate-glass window at the sea crashing somewhere out in the darkness. The color had drained from her face, and her skin looked drawn, taut. She blinked her eyes, several times, then sniffed. The shock of the last week was still a force to be dealt with, which she evidently was trying to do as best she could. Eventually she returned her gaze to Logan and held his eyes with hers.

"Jenny tried so hard to keep everything a secret," she said, shaking her head. "Until after her two years were up."

Logan looked at her quizzically, but said nothing, hoping the silence would lead her to continue.

"I don't know what your relationship with Jenny was . . .

and I don't care," Corie went on, her voice tentative, coming out in short bursts. "But one thing you probably didn't know was that she was married."

"Not until I saw it in the paper." He thought back: she hadn't been wearing a ring last weekend when she'd sat down beside him at the bar. It was the first thing he checked.

"She had to."

"You mean?"

"No," Corie quickly said. "There's more than one reason to tie the knot these days."

Outside of love, money, or necessity, Logan drew a blank.

"Immigration. She was from Auckland."

"And she was here illegally," Logan finished for her, the picture suddenly coming clear like a Polaroid snapshot. "So she got married."

"Exactly. She came up here seven years ago. Her visa had expired, but she stayed on. She'd worked at a few radio stations in New Zealand in the mid-eighties, and when she arrived here she landed a good gig over at Pacific. Got a Social Security number, driver's license, paid taxes, everything. But she always knew the INS would catch up with her eventually."

"What about amnesty?"

"The amnesty plan only worked if you could prove you were here continuously since 1982. But she had to go home for a few months in 1986, screwed it all up."

"So she married some gay friend."

"James is a very nice man," Corie said reproachfully, casting him a scolding eye. "And don't worry. Their marriage was strictly for appearance's sake."

So how did it work? Did Jenny keep her clothes and car at the condo in Studio City, then go off and play while her husband invited his boyfriend over? Only in L.A.

"It happens more often than you might think," Corie said, as if reading his thoughts. "Getting married to stay in the States, I mean. As long as you don't have an FBI record and can get someone to help you, it's pretty easy."

Corie selected another clam from the bucket, inserted her knife between shell halves, and viciously twisted it open. She glanced up at Logan, flashed him a pretty smile, and stabbed at the tidbit waiting inside.

"And now, if you think we can change the subject for just a little while, I'm going to try to enjoy my meal." She

drenched a morsel in butter, then flashed him a tempting
wink as she slurped it into her mouth.

Lucky clam, Logan thought.

22

Sometime during the evening their conversation drifted away
from murder and mayhem. Logan found himself holding
Corie's hand across the table, gently rubbing her soft fingers.
Dinner ended late, the hour was growing later.

The surf hammered the beach. A swollen moon framed
them in shadows as they strolled along the sand. Shallow
breakers raced up and tickled their bare feet, then washed
down from where they stood, hand in hand, facing each other.
Closer, coming together until their lips touched, testing at
first. Then they pulled apart, just enough to let the moon slice
through again.

Corie reached for his fingers, lightly squeezing them, then
tugged him back up the beach the way they had come.

"I know a place," she breathed. "It's private."

"Your wish is my demand," he whispered.

"Then follow me," she commanded him as they slowly
wandered up the slope from the sand, still warm from the
day's heat. As they neared the valet parking booth, she added,
"Stay close. You get lost, it's your loss."

He followed her north on Pacific Coast Highway, past the
surf shops and taco stands and gas stations and overpriced
beach houses and the Colony and Pepperdine University. The
taillights of her blue Honda closely hugged the road as she
raced ahead of him, almost disappearing around the curves.
He dared not lose her, not tonight. Tonight he needed her.
Maybe tomorrow, too. But tonight he needed her most—her
touch, her warmth, her kiss, the feel of her against him, close,
wrapping himself in her.

His thoughts drifted dangerously close to Molly, two years
ago, the way they'd made love that last night, that last time,

so perfectly. He remembered how she felt next to him, their skin gliding smoothly, the electricity between them in the dark, her body curled up, the sheets scrunched up at the foot of the bed. Her silky legs, not as tan as she wanted them. Her heart-shaped face, like the heroines' in the romance novels she read. Her cute little ears and tangled hair. Her form fitting his, and his body filling her every curve.

And why the hell was doing this to himself, thrusting himself into melancholy as he followed Corie up PCH, knowing when he got where they were going he would be with her, not Molly, and whatever it was would be new and different and good.

Corie finally slowed at the entrance to Paradise Cove. Logan edged his Plymouth down the serpentine drive, following her past the eucalyptus and oleander, through the gate and up a small road that wound to the top of a bluff. She pulled into a small driveway next to a double-wide mobile home parked near the edge of the ridge. Home sweet home.

He climbed out of his car and stood at the edge of the precipice. Waves battered the sand and rocks, a sheer drop of a hundred feet to the sea-swept shore below. The roar of water on sand, washing in and out in hypnotic rhythm, blending with salt, seaweed, and meadow sage. A light breeze stirred up from the surf, wrapping him in a tranquillity he hadn't felt in a long while.

"Another perfect evening in Paradise Cove," Corie whispered as she joined him in his serenity, slipping her arms around his waist and drawing him against her.

"You live all the way out here?" he asked as his tension seemed to float away on the wind.

"Great way to leave your troubles behind," she breathed, relishing the freshness, the aroma of a world far removed from the asphalt and soot and grime.

"Troubles?" he sighed. "What troubles?"

"Come with me," she invited him, taking his hand. "You ain't seen nothing yet."

A distant tremble from deep within him told him she was right.

She led him down the road, corroded and crumbling from the salt. They sidestepped along the cliff until they were standing over the ocean cascading up on the polished sandstone and empty beach below. Only a faint glow in the southern sky reminded him that L.A. was just a rush hour away.

The moon and stars—plenty of stars—shimmered off the sea, rising and falling in swells rolling in to shore. "Let's go down to the beach," he suggested, the sweet smell of heather enveloping his system.

She squeezed his hand, and they started down.

"Be careful," she warned, her voice a breeze. "It's a little treacherous in the dark."

He gripped her hand tighter as she led him down a dirt path to a dry drainage gulley. They steadied each other as they inched down through the dark, then stepped onto a small dirt trail that wound into the blackness. The footing was tricky as they climbed over the rocks and descended to the beach, where the sand quickly spilled into Logan's shoes. He slipped them off, the second time this evening, and left them on an outcropping of dry sandstone. She placed hers next to them.

"So this is where you take all the guys." He laughed nervously as he scuffed the sand with his toes.

"Only the ones with great hands. Did anyone ever tell you that you have great hands?"

"How can you tell in the dark?"

"I have a good sense of feel."

They strolled down to the water's edge, where the waves pounded up on the sand, then flowed back to meet the next curl. They walked along the waterline, both of them dancing as the cold gripped their feet and an occasional strong wave washed past.

"How long have you lived out here?" he asked after a long, peaceful silence.

"Three years. My brain tumor and I bought it, right after we were married. It was a sort of escape, a last resort."

He grinned, but it was lost in the dark. "And?"

"And now it's mine. He got the condo in the marina, I got the battered old trailer in Malibu."

"I think you got the better deal."

"So do I. Still have payments on the trailer and a monthly lease on the land, but at least I can see stars at night." She stopped walking and stared out at the dark, distant horizon. Then she started walking again, slowly, this time lightly brushing her body against his.

"Come with me," she whispered in his ear, settling her head softly on his shoulder.

"Where?"

"Shhh." She pressed a finger against his lips and led him back up the path. They helped each other over the rocks as they slowly climbed the bluff. He trailed after her, still holding her hand as the dry scrub grabbed at his trousers and scraped his bare skin. They worked their way over a small knoll, then into a little clearing—a dry, grassy meadow closed off from curious eyes but with a peek of the cove and the dark ocean beyond. And the stars above to keep them company.

Corie knelt down and Logan slowly followed her lead. "This is my secret place," she said softly as she gazed off over the silver sea and soaked it all in.

Logan's eyes followed hers to the horizon, then turned and absorbed her profile, backlit by the glow of distant moon. Lovely, intense, serene; he leaned over and lightly kissed her satin cheek.

She faced him, her eyes studying, her lips tempting his. She leaned forward and they touched, softly at first, then harder as he tasted her tongue. Tentative, feeling the newness, nibbling her neck, her ears, her lobes, she running her hands through his hair, drawing him closer, harder, stronger as the sea breeze quivered around them, feeling the excitement, the unknown, the anticipation.

Then they were lying on the grass, soft and dry around them, her coral dress billowing beneath her as she looked up at him, her dark eyes glazed and deep. He lowered his body to hers and tasted her lips again as two became one, the moon smiling down, the sea murmuring in vicarious approval as it lulled the senses.

Afterwards, silence. They lay there, side by side, Logan leaning on his elbow, gazing over her pale skin as he memorized her form with a wandering finger, neither daring to break the spell. The breeze caressed them gently as the moment lingered, the memory formed.

He leaned over and kissed her breast. Then he lay back and gazed up at the watchful stars, waiting for the rush of guilt to course through his body.

It came, but it was not the same rush. It was not the guilt he expected to feel because he had thought about Molly while he was making love. The guilt he felt was because, for the first time in two years, he hadn't.

* * *

In the rested light of the morning after, Corie's home didn't even seem like a trailer.

Her ex had taken most of the furniture, whatever they'd had, and she hadn't yet bothered to replace it. The living room focused on the couch, a standard off-white sleeper with a pseudo-teak Scandinavian coffee table in front of it. A portable TV topped a small stereo rack, and several crates of records were stacked in one corner. A folding futon chair sat in the other. A glass table and two folding chairs occupied the small dining area, which opened through sliding-glass doors to a small deck with a panoramic view of the ocean. A freestanding wood stove, which looked like it hadn't seen a fire in years, separated these two rooms. A large kitchen opened off the hallway that led to the master bedroom.

They stood on her deck, wrapped in the fog and each other, both quiet and very still. Then, very slowly, she reached out a hand and found his. He touched her skin lightly, moving up to her shoulder, then down between her breasts. She inched next to him, and he slipped his arm around her and pulled her close. She turned and their lips met, testing again, the fire building until she squeezed his hand and led him back inside.

Afterwards, they lay in bed, silent, savoring. She nestled against him, tucking her head under his chin like a violin, draping her arm over his chest. Neither said a word, not for a long time. Finally Corie broke the spell; she rolled off him, clasping her hands behind her head and staring at the ceiling.

"What about Roger McNulty?"

Logan suppressed a laugh, then turned to look at her. "Oh, God . . . what have I done to you?"

"Everything wonderful." She giggled, kissed his ear. "But really . . . he could be a suspect."

Logan sighed, kissed her back, and more. " 'Suspect' sounds so . . . so melodramatic. But you're right . . . he may have had a motive."

"He and Novak were like this," she said, crossing her fingers.

"And he and Mrs. Novak were like this," Logan added, making a circle from his thumb and index finger and inserting his other index finger through it.

"And that's enough to want Neil dead?"

"Men have killed for less." Logan shrugged under the sheet that was covering their naked bodies. "And Leslie stood to win a lot of cash and prizes."

"Greed?" She shook her head. "McNulty's a prick, but he's also a rich prick. He's not the type to risk jail for more of what he's already got."

Logan folded his hands behind his head. "Well, whatever the case, now that Neil is dead, what do you bet the thrill wears off?"

"For Roger or Leslie?"

"Does it matter?"

"You tell me, Mr. Stuart Logan, P.I."

He laughed. "Okay. Why does a person kill another person?" He looked at her expectantly, as if the question was more than just plain rhetorical. "Greed, sex, revenge."

"It's not the money," Corie assured him. "The money's nice, but it's just not her. She didn't give a shit about Neil—but she'd sooner divorce him than kill him."

"So then you've got sex," Logan suggested, turning on one elbow to face her.

"So do you." Corie giggled, reaching a hand under the sheet and squeezing. She snuggled close. Her skin felt like velvet against his. "But you're right. As far as Neil was concerned, there was no shortage of young flesh. Use 'em up, spit 'em out. That was his creed."

"So I heard." His nerves tingled at the feel of two mounds of soft skin pushing against his ribs.

Corie drew a design on Logan's chest with her finger. "Maybe someone wanted to buy him out, and he wouldn't sell, so that someone bumped him off. Figured if Leslie got her hands on his share of the company she might be easier to deal with."

Logan thought this over, then shook his head. "Nice theory, except they had him where they wanted him. Neil Novak *was* Rhapsody Records. With him out of the picture they'd be scrambling like mad to shore it all up."

"Revenge, you think?"

"The mob's creed."

"Rats eat their own young," she pointed out.

"Especially when they talk to the grand jury," Logan said, staring at the dark ceiling. He ran a hand down the cleft between her breasts, watched as the goose bumps formed. "And they usually leave no trace."

"But the gun in Jenny's car—"

"Exactly. Not the Carbone trademark." He rolled over,

propped himself up on one elbow, and studied her intently. "What about Leo Gold?"

She shook her head. "They were good friends."

"Not after Neil uncovered the counterfeit scam."

Corie stared at Logan, then slowly shook her head. The look in her eyes told him that he was on the right track about Gold's relationship with Novak. "You *do* get around, don't you?"

"That's me." He smiled. He kissed her on the nose, then ran a finger down the sheet that seemed molded to her luscious curves. Then he sat up and swung his legs to the floor—a far shorter distance than he expected.

"What? Leaving so soon?" Her voice was a blend of carefree playfulness and genuine anxiety.

"Places to see, people to do," he said apologetically. He didn't want to be leaving any more than she appeared to want him to. "You just save some of that for me . . . for later."

She thought this over, frowned for a moment, then seemed to accept it. "Will she ever see him again?" she asked with a smile in her voice, her question sounding like a headline from *Cosmopolitan*. No anxiety, no strings, no more than last night and this morning. "Or was this a fleeting memory that will fade into the sunset?" She gracefully rose to her feet, the sheet wrapped around her, her naked body pushing at the fabric in all the right places.

Logan fixed his eyes on what tempted, and shot her a glimpse of what she'd called his bedroom eyes last night.

"Sweetness love, I do not go in weariness of thee," he whispered as he touched his lips to hers.

"Donne again?" she breathed.

"Far from it," he sighed. "Just beginning."

23

Logan waited for a string of cars to pass, then joined the southbound flow of beach traffic pouring up from the city or pouring down through the canyons from the Valley. The light summer fog was releasing its grip on the beach, giving way to a few voluminous clouds trundling in from the Pacific, filling the deep blue Saturday sky with kingdoms of white puffs.

Corie had injected him with a spark, the faintest glimmer of future, a turn away from the sorry plodding of the past that had cast itself upon him. He sensed a churning deep within, but he did not know or care where or why. For a brief shining moment here was Camelot, a double-wide mobile home perched on a bluff above the romance of Paradise Cove.

He drove past the same landmarks he'd passed the night before. Ubiquitous T-shirt shops advertising three for ten bucks, scuba shops where summer crowds of young turks hung out with bikini-clad babes. Microcosmic shopping centers, each housing three or four small boutiques or galleries or pizza joints. Beach houses clung capriciously to the small wrinkle of land on the ocean side, slung out over the sand.

He pulled into the parking lot of a Jack in the Box and came to a stop alongside a telephone booth. He dropped a quarter in the slot and dialed a number from a slip of paper he dug out of his wallet.

"Novak residence," came a voice with a thick south-of-the-border accent. Gruff yet female.

"May I speak with Leslie Novak, please?"

"I'm sorry, Meesus Novak no come to phone. Goo'-bye."

The accent hung up, leaving Logan holding the receiver. He steamed, dug through his pockets for another quarter, found only a dime. He went inside and bought a taco and begged a dollar in change, then returned to the phone and dialed again.

"Don't hang up!" he barked rudely when she picked it up again. "I know she's there, she's expecting—"

"Mr. Logan! Is that you?"

"Mrs. Novak?" he asked lamely through a bite of tortilla and cheese, the best fast-food Mexican grease in town. "I'm sorry—"

"No. It's my fault. I forgot to tell Maria you'd be calling."

Logan accepted her polite apology and pleaded for a few minutes with her. She agreed, and he eagerly consented to drop by for an early-afternoon gin and tonic. From where he stood, she sounded as if she was already sucking down her second or third of the day.

* * *

Logan raced back to the motel, showered and shaved, ran a comb through his hair, and slipped into a combo of white slacks and blue tropical shirt. Then he dashed back downstairs to his car, where he got to once again tackle the crosstown traffic.

This time, instead of sneaking up into the Bel Air hills and parking down the street from the Novak estate, Logan drove directly up to the gate and pressed the intercom button. The old Plymouth Fury seemed out of place in the neighborhood, as if it belonged to the pool man rather than an invited guest. He waited a few moments before Maria's static voice came over the speaker and eventually agreed to let him in.

He pulled up the cobbled drive, past an ornate tiled fountain shooting streams of water through little boys' penises. The sloping lawn could only be described as expansive and manicured, edged with flowers that somehow defied the penetrating heat. The Mediterranean-style mansion itself seemed freshly painted, its pseudo-adobe walls newly whitewashed. The tile roof appeared ancient, covered with lichen and moss, a decorator technique no doubt designed to fool guests into thinking it dated back to the Spanish settlement.

Logan pulled the Plymouth alongside Leslie's yellow BMW and a British racing-green Aston Martin Volante. Neil's car, no doubt. He gathered the roses he'd picked up at Conroy's and mounted the tile steps leading to the massive oak door. He touched the Florentine doorbell and waited a few moments before a shadow appeared through the panels of red floral glass. Finally the door sneaked open.

Maria's eyes came to his neck. She looked up at him, her dour eyes piercing his with protective skepticism.

"Meester Logan?" she asked, glaring suspiciously at the roses. "Thees way."

"*Gracias,*" Logan said, almost bowing.

"*Un momento, por favor.*" She disappeared through a door and returned a moment later with the lady of the house.

"Stuart . . . you found us." Leslie Novak shook his hand as if she was reaching for a Kleenex. She was dressed in a white strapless sundress cinched at the waist and exposing great swarms of freckles to the sun. "It's such a hot day."

"Indeed," Logan said, handing her the roses. He glanced around the entry hall; the place was stuffed with floral arrangements of all shapes and sizes. His roses seemed like child's play among real toys.

She accepted them graciously and smiled, then handed them to Maria. She plucked several dead petals from the dozen, then disappeared through a set of heavy double doors to locate a vase.

"Thank you for agreeing to see me, Mrs. Novak. Again, I want to express my deepest sympathies—"

"Of course," she said with detached chill, waving off excess sentiment. She ushered him through the two-story entry hall, edged in hand-hewn timbers and more stained glass. Blue and yellow imported tiles were artfully imbedded in the white plaster walls, and a massive chandelier hung from the cathedral ceiling. The hall extended to the back of the house, with stairways on either side leading up to the second floor and connecting in a clerestory balcony at the rear. Paintings, which Logan assumed were the real thing, were expertly positioned on the walls as in a museum. Two antique chairs sat on the red tile floor, one at the base of each of the two stairways.

He offered his compliments on such a fine house, approval which she shrugged off as she led him into the front living room.

"We had to choose between Spanish and Tudor," she explained with the whimsy only idle money can afford. "Finally decided this was more in keeping with L.A."

The living room was as expansive and impressive as he expected it to be, again towering up two stories before the ceiling peaked with exposed, hand-hewn beams. An enormous adobe fireplace consumed the far wall, guarded by a set of crossed swords set above the mantel. The furniture was all Spanish oak: two long sofas with dark oak arms and matching Mediterranean floral prints flanked possibly the largest coffee table Logan had ever seen. Four antique chairs, identical to those in the entryway, were stationed at either end of both couches. A wool rug of Mexican origin protected the polished oak floor from this antique collection, and several pieces of artwork that looked suspiciously like Picassos broke up the expanse of white walls. A second-floor balcony loomed above the far wall.

She led him through beveled glass doors out onto the back patio. The yard, if it could be simplified as such, stretched back to a stand of trees, a perfect fairway of manicured Bermuda grass carpeting the acreage. A north-south paddle-tennis court was set off on the far side of the lawn, while a large, freeform, stone-rimmed pool—fed by a trickling waterfall—hugged a man-made hillock with a bubbling spa and gazebo at its crest. The patio, a mix of red and yellow Italian tile, stepped down to the poolside, bordered by a row of freshly pruned roses. An outdoor bar and barbecue pit, also lined in tile, could easily accommodate the throngs of guests for which the house was designed.

"Gin and tonic okay?" Leslie Novak asked as she swept to the bar where ample doses of Tanqueray and Schweppes were lined up.

"Fine," Logan answered as he steeled himself for the hair of the dog. "This is an absolutely beautiful place, Mrs. Novak."

She nodded as she dropped ice into two highball glasses. "Amazing what a shitload of money will buy, huh? And please . . . call me Leslie. Mrs. Novak is Neil's sweet, gracious mother." Her tone suggested she could easily have added "the bitch" without feeling even a touch of remorse.

Logan nodded and let her do her thing. She was mesmerizing; no other word would suffice. Her face was soft and lightly tanned, just enough makeup to accent her features but not mask her natural beauty. The sun glinted off her auburn hair, styled in a way that could only be described as completely fuckable. Even more so than when he'd spoken with her on Rodeo Drive last Wednesday. He could easily see why Roger McNulty hung around.

She dragged a chair into the sun, then pulled a small table alongside and sat down. Logan did the same, positioning his chair at a strategic angle, neither beside her nor facing her. He wanted to look at her but didn't want his visit to appear too much like a formal interview.

"Saturday in the country," he sighed as he stretched his legs out and let the sun go to work on his face and arms.

"A little piece of heaven in a hellhole of decadence," Leslie agreed as if she were quoting someone. She allowed a hearty sip of gin to flow down her throat, then looked at him intently.

"A good friend of mine thinks I'm crazy to even be talking with you," she continued. "I hope he's wrong. He usually is."

"Roger McNulty." Logan easily guessed as he tipped his head and took a sip. "Seems a bit jumpy, if you ask me."

"That's my Roger. Impetuous and arrogant. He said I should kick you out on your ass. But I'm intrigued." She swallowed again. "Aren't you going to ask my why?"

"Why?"

"Because." Her lips quivered as she said it. Like a rich schoolgirl giving some vague reason for why she'd stolen a lipstick from the drugstore. A reason no one would ever understand, least of all herself, but a reason just the same. Logan's instinct told him that Leslie Novak probably never knew why she did things, why she felt what she felt. She just *did*, and that alone was good enough. She obviously was intrigued by how Logan found her at Jean Michel's, and equally intrigued by what he must be thinking of her grieving widow act. And she was intrigued by the mere sight of Logan, six feet without shoes, hands that could work her every passion to the surface, eyes that could squeeze out a flurry of fantasies just by fixing on her own for one second too long. Imagine what the rest of him could do.

"Actually, if anyone was intense, it was Neil," she added.

"And do you know anyone who may have had a conflict with his intensity?" he asked.

"Practically everyone at one time or another." She shrugged her bare shoulders, and a strap slipped. She ignored it. "Even me. Neil was ... unpredictable. Had very few friends, and rarely trusted those he had. Kept to himself, and as a result he thought only of himself. If he wanted something ... or someone ... he didn't care how far he had to go, or who he had to step on, to get it. Flattened a lot of feet to get where he was. That was his image. So do I think he screwed enough people over to the point that someone would want him dead? Yeah. Christ, sometimes I even wanted to wring the little shit's neck."

Logan eyed her with calculated bewilderment.

"I know what you're thinking," she continued, her fluidity of speech quickly balancing out the level of gin in her glass. "Here's poor Leslie Novak, grieving widow, just a week after her husband's death, sipping gin on her back patio and confessing how her late husband's death is anything less than a total tragedy. So let's set the record straight: I'm no coldhearted opportunistic bitch. But hell, it's no real secret—nothing really is in this G.D. town. Neil and I, we didn't exactly live in ultimate marital bliss, you know what I mean? He went his way and I went mine. And sure, I'm sad and

grieving . . . in my own way. But I used up most of my sadness years ago, so there's not a whole lot to tap into now. Do
I shock you?"

"Not at all," he said with considered vagueness. "Nothing
shocks me anymore. Not in this, as you say, G.D. town."

She nodded, as if he'd just scored a three-pointer. "Sounds
like we're on the same wavelength."

"Sounds like."

"Then where do we start?"

"You tell me."

Leslie sipped her drink as she dredged up an episodic past.
"How 'bout the sex and drugs of rock and roll. That's what
this town's all about, right?" She didn't wait for an answer.
She started by recounting a wandering, wondrous series of di-
gressions, little vaudevillian blackouts and orgiastic moments,
details of the life of a wife of a show-biz tycoon.

"Just for example, we had this party one night," she said,
her voice animated, excited. "Little get-together. Two, three
hundred guests. Close friends and colleagues. Neil was introducing a new act, some group that never made it out of the
starting gate. He touted them as the next Beatles, but back
then everybody was supposed to be the next Beatles. Anyway, it was a hot summer night, maybe six years ago. By the
time the band started playing, everyone was pretty well
toked, one way or another."

"And the rest is history?" Logan conjectured.

"Hysterical, actually." Leslie giggled giddily. She sucked
her glass dry, then set it on the table next to her. "It was one
of those awful heavy-metal acts Neil loved so much, and they
were awful. And when the band cleared out, there were about
thirty of us left, some in greater stages of dress than others.
Everyone sort of drifted over to the pool, the only cool place
around, even that late at night. I don't have to tell you what
happened after that."

No—but Logan wanted to hear it anyway. She read his
mind and paused, teasing him while she returned to the bar
for yet another refill, picking up his glass along the way.

"How we lived to talk about it I'll never know." The legendary Hollywood orgy, in the flesh.

Logan pictured the scene as Leslie intended him to, while
she filled in every detail, every fantasy. An assembly-line
party with interchangeable parts. Logan had heard of them,

even written about them on occasion. But he'd never witnessed one up close.

"And your husband?" he asked cautiously.

"Aren't you just a little bit curious about me?" She smiled as she handed Logan his glass and reclined in her own chair.

"Absolutely."

"Good," she said, running a teasing tongue over her lower lip. "Well, while Neil was out at the pool with his groupies, I was in the cabana with a couple of mine. He didn't seem to mind." The gin and the shock value were knocking down Leslie Novak's inhibitions right and left.

"And what did you think . . . ?"

She shrugged. "I never gave it much thought."

Logan did, and he fell silent as he contemplated the fantasy of entwined flesh. "How did Lynn Sutton fit in?" he asked gingerly, now treading an active fault.

"Wherever Lynn Sutton went, Neil was sure to go," Leslie Novak said very matter-of-factly. A slight breeze rustled over the patio, and she tossed her hair in the sun.

"And you didn't give it a second thought."

"It was a gradual thing. We sort of drifted apart. Sex became a footnote. We started sleeping in separate beds, then even in separate rooms."

She began elaborating again, this time on the dissipating marriage, how she had considered divorce a half dozen times but never quite got around to it. Life with Neil Novak had been unbearable, but because he spent so much of his time away from the house her time with him wasn't quite hellish.

"And then he bought the boat," Logan pressed.

"Best thing that could have happened. Got him out of the house, kept him out of my hair. So to speak." She sucked on an ice cube with a subliminal, if not altogether subtle, ferocity.

"The boat was his second love?"

"Right behind Rhapsody Records, and far ahead of me." Again her voice oozed with sexual tension, but fueled by resentment.

"Did you ever go out with him?"

"On the boat? Once, maybe twice. I'm a landlubber. Didn't see the thrill of it at all. Cramped quarters, always rocking about, toilet was too small. And we were always running out of ice."

"You ever go out to Catalina with him?"

Her eyes opened wide, part of a knowing grin. "Him and me? You got to be kidding. That was his . . . love nest. Wives need not apply. But it was kind of handy. When he went off to the island, I knew he wouldn't be back for the night." She winked lasciviously.

"So while he was out you stayed home?"

"I stayed discreet. Funny how horny you get when you're locked up at home all day with nothing to do. It's true what they say in this town about housewives. And widows."

Leslie Novak stared off at the trees, momentarily lost in fantasy. Then she drew her gaze back to him, her deep-blue eyes bent on mesmerizing his. She licked her lips again, and Logan sensed a shift in the Bel Air breeze.

"You're not married," she announced with expectant hope.

"Nope." He took a stiff swallow of gin and tonic.

"You probably think I'm too old for you." She nibbled at the rim of her glass, teasing, testing him.

"Actually, *I'm* probably too old for *you.*"

Jesus. She was coming on to him, this lean, tight, toned widow of independent means. In fifteen minutes he could have her upstairs, wrestling her slick body on whatever bed she had up there, tasting the pleasures of her flesh. Pure physical pleasure, an adventure in moving.

"Well?" she purred. "Are you game?"

He said nothing. Game? Sure, he felt game. But he also was prudent. To say nothing of confused. And faithful?

She sensed his reluctance. "You probably have a girl? Don't want to screw things up with her, pardon the pun."

He didn't know if he had a girl, and he didn't know if there was anything to screw up. But he knew this scene, he'd seen the part before. Both parts, in fact. When Molly had died he wanted to cut loose, make love until his whole body ached. He wanted to release the energy, span the chasm that cut him off from where his life seemed to be. It hadn't worked quite that way, just a few fleeting moments when opportunity had been gracious. But now he sensed that Leslie Novak needed the same thing. She needed release, she needed to leave her brains on her pillow upstairs.

"Rain check?" he reluctantly suggested.

"It never rains in L.A.," she observed, not without a not-so-subtle look of disappointment that Logan suspected, all modesty aside, probably lingered long after she walked him to his car and he drove off down the driveway.

24

Logan was sitting on his balcony again, staring out at the pewter-colored surf, working his way through a soggy roast-beef sandwich and a gin and tonic. The two he'd had at Leslie Novak's had primed him for the day, and he continued to feed his thirst when he got home. His aviator shades were tipped down over his eyes, and the ceaseless sun was burning circles around the rims.

He'd bitten off another bite of roast beef and lettuce when the phone rang. He wiped the mustard from his mouth and answered it on the second rude burp.

"Yo." L.A. definitely was setting in.

"Hey, Logan. Chick Tedesco."

"Chick." When he'd handed the ex-junkie his card he really never expected to hear from him. "Figured you'd be tending bar at some ritzy wedding reception somewhere."

"Listen to that," Tedesco said as he evidently held the phone up so Logan could get an earful of clinking glasses, people shouting, party sound effects. "Look, man. I only got a minute, thought you might be interested. Morgue's got a stiff comin' in."

"Yeah? What's up?"

"You know this dude McNulty?"

"He's dead?" Logan sat up, almost choking on his sandwich.

"No such luck. But his little red Mercedes is. Heard it just up and blew, right in the middle of Wilshire. Couple hours ago."

"Roger survived?"

"He wasn't driving. Some kid from some detailing shop bit it. Dude was returning the car and it just went up."

"You're sure 'bout this?"

"Bet your ass. Number one topic of convo 'round this boring little soir-*ee*."

175

"Jesus." Logan whistled. "Car must be in pretty bad shape—?"

"We're talkin' McNuggets. Looks like it may have been the car phone. They found the handset along with part of the guy's right arm. Talk about long distance. Look, I gotta get back to the bar, see to it these rich folks get properly tanked."

Logan thanked Chick quietly and hung up. As he gently replaced the receiver his stomach started doing wild back-flips, churning at the thought about that split second of pain when the body is ripped apart, before the brain is dead enough to discount the agony.

He picked up the phone, thought for a moment, then dialed. The voice that answered sounded tinny and hollow, a voice filtered by the weak signal of a backyard cordless phone. It was Jeff Rhodes' voice, cooked and softened by the pervasive Southland sun.

"Logan," Rhodes greeted him over a cold backyard-barbecue beer. "To what do I owe the pleasure?"

"Roger McNulty," Logan said simply. "What gives?"

A long silence followed as Rhodes contemplated fact or fiction. Eventually he settled on the first option and offered up an edited synopsis. McNulty's car exploded some three hours ago, the kid who was driving it was killed instantly. The explosives apparently were placed in the handset of the car phone, rigged to go off when the receiver was picked up.

"Any link to Novak?" Logan asked.

"Novak's dead," Rhodes reminded him with blatant sarcasm. "But speaking of the dead king, remember the gun? The one they found in the Baxter woman's car?"

"What about it?" Logan mumbled through a mouthful of beef, bread, and mustard.

"It wasn't Jenny's gun," Rhodes said slowly, drawing out each word. "It was Novak's."

"Jeez . . ." He paused a beat, mid-chew. He waited until he could swallow, then said, "Killed with his own gun."

"Wrong, Logan. Guns don't kill people, people kill people." Rhodes allowed him time to suppress a laugh. "Novak reported it stolen five years ago."

Logan thought for a moment, swallowed the remains of his sandwich. "How 'bout prints?"

"Jenny's, like I told you before. Some partials, unidentified. And a few smudges of latex rubber."

"Gloves?"

"Looks like."

"A pro job, you think?"

Logan could sense Rhodes shaking his head. "A screwed-up job is more like it," he said. "Autopsy report said she died from a broken neck when her car hit the tree. What it doesn't explain is the massive dent in the back of her skull, or all the bruises and welts on her arms and legs."

"Ligature marks?" Logan guessed.

"Bingo." Rhodes hesitated, as if searching his brain for anything more he could leak. "What gets me is that your red-head probably didn't know a damned thing that's going on, really. She gets her head bashed in, while sleazebag Roger McNulty sits on his fat ass while his friggin' car get blown to bits."

"And your friends at the Sheriff's Office?"

"Don't worry. They did their scripted part. Found him down at his restaurant in Beverly Hills, what's it called—Piccolo—and ran a few standard questions by him. And all he does is giggle and shrug. That's what gets me."

Logan offered gratuitous thanks for the information, realizing it included the barest of details that Rhodes thought could be leaked. Still, it was enough to push forward one more step, see to what dead-end street he might travel this time.

He stared at the legal pad balanced on his knee, the network of relationships and cross-relationships. He connected a solid line from Jenny Baxter to Neil Novak, still unsure of the nature of the relationship. Leslie Novak had told Logan that Neil's trips to Catalina were reserved only for special, intimate guests. Yet Jenny Baxter had been Billy Keenan's manager, and Logan recalled that Leo Gold had said she had met with Novak and Keenan at Sonnet Sound the afternoon before they set out for their island cruise. Was Novak breaking his own rules, merging business with pleasure aboard the *Rhapsody on Blue*?

Another question nagged him: how did Lynn Sutton get out to Catalina, and why was she there? Did Novak invite her out, and if so, did she accompany Novak and Jenny for some sort of wild sexual orgy? What was it that Jenny had told Logan at the bar the night he picked her up, or vice versa? Three's a crowd, and she preferred duets. And what motivated her to sneak out of Logan's apartment that night to return to the *Rhapsody on Blue*? And while she was on the boat, what did she witness, and who or what did she see?

Further, what did she know that she might have revealed to Logan had she not been killed just hours before she had a chance to get to him?

Which brought his thoughts back to Corie. How many secrets had they shared? How much did Corie know, beyond the fact that Jenny had entered into a marriage of modern convenience? Maybe she knew lots more than she was letting on, and maybe Corie still was protecting her dear friend from postmortem examination. And maybe Logan should have called her earlier, to check on how she was doing. And to reassure her that last night was not just part of a passing sexual shuffle.

So he made up for lost time, dialed Corie's number.

"Hi, sweetcakes. How's the world of the leisure class?" he asked when she answered the phone.

"Leisurely," she said. "Packed a little lunch, went down to the beach."

"Life-styles of the rich and famous."

"More like the idle and unemployed," she purred. "Why don't you come out and join me?"

"Don't tempt me."

"That's the point. A cool drink under the sun, water lapping at your toes, cool breeze on your skin. Paradise found at Paradise Cove. Champagne wishes and caviar dreams."

"What's for dessert?"

"The sweetest tart you've ever had." She laughed.

He wanted to give in and join her, to ease his mind and purge his soul. Forget Neil Novak and Lynn Sutton and Jenny Baxter, leave them behind for a day. To hell with Frank Kennedy and Leo Gold and Roger McNulty and Leslie Novak and even the Carbone family.

"Sounds like a plan. But I've got a few things I've got to take care of first."

"Ah, yes . . . the man of mystery. Well, try to hurry. I'll just chill a little chardonnay, peel the shrimp, and bronze my taut flesh until you get here."

"I can hardly wait."

"Haven't you heard? Patience is a virtue."

"*Virtue?* I hope I'm not giving you a wrong impression." He felt a cold rush kiss his skin as she giggled, light as crepe, and hung up.

* * *

He passed the restaurant four times as he circled the block, looking for a parking space. The pink-and-blue sign spelled out PICCOLO in cursive neon lettering, and at the curb in front a green Rolls-Royce Corniche was off-loading a man and woman who looked like storefront mannequins. Under normal circumstances Logan would have cruised the block until a space opened up, but the squall of afternoon rush-hour traffic forced him to concede defeat. He exchanged his keys for a pink parking stub from a kid with a Middle Eastern accent, who told him to "aff a nice lutch."

It was too late for lunch and too early for dinner, almost three o'clock. He stepped through the double doors of frosted glass etched with intricate Art Deco designs.

Whatever designer had been commissioned to define this latest trend in fine dining was partial to coral and lime pastels, black-and-white checkerboard marble floors, brushed aluminum tubing, and indirect lighting. The dining room was set off on several levels, levels which Logan imagined were assigned depending on a customer's social status or power tier. Floor-to-ceiling mirrors lined the far wall and had the effect of doubling the size of the restaurant.

The tables in the nouveau-chic bar were already beginning to fill with a crowd of meat-eaters, eyes constantly drifting up to check out each new face like a contest entry. Logan gazed across the bar, then glanced around the dining room. His bearings found, he relaxed—just as he felt a presence rise up behind him.

"Table, sir?" inquired the maitre d'. He was a short, thinnish man with a pretentious yet sterile manner.

"I'm here to see Roger McNulty," Logan explained curtly.

"Yes, sir. Who shall I say—?" So the prick was in residence.

"Stuart Logan, Justice Department." Logan casually flashed a bogus I.D. in his wallet and the maitre d' scurried off. He thought about sidling up to the bar and ordering a Tanqueray on the rocks, but didn't know how long he'd have to wait.

As it turned out, not long at all.

McNulty seemed older than he did just three days ago. His face was craggy and weathered, his eyelids sagged, and his forehead looked as if someone had raked wrinkles with a lobster fork. He wore an off-white sport jacket, and the unbuttoned collar of his pink polo shirt exposed a heavy gold neck chain with some sort of jeweled pendant dangling from it. An anachronism in the flesh.

McNulty grunted his displeasure with the maitre d', who looked confused and then glanced over where Logan was standing.

Logan heard parts of words which, added together, sounded like "I'm sorry, Mr. McNulty, but he said he was waiting for you."

"It's okay, Roberto. I'll straighten it out." McNulty strode into the bar and approached Logan.

"Roger." Logan raised a casual brow in greetings. "Too bad about your car."

"Get out. Now."

"You have a nice place here," Logan said, ignoring McNulty's attempt at verbal persuasion. "You know, you're a hard man to track down. I've got a few questions I'd like to run by you ... nothing difficult, mind you. And there are no right or wrong answers."

"You don't listen real good, do you?" McNulty rasped, his anger mounting. He placed a rough hand on Logan's shoulder and began to back him toward the wall. "Now, if you'll just leave before you create a scene—"

Logan shook McNulty's hand free. "A scene like the one between you and the poor grieving widow Novak?"

"That's it, you bastard—"

McNulty's hand reached for Logan's collar, but Logan caught it with a firm grip and twisted it back.

"You already ripped one shirt, and that's enough," he sneered, conjuring up his best Doberman impression. "Besides, I'm sure you're just dying to know who blew up your nice little red Mercedes. 'Cause if you knew that, you'd know who was trying to kill you."

Heads in the bar were beginning to turn. McNulty fumed. "Listen, you son of a bitch—"

"*You* listen ... it might save your slimy little neck."

"*My ass*—"

"That too. Look, Rog. Can I call you Rog? As you may have already figured out, I've sort of taken an interest in the death of your main squeeze's late husband."

"I'm not involved with any of this shit—"

"You sure as shit *are* involved. You're involved because Neil Novak is involved, and because his vices are involved. His wine, his women, his song. You're involved because someone this afternoon tried to pick you off. And you either know who it is, which has got you shaking in those two-hundred-dollar shoes of yours, or you *don't* know who and you're about ready to piss your pants."

McNulty stepped forward, tightening his fists. Then he sensed the eyes of at least a dozen attentive patrons piercing him with curiosity. He backed down. "Five minutes, then you get the hell out. Understand?"

Logan nodded. He followed Roger through the dining room to a small door carved out of the coral wall, next to the men's room. "I'll have my decorator call your decorator," he quipped as McNulty closed the door and sat on top of his immaculate marble-and-chrome desk. His throne of power.

"The clock is ticking," McNulty reminded him, his voice quavering on a note of suspicion. Fact was, Logan was right: Roger *was* worried about who blew up his car. Damned worried, and Logan's suggestions did little to calm his nerves.

Logan fixed his eyes on McNulty's. "You think it's just a simple twist of fate that Novak is dead?" he asked slowly.

"You don't get anywhere in this town without making yourself a few enemies," McNulty said flatly. "But I really didn't know him well enough—"

"Shit . . . don't waste my time." Logan pulled an insulted look out of his emotional repertoire. "You supplied his habit, provided his women, and boffed his wife on the side. You have a business relationship with Frank Kennedy that's got the feds circling the wagons, waiting for the word from the grand jury."

McNulty's lip curled up in a snarl. "You're fucking crazy if you think I killed Neil."

Logan shook his head quickly. "He was too good a customer for you to even think about wasting him. You'd be stupid to have anything to do with it—but you probably know the folks who did."

McNulty slid off the desk and sort of shook himself into place, then paced toward the window and gazed out on the parking lot full of Jags and Bentleys and the occasional Maserati. "Look, Logan, whoever or whatever you are. A lot of people didn't like Neil. In the long run, he was a shit. Most of the people in this business are. But shits learn to put up with shits. And you quickly learn who your friends are . . . and your enemies."

"And Novak?"

"Neil Novak didn't have a whole lot of friends, and those he had really were enemies in drag. They were friends more out of necessity than friendship. You gotta understand one thing: to these guys, this business is a sport."

"So what do you call blowing up a car?"

McNulty said nothing, and for a moment Logan thought he might see a tear form in the corner of Roger's eye. Then he growled, low but distinct, "No respect for German technology."

"It was supposed to be you," Logan pressed. "In the car."

McNulty lifted his gaze to Logan's eyes, the dark fear steaming within betraying his composure and stoicism. The intent of the blast certainly was not lost on him. "Your five minutes are up," he informed his unwelcome guest.

"This time they missed, maybe even on purpose," Logan prodded. "Gave you a warning, a head start. But they're gonna come back and do it right, no more fuck-ups. And you know who these people are, and you know they're good."

"You son of a bitch . . . get out!"

Logan calculated the fury in McNulty's eyes and decided it was time to split. He moved toward the door and pulled it open, stepping into the short hallway that led back to the dining room. Then he turned and flashed McNulty a knowing grin.

"Just remember, Rog: they'll try again." Logan looked deep in his eyes. "And when they do, I'll send flowers."

He turned and eased the door quietly behind him, wondering just how quickly his words would ring true.

25

The faintest of faint wisps of fog danced across Pacific Coast Highway, obscuring the sea with a ghostly lace curtain. The air was heavy and wet and still.

The mist drew Logan into its depth, inviting him with its

cloak of comfort. It reached him where he always felt the coldest: the ulcerating images of the past. There had been a time, a very long time, when Molly graced a gallant pedestal, kept there by a relentless need to preserve the past, every precious moment seemingly suspended by glass threads. He'd fought to keep it that way, an easy task in the beginning and one in which he could feel great accomplishment for extending as long as he did. He had tried to prolong the agony, to sabotage the healing process and reject the inevitable. But time was an arrogant elixir of health. After enough time, wounds really *do* heal, and life really *does* go on. With only a slight scar to remind of earlier pain.

And time finally was beginning to perform its task with Logan. An old, familiar tide was surging through his veins, an excitement drawn from hope and promise. Out of death— Neil's, Lynn's, Jenny's—Logan had found a fiber of his own life and a purpose that had languished far too long. And in Corie he had snared a passion he thought he'd cast to the sea along with Molly's ashes.

He loosened his grip on misery and all its accumulated company, ever so lightly but still enough to let in a rekindled spark. The loneliness, the loss, could now be touched, eased by a soft hand and not the lingering faint hope that this was all a terrible dream. Memories remained strong and eternal, but the sharp pain now was only a dull sedative. He felt a future again, a future that offered much more than pain and sadness. It was time to close one door and allow another woman to step through another.

Corie had left word with the guard to wave Logan through the gate. The amber sun had long since succumbed to the afternoon fog, now quickly loping in from the sea and swallowing the beach and rocks and scrub and the steep coastal cliffs. Logan pulled his car into the driveway behind Corie's and turned the key off. He sat in stillness for a moment, letting himself disappear into the gray curtain that washed in around him. Then he mounted the front steps and knocked.

She opened the door. "You missed the sun," she whispered.

He wrapped his arms around her from behind as she sank against him. "I missed you more," he told her.

She took his hand, lightly, and led him inside.

Later he felt his own soft tears as he lay with her in her warm bed. Her touch played down his body like the determined fog outside, swallowing him, enveloping him in a world emerging from the glowing embers smoldering within.

"So . . ." she breathed, unable to contain herself any longer as she nuzzled against him, the thin cotton sheet scattered to the floor. Her legs gripped him gently and she ran a teasing finger down his chest. "It's time to expose the mystery man."

"What we just did, my dear, was anything but a mystery."

"Mmmm," she purred, as if the last time her senses had been exposed so thoroughly was but a distant memory. "Better than my greatest fantasy, which is just about all I've had to live on lo these many months."

He kissed her forehead and inhaled the soft scent of her hair. "Champagne wishes and caviar dreams," he reminded her.

She nibbled his ear, then pulled back far enough to focus on his eyes. "Speaking of which, was that a bottle of champagne I saw you sneaking into my fridge?"

"Two bottles, in fact." Logan rolled onto his side and touched his lips to hers. Then he rose from the bed and dragged his trousers on and padded down the hallway to the kitchen.

Moments later they were sitting on Corie's small deck, the cove obscured now by the dark fog, the distinct salty aroma of kelp churning with the plunging surf on the distant rocks.

"So . . . out with it," Corie said as she smiled at him through her flute of champagne.

"Out with *what?*" Logan's face was turned toward the bank of fog, and he breathed easily, relaxed.

"Your story." Corie stretched out her legs as she savored the night air on her face.

"What story's that?" he mumbled lazily, his eyes closed to the outside world . . . and to her curiosity.

"How a nice guy like you got into a life like this."

"I wouldn't want to bore you."

"You could never bore me."

"Don't tempt me."

Corie gave him a playful kick in the shin that was too sharp to just be playful. "Come on, Logan. Open up."

"And spoil an otherwise beautiful day?"

"Day's over. Now it's even tide."

Logan shook his head and stared out at the fog. "Sorry."

"I see." She shot him a glance of hurt and anger, a perfect blend. "The tortured, tormented man of mystery. The man with a hidden pain lurking in the dark recesses of his self-pity."

He folded his arms tightly across his chest and sat back hard. "Ancient history," he grumbled.

"Not the way you seem to dwell on it."

"A man's privacy is his castle."

"Sometimes privacy is meant for sharing," Corie grumbled back. "Especially with someone you're beginning to care about."

They sat in silence as seconds felt like minutes drifted into hours. Evidently, Corie knew when to keep quiet. And, despite his inner reluctance, Logan knew when to open up.

"Okay," he finally relented. He took a deep breath, let it out.

"Okay what?"

"Okay, I'll tell you. If you really want to know."

Corie could have responded with something sharp like "Don't do me any favors," but such a response could destroy much more than just a momentary mood. "Please," she whispered.

Logan fell silent again as he sorted through the memories he'd known someday he'd have to call into play. Finally he turned his head and drank in Corie's azure eyes.

"Okay. I was married, until a couple years ago."

"It happens to the nicest people," she said, nodding. "One out of two marriage ends in divorce."

He shook his head, sipped his champagne. The sharp bubbles distracted him as they floated over his tongue. People always assumed young marriages end only in differences, never death. It was an assumption that didn't do justice to their life, not to his and Molly's.

"We weren't divorced," he finally said, slowly, looking out at the massive wall of gray.

Corie said nothing, just sat motionless, watching him. Was he kidding, pulling her leg? No, this was not the sort of thing one joked about. If not divorce, then what? And then it hit her. She reached out, tentatively, touched him on the shoulder. He looked at her with a sad smile, and tears welled up in her eyes. "I'm sorry," she finally breathed. "I didn't know."

He shook his head, meaning of course she didn't, meaning no one ever did, meaning it was all right.

"I had no right—"

"She was killed by a burglar," he said coldly, separating fact from emotion. He looked at the champagne in his glass and set it on the deck rail. He stared out at the fog, then launched into his tale, what happened that afternoon. His first evening two years ago as a thirty-one-year-old widower, and how he spent a year wondering when the goddamned L.A. police were going to call and say they'd caught the no-good son of a bitch who did it to her. To him. And how, when they never did, his life dissolved into endless days of searching and finding nothing, and eventually finding less and less.

"Funny, how you never give a second thought to death," he sighed as he finished, a long time later. "I mean, we all think about it. It's only natural. I don't think there's anyone who doesn't wonder what its like, how empty it must be, what the final split second of life is like before it blacks out forever. If it actually does. But you never figure how something like that can affect you. And when it does it hits hard, and you have to find the strength to hit it back even harder. Like getting back up after a knockdown and going the whole fifteen rounds."

He bit his lip and stared off at the horizon, squinting back whatever part of the past was welling up in his eyes.

"Looks to me like you've won the fight."

"Hardly. What you're seeing is the edited-for-TV version. Once that self-pity started to creep in I really did a job on myself. Denial, sorrow, anger. All the textbook stuff. I couldn't eat, couldn't sleep, couldn't work. Didn't give a shit about anything. Nothing to keep me going and nothing to stop me. All the experts say, don't make any major decisions for two years. Let things settle. Adapt to the changes. But did Mr. Logan listen? Hell, first thing I did was sell the house. Too many memories, too hard to come home at night. Emptiness all around, all that shit. So I dumped it all and dropped off the planet."

"You can't beat yourself up over it forever," she reminded him, not knowing where all the mines were placed in this room they'd gingerly entered. "There comes a time when you have to let it go, realize there was no need, no meaning, for any of it."

Logan turned toward her, regarding her with a hard look, rejecting the dime-store therapy but recognizing it for its genuine sincerity. "You sound just like Dr. Gillette."

"Who?"

"Gillette. The high-priced shrink who tried to put Humpty-Dumpty back together again."

Corie slowly shook her head as she gazed into the blanket of fog. "I think he did a good job."

Logan shrugged at the condescension, or maybe sympathy. By now it was hard to tell the difference. "I'm no hero. After it happened nothing was enough, especially work. The cops couldn't find him, and neither could I. The bastard left one set of footprints, one lead slug in my wife's brain. Hardly enough to go on. The guy went free, and I crapped on every uniform I could find down at L.A.P.D. And then I crapped all over my job. Had to destroy everything that was a part of our . . . my . . . life. I'd already put the rest of my world in self-destruct, and this was the last domino."

"The guy's still out there?" Corie looked at him with more alarm than disbelief.

He nodded dumbly. He picked up the bottle and dribbled more champagne into both their glasses.

"So you fled to Catalina."

"The great escape," he mumbled.

"If you can't allow yourself the latitude to make a few errors then you'll never give yourself room to live."

"I've made my share of mistakes."

"Not lately, I hope." She smiled, squeezing his hand.

He glanced at her but said nothing. Then their eyes exchanged truths, and she leaned forward and lightly touched her lips to his. She pulled away and gazed up at him.

"I'm beginning to feel things that probably are going to scare the hell out of you," she whispered.

"How do you know?"

"Because they're scaring me."

"Mmmm."

She rested her head against his shoulder, neither of them uttering a word, not wanting to spoil whatever was being said between them. He was beginning to feel a few worrisome stirrings of his own, but now was not the time to bring them up. In her he sensed much of the same, a tentativeness in the touch of her skin on his cheek, a slight tremble rooted more in anxiety than expectation. Maybe things were moving too soon, too far. Too easily.

Suddenly she sat up, nudging Logan from the comfort of the damp fog. "I know what . . . let's go eat!"

"What?"

"Breakfast." She playfully poked his shoulder. "You know . . . first meal of the day, bacon and eggs and home fries and black coffee."

"It's not even midnight," Logan protested.

"But it's morning in London," she prodded. "Come on. Have some adventure, show some spirit."

They ate at Du-Par's in Santa Monica, two cholesterol specials with a side order of grease and unlimited caffeine. Sometime around the second refill Logan leaned back in the booth, staring at Corie with wide eyes that were starting to zing from the coffee.

"You realize, of course, we'll never get to sleep now," he remarked her as he sipped from his mug.

Corie nodded. "That's the general idea."

Logan dipped his head in understanding. He glanced around the restaurant; another couple in the opposite corner was hunkered down over matching plates of early-bird specials, heads bent together, voices whispering in conspiratorial tones. A scraggly kid at the counter was finishing up a slice of warm pie, poring over a copy of *Guns & Ammo* magazine.

"So," Logan said, drawing his leg up, hugging his knee.

"So, what?"

"So . . . I showed you mine. Now you show me yours."

"My what?"

"Come on, Corie. Open up." Logan raised his brow in a subtle grin of impending persistence.

"Ancient history?" she begged, stalling playfully.

"Now where have I heard that before?"

She grinned then, rubbed her head with her index finger. "Where do you want to begin?"

"Your brain tumor, for starters," he suggested.

She rolled her eyes toward the ceiling and laughed. "Every woman is allowed one mistake in her life," she said.

"A real turd, huh?"

"Not in so many words," she agreed as she played with the scalloped edge of the paper place mat. "He had nicer words for you."

"Me?" Logan eyed her curiously.

"You've met him."

Logan sipped his coffee, which by now was almost cold.

"He told me he had a good talk with you just the other day," she continued. "Down at the Santa Monica Pier."

"You mean—" He considered the notion for a moment. Scarface was her husband? "You were married to that slime-ball?"

"He had nicer words for you."

"I'm sorry. I just . . ." He faltered again. "He's your ex?"

"It was a long time ago," she said wearily. "In a galaxy far, far away."

"So that's how he got my name. You talked to him."

"Guilty as charged. I wanted to . . . check you out. See if you were on the level. You have no idea how much press was hanging around, bugging the shit out of me, trying to get an inside scoop."

"Chapin." He searched his brain, sifting through old garbage before the name rang a bell. "Peter Chapin. He used to do afternoon drive on Q-Rock, right?"

Corie nodded. "I told him what you were up to, said you were persistent . . . but somehow different. He agreed to meet with you. You scored pretty high."

"You got approval from your ex-husband to sleep with me?"

She grinned. "That was my score."

His mind raced through layers of thought. Los Angeles really was just a little town, tightly wrapped by a ribbon of massive freeway. He held his cold coffee in both hands and studied the lovely woman sitting across from him, a sly twinkle in her eyes.

"So tell me about this obviously good-for-nothing oaf you once loved, then left to slide down the sewer."

She giggled and kissed his hand. "He was your basic prick, the sort of man women always fall for. Charming, gallant, funny—and empty. Disc jockey, liked to call himself an air personality. More air than personality. Typical man: Full of lines and quips, always putting on a show. I shoulda figured. You know the sort—they use their wit to lull the woman into a fantasy, but when the show's over, lights out."

"So you were duped."

"Typical female excuse, huh? He was everything I thought I'd ever dreamed of. Until I married him. Then he changed, became whatever he was before we met. His own self. And self is the word: selfish, self-centered. No more chivalry, no more sensitivity, no more funny lines, even. And that face, so gorgeous and rugged and masculine in the beginning, it became transparent. I started to see right through it, right through everything."

Logan didn't think that face was so gorgeous, even for a guy. But then, he'd only seen the ironed-out version.

"Let me guess . . . you met him at one of Novak's famous parties?"

"Of course." She gave him a how-did-you-know look. "This was a listening party, one of those ridiculous things where some record label gets a bunch of radio and promotion people together to listen to the latest release from some group, and everybody says things like 'Power, dude' and 'Man, that's bodacious,' or 'Really awesome, babe.' Then they all go out and get high, maybe find another party and get higher still."

"And it lasted how long?"

"The party lasted all night. The marriage lasted a little less than two years." She grinned sheepishly; another statistic in the book. "It fell apart last November. He was in over his head. Drank too much, did a few lines now and then—nothing really unusual for the biz. But he had a penchant for gambling. Always trying to get me to go to Vegas for the weekend, certain he'd strike it rich. I went once, only because he said I'd be good luck for him at the tables. I watched him blow twenty grand in an hour. Twenty thousand bucks—that's more than I made in a whole year back then."

"And that's when you started to realize he had a problem?"

"The wife is always the last to know, or at least the last to see." She nodded glumly as her memory dredged up the past. "I tolerated it for a while, the phone calls and the threats. Then one night he came home with two dislocated thumbs because he fell behind on a bad debt. That sealed the deal. I packed, found myself a lawyer, and the rest is public record."

"So it goes."

"Right. A month after I moved out, his chits were all paid up. He was put in charge of all programming at Q-Rock, and before you know it he was Frank Kennedy's biggest buddy."

"They covered his debts?"

"Tabula rasa," Corie concurred. "At what price, I don't know."

"Nice people to get into bed with."

"I can think of better." She reached across the table, found his hand, slipped her fingers between his, squeezed gently. Her eyes met his in a warm daze, and he squeezed back.

26

Sleep was out of the question. After three cups of coffee apiece, Logan and Corie were wired for sound. From Du-Par's they cruised through the barren early-morning streets of Santa Monica, parked the Plymouth in a space at the far end of the motel lot, and retreated up to his room.

"Nice digs," Corie commented sarcastically as she glanced around the room, gingerly stepping over a stain on the worn shag.

"Home away from home," Logan agreed.

She wandered over to the bed, inspecting the spread before sitting on the corner. Logan sensed her caution and lunged at her, pulling her backwards onto the bed, pinning her arms, kissing her hard on the lips. She struggled at first, more to escape whatever vermin might be lurking in the fabric than to elude his burst of wild pleasure. Then she let up, eventually giving in altogether, all thoughts of mites and dirt evaporating in their own heat.

When they finished, moments later, Corie edged up on the bed, leaning her head against the wall. She rearranged her pink panties and tied her unbuttoned blouse in a knot just above her navel. Then she hugged her knees to her chest. Logan swung his legs to the floor as he tugged on his jockey shorts.

"So what do you think?" she asked after a long silence.

"On a scale of one to ten, I'll give it a nine."

"A nine?" She tossed a pillow at him.

"Never close the door on perfection or imagination," he said.

She thought about this for a moment, then shrugged. "Actually, I wasn't looking for a critique," she said. "I meant, what do you think of McNulty?"

"McNulty's a prick. What about him?"

191

"You think it coulda been him? You said you talked with him this afternoon."

"You're beginning to sound like me." Logan laughed. He picked up his shirt that moments before had been tossed haphazardly on the gritty floor. He draped it over a chair, then returned to the bed and sat next to Corie. "But it just doesn't figure, you know? Can't see him blowing up his own car."

"You've got a point," Corie admitted. "Unless—" Her voice broke off as she allowed the cogs to turn.

"Unless what?" Logan pressed after a moment.

"I dunno. Maybe this thing is layered in ways we don't understand. Maybe McNulty did kill Neil and Lynn, and someone who wasn't too happy about it figured out what was going on."

"What goes around comes around?" Logan said slowly, a puzzled look etched on his face.

"It's a thought."

"And a pretty one at that. But it doesn't make sense." Logan shook his head, took a long breath. "I mean, why would McNulty want to kill Novak? And Lynn Sutton? Aside from the fact that he was balling Leslie, Novak was one of his best customers. And Lynn was the backbone of his little ring of call girls. She practically ran things, from what I hear."

"McNulty acts on impulse, not logic." Corie sighed tiredly. "What I don't understand is whether Jenny went out to Catalina with Neil alone, or if Lynn was with them. And if she wasn't, how did she get out there?"

Logan had mulled this one over too, and was still mulling. It was a good question. And the more he mulled it, the more it led to a better question. Two, in fact.

He nodded. "Why Catalina? Why kill them out there, rather than right here in L.A. and—" Now the tumblers began to click. "—who the hell knew Neil Novak was going to be out there to begin with?"

"Neil goes . . . went . . . out to Catalina a lot during the summer."

"Sure," Logan said. "But this was no random murder. It had to be planned, and if it was, then the killer had to know when he'd be out there. He had to know dates and times, and he had to know where Novak moored his boat." He paused, framing his thoughts carefully. "And whoever it was knew who was going to be with him."

"You mean . . . whoever killed Neil also planned to kill Lynn from the start?" She looked at him skeptically. It was a farfetched idea, conceived from circumstantial odds and ends. Or was it?

"Could be. Maybe Jenny Baxter mentioned it to someone, and—" A sudden jolt of realization singed his spine.

"—And she just happened to be conveniently off the boat when they were killed?" Corie finished for him, her steadied voice suggesting she didn't like the implication any more than Logan did.

"It could have been mere coincidence," Logan said doubtfully. Mere coincidence that Jenny Baxter had left the Albacore Lounge with Neil Novak, only to return minutes later alone. Coincidence that she had chosen the seat next to Logan at the bar, and had accompanied him home to his apartment not five minutes later. Coincidence that after they got there, he passed out and remembered nothing of the previous twelve hours.

"So how did Lynn get out there?" Corie pondered aloud. "I mean, did they all meet by accident, or was it a setup from the start?"

"I don't know," Logan said, taking a deep breath. "Neil was into kinky sex, maybe he'd planned a ménage à trois. If Lynn just happened to show up innocently maybe he thought he could talk Jenny into something. Who knows? Maybe it *was* just a coincidence. Maybe Lynn just happened to be out there and ran into them."

"And pigs can fly."

"Well, whatever the arrangement, it got all three of them snuffed," Logan observed grimly.

"And I want you to watch your step," she cautioned him. "Roger McNulty means business. He's got his fingers in so many pies that he needs more hands."

Logan thought of the poor kid who lost his own hands while returning McNulty's car that very afternoon. "Rog knows I'm no threat to him. Not if he's innocent."

"My sweet crusader." She hugged him close.

"That's me. Neither snow nor rain nor dead of night can keep me from my self-appointed rounds."

"They could shoot your kneecaps."

"That might work," Logan agreed.

"You know something . . ." The tired cogs in Corie's head

were still turning, however slowly. "Whoever killed Neil and Lynn had to be out there that night. All night."

"I'm sure the cops have covered that angle. Checked all the hotels and guest houses, every boat moored in the harbor."

"Maybe they missed something."

Logan looked at her doubtfully. With the Sheriff's Department, the Coast Guard, and a horde of feds converging on the island, virtually no stone would have been left unturned. Still, it was a possibility. As far as Logan was concerned, the cops had a less than exemplary record in tracking down cold-blooded killers.

"Maybe they missed the obvious," Corie continued.

"Which is—?"

"Why Catalina? As you said, if someone wanted to kill Neil, they could have done it here just as easily. Lynn, too. Unless—"

"Unless Catalina was more convenient. Unless—" He stared at Corie as the obvious settled in. "Unless whoever did it just happened to live out there!"

Corie grinned modestly, then frowned. "But what about Jenny?"

Logan shook his head quickly. "Easy. Something got screwed up, and she split the scene." And then lured a lonely piano player back home for a couple of hours of ivory-tickling, he failed to add.

"So all we need is a telephone book for Catalina, right?"

"Right."

Avalon wasn't a big island, with a summer population of only several thousand restful souls, but the task of checking out every one of those several thousand was monumental. Especially when the nearest volume probably was located in the bowels of the L.A. Public Library, which wouldn't be open again until Monday morning. And that's when his eyes fell on the chair in the corner, where he'd scattered his pads and papers and odds and ends from the last few days. Odds and ends that included Neil Novak's purloined ebony address case. He trudged across the room and picked it up, then returned to the bed.

"Hey . . . that's Neil's," Corie gasped as he tentatively opened it to the letter A.

Logan shrugged. "He won't be missing it. And it might just make our job a hell of a lot easier."

"How . . . oh, shit. Never mind," she sighed as she huddled close.

She peered over Logan's shoulder as he began poring through the entries Novak had scrawled in the book over the years. Most were scratched in pencil, with numerous erasures and strikeovers, and in no particular order. Adams was followed by Arkin, followed by Abrams, then Anderson, and so forth.

"What are we looking for?" Corie asked impatiently as Logan turned the page to the B's.

"A long shot, at best." He scanned the page, then turned to the next. "Catalina's a small island. All phone numbers begin with the same prefix: 510."

"So all we have to do is find one that starts with 510, and we've got our killer?"

"I know. Sounds too simple, right?" He shrugged it off. It was elementary, too basic for clever police work. Even with all the computers and lab work and spectography and other state-of-the-art technology, everything still boiled down to simple facts. But the cop who overlooked the obvious often was looking far too hard.

"You really think Neil would have known his killer well enough to have written down his number?"

"Or *her* number," Logan reminded her as he turned to the C's. "As I said, it's a long shot. But remember: Novak was killed with his own gun, the one he reported stolen five years ago. Now, he could have been lying when he reported it missing, or maybe he later found the gun and just didn't think to tell the cops. But it's also possible whoever took it had known Novak for a long time, and only now decided to bump him off."

Corie considered this possibility and said nothing. She rested her head on his shoulder while he turned to the D's, then the E's, then the F's.

"There!" she gasped in his ear, a giddy whisper. She pointed at a name halfway down the page. "Finch!"

Logan dropped his eye to the listing. No address, just the name "Finch, Barry," and a phone number—beginning with 510.

"Who the hell is Barry Finch?" he asked, glancing up at Corie. Obviously the man was somebody, judging from the excitement lighting her eyes.

"Barry Finch," she repeated, shaking her head as if she couldn't believe it. "He was part of the old Lilac Tradewind."

"Johnny Rand's band?" Logan regarded her doubtfully.

She nodded. "Played bass guitar, I think. He and Rand were friends from way back. When the band broke up they both went solo. Johnny Rand had some success on his own, but Barry Finch hit bottom. Then Johnny Rand hit bottom, too, and nobody even thought about them until 'We Are the World.' "

Logan recalled the industry-wide musical appeal to help save the starving children in Africa. When would that have been? 1985? "They were involved in that?"

"Johnny Rand was. Barry Finch got in a car wreck on the way to the studio that night. Barely pulled through, and he never really was the same since."

"Was?"

Corie nodded, the glimmer of hope fading. "He died last spring. Complications from the crash."

"Well, I doubt he had much to do with Novak's death," Logan said with more than a fair share of sarcasm. "Unless, of course, he came back from the dead."

Corie shot him a look of mock contempt, which turned into reflection. "Or unless . . ." She paused to consider another remote possibility. "Unless Finch had a friend."

"A what?"

But Corie wasn't listening. Instead she grabbed the address case from Logan and quickly flipped through it to the first R page.

She drew her finger slowly down the page. "Johnny Rand dropped out of sight right after that," she explained, her enthusiasm rekindled. "He'd hoped the 'We Are the World.' gig would kick-start his career, but it didn't. He got more into booze and drugs and dropped out of sight. Speculation had it that he was drying out somewhere; all the checkout rags had photographers camped out at the Betty Ford Clinic for weeks, just to get a shot of him."

"You think maybe he moved twenty-six miles out to sea?"

She lifted her shoulders in a slight shrug. "I figured he was living up in a canyon somewhere, or maybe out in the desert. Never gave it much thought, I guess. But sure . . . what if he and Barry Finch just quietly slipped out of town to Catalina?"

She jabbed a finger at a faded entry and turned the address

case toward Logan. "There," she announced triumphantly. "Johnny Rand, 510-3556."

Logan looked and recognized the seven digits instantly. It was the same number that belonged to the late Barry Finch, on the island of Santa Catalina.

27

Logan switched off his headlights and edged the Plymouth down the narrow alley. He glided past a monstrous dumpster that was overflowing with shredded cardboard boxes and palm-tree prunings, then tucked the car behind the abandoned trailer of a rusted eighteen-wheel rig. A lone street lamp at the far end of the lane painted deep shadows in the night but offered little visibility.

"You sure you feel up to this?" Logan whispered.

"No, I don't." Corie glowered as they sat in the dark. "It's three o'clock in the morning, I haven't had any sleep—"

"You will," Logan assured her. "After we finish burglarizing your former place of employment."

"You really think this is all a game, don't you?" she fumed.

"What're they gonna do, fire you or something?"

"For starters, they can arrest us for breaking and entering."

"We're not breaking in," Logan reminded her. "You still have a key."

She exhaled a sigh of exasperated protest as he opened his door and cautiously slipped out of the car. He walked around the front end, keeping his head low, and helped her out. He squeezed her hand reassuringly.

They worked their way through the shadows to a side door tucked behind the pregnant dumpster. Corie fumbled in her purse for the key and tried it in the lock. No luck.

"Shit. We have to go around front."

Logan followed Corie through the dark alley to the front door. Neil Novak couldn't have picked a better place for stealth, a corner of Culver City where the fringes of life hugged the black recesses of night and no one paid any mind. When they reached the corner of the building they slipped into the recessed front entryway. Logan peered through the smoked-glass double doors. The lights were off, all except for a distant fluorescent glow coming from somewhere deep within the building.

"Someone's working late," she whispered. They waited a few seconds for the faintest sign of movement from within; then Corie inserted her key in the lock and waited for the bolt to click.

It did. They exchanged glances of mutual commitment; then Logan opened the door and ushered Corie inside. He followed her, then pulled the door closed again and snapped the lock shut.

They worked their way through the darkened central work pit. The computer terminals cast an eerie green glow on the cubicle partitions. The soft carpet hushed their footsteps as they stole past the open door of the single lighted office.

"Howie Nunn," Corie whispered once they were out of earshot. "Consummate workaholic."

Logan said nothing as he followed her up the stairs to the mezzanine suite that consisted of Novak's and her former offices. Corie hesitated at the top of the stairs, reassuring herself that they were alone in the darkness. Then she edged over to her empty desk and sat down. She swiveled her chair to face the terminal, then flipped the power switch.

"Let's just hope they haven't gotten around to deleting my data files and entry code," she said as she punched a few keys and waited for bells and sirens to go off. The on-line computer beeped twice, then a message flashed up on the screen:

ENTER PASSWORD

She typed her password, pressed *execute,* and prayed a silent prayer to the god of microchips. The terminal again beeped twice, then another message replaced the first:

MAIN MENU
SELECT ENTRY AND PRESS RETURN

"Bingo!" she whispered excitedly. "We're in!"

"Beautiful," Logan breathed, kissing the nape of her neck.

She scanned the menu, selected the entry for ARTIST FILES, and hit the return key. Another message flashed on the screen:

ENTER CONFIDENTIAL ACCESS CODE

Corie hesitated, then typed a short message and waited for a response.

ACCESS DENIED

"Damn!" she cursed.
"Try it again," Logan pressed.
Corie shrugged and typed her code again and waited. This time the terminal beeped twice and flashed:

ACCESS GRANTED

Logan leaned forward as Corie's fingers flew across the keys. Again the terminal beeped, and the first page of the desired file flashed up on the screen. At the top was the heading:

JOHNNY RAND. ACTIVE FILE #R0001A. FILE START DATE: 2/28/75

Underneath the heading was printed Rand's Social Security number and a mailing address on Avalon Canyon Road on Catalina.

"This is it," Corie whispered.
"You're a genius." He kissed the top of her head; he sensed a shudder of excitement run through her.
"Of course." She grinned. "So what are we looking for?"
"I don't know. Let's just take a look."
He watched while she scrolled through Johnny Rand's files, page after page. Little bits and pieces of numbers and names, album and song titles and recording dates. His mind raced as the pieces blurred together; then, like a Polaroid snapshot, the picture began to come clear.
"Okay, try this," he said after Corie had scrolled through the last page. "Rand was the first artist Neil Novak signed to Rhapsody Records, right? Back in 1975. So suppose Rand has a score to settle with Novak, something that goes way

back. Maybe he even stole Novak's gun and planned to do something about it at the time, only he never got the chance. In any case, something triggers this old grudge and Rand goes gunning for Novak. He finds out—maybe Jenny tells him—that Novak is going to be out on Catalina, and he hatches a plan to kill them both. How does that sound?"

"Fine. Except for one thing."

"Which is?"

"Which is that Johnny Rand is dying. Leukemia. I saw him at Neil's funeral, and I doubt he'd have the strength to even lift a gun, much less pull the trigger."

"So he had someone to do it for him," Logan said, without a moment's hesitation. "Whoever did it waited while Neil and Lynn rowed out to their boat, then sneaked aboard and shot them."

He pondered his own scenario, searching for loose ends. At least he had a suspect, however circumstantial. Not enough to convict, but adequate to move from point A to point B. What he needed now was a motive, which was why Corie was sitting in front of a computer screen at quarter to five on a Sunday morning.

"I say we keep looking," she suggested.

"It's your machine," he said, raising his palms in surrender.

They continued to search through the computer file. The first few screens accounted for seventeen-plus years of Johnny Rand transactions. Performance fees, advances, royalties paid for the three albums Rand recorded for Rhapsody between 1975 and 1980. The first of these did quite well, selling slightly more than a million copies and earning platinum status. The second sold just over a half million, still a respectable volume and enough retail sales to qualify as gold. But the third album was a dismal failure, just over a hundred thousand pressed, twenty thousand returns. An early candidate for the discount cutout bin.

Each of the three album files was accompanied by a detailed accounting of Rand's publishing earnings. At the start of his relationship with Rhapsody, his combined gross income was easily into seven figures, and his net earnings made him a millionaire several times over. But in 1980—the year his career took a nosedive—his income fell below a hundred grand. Most of his production advance was wiped out by the poor performance of the third album. The only entry that seemed to keep him off the streets was the 1986 sale of his own independent publishing company—Lilac Windsongs—to Rhapsody Blues Music. The entire catalog of songs brought him just over two hundred grand, five times what he'd earned from his songwriting the first two years combined.

Corie shook her head when she saw the figure. "That can't be right. No way Rand's songs were worth that much."

"The man *was* a rock and roll idol."

"Big deal. I've seen the files. Neil bought the entire Lilac Windsongs catalog—thirty-five, forty songs, tops. Hardly enough for Neil to pay a king's ransom. It's gotta be a mistake."

"Thirty-five songs?" Logan questioned. "That's barely enough for the three solo albums, let alone all the records he recorded with the Lilac Tradewind."

"The Tradewind songs were all published by Pacific Music. That was Tradewind's label, and their publishing wing took care of all their music. Until the group broke up and Neil stole Rand away."

"So there's got to be something more."

"Something like what?"

Logan straightened his back and stretched, then glanced back down at the screen. "Something that's not in the files. Maybe Novak paid him off. Maybe Rand had Neil's tit in the wringer."

"Blackmail?"

"Let's just say Neil had to pay Rand off for something, but he didn't want to just slide the aging hippie a wad of cash under the table. So he hid the payoff as part of the publishing deal. And saw to it that Rand never worked again."

"Rube Goldberg reasoning." Corie tipped her head back and looked at him skeptically.

"Complexity is the mother of invention," Logan persisted. He moved around to Corie's side and kneeled on the floor. "Come on . . . think. What else could Johnny Rand have done that would have netted him two hundred grand and destroyed his career, in the same one-two punch?"

"Well . . ." Corie said, rubbing the sleep from eyes that felt gritty and droopy. "We already know Neil bought Johnny Rand's publishing company and all copyrighted works registered with it. So maybe he bought more than meets the eye."

"What more could there be?"

"I don't know." She pushed back from the terminal and looked at Logan. "Most times when one publishing company buys out another, they buy all rights except for copyright and royalties. Look at Michael Jackson: he bought up scads of music, including a lot of the old Beatles songs. Every time one of those songs is played on the radio, he gets a cut. The songwriter also gets his share. But just suppose the songwriter is strapped for cash, or is stuck in a bad setup and can't get out. And just suppose that the songwriter can clear the books with one quick signature . . ."

"Can you do that?"

"You can do just about anything. No one in their right mind would sign their entire life's work away, but Johnny Rand . . ." Whatever thought was forming in her head trailed off. She glanced at the green screen, then shook her head doubtfully.

"Mind if I ask a dumb question?"

"Go ahead," Corie said wearily.

Logan picked up a pencil from what used to be Corie's desk and rolled it between his thumb and forefinger. It gave him something to do while he framed his thoughts. "Exactly what does a publisher do? I mean, what's his relationship with the songwriter?"

"In most cases, it's just like getting copyrighted," Corie began. "It protects the songwriter against someone ripping him off, and the publisher acts as the intermediary between the songwriter and whoever else might want to record or perform the song."

"And the publisher takes a cut for his services."

Corie turned toward Logan and looked at him quizzically, wondering where his thinking was going. "Of course. That's why a lot of artists set up their own publishing firms."

"Artists like Johnny Rand," Logan said.

"Exactly."

Logan leaned back, allowing this information to sort itself out. "You said you saw the files, the songs that were part of the Lilac Windsong catalogs."

"That's right. They were all from his three solo albums."

"So . . ." He paused, inserting the pencil in his mouth and chomping down on it like a horse might clench a bit in his teeth. "So, if Johnny Rand was such a prolific writer, where were all his songs? Unless he stockpiled them somewhere without ever thinking of copyrights and royalties and rip-offs?"

"You think—?" Corie's eyes lit up with a spark of discovery.

"Is there any way to check?"

She thought for a moment, then turned toward the row of file cabinets that lined the wall between her office and Novak's. Now Minetti's. She rolled the chair across the room, pedaling with her feet, pushing her way to the last cabinet. She pulled out the bottom drawer, then hauled out a hanging file with the name "Johnny Rand" typed on the little tab. She opened it on her lap and rifled through the pages.

"Hmmm," Corie pondered as she perused the list. "Interesting."

"Spill it."

"Well, looks like I was right. Thirty-six songs." She pored through reams of business transactions, royalty disbursements, and financial statements outlining Johnny Rand's history with the company. She was three-quarters of the way through the file when she came across a sheet with handwritten notations on it. She recognized the handwriting and pulled it out.

"That's funny," she mumbled after considerable silence. "Take a look at this."

Logan glanced at the sheet. It was a list of titles, hastily scrawled in pencil.

"What is this?" he asked.

"A roster of Billy Keenan's songs that were included on the last two Metric Geese albums."

Logan whistled softly, momentarily forgetting where he was and what larceny he was committing. He smiled at Corie apologetically. "Novak's handwriting?"

"Exactly."

"And you're sure these are Billy Keenan's songs?"

Without answering she rolled back to the computer and keyed in Keenan's name, then waited for the file to flash up on the screen.

"Take a look."

Logan glanced at the screen. What he saw sent an icy stab through his skin. Every song on the list showed up on the list of songs Keenan had published through Rhapsody Blues Music.

"Jesus Christ," he whispered.

Corie began scrolling through the list. "Look at some of these songs: 'Maybe My Baby,' 'Five O'Clock Shadow,'

'Dawn of Time.' What the hell are they doing in both Johnny Rand's hard file and Billy Keenan's computer catalog?"

"A lot of artists cover other people's songs."

She shook her head. "Billy writes all his own stuff. It's part of his mystique, his alleged genius. But look at these. 'Remember December,' 'Hot Foot,' 'Blind Vision,' 'Delicate Haze.' They're all from his *Appointment with Dentistry* album."

Logan watched as Corie went down the list and pointed out a total of eighteen songs bearing the same title as those released on the last three albums by Billy Keenan and the Metric Geese. Three of them—'Boxed In,' 'Everything's Not Enough,' and 'Local Lover'—were the group's last top-five hits.

"Are you thinking what I think you're thinking?" he asked.

"You mean that Billy Keenan, rock and roll prodigy, artist extraordinaire, and songwriter supreme, is a fraud?"

"Something like that." To Logan it was plain and simple: Billy Keenan was making it rich off Johnny Rand's work. For whatever reason, Rand had sold out to the devil, a twenty-year-old hairball who probably knew only a half dozen simple guitar riffs.

Unbelievable. Corie blinked at the concept. Neil Novak and Billy Keenan, right under her nose. She felt like a fool, and Logan saw it in her eyes. She'd prided herself on knowing what was going on in the office at all times, but here was proof that Novak was not exactly the man she had trusted with unquestioned loyalty.

"There's no way you could have known," Logan told her.

Corie nodded doubtfully. She sat back in her swivel chair and stared up at him. They exchanged silence for a few moments, then Corie dealt him a plaintive look.

"Johnny Rand killed Neil," she said impassively.

"Looks like."

"But why Neil and not Billy? My God, they even sat together at Neil's funeral."

"With your friend Jenny Baxter, no less," Logan reminded her, recalling their mutual conversation outside the chapel at Forest Lawn. "Billy's Keenan's manager."

"Shit," she whispered as the implication hit her. She shut down the computer and sagged tiredly in her chair.

"Let's get the hell out of here," Logan suggested as he helped her to her feet, wrapped his arm around her.

28

The sun was inching up over the distant downtown high rises as Logan pointed the Plymouth west on the Santa Monica Freeway. Dawn came like a great orange stroke across the sky, its hue deepened by the first hint of ozone swelling up from the waking city. Even at this hour the freeway was starting to choke with traffic, early risers headed for the beach or, by some slim chance, church.

Logan dug at his eyes with his hand, wiping away the sleep and smoggy sting. He glanced over at Corie, her head lolled back against the seat, her mouth gaping as she slept. He could see her chest rise and fall, her heart pumping through the exhaustion that finally had overtaken her body. He squeezed her hand, then ran his hand through his hair, brushing it out of his face. The wind pouring in over the windshield blew it right back in place.

Suddenly, without warning, she sat up and blinked her eyes in the hazy dawn.

"Oh, my God!" she cried.

Logan wildly swerved to avoid the Corvette ahead of him, then pulled back into his lane. He shot her a rabid glare.

"Jesus, Corie."

"What?" she said, her mind obviously somewhere else. "Oh. Sorry." She paused a beat, then shook her head. "God, sometimes I'm so stupid."

"Huh?" he mumbled, as he read the sign that announced LINCOLN BLVD. 1 MILE.

"Lynn Sutton," she stated. "She's the link."

"What the hell are you talking about?"

"Listen." She turned in her seat, gripped his arm as if he might blow out of the car. "You . . . we . . . have been so intent on tracking down Neil's killer that we've overlooked the obvious."

205

"Which is—?"

"Johnny Rand's sister."

"Say what?"

"Lynn Sutton and Johnny Rand are . . . were . . . brother and sister."

"Christ!"

Corie sighed a faint apology as she pulled her knees up to her chest. "It didn't hit me until just now. Mental glitch, maybe the lack of sleep."

Logan glanced down at the speedometer; it read seventy. Typical L.A. speed, but he was feeling too tired to keep up the pace. He let up on the gas pedal and slipped into the right lane. He glanced over at her, then back at the traffic flowing up from an entrance ramp. His mind focused on the diagram he'd scribbled, the lines he'd used to connect Novak with Lynn, Jenny, Johnny Rand, Kyndall Wyatt . . .

"Then that means Kyndall must be Johnny Rand's daughter."

"Who?"

"Kyndall Wyatt." He hesitated, wondering how much he should reveal about the little interlude he'd shared at the Century Plaza the night before his tryst out at Paradise Cove. No harm done: it was all platonic, all in the line of duty. He briefly described the rendezvous, carefully omitting the details of lingering lust.

"She said her father was a musician . . . but I had no idea." He sighed, cursing his own blindness.

Corie nodded absently. "Yeah . . . I think I met her once, last winter sometime. Some industry party. Neil had a lot of girls wandering around, like always. If I remember, she was just a kid."

"Still is," Logan said.

She stared blankly through the window at the orange glare shimmering off the distant Century City twin towers. "Lynn didn't make a big deal about her relationship to Johnny."

"Kyndall said they had some sort of falling out years ago."

"A big one. Lynn sang with him in the beginning, before the Tradewind. When he split town she hit the streets hard."

"And resurfaced years later on Hollywood Boulevard in hot pants and a halter top." Logan contemplated the picture; he wondered what anger Lynn had felt toward her brother back then, and how well it had traveled over the years.

"You think he could do it?" he asked absently as he pulled to a stop at the light.

"Do I think who could do what?" she asked. She pulled down the visor, checked her face in the mirror, winced at what she saw. She was too tired for this. She needed sleep, a lot of sleep, before she would be able to jump-start her brain.

"Do you think Johnny Rand could kill his own sister?"

"Sometimes blood is thinner than water," Corie pointed out as she flipped the visor up. "It all depends on what dilutes it."

Logan followed the freeway to the end, where it merged onto Pacific Coast Highway and headed north along the beach. He hugged the right lane as he headed toward Malibu, past Gladstones, past the Colony, past Pepperdine, through the early-morning mist that clung to the coast. Corie nodded out again, her head this time lodged in the gap between her seat and edge of the door. Her lips moved slightly, just a little quiver, as if she were speaking to someone in a dream. Logan stole a glance at her, longing to reach out a hand and run it down her tender cheek, to feel the softness of her milky skin.

Thirty minutes later he pulled into her driveway. He cut the engine and studied her while she dozed. She was lost in the depths of much-needed sleep, and didn't stir at the sudden lack of motion or noise. He sat there for a long moment, then got out and walked around the car. He quietly gathered her in his arms and started to carry her toward the short flight of steps that led to her kitchen door. She wrapped her arm around his neck and clung tight. He lightly kissed her nose, cold from the convertible ride back from Culver City, and she blinked her eyes open and looked up at him. Instinctively she knew what he was doing, where he was taking her. She unfolded her arm and twisted her body until her feet touched the ground.

"Let me just get you inside and in bed," he whispered, squeezing her hand.

"Just like a man." She hesitated. "You'll stay?"

"No." He shook his head tiredly. "I've got to go."

"You've got to stay," she corrected him.

"Can't. I've got things to do."

"You're doing nothing until you get some sleep."

"That's first on my list. Where're your keys?"

She looked around nervously, glanced at her empty hands. "Where's my purse?"

"Guess I left it in the car." He steadied her against the wall of the trailer while he retreated to his car, returning with her purse and key ring.

"Please—"

"Later," he told her. "Tonight."

She started to lodge further protest but decided to honor his wishes. A protest would doubtless be futile anyway. "Promise you'll call me later?"

"Promise." He walked her inside, helped her out of her clothes, tucked her in, kissed her cheek. She reached out, wrapped her fingers in his. She held his hand to her lips and kissed it softly, then just as softly let go.

"I'll go with you—" she started to say.

He shook his head wickedly. "You get that body some sleep. I'll be back for it later."

She considered the threat, treated it as a promise. "Just see that you do."

"Count on it." He flashed her one last lusty look.

"And remember, Logan," she said, her tone taking on a warning tone. "Don't do anything I wouldn't do."

"That's what I like about you," he said with a sly grin. "The possibilities are endless."

When Logan returned to his room he didn't go to bed. Instead he fixed two cups of motel coffee and retreated to his perch on the balcony. There he sorted out his notes and his diagrams, and the coffee and salt air sorted out his head. Yet despite the fresh infusion of caffeine in addition to that already in his system, he fell asleep. And that's how he stayed for a good three hours.

He was jolted from a slumber by the phone, snagging him from the faint scraps of a dream he hoped to re-create later. He blinked his eyes open and covered them with his hand to ward off the blast of sun. He groped for the phone, picking it up on the umpteenth ring.

"What?" he snarled as he held it to his ear.

"Now, is that any way to speak to your friendly neighborhood butcher?" It was Langston Post, and he sounded as drained as Logan felt. Probably up all night too, except Dr. Post got paid for it.

"Sorry, Postman," Logan mumbled. "What's up?"

"McNulty."

"Shit." Logan was getting damned tired of that man. "What's he done now?"

"He showed up on my breakfast table about an hour ago."

"Huh?" Logan was too tired for anything but straight talk.

"Meat wagon just brought him in. Thought you'd want to know."

"McNulty's dead?" A giddy spark shot through his skin.

"Last night, late. Bel Air Hotel, of all places. They got a phone tip. Creep must've checked in under a fake name, 'cause he's not listed as a guest."

"What . . . how?"

"Apparent sharp blow to the head." Post sounded like he was reading from a police report, which he probably was. "Five or six blows, actually. Then he got his belt wrapped around his neck."

"Thorough job." Logan pictured the scene and shrugged it off. Couldn't have happened to a nicer guy. "Any idea who?"

"Sorry," Langston Post apologized. "Couple next door said they heard a struggle sometime last night but didn't do anything. They were from New York, the last people you'd want to invite to a killing. They said they thought it was some sort of L.A. thing. Other than that, nothing."

"When's the autopsy?"

"This afternoon. Figure it'll be pretty cut-and-dry." he chuckled heartily; a touch of gallows humor in a humorless job.

"Cops find anything?"

"The place was pretty clean," the medical examiner said dryly. "But there was one thing."

"What's that?"

Langston Post was silent for a long time, either contemplating the consequences of leaking confidential information, or making sure no one was within earshot.

"They found a charge-card roller."

"Like the ones they have in department stores?"

"Exactly." Post thought for a moment, then added, "Except this didn't belong to May Company."

"Who, then?"

"The Sachet Social Club."

Logan whistled a feeble whistle. "That's McNulty's place."

"But it wasn't McNulty's handbag they found it in."

"So whose?"

"Girl named Kyndall Wyatt. She worked for Sachet, part-time."

Kyndall Wyatt and Roger McNulty? What was it she had

told Logan as she was leaving the hotel room a few nights back? She'd be getting out of the business soon, if she could just get away from old Roger. "This girl—Kyndall. Any idea where she is?"

"*Nada.* Cops're tryin' to track her down, but she didn't have a hard address. The girl who was on the phones last night at Sachet said that Kyndall had gone to the Bel Air for a date, but never called in to report she'd arrived."

Some date. Logan sighed and shook his head, said nothing.

"Stuart? You there?"

Logan realized he must have been silent much longer than he thought. "Huh? Oh . . . yeah. Nothing."

"Yeah. Well, like I said, just thought you'd want to know. Keep you posted. Ha-ha!" He laughed at his pun and hung up. Logan replaced the phone in the hook, soaked in the scent of fresh air breezing in from the sea, as clear and salty as it ever smelled out on Catalina. He felt his muscles start to droop, aching for a few more hours' sleep, but priority grabbed him and hauled him to his feet. He collected his papers and his wits and wandered inside. Then he stripped off his clothes and treated himself to a shower, alternating hot and cold.

Corie called just as Logan was heading out the door. Just checking, she said. Checking on what she didn't say.

"You get some sleep?"

"A little," he assured her. "All that coffee kept me up."

"I probably woke you."

"Nope. I was on my way out to the pool," he lied uneasily.

"Promise?"

"Promise what?"

"Promise you won't do anything dumb."

"I promise, sweets. Nothing rash."

"I'm not worried about rash; I'm worried about dumb."

"Okay. Nothing dumb," Logan insisted, maybe a little too hard. "I'm just going for a swim, soak up some rays. Meanwhile, you get some sleep. If you're a real good girl, I'll call you later."

"And if you're a real good boy," she purred, "I'll invite you over so we can play."

29

The craggy peaks of Catalina loomed out of the sea, a jolt of gray rock stabbing the virgin sky. The hills, dry and matted with scrub and parched brown from the long summer, proferred a barren tranquillity, a cryptic solitude.

Logan was seated in front, next to the pilot. The helicopter had taken off from San Pedro just twenty minutes before, and now was circling in toward its landing pad just south of Avalon. The chopper's nose dipped toward the sea and the tail swung around in a lazy arc; the pilot eased forward on the stick and the loud machine began to settle as its broad blades chopped at the still air. Finally the bird touched down, leaning into the turbulence, and the pilot immediately eased back on the throttle. Outside a typhoon of dust kicked up, scattering sticks and twigs and a few shreds of stray litter around the perimeter of the landing pad.

During the short cab ride into town he worked on the mental squibs that still didn't quite fit. Johnny Rand somehow had killed Neil Novak and Lynn Sutton. Someone had tipped him off that Novak was going to be on the island. Was it his sister Lynn, maybe Jenny Baxter? But Jenny was Billy Keenan's manager, which hardly made her an innocent party in whatever had gone down. Also, according to Corie, Rand was ill, dying in fact—so he probably wouldn't have the wherewithal to push Jenny's car over Mulholland Drive. So if not Rand, then who? And who had killed Roger McNulty last night? And what about Kyndall Wyatt: where the hell was she, and how did she fit into all this?

The cap to all this was the short visit Logan paid to the Long Beach offices of Starwood Limousine, conveniently located just a mile up from the cross-channel heliport. A quick check with the overnight dispatcher, plus two crisp twenties, revealed that the limo bearing the plates STRWD 23 had been rented last Wednesday by Rhapsody Records and ordered to stand by for a passenger coming over from Catalina. Irony of ironies: Neil Novak posthumously had paid for his killer's trip to his own funeral service.

The sun was pale, almost directly overhead, dry and threatening. The rocky canyon wall choked off the ocean's breath. Mounds of crumbled rock lay beside the road, remnants of tiny spills trickling down the hillside during the dry summer months, gentle reminders of the more perilous slides to come during the winter rains. The canyon was a subtle rip between the barren wasteland and the graceful, natural beauty of the sea. Dry scrub clung tenuously to the parched earth by stubs of root, ready to pull up and tumble off with the wind. Boulders lay scattered where they had fallen thousands of years ago, washed clean by subsequent flash floods and then baked in the scorching summer heat. The sky was a deeper blue than any he had seen in over a week.

The narrow lane was poorly marked and he almost missed it. He braked, in a skid of loose dirt, then pondered the signpost, faded by years of neglect: VENTOSA DE MAR.

"Wind of the sea," Logan translated from the Spanish. Crude, hand-lettered notices posted below this warned PRIVATE PROPERTY and NOT A THROUGH ROAD.

Four hundred yards up this gravel road he came to a steel gate that sagged on rusted hinges, chained open against an equally sagging barbed-wire fence that had long ago suffered the merciless ravages of the elements. Beyond this the road became a two-rut track. Logan leaned his Fuji against the fence and decided to travel the last hundred yards on foot. A dirt track led up to a massive stand of trees that cloaked the crest of a small hillock. A steep wall of gray granite cut into the thin, blue sky. Grizzled eucalyptus and oak trees pimpled the rolling fields of golden brush. If solitude was what Barry Finch and Johnny Rand had sought, they certainly found it here.

Under this forested dome was Rand's house, a cross of contemporary and old West styles. Whitewashed post adobe, polished hand-hewn timbers, a pueblo effect. A decrepit Spanish tile roof languished over the squat hacienda. Cracks split the foundation, and a thin layer of dust lightly masked the neglected walls. A porch stretched along the front of the house, its roof serving as an arbor for the jungle of crimson bougainvillea extending around the far side. Faded oleander and cactus sprouted wildly around the perimeter of the yard.

Logan approached the house with caution, remaining in the shadows, keeping an eye and an ear over both shoulders. He hadn't come this far just to get his head blown off. His hand felt for the Smith & Wesson snub-nosed .35 under his jacket: still there. He moved alongside the house, ducking as he slipped past the two front windows, then tiptoed up the flat stones that led up to the front porch. He knocked on the door, waited, knocked again.

Finally he heard footsteps shuffling across the floor inside.

Johnny Rand, or what was left of him, opened the door. He was tall, gaunt, shriveled to the point of emaciation. He had the look of a man at one time hefty and strong. Now his arms sagged from muscle turned to flab, and his face was distorted by folds of vacuous fat cells. His eyes were recessed deep inside his crevassed, wrinkled forehead, and peered out past pockets of flesh that drooped from his pasty brow. A thin mustache hid his quivering upper lip.

"Yeah," Rand wheezed, like a man who had just swallowed a mouthful of feathers. "Who're you?"

"Stuart Logan," Logan replied. "You're expecting me."

"Hell I am," Rand grunted with the same breathy wheeze. "What the fuck am I expecting you for?"

"Neil Novak and Lynn Sutton."

Whatever color remained in Rand's blanched skin drained away. His shoulders sagged even further, and for the briefest of moments Logan thought he'd have to catch this sick man in his arms. Then he realized that Rand simply was just studying Logan's face, like a man who couldn't believe he'd just found his long-lost brother. He peered deep into Logan's eyes, then drew back in a defeated sigh.

"Goddamn." He coughed in a dry rasp. He looked out the door past Logan, then moved aside. "Come on in."

Logan stepped through the door, which quickly slammed shut with an ominous thud. He followed Rand into the large living room, a cross between early Louis L'Amour and modern dude ranch. The walls were constructed of unvarnished beams and barn boards, hung with aged ranch equipment and "Wild Kingdom" animal trophies. Deer, moose, and elk eyes cast glassy, forlorn glances at him. A large oval hooked rug protected the wide board floor from a haphazard collection of mountain furniture: ragged couch, rough-hewn tables, several

old oak rockers, and a warehouse of kerosene lamps. Two ancient flintlocks were mounted above the rustic stone fireplace,
and a Remington original was hung above a long oak library
table at the far end of the room. A wagon-wheel candelabra
suspended from the exposed-beam ceiling finished off the er-
satz Western motif.

"You a cop?" Rand asked, his voice tired. His lips and eyes
seemed drawn on white parchment stretched over a knobby
skull.

Logan shook his head but didn't explain. He waited for
Rand to continue, wanting to see where the aging rock idol
would try to lead him.

Rand grunted as he nodded Logan toward a rickety old
chair. Then he sank into a well-worn overstuffed chair across
from him.

"So . . . how'd you figure it?" he said after a long pause.

"Just like that? No small talk?"

"I'm a sick man, Mr. Logan. I have no time for small talk."

"You had enough time to kill five people, Mr. Rand."

"Que será será." Rand hacked. He chewed on his lip,
which looked like it recently had suffered many such chew-
ings, then ran a finger to it to dab up whatever blood had
formed. Did this man feel no pain? Or maybe a tinge of guilt
or remorse, for that matter?

"You killed your own sister," Logan reminded him.

"Yeah, well . . ." He stopped mid-thought, stared off at a
distant vanishing point before he continued., He coughed
again, a sickening gag. "Accidents will happen."

"She caught a bullet in the brain, Mr. Rand. And she died.
That was no accident."

Rand shrugged, the corners of his mouth turning up in a
slight grin that just barely hinted of sorrow. "Wasn't part of
the plan, bitch just got in the way. But you know, the little
whore deserved it. She corrupted my girl, you know. Turned
her into a whore just like herself."

And just where were you all these years? Logan wanted to
ask. Where was self-righteous Johnny Rand while his little
girl was getting banged in an old Airstream trailer up in the
redwoods?

"So you were after Novak and Jenny Baxter from the
start," he said instead, a statement more than a question.

Rand's grin erupted into a full, sick smile. "My, we're
quick," he said, nodding. He wheezed and hacked again, like

an old two-stroke engine struggling for life. "So what are you going to do about it, Mr. White Knight?"

Johnny Rand rocked forward in his chair, then threw his head back in one violent motion. Logan felt his muscles stiffen at the sudden movement, found himself reaching for his gun when he realized that the old bag of hollow bones was using the whiplash effect only to clear a wayward glob of sputum from his throat. Rand's lungs rattled viciously, then he settled back in his chair. He looked up at Logan and found himself staring down the barrel of a .35 snub-nose.

"What the hell?"

"I think it's time to call in the cavalry," Logan explained. He rose from his chair, crossed to the library table, and picked up the telephone. Rand eyed him glumly but sat still, seeming almost relieved that the whole ordeal was coming to a close. Whatever had grabbed hold of his body was sucking every last bit of life from him. Death was imminent, and with the L.A. courts backed up as they were, Rand's case wouldn't come to trial for a year, probably two. What did the old guy have to lose? He'd probably be dust long before any prospective jurors were ever called.

The Avalon sheriff's number was pasted to the handset. Logan dialed quickly and waited for whoever was in the office to pick it up. A pert voice answered and politely inquired whether she could be of assistance. Logan knew the voice but not the name.

"Deputy Woods, please," Logan said, forcing a note of urgency into his voice.

"I'm sorry, sir. He's out of the office at the moment."

"Is he near a radio?" Logan demanded.

"Well . . . yes, he is. But—"

"Then get him! Tell him Stuart Logan says it's critical! Give him this location . . ." Logan unfolded the scrap on which he'd scribbled the address and read it to her. He glanced up at Johnny Rand, still sitting patiently in his overstuffed chair, still unperturbed by the presence of Logan or his gun.

Logan hung up and held the snub-nose on Rand. He returned to his chair, but instead of sitting he placed one foot on the seat and steadied the gun on his knee. The two men stared at each other, Logan trying to divine some sense of remorse from the former teen idol huddled in his chair, Rand peering back through blank eyes that had been ravaged by disease.

"Why didn't you just kill Billy Keenan while you were at it," Logan finally asked after a few moments of silence. "He's the real culprit in all this."

The sudden mention of Billy Keenan brought a tangle of anger and forgiveness onto a face that otherwise seemed void of passion, resolved to death. Rand's upper lip quivered, the only evidence that any facial tissue had any life left in it.

"Billy's just a stupid kid," he observed with a touch of sadness. "Pity the fool, for he knows not what he does."

Logan lowered his foot from the chair and faced him squarely. "Neil Novak and Jenny Baxter weren't fools, were they?"

"Just devils, his and hers," Rand proclaimed, as if reciting a quote. "I sold my soul, and they turned a profit on it."

"Isn't that what the business is all about? Profit and loss?"

Rand hacked again, then transferred his gaze from the gun to a point halfway to the ceiling. Thinking, remembering, rationalizing. Then he spoke.

"You know what it's like being on top and having nowhere to look but down?" His self-pitying words came out interspersed with two or three throat-clearing gags. "Three albums in three years, two national tours, five top-ten hits. All the groupies I could want, hotel rooms to trash, more money and dope and booze than I could have ever imagined. It was a great life, pissing away everything I had. Really fried some cells."

"The good old days."

"Whatever," he said, pausing for a moment of fond memories. "Then Novak pulled the plug, and it all stopped cold."

"Novak pulled the plug? Why, if you were such a hot ticket?"

"Said he needed new blood. He was adding to his roster, he needed to support his new talent." Rand considered this for a moment, sorting through the fact and fantasy of his failing memory. "He didn't cut me off, not right away. Just let me kill myself in my own time. Put me in the studio with no money, told me to produce a million-seller."

"Did you?" Eighty thousand units was closer to the truth.

"Under that sort of pressure? Hah! It sold a fraction of that, counting the freebies and cutouts and all. But Novak was moving on, and he wanted to cut the deadweight."

Johnny Rand was beginning to loosen up, letting his guard down. The good old days served as a tonic.

"I thought the two of you were friends."

"You don't know shit." He coughed, grinning. After all, the bastard was dead.

"But you kept writing songs."

"I tried, but the juices wouldn't flow. I'd burned out, I didn't have a song left in my heart." Rand's eyes flickered like dying campfire embers.

"But the songs you'd already written?" Logan pressed. He glanced at the clock on the wall: where the hell was Woods?

"I was hard up for cash, so I made a deal. Sold all my songs, published or not, to Novak." He paused a moment to catch his breath, which was being exhausted by so much talk. "And all it got me was—"

"Two hundred grand," Logan finished for him.

Rand glanced at him with dumb surprise. Then he raised a limp shoulder in a feeble attempt at a noncommittal shrug. "Hell, I'd had my peek over the hill, and I was on my way down again. I figured, what the hell do I need all these dog-shit songs for? I'd scribbled them wherever I was: on napkins, record sleeves, airplane schedules. Those songs were all I had left. Everything else I managed to snort up my nose or shoot into my veins."

Logan suspected a great portion of the former rock star's earnings had been thus consumed.

"So what goes around comes around," Logan probed.

"More or less. Novak and that Baxter bitch hatched a plan. He owned Johnny Rand's songs; she owned Billy Keenan's career. And together they made a perfect match."

"And a perfect target."

"*Que será, será,*" Rand said again. He folded his hands in his lap and smiled smugly. The look on his face, etched in his pink eyes, said, *Now what, sucker?*

The distant sizzle of rubber on gravel caught Logan's ear. He cocked his head, training his senses on the sound. Outside, down the winding driveway, lumbering up the dirt drive. Logan glanced at Rand, leveled the gun at him to remind him who was in charge, then edged over to the front window. He pulled back the curtain and stared out at the dusty yard. The scrape of tires on hard earth drew closer; then one of the two Ford Broncos belonging to the Avalon Sheriff's Office rolled into view. Logan watched as Deputy Woods opened the door and grabbed the double-barreled Remington from the seat beside him. Woods checked to see if it was loaded, then started toward the house.

At the sound of the deputy's footsteps on the front porch Logan called out, "Come on in, Jack. Door's open."

Logan sensed a moment's hesitation before Woods turned the knob and slowly pushed the old oak door inward. Rand leaned forward in his seat; he tensed as the deputy cautiously stepped from the sunlight into the darkness. Logan motioned Rand to sit back, relax, hold tight.

"Jesus, Jack. Where the hell were you?" Logan demanded as he slowly lowered his gun and turned toward Woods.

"Out of range," Woods explained tersely. He glanced at Rand, a spark of recognition in his face, then shot Logan a sour look. "So what the fuck do you think you're doing?"

"Just your job," Logan sniped. "Found you your killer. Mr. Johnny Rand, former rock star and teen dream, has admitted all."

Jack Woods eyed Rand curiously, his brow creased with deep worry as he tried to sort out the situation. He glanced over at Logan, then looked back at Rand.

"That true, Jay?" he finally asked, raising his shotgun and pointing it at the wheezing, hacking singer. They shared a long stare, and Rand nodded glumly. Then Woods lowered the rifle. "You tell him everything?"

"Just enough to stall him till you got here." Rand coughed.

"You take care of that other business?" Woods asked.

"Safe and sound. Sleeping like a baby."

Logan moved forward, caution in his step. He didn't like what he was hearing, and he liked even less what he was thinking. Instinctively he started to raise his gun.

"Hold it right there," Woods ordered, bringing the shotgun around until it was pointing in the general direction of Logan's head. The deputy glanced at the Smith & Wesson, then nodded toward the coffee table. "Put it down."

"What the hell—?" Logan stammered as his arm froze.

Woods stepped forward, the gun steady in his grasp. Logan saw a finger tighten on the trigger. "I said, put it down."

Logan eyed the deputy with contempt. He drew his gaze over to Rand, who smiled viciously. Then he focused again on Woods, the twin barrels staring him in the face, and understood the situation as it was shaping up.

Helpless, he let the gun slip from his hand.

30

Woods handed Logan's .35 to Johnny Rand, then waved the shotgun at Logan. "Move," he barked.

"Move where?"

A fierce jab in the ribs told Logan not to try to be funny. Logan got up, holding his arms away from his body, refusing to put them in the air or rest them on top of his head, or anything even remotely resembling compliance or fear. Woods dug the shotgun into his back, and the thought of hot bird shot ripping through his body drew a river of sweat to his forehead.

"Where we takin' him?" Rand wheezed as he rose on thin, wobbly legs, dutifully holding the .35 on Logan.

"Up the hill." Woods jammed the gun deeper into Logan's kidneys, bringing a grimace of pain to his face. Woods grinned viciously, then glanced over at the library table set under a large window. A bottle of Jack Daniel's, almost full and inviting no good, was its sole occupant.

"Grab that bottle," he ordered Rand.

They marched down the front steps and around the corner of the house, scuffing along a hard-packed dirt path. The trail was littered with old watering troughs, part of an old tractor, a small shed, a rusted water tank. It led through a small passage carved into the thick tangle of khaki-green oleander. Dry briars grabbed at Logan's legs as he was prodded forward. They emerged into a field that next winter would be a green meadow, but which now was a dry field of dead grass and scrub. A passel of oaks and low brush defined the far side of the clearing. Tucked along the far side of the clearing was an ancient shed, measuring some ten feet square, weathered and parched. Its roof buckled from the intense inland heat, but otherwise the structure looked solid and sure.

Woods jabbed the barrel harder into Logan's back, pushing

him toward the shed. "Inside!" he barked, as if he were operating on automatic.

Logan turned and fixed him with an angry glare, buying a
moment of time, time to think.

"Inside! Now!"

Logan trudged up the single step and pushed the door inward. The cabin was dark, dry, smelled of dust and dead vermin. Woods pushed in behind him, and Johnny Rand brought
up the rear, Jack Daniel's in one hand, the .35 in the other.

"So we're inside. Now what?" Logan asked. "You know,
any medical examiner worth a shit'll figure out all the goddamn bruises in my ribs—"

"Sit," Woods demanded, quickly pulling the shotgun away.
Logan lowered himself into a rickety chair set against the
wall as Woods turned to Rand and said, "Let me have that
bottle."

"Oh . . . I get it," Logan said, a little too bravely. "You're
gonna do me the way you did Jenny."

"Shut up!" Woods growled.

"What'd you do? Hold her down and pour the booze into
her, then beat her up real good before you drove up to
Mulholland?"

"I said *shut up!*' "

"Hey, Jack . . . chill out," Johnny Rand intervened. "Man's
dead meat. What the hell's the harm—?"

Woods thought it over for a moment, then eased off on the
gun a bit. He ran a hand through his damp hair. The hot sun
outside was nasty, but the air in here was stale. He growled,
then uncapped the bottle of Tennessee sour mash. He handed
the bottle to Logan.

"Drink!" he ordered.

Logan drank, shuddering at the first sting on his tongue.
"Come on, Jack," Logan said as he made like he was taking
a healthy sip, gulping air. "How'd you do it?"

"Easy," Deputy Woods began, a note of indifference seeping into his dry voice. "She left work, stopped at a light, and
found herself staring down the barrel of this gun. Took her
back to a motel, one of those cheap places with those Magic
Fingers and paper bath mats, and forced a bottle of Black
Velvet down her throat. Coulda put something else down
there, too, but it woulda left traces. So I just beat the living
shit out of her instead." He raised the gun slightly and
grinned. "Keep drinking."

Logan took another false sip, then wiped his lips. He tried to force the scene from his brain, the power behind Woods' water-buffalo arms as Jenny's life was battered from her body. "So ... you gonna take me for a little drive up the shore, maybe push me off the rocks?"

"Something like that," Woods grumbled. "Haven't quite figured the tacticals yet. Come on, 'nother sip." He reached with the gun and tipped the bottle with the barrel, spilling a few trickles down Logan's chin. This time he got a full mouthful, some of which he gagged down with a hearty choke.

He glanced from Woods over to Rand, who was leaning in the doorway, the Smith & Wesson aimed more at the floor than at Logan. "So ... how'd you get Novak's gun?"

"Neil gave it to me." Rand hacked. "Years ago."

"Cops said he reported it stolen."

"So maybe I stole it," Rand shrugged.

Logan regarded him curiously, then took another forced swig from the bottle. To no one in particular he said, "If I turn up dead the cops'll be crawling all over this place by nightfall."

"You're forgettin'," Woods said, snickering, a wry bite in his voice. "I *am* the cops 'round here. Now drink!"

He drank. Slowly, not too eager to go to his grave any earlier than necessary. His head ached, too soon for the effects of the booze. Lack of sleep, all that coffee, all those eggs. Woods had backed off a pace or two, resting against the wall. Rand was still leaning in the doorway, the gun hanging lazily in his hand.

Logan took another long gulp, draining most of his intake back into the bottle. Then he looked up and wiped his lips. On cue, Woods looked up and raised the gun.

"No one told you to stop, shithead."

"Go to hell." Logan spat defiantly. He gulped a lungful of warm air and dust, then let it out slowly. He looked at Rand, then cocked his head toward Woods. "Where the hell'd you get this guy?"

Rand thought for a moment, sniffed. "We go way back. San Francisco."

"Shut up!" Woods snarled.

Rand raised his hand, waving the deputy off. What the hell did it all matter now, anyway?

"Our pad was on his beat, and he sold us shit," Rand said

longingly. "He had access to all the goodies in the evidence room."

"Cram it, Jay!" Woods exploded. He drew the gun around until it was pointing at Rand, who in turn raised Logan's purloined snub-nose to remind the deputy that, for the moment, they were on equal ground. Logan's eyes shifted, just for a second, to Woods, who looked as if he was still deciding if he should permit this discussion to continue. The standoff continued for a good thirty seconds before Woods finally caved in.

"Fuck it," he finally growled. He lowered the Remington, but not his guard. "Man's snack food, anyway."

The negative vibes made Logan nervous. He glanced from Woods to Rand and waited for whatever explanation was due to unfold.

"Jack was a cop, a fan, and a junkie," Rand continued, glancing expectantly at Woods, as if for some sort of confirmation. "When the pigs got wise they cut him loose, so we took him on. Security manager, procurement agent, and overall utility infielder. Ain't that right, Jack?"

Woods dipped his head once, his only reply, then waved the shotgun at the bottle.

Logan took another sip. "So what brought the lot of you out here? You and Marshal Dillon there, and Barry Finch—"

The sudden mention of the name jolted Johnny Rand to silence. He stood motionless for a long time, head drooped, staring at a spot somewhere halfway across the floor. Then he finally looked up and announced, "Barry's dead."

"I know," Logan said softly, playing the moment, latching onto whatever latent emotion Rand still was capable of.

Rand glanced at Woods, who was standing rigid against the wall, his legs slightly apart, the gun braced in his arms. The look on his face was fierce, mean. It was a look that said, *If Rand needs to confess, let the poor fool talk.*

"We were friends, like brothers," Rand began. He thought back, his thinned brain capturing shards of memory that he'd stored up but hadn't opened in a long while. He began by regaling Logan with tales about Lilac Tradewind, about Barry Finch and the other members of the band—one who now sold computers in New York and the other who wasted her life away in a trailer court in Southern Comfort. He talked about their years playing San Francisco clubs for drinks and tips, long before they hit it big in L.A. He recounted the ups and downs of fame and fortune, mostly the down and outs. He skipped most of the Rhapsody years, skipping forward to the near-fatal car crash that crushed Barry Finch's spine and legs and for six hours left him dying on a remote highway up near Big Bear the night "We Are the World" went down.

"It was my fault," Rand concluded, now moved by the guilt that earlier had been missing, the remorse that should have been felt for five other deaths. "He didn't want to do it, but I talked him into it."

"Let go of it," Woods said gruffly, as if annoyed once too often by Rand's constant indulgence in self-pity.

Rand glared at him, then dropped his gaze to the floor. For a moment he said nothing, then looked up at Logan. "He was in a lot of pain," he said slowly, as if the mere mention might rekindle some lost sympathetic agony.

"Morphine," Logan said, a statement more than a question.

Rand nervously glanced at Deputy Woods for reassurance. A brief conspiratorial look passed between the two, more than the simple collusion of partners in crime. It was a look rooted deeply in the past, reflective of the bond of brothers who share in the spoils of past torment and adventure.

It was in that brief flash that Logan understood. He brushed his limp hair from his eyes, wiped the sweat on his pants. Then he regarded Woods with the contempt due a school-yard pusher.

"You . . . had the contacts."

Woods nodded with benign indifference. "Guilty as charged. Old habits die hard."

"Finch OD'ed?"

Woods lifted his shoulders in a capricious shrug. He shifted his gaze to Johnny Rand, busily mulling the warped floorboards in front of him.

Rand continued to mull for some twenty seconds, not lifting his head. Then he gave forth a low gutteral wheeze which came out as "AIDS."

Logan eyed the withered man suspiciously. AIDS? Barry Finch? Barry Finch, ex–lead guitarist for Lilac Tradewind, was a closet fag? If so, what about Johnny Rand? Were they sweet on each other, some long-kept secret stored away out here on Catalina, far from the probing snouts of the supermarket tabloids and the record-biz whores and the countless Tradewind fans who mindlessly placed Johnny Rand and Barry Finch on porcelain pedestals?

Johnny Rand shook his head slowly, as if reading the inner recesses of Logan's mind. "Not that," he whispered. "It was the accident. He almost died . . . he lost a lot of blood."

Of course, Logan thought. It all fit in. Massive loss of blood and subsequent transfusions, supposedly screened but always suspect. Somehow the HIV virus had been introduced into his body, and over time had brought the shades of death down around him.

"He found out last summer." Rand hacked, drawn out with sadness and pain. "And he died in March."

Logan studied the man's pale skin, his drawn face, his loose bones and scraggly hair. He hadn't drawn the connection before, but now it seemed obvious.

"And now you have it."

Rand aimed at Logan, but his eyes seemed heavy, weak and wasted. "They always said needlepoint was safe."

Logan felt the barest touch of sympathy for him, this man condemned to a withering death, having seen in Barry Finch's passing five months ago his own ultimate demise. Both men addicts, both men condemned by their own frailties. Logan graced him with a look of pity, but not so much that he forgot his own condemnation. Hard to feel much remorse for a member of your own execution party.

"That's why you went after Novak. Had nothing to lose."

"Enough!" Woods bellowed, interrupting the free flow of emotion. He grabbed the shotgun by the stock and pointed it at Logan's head and took a step forward. "Drink."

Logan ignored him. If he was going to die out here in some small cabin tucked away in the island interior and be left for the vultures and rats to munch on, he at least he was going to know why. And if, by chance, Rand and Woods lowered their guard, just for a split second.

"Novak knew," Logan continued, staring intently into Rand's sad eyes. "He put two and two together, right? He lays it all on the line. Johnny Rand signs over every song he's ever written, or he blows the old whistle. That the way it worked?"

"I needed the money," Rand blurted with a cough, a long-dormant grin of confession working across his face. "For Barry."

"For the morphine."

The silence that followed confirmed Logan's suspicions.

"And the gun?"

"Incidental protection. That was a few years ago. Reporters started nosing around, asking questions. Figured a gun might keep the vultures from circling."

Rand inhaled deeply, his lungs gasping for air. He warded off another coughing fit, and seemed relieved at his accomplishment. He turned Logan's gun over in his hand, fingering the trigger, massaging the barrel, as if recapturing lost thrills.

Logan studied Rand's face, shriveled with fond memory, etched with the pain of loss. And in all the memory and pain Logan sensed in the dying singer a triumph, a hollow victory over the empty ghosts of paranoid psychosis.

And that's when the confusion erupted.

None of them was expecting the interruption, least of all Logan. Not out here, tucked away in the hills, far from the milling throngs of Avalon and the intermittent hikers trekking out to the western reaches of the island. So when the footfalls first scraped up the path, amplified by the silent, still air, the three of them shared a brief sense of curiosity. Logan started to rise from his chair, but Woods waved him back in. Then the deputy crossed to the door, brushed Johnny Rand aside, and peered out.

Kyndall Wyatt looked exhausted, pale, much younger in the jeans and Guns N' Roses T-shirt that clung to her lithe body. Her hair hung in strands, and her face was smeared with traces of day-old mascara and eye shadow and tears. She recoiled at the sight of Woods, a confused look of gratitude and hatred darkening her eyes. Gratitude because he had saved her from McNulty's wrath, hatred because she had seen him kill with such coldness. Then she saw Johnny Rand.

"Daddy." She stepped up into the small shed, which quickly was becoming overcrowded.

"Kynnie—" Her father gagged.

"Shit," Deputy Woods cursed, then quickly caught himself. He smiled benignly at the girl, who had stumbled into this mad conspiracy and now only compounded the problem. Probably should have killed her along with the McNulty creep, but Johnny Rand wanted her out here, with him. "You oughta be resting," he admonished her with a protective kindness. "You been through a lot."

For a moment none of them knew what to do, where to turn. Kyndall was too dazed, too confused to fully comprehend what was in the works. Then she saw the two guns, who was holding each, and the direction in which both were un-ceremoniously aimed.

And then she saw Logan, or the fuzzy image she somehow recognized without her contacts. She squinted, staring through the dim light of the cabin, sorting out where she might recently have seen this man, one man among so many. She held her gaze for a few seconds; then the recognition seeped into her face.

"I know you," she said brightly.

"Jesus Christ!" Woods blurted as he lined Logan up with the gun at gut level.

Kyndall started to speak, then shrank back. She stared dumbly at Logan, then at her father. Both were at a loss. Woods sensed this hesitation, a fragile moment. His finger gripped the trigger and began to pull it back.

"No!" Kyndall screamed in the brief instant that the flame exploded from the gun barrel. Logan dived to his left as a blast of bird shot ripped into the chair and the wall behind it. He felt a hot spike of pain tear into his right foot as he tucked into a somersault and rolled as far as he could, up against the far wall. Momentarily he lost sight of Woods. He waited for the second, final blast, wondering in that instant whether pain or death would come first, wondering if Molly had had time to wonder the same thing before her life was gone.

The second blast came, but this time Logan felt nothing. In death is there no pain? Then he felt a shower of splinters cas-cade down on him, tasted dust and dry wood, realized he was still alive. He scrambled to his knees, the pain driving into his leg, up through his body into his head. His dirty Nike sneak-ers were crossed with red rivulets of blood, but it was coming out in a trickle, not a stream. The pain was severe, sharp, as if he had just been mangled by the spring-loaded fangs of a trained pit bull.

He glanced up at Woods, who frantically was jamming two more shells into the barrel of his shotgun. Johnny Rand had retreated to a corner of the shed, still holding the .35 but not knowing what to do, where to aim. Kyndall was frozen in horror in the doorway; she obviously had seen enough blood, enough death, in the last twenty-four hours to last a lifetime.

Logan's roll had landed him against the wall, nowhere to run or turn. He looked up at the fear drawn on Rand's face, and realized the sick rock and roll idol was his only chance. He hoped the languid former rock idol was too weak and twisted to be effective with a gun, and too confused at the moment to give it much thought. As Woods jammed the second shell into the barrel and cocked it, Logan made a mad dash for his Smith & Wesson.

He collided with Rand head-on. Rand's head snapped back against the wall as Logan's hand grasped the .35. In one desperate pull he ripped it from Rand's tired fist as he crashed through the side of the shed, tumbling outside into a parched tangle of oleander. He scrambled to his feet, brought the gun around with one sweeping motion toward where Woods was lunging from the doorway. Logan fired twice, but at the last moment the barrel caught on a thick stump of oleander. Both shots went wild.

"You're out of shape," Woods growled, taunting him as he cocked the shotgun and leveled it at him.

Logan crouched low in the dry thicket, saying nothing, knowing his ass was fried.

Woods yanked on the trigger, but at the last moment the shot went astray as Kyndall flailed into him from behind. Woods stumbled forward, cursed, wheeled around and grasped the girl around the neck in a practiced choke hold. Then he pressed the muzzle of the shotgun against her throat.

"Drop it, sucker," he snarled at Logan as terror swept across Kyndall's face. He jabbed the muzzle harder against her skin.

Logan eyed them both, sized up the situation. In order for Woods to make a clean break, the deputy would have to kill him, and probably Kyndall. Maybe even Johnny Rand. A string of eight bodies, all in just over a week. Could he do it? Probably: you only hang once, and usually never in the state of California. So, who would Woods kill first? Preferably Logan, but Kyndall if he had to. Then maybe Logan, then Rand. Or maybe he'd save Logan for last.

"I warned you, Logan!" Woods exploded. "You're fuckin' dead!"

"Daddy!" Kyndall screamed.

Woods pulled her tighter against him and pressed the shotgun against her face. "Drop it!" he roared. He pushed Kyndall away, swung the gun down, pulled the trigger, all in one move.

Logan expected it, saw it coming, and had no plan except to count the odds, pray they were in his favor. He tumbled to his left just as Woods' finger inched forward and the ground

erupted, just beyond where Logan had been standing. A few
stray pellets caught him in the thigh, the instant pain matching that just a little lower in his leg, but he managed to fall
off to one side as Woods calculated his next move. Reload or
run: which would he choose?

Logan lunged forward as Woods again grabbed Kyndall,
clamping his arm around her throat.

"I'll break her lovely little neck!"

Logan ignored him, took another step. Woods tightened his
grip to emphasize he meant business, but Logan wasn't having any of it. The rage in his eyes was matched only by the
hatred in Kyndall's, and the fear in Woods'.

"Let her go," Logan ordered calmly. "It's over."

With his free hand Woods fumbled in his pocket for more
shotgun shells.

"I said, let her go."

Suddenly Woods pushed her toward Logan. He backped-
aled around the corner of the shed and slipped through the
brush. Logan ripped off a shot just as Woods broke for the
trail leading back down toward the house. He heard a sharp
scream: the shot had connected.

"Give it up, Woods," Logan called calmly.

Woods answered by making a limping dash around the corner of the adobe house. Logan took off after him; he knew
where Woods was headed. He got off another shot as Woods
dived behind his Ford Bronco and pulled open the passenger
door. In an instant he'd crawled in and grabbed a gun from
the glove box. He checked to make sure it was loaded, then
dropped to his knees and fired into the ground at Logan's
feet. Logan jumped for cover behind a rotting watering
trough that looked like it hadn't seen water in years. Some
cover, he thought.

Logan peered around the edge of the trough, saw Woods
doing the same around the edge of the Bronco. Logan fired,
blasting the headlight just inches from Woods' eye. Woods
pulled back, allowing Logan to dash out across the barren
yard. Logan tucked himself into a roll and ended up behind
the stump of an old oak, just barely high enough to cover his
head. Then he slipped down to his knees and inched toward
the truck, glancing down under the chassis to keep an eye on
Woods' position. Woods was on his knees, massaging his in-
jured leg, calculating his options. Logan edged closer, trying

to ignore the surge of adrenaline as he stretched out on the ground.

He sighted down the short barrel, pulled his finger forward on the trigger with measured determination, and squeezed.

And when he saw Woods still moving, he squeezed again.

31

The night was young, the air freshly scented with salt and melted wax and gin, the soft hint of perfume. A light breeze sifted in from the dark bay, pocked with the winking lights of sloops and power cruisers gently rocking at their moorings. The light was low, strange shadows dancing off the netted walls. Hushed voices mixed with the clink of ice and the street sounds outside: revelers laughing on the beach, singing along Crescent Street, music drifting down from the hotels and the other varied night-spot bars that made this the island of romance.

Logan liked to believe every note he played hung on the billow of smoke swarming near the ceiling, and every patron hung on his every note. But he wasn't that dumb, and he wasn't that much of a dreamer, either. All he was, was just a writer—a writer who played piano two nights a week at the Albacore Lounge for drinkers and lovers who wanted to hear music that tested their memories. Elevator melodies and pop favorites like the one he was playing now: "Strangers in the Night."

His fingers touched lightly on the keys as the sound ended. He bowed his head at the polite applause, checked his watch, announced he was going to take a ten-minute break and please, please don't go away. He lowered the lid over the keyboard, sipped from his glass of tonic and bitters, and slowly limped over to the small table set to the side of the smoky lounge. The lingering pain in his leg was dulled by the late hour and his anticipated company.

Corie flashed him a pretty smile as he approached. She

reached out her hand and touched his, then pulled out a chair for him. He set his glass on the table and settled in beside her. She kissed him on the cheek and inched her chair closer.

"You play very nicely," she said sweetly, politely encouraging his future avocation. "Every bit as good as Liberace."

"So look what happened to him," Logan reminded her.

It was the weekend after the "shoot-out on Catalina," as the media had dubbed it. The story had broken open last Sunday; Logan was interviewed by all three networks as well as the local news crews. Cameras caught him as he emerged from the police helicopter in Long Beach, crudely swathed in bandages where the hot pellets had pierced his skin. After a few hours of close medical scrutiny, he was released to Corie's able and willing care.

The following morning every daily newspaper in the country ran some version of how former (and future?) reporter Stuart Logan, with Corie's indispensable and irrefutable assistance, nailed the goons who killed Neil Novak, Lynn Sutton, Jenny Baxter, Roger McNulty, and auto detailer Crit Jackson. Deborah Norville and Peter Jennings did their interview thing, and he answered callers' questions for an hour on "Larry King Live." The local media hounded him, asking questions that didn't need to be asked, questions that made him thankful that fame was fleeting. Now, seven days later, his brief bout with Warholian fame was ebbing and life was returning to normal.

Whatever normal was. He'd received calls from the *L.A. Times* and the *Daily News* "pursuant to employment," and he told them both that he'd get back to them later. He'd been approached by two studios and two networks to option the rights to the story. To them he said, "Don't call me, I'll call you."

Logan felt relaxed for the first time in a week. No cameras chasing him, no telephone ringing off the hook. Just a dark corner in a dark bar on a dark night. And his girl.

And she really was his girl. He knew it from the look in her eyes when he stepped off the helicopter a week ago, the tone in her voice when she ran up to him and demanded what the hell was he doing running off like that without even giving her the courtesy of a hint. The little shithead could have gotten himself killed, and deserved it if he did, Corie fumed. But she'd held his hand at the hospital while the doctors scoured his wounds, stood patiently beside him while he dealt with his fellow members of the press, and drove him back to the Bay View Inn for a careful night of tender loving care.

She was something, someone, he needed. She filled the void in his heart as completely as he could ever hope for. A space in there was still reserved for Molly, always would be. But the fragile thread between hope and despair had been strengthened by Corie's touch. He finally allowed himself to close the door, to stop clinging to porcelain dolls and to allow his heart to lead him again.

Lydia wandered over and asked if they wanted another round. Logan ordered another Black Russian for Corie and another tonic and bitters for himself. Corie rested her head on his shoulder and squeezed his arm. Lydia took the not-so-subtle hint and quickly swished her ass back to the bar.

Corie gave him a playful jab in the ribs. She knew he wasn't the slightest bit interested in Lydia, but she still felt the first pangs of new romance—and all the embarrassing uneasiness that went with it. "I think she likes you," she observed, trying to hide her blatant jealousy.

"Girl has good taste." Logan grinned, then added, "You too."

Corie leveled a cutting glance at him, then smiled. She seemed to lighten up then, settling more comfortably in her chair. "My hero—even if he is vain."

"Don't forget alive," Logan said. "That's the important part."

"So how is my great crusader, anyway?"

"Still in one piece," Logan said, trying to push the dressings on his thigh and calf from his mind. "More or less."

"At least the whole ordeal's over."

"Not quite." Logan shook his head. "The Carbone trial's coming up. Racketeering, wire fraud, conspiracy, taxes, all that shit." Three days before, the L.A. grand jury had handed down a flurry of indictments, dispersed evenly among Niki, Luigi, and David Carbone, as well as Leo Gold and Frank Kennedy. Roger McNulty had been named as well, but since he was dead the charges meant very little.

"And you just can't keep away," she said with equal measures of concern and sarcasm.

"Might not get a choice." Logan glanced up as Lydia returned with their refills. He waited until she was out of earshot, then continued. "Grapevine tells me I might be called."

"Why you?"

"My own fault. Guy in the D.A.'s Office, politico named Cal Mitchell, thinks I know more than I do. Keeps threatening to put me on the stand. We'll see." He lifted his glass, clinked it with Corie's in a silent toast, and took a long sip.

"These Carbone creeps I can understand." Corie shrugged after she set her glass back on its warped cork coaster. "The mob's the mob. But what I don't get is Leo Gold's role in all this."

"As they say, you never really know your friends." Logan shrugged. "I'll tell you one thing, the man's got big kahunas. Helped the mob scam Novak with this counterfeiting deal, then skimmed the mob off the top. Just goes to show—"

"I know ... crime doesn't pay." Corie stirred the vodka and Kahlúa in her glass, then looked up at him. Her eyes glimmered like sapphires in a dark cave.

"What about Kennedy?"

"Tax evasion," Logan said, with no emotion. Hard to feel sorry for any of these pigs. "Same way they got Al Capone. From what I hear, Treasury's got him, open and shut."

"Good riddance," she whispered.

"We'll see." Logan scowled. "They'll probably all get off with little wrist slaps. Fines, maybe probation." He thought for a minute; reflecting on the notion that sometimes justice is not blind. "Except for McNulty. He got what he had coming to him."

"No one's gonna fly their flag half-staff for that little prick," Corie agreed bluntly. "What about the girl?"

"Kynnie?" Logan had visited her in the hospital the day after the shoot-out, and dropped in again yesterday. "She's taking it pretty well. A bit shaken-up and all, but she's going to be okay."

"She claiming self-defense?"

"With McNulty, you mean?" Logan shook his head. Hadn't Corie watched the news? Then he realized he hadn't really had the chance to have a long, cozy, heart-to-heart, face-to-face talk with her since he released himself to his own care and fled out to the isolation and clean air of Catalina three days ago. Except for the luxury of long-distance, their lives were traveling parallel paths, twenty-six miles apart. "Kynnie gave her statement yesterday."

"Statement?"

Logan nodded. "The way she tells it, Woods developed a real crush on her the second he saw her. He accompanied

Johnny Rand out to Malibu for Lynn's memorial service, and fell for her on the spot."

"The same day he killed Jenny," Corie recalled. She chewed on the end of her cocktail straw, then tossed it angrily on the table.

"That's right. Anyway, according to Kynnie, he was obsessed. Started following her. He followed her to the Bel Air Hotel, where McNulty had lured her."

"Lured?"

"She says she told him she was quitting. He didn't seem to take it too well, started to beat the crap out of her. Teach her a lesson, of sorts. And along comes Deputy Jack Woods—"

"And the rest is history," Corie said. She touched her glass to his, then drowned any lingering sorrows in her Black Russian. She studied him over the rim of her glass. "Good thing he didn't follow you to the Century Plaza."

"Damn." Logan shuddered. He hadn't thought out that angle, and didn't care to imagine it now. He felt a stab of pain shoot up his neck, a reminder of his midnight intruder some ten days ago. Could that have been Woods?

"Gotta admit ... Woods had balls."

"Big balls," Logan agreed. "Really had me going, right up to the end. He even used me to track Jenny down."

"How do you mean?" Corie wondered aloud, Corie's eyes tightened, her wide eyes dancing in the red glow of the flickering candle.

"Well, if Johnny Rand meant to rub out Neil Novak and Jenny Baxter for whatever crimes they committed on behalf of Billy Keenan, Woods knew damn well who his missing redhead was. But what he didn't know was what she might have told me. He also wanted to finish what he'd started, but he couldn't find her."

" 'Course not," Corie said nervously. "She was with me."

"You?"

Corie lowered her gaze to her lap as if ashamed of her part in the truth. "She showed up at my place that afternoon, Sunday, said she needed to crash for a few days. She was pretty drained. I figured it was something to do with Immigration or something. I dunno. And then when you started sniffing around, I got worried."

"So you got your brain tumor to track me down and find out what I was up to."

Corie nodded. "Something like that." She stared at the red

checkered tablecloth, then at the stuffed fish hanging on the wall. Eventually she drew her gaze back to Logan.

"So . . . what happens now?" she asked tentatively.

"Now?"

"Now. Us. You, me."

"I've got plenty of room," Logan offered, more than just a touch of hope in his voice.

"Can't." She smiled as she drained the remains of her Black Russian and set the glass on the table.

"Can't or won't?" Logan pressed.

"Can't," Corie said firmly. "It's too soon. Besides—" She leaned forward and gazed deeply into his dark eyes. "My new job starts a week from Monday."

"Your . . . job?" he gasped. "You should've told me. They've got great cheap champagne here."

"The night's still young." She giggled.

He clinked her empty glass again with his, a silent toast. Then he leaned over and kissed her, much more than just a friendly peck. "Another record label?"

"Hell, no. I'm done with the business. No, it's a publicity gig over at Fox. Television development."

"You'll come out and visit me?" Logan asked, flashing sad puppy eyes at her.

"Every weekend," she said in a warning tone. "If you promise you won't get tired of seeing my face."

"Promise."

Corie smiled, took a deep breath, swirled a lone cube of ice in her glass. Pondering something. She studied Logan, almost revealing her thoughts, then hesitated.

"Out with it," he ordered.

She grinned. "All right . . ." She thought again, and set her glass down. Then she blurted, "Did you sleep with her?"

"Sleep with who?" Logan glanced around the lounge, but no one seemed to have heard. "Jenny?"

"Kyndall. In the hotel. The night before we . . . you . . ."

"No, I did not," Logan assured her with a wicked grin. "It was strictly business."

"Hers or yours?"

"Corie!"

"Okay, sorry," she said sheepishly. She fixed her eyes on his, making sure she saw honesty in them. Then she said, "What's she going to do now? Kyndall."

"Well, not that you genuinely care, but with Roger out of

the way, she's done with her former career. And she says acting is out because no one is going to cast a hooker in anything except porn. Same thing with modeling. All this publicity's ruined her for that sort of thing. So now she's talking about taking some of what Lynn left her and going to school, maybe fashion design. She's a bright kid, she'll do all right."

Corie shrugged. "If you say so."

Logan sipped his drink. He thought for a minute, about Kyndall Wyatt and Johnny Rand and Jack Woods, and all the bodies that lay scattered about.

"You know what's the irony of this whole thing?" he said.

"Irony?"

Logan nodded. "Exactly. Rand knew he was dying, and he wanted to leave something to his little girl, get back some of what he figured Novak stole from him years ago. So he killed him, killing his sister in the process. He never got his songs back, but in the end Kyndall got her aunt's life savings anyway."

"Life's funny little twists," Corie observed wryly. "But I still don't understand why Lynn was out here with Neil and Jenny that weekend."

"Three's company, they say."

"Neil was a bit kinky," Corie had to admit. "But I don't think that was Jenny's style."

No, that wasn't Jenny's style; she preferred duets. That's what she'd told him, just before she returned with Logan to his apartment just two Saturday nights ago. Maybe Novak had made what she considered an inappropriate demand, and she bolted. And maybe Logan was the next best thing . . .

"What about Woods?"

"What about him? He'd devoted his life to the Lilac Tradewind, Johnny Rand, and Barry Finch. Crooked cop, number-one groupie, the loyal fan to the end. Monumental psychosis notwithstanding. He supplied Rand with his drugs, Rand provided him with a purpose." Logan turned his palms up, indicating that this sort of psychoanalysis was way beyond him. "Let the shrinks sort it out."

Corie mulled this over, seemed to accept it. Every once in a while it's best to let the unknowns rest with the dead. Logan checked his watch; his ten minutes were more than up. He kissed her on the forehead and stood up.

"Time for Act Two," he said apologetically as he picked up his glass. "Keep my seat warm?"

"If you do me a favor—"

"Anything."

"Play me a song."

He hesitated, staring into her blue eyes, now a deep purple from the red candlelight. He said nothing as she stared back, plaintive love reflected on her soft cheeks, her lips. A flow of energy spread between them.

" 'The First Time Ever.' " She smiled.

Logan crossed back to the piano. He set his tonic and bitters on top, flexed his fingers, sat down, raised the lid from the keys. He adjusted himself on the hard seat, wet his tongue with a sip of his drink, then looked out over the lovers and friends sharing tables in the dark lounge. Kind applause erupted from a few tables where his presence had been observed.

"Thank you," he said with a smile as his fingers began trickling up the ivory in faint, rainlike trills. The first few notes of a familiar song, even the way Stuart Logan played it.

"Tonight we have a request," he began, as he introduced the second set of the evening. And maybe his life.